Liberty's Dagger

by

G.W. Barnes

Dedication

To my wife Elizabeth for whom this book would never have been written without her endless patience and support.

Prologue

In 1786, representatives of the several states decided to meet for a convention in Philadelphia, to discuss fixing America's first Constitution called *The Articles of Confederation and Perpetual Union.* What happened during this great debate was penned by James Madison and is part of America's long history of the Federal Government.

What was also written, in secret, was what really happened; how the new Republic was being torn apart from within through a lust for power and glory. These secret documents were hidden away in the hope that one day, the truth could be told. A conspiracy of power grabs, treason, and murder.

Be warned. What you've been taught about American history is a lie. A lie so big it has transformed what was once a Federal Republic into a democratic tyranny of the elite. The total control of the people by the two-party political system is complete.

This was not the America many Founders envisioned during and after the Revolution against England. In fact, our current Federal Government is what they fought against; the stripping of liberty and freedom from the people by its own centralized government.

Tyranny comes in many forms. The American tyranny is disguised in democracy and the politicians use partisanship to divide us and keep us enslaved. They stop at nothing to protect their power and they have the means to suppress any attempt by the people to regain control.

As the young American Republic of thirteen colonies try to unite in the form of a Federal Government, England struggles to keep control.

Revolution is in the wind and King George means to crush it. He has no doubt his great military might will bring these stubborn colonists to their knees. But just in case, he has a backup plan. A plan no one knows about save his most trusted court.

If the Americans manage to break free from the Imperial Crown, he will destroy them from within. For there are always those looking for power and glory. Those who wish to stay a part of the English Empire. Those in the very heart of the new American Federal Government.

Who are these people and what means can they use to tear the young Republic apart?

Those you would least expect, as they have become heroes in American history. They managed to change the very fabric that was established in the beginning.

This is a reckoning. The past and the present coming together in a tale of epic proportions. Without the knowledge of the past, no one in the present has a chance to restore what was taken. This account shows what happened then is influencing today's America. The groundwork must be laid for the truth to be revealed.

The battle for the American Republic begins in a most unexpected way. There are already traitors amongst us…

Chapter 1

<u>*September 1993 - Staunton, Virginia*</u>

We begin our journey in the brownstone home of Richard and James Yates, on Stewart Road, in downtown Staunton.

"Now, where were we?" Richard pulled his son's desk chair up close to his bed and sat as James lay on top of the covers.

"Well, last night you told me about the different taxes England had pressed onto the colonists. It was pretty boring." James was looking for another story line that had some punch, some action.

"Oh, so now you're a critic?" Richard responded smiling.

"Dad, I'm eight. How many eight-year-olds think taxation is a thrilling subject?"

"Now never mind. Just think how lucky you are. Most fathers don't even know American history; much less share it with their children."

Richard and James had a very close bond. They did everything together, that is when they were together. Richard was often away from home on one of his expeditions.

"Okay, let me see. Oh yes, of course. This part gets quite exciting. It was 1772; Mr. Stevens had arrived from the Caribbean, and was presented to King George in the royal palace."

◊ ◊ ◊

"Your Royal Highness. I present to you the good Mr. Thomas Stevens." Lord North declared, second Earl of Guilford, and Prime Minister of Great Britain.

"You may approach me." King George III responded, ruler of Britain.

Stevens approached the throne and bowed properly.

"You have news for me?" the King asked.

"Yes Sire. I have finished the arrangements for my apprentice to emigrate to the colony of New Jersey."

"Is he ready for his assigned task?"

Stevens answered in a proud affirmative tone. "He is. Mr. Arnold has seen to his education these last two years and his ability to learn is far past his peers. He also desires the fame and glory you offer him."

2

The King turned to Lord North. "See to this matter, North. I trust you will make sure he works within the confines he is given?"

"He shall, Sire." North assured the King.

"Very well then. Until these disputes with the Colonies are rectified, I find it necessary to have other options in place."

"A very wise decision, Sire." Stevens added.

"Yes, yes…" The King motioned North to dismiss Stevens. Once alone the King spoke. "Tell me North. Do you really think this plan is necessary? What if the colonists find out?"

"Sire, having a boy emigrate to the Colonies shall not raise any alarm. Further we have made all the arrangements to continue his upbringing and once of full age, he shall be able to effectively control your most outspoken province."

"I hope you're right North. Having to repeal the *Stamp Act* was one thing. Having to accept the Colonies' right to exist independently is quite another. These colonists are a stubborn bunch."

"Most of the colonists are loyal to the Crown, Sire. But many do feel they should have representation in Parliament. It was wise to have Parliament pass the Declaratory Act as the Stamp Act was being repealed. Having the colonists' praise your Highness for stepping forward to protect them from unfair taxation, while putting forth our will to enact all binding laws affecting them was a master stroke."

"They are represented. Virtual representation is the same as having a political figure sit in Parliament. Most of the Empire is represented this way. Why should they be any different?"

The King picked up a parchment from his desk. It was a copy of the Declaratory Act.

"The Parliament had, hath, and of right ought to have, full power and authority to make laws and statutes of sufficient force and validity to bind the Colonies and people of America ...in all cases whatsoever."

"They do believe the British Constitution gives them the right to refuse." North said rather softly.

"The British Constitution is not even written and besides it is based on our monarchy. They should do well to respect the wishes of their King. It is bad enough I have little influence in the Parliament. I will determine the fate of the American colonies and Parliament shall be bound by my decisions."

◊ ◊ ◊

"Dad…come on. Where's the good part?"

"Now be patient. It's hard enough telling you how events took place. If I just skip important parts, even if they seem boring, it will ruin the exciting parts."

"Well…okay." James replied, resigned to the fact that his history professor dad just couldn't leave out important, even minute details.

"Now let's see, where was I? Oh yes…Lord North had to tell the King about a very important issue."

◊ ◊ ◊

"Sire, there is another matter on which we must act and perhaps we can tie these two together."

"This is not about the East India Trading Company again, is it?"

North gave an uneasy smile and nodded.

"What is it now? Have they bankrupted the company, wanting me to bail them out yet again?"

"Sire, since the government has a large stake in the company, and the company uses its resources to help build the Empire, we must intervene."

◊ ◊ ◊

"But the East India Trading Company is really evil, isn't it?" asked James.

"Ah…no, not really evil, but perhaps they did some bad things back then. Now, King George was not fond of this bonding between the world wide trading company and his monarchy. It was an enormous corporation and, in addition to trade, it was setting up English governments throughout the Empire, the largest being in India."

◊ ◊ ◊

"Then this is the proposal." the King answered. "We shall cover the company's debts, but in doing so, we shall appoint a board of directors to run it. I will not leave the fate of our Empire to these bumbling fools."

"And with respect to the Colonies, Sire? A way to placate them into submission and end all this talk of breaking away from the Empire."

"What do you suggest?"

"First, the East India Tea Company must be allowed to sell tea in the Colonies. Second, we must protect our investment. Our company cannot compete in the open market with the local merchants and importers in the Colonies. I believe we must give the corporation special benefits so that it can prosper in the Colonies."

"You want to create an unfair advantage?"

"Perhaps more of a protectionist advantage. We must protect our interests without the colonists knowledge."

"If you tax the already fixed prices on all the other importers, it will raise their ire even more."

"Perhaps I can suggest an alternative. The Tea Tax is the only piece of the Townshend Tax Acts of '67 that remains. If we give East India Tea a credit on the tea it sells to the Colonies, then it can sell at a reduced price. We will be able to undercut the prices of our colonial competitors and so control the entire industry in the Colonies."

The King thought hard on this. "We do need to have some tax on the colonists, just to show it is the right of the Empire to do so. Our previous measures have not worked, so perhaps this will."

"And having tea sold at a discount will not seem like a tax at all." said North.

◊ ◊ ◊

"And so the Tea Tax was imposed in 1773, but the colonists saw through the scheme. Local merchants all across the eastern seaboard objected to the new tax, not so much as the tax itself, but the fact that East India Tea was being sold at a discount. This was the linchpin towards the beginnings of the American Republic." Richard was very animated in his presentation, or at least very animated for a history professor.

"More taxes? Why is it every person in government wants to tax, tax, tax?"

"Taxation is what funds government."

"Whatever." James said as he rolled his eyes. "So what happened?"

"The Boston Tea Party."

"No, no…what happened to the boy?"

"Ah yes…the boy was not within the Colonies yet and was

still young, however, he was looking for power and glory. He emigrated to America only a few years before the war started and soon, as predicted, he found his way into the very heart of the young government. And with him the desire for power that had taken the King and Parliament, soon took him. Once the boy was learn-d past his years, they set him to task. Malice was in his heart and he would use the power of government for his own and rule as the King's greatest ally; all the while confounding the people into thinking all he did was just and right. The boy amazed those around him with his skill of the pen and knowledge of history and governments."

"Learn-d? What is learn-d?" James queried. "No one talks like this, Dad."

"You know, when a student is in accelerated classes or perhaps skips a grade because they are very smart."

James did love history, though no other eight-year old he knew felt the same way. Perhaps it was because both his parents were very intense in their research. Perhaps it was the accident. He was compelled, driven, to find out facts; facts that no one was learning in school, even in the higher grades. He got the information first hand. His parents had found so many hidden truths, so many errors that needed correcting.

Richard enjoyed telling the stories. It gave him a chance to step into the shoes of all those people he was talking about. It helped him work through many of the facts and get a firsthand emotional response to all that was done. And, of course, he loved his son more than anything on earth and wanted to prepare him for what lay ahead. He was always animated in his delivery to spark an excited response.

"His situation was perfect for the King to ensnare. His father was corrupt and soon abandoned his mother. She fell sick and died before his tenth year, leaving him orphaned. The King used others like Mr. Arnold to teach the boy in the ways of the world and the King's evil. The boy embraced these teachings and wanted glory and power above all things…and Caesar was his idol."

"You wouldn't abandon me would you?" James asked with a serious look.

"Never." Richard smiled as he picked up his eight-year old and tucked him under the covers. "Think of this, James, what would America be like, had that boy never emigrated to the Colonies?"

"How come they don't teach this in school?"

"That, my young one, is for another discussion." He fixed James' covers just right. "Now off to sleep with you."

Richard stopped and looked at James before he left the room. He smiled, turned off the light and closed the door.

A rush of memory hit him and he leaned against the wall in the hallway. Visions flooded his mind. An accident, a car accident. He rushed to the car. She called to him to help. She reached for him, but he couldn't grab her hand. She screamed and the vision vanished, but the sound of her voice lingered in his mind.

His face showed the loss he shared with his son.

Chapter 2

May 1997 - Monticello, Virginia

It was a typical school field trip. James Yates was looking out the window as the bus made its way towards Monticello, Thomas Jefferson's historical home. He'd been on trips before to see many historical sites; his dad was a true historian.

He'd seen drawings of buildings with notes scribbled on them in his father's study. His dad had been searching for something, something that had eluded him for years. He told James he was seeking the truth about America's past. Richard brought his son along on many adventures in search of clues. He told him about the three key pieces of information that he kept secret. Perhaps James could help him by keeping an eye out during this trip.

As the bus moved, he watched the buildings go by and soon he was looking at trees, hills, and fields. It took about forty-five minutes to make the trip from Staunton, Virginia. The bus wound its way up the drive towards Monticello. It was a bright crisp day in early March with only a few wisps of clouds slowly moving across the sky.

The children and their teachers got off the bus in front of the guest center. The scene was one he was familiar with from previous trips both with school and his father.

The school group was shuttled up to the house and started the tour at the front path. The tour guide was explaining several items of historical information, but James wasn't listening. He was eager to get inside and start his search, hoping to find something out of place. The group followed the guide to the East Portico, which was the large front porch.

Their tour guide started. "And as you look up, you can see the outside face of the Great Clock. Notice it has only an hour hand. This clock is attached to the clock inside, with both running off the same works. You can hear the great gong from almost every corner of the estate.

"Looking at the ceiling above, you can see the lower section of the weather vane. Jefferson had this attached to the vane on the roof. This allowed him to know which way the wind was blowing from right here, without having to go out into the yard and look at the roof."

It was a flat circle hanging just below the ceiling on the entrance porch and was marked with the four directional letters. James could see it move as the wind changed. He thought. *That's quite a gadget for the 1700s.*

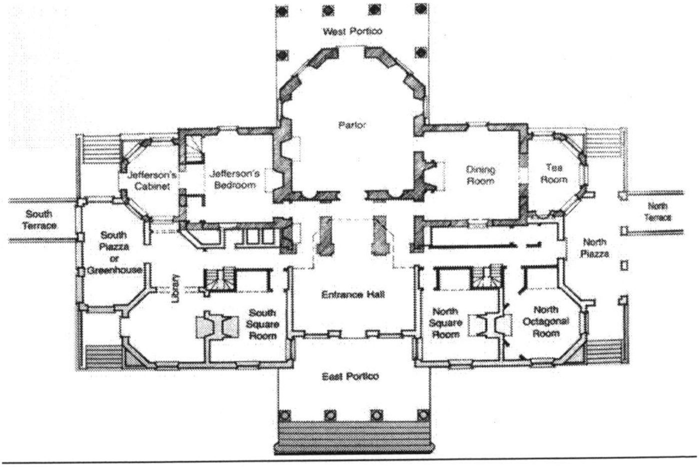

Thomas Jefferson's Monticello Home - Main Floor

Soon they were escorted into the entrance hall. James, having been on this tour with his dad before, started looking intently at every detail. They went up the stairs to the second level and the class was being shown all the areas allowed for the tour. Some of the rooms were off limits but one could glimpse them walking by. Nothing presented itself to him.

"James," called out one of his school teachers. "James, keep up with the group."

He'd dallied too long in one of the rooms. He was so focused on the details of the areas; he'd lost track of staying with the other kids.

"Yes, ma'am," he answered and hurried down the hall to join them.

As the tour progressed he was getting more and more frustrated that he couldn't find something his father might have missed.

Why would I? Dad hasn't found anything. Yeah, right, I'll solve the puzzle in just one visit.

The Jefferson bedroom suite included a small office. There was a pantograph machine the desk.

The guide continued. "It has pens set in it with wooden arms attached. One could start writing a letter and the other pen would move with the author's. A copy on another paper was being made as the letter was written. This allowed Jefferson to keep copies of all he wrote without having to rewrite the same letter."

The tour proceeded to the parlor in the back of the house. The guide continued. "Jefferson truly enjoyed science and agriculture. But many don't know how much of an inventor he was. Notice what happens when I close the double doors facing the main entry." She grabbed one door knob and pulled it shut. As it was closing, the other door was also closing. "Jefferson incorporated moving devices into the wall so both doors would close together."

"Wow, that's cool." one of his classmates said.

"Can you even imagine?" another responded.

James, of course, had seen this before, but he did enjoy thinking about just how Jefferson set up the machinery inside the walls. Next was the dining room and yet another gadget.

"If you look at the sides of the fireplace, you'll notice he incorporated four narrow dumbwaiters, two on each side. This allowed for wine to be sent up directly to the dining room from the wine cellar below. When the doors are closed, it just looks like the fireplace sides are paneled. Jefferson incorporated many other devices. There are even doors going nowhere now, but might have been used for secret passages in the past."

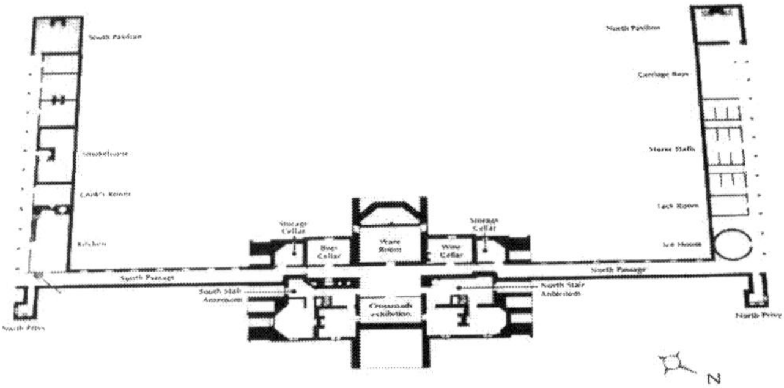

Overhead sketch of Monticello layout

The final leg of the tour was the lower level, which was partially underground. They passed through the all-weather passage into the Northern Dependency. There was the old ice house, stables, and carriage house. James continued to look, but found nothing.

They finished up in the Southern Dependency, going through the kitchen and outside on the southern slope of the hill. From there they could enter the cook's quarters and smoke room. The last few rooms had been turned into public bathrooms, with the last being the men's room under the South Pavilion. The old interior staircase going up to the second floor of the Pavilion was closed off by a locked door in the men's room so the group had to go around outside the building to reach the back yard on the main level.

The Pavilion itself was one story above the lower level. This was indeed the very place Thomas and Martha Jefferson had first stayed. The class climbed the slope of the south hill and went out into the back-yard area.

Still nothing was presenting itself to James.

There must be something here. What am I missing?

He was exceedingly good at math and science. He glanced at the Pavilion. The top floor was being restored to its original design and intent, but it was closed to the tour.

Deciding to leave the tour once again, James went over and looked through the Pavilion's the double glass doors. Did he see something? The stairway in the back-left corner was there.

He went back around and down to the lower level, and entered the men's room. The locked door was directly in front of him as he entered.

They must have removed the lower part of the staircase.

He looked around, thinking about where the stairs would have ended before the door was put in. As he spied out the rest of the room, he didn't see anything unusual.

It's just a bath renovated into the lower room.

He went back outside and looked closely at the building as he made his way to the back yard. He eyed the brick wall to the west and east of the Pavilion.

What is it? What am I looking for?

There was nothing special, but something seemed out of place. The stairway he figured out, but this was something different. The structural math didn't quite add up, though looking at it didn't reveal anything of importance.

"James, where are you now?" called one of his teachers from the back yard.

"I'm just here." He hurried up the hill to the yard.

"Hurry up, James. We need to be going."

He glanced back several times as he was leaving the Pavilion. The tour returned into the house through the back parlor and into the front entrance hall. As they were leaving, he looked up at the Great Clock above the front entry. It was nearly eleven as they filed out and into the shuttle.

He was in deep thought the whole ride back, looking out the window, but was not seeing the landscape anymore. It was a puzzle in his head. He needed to look at the drawings and sketches on his dad's desk. He could hardly wait to get home.

The school day had ended and the bus stopped in front of the Yates' home, a brownstone in a nice neat neighborhood. James came running off and into the house. Susan Jennings, the *au pair*, was there waiting for him on the front porch.

"What's the rush?" Susan asked as he flew by.

He kept going without a word.

She followed him into the house. "James? I have a snack for you on the kitchen table."

He barely heard her as he ran upstairs to his dad's bedroom. He knew the key was hidden here. He just had to find it. Dad was quite clever at hiding things, yet James was a master at seeking them out. He looked in the dresser drawers, making sure he kept things neat and as they were, yet found nothing.

Next, he checked the night table. Then he sat on the edge of the bed and looked around the room. He knew all the hiding places. He closed his eyes.

It's Tuesday. I know he uses the days of the week to change hiding places. Where is Tuesday?

This was a game his dad came up with, using days of the week to locate certain hidden objects in the house. As he got older, his dad would mix it up and make it more difficult. Ever since his mother died, his dad was obsessed with training James in the art of discovery.

A smile crossed his face as he opened his eyes and looked at the small painting hanging over the night table…*Tuesday.* He got up and reached behind the lower left corner. A key was taped against the back of the picture frame.

A level of satisfaction came across his face as he headed back down stairs. Susan was in the kitchen, watching the small TV on the counter. He silently passed the kitchen undetected and came to the study. Using the key he had just recovered, he unlocked the door, slipped inside, and relocked it behind him.

It was an ordinary looking den with a throw rug over the hardwood floor. A desk was positioned on the back wall flanked by two windows. To the right was a fireplace, cold and dusty. On the left was James' favorite dark leather wing-back chair. He didn't get the chance to use it as often as he would have liked to, but still he enjoyed the plush feel of the leather and softness of the cushions.

Moving to the front of the desk, he began sorting through all the pictures and sketches. There were dozens, mostly of Monticello, and they were in small semi-neat piles that covered the entire desktop.

His nerves tingled as he organized all that he found and then sat in his favorite chair. A shutter ran up his back as he started reading his father's notes and carefully looked over the pictures and sketches.

He went through page after page, but couldn't find anything that was out of order or of special note. His dad's written notes were everywhere on the drawings. The notes on one of the pages containing the sitting room read: *Inspected the sitting room extensively on the main level. Nothing found.* There were several small circles on the sketch identifying possible locations for something, but they were all crossed out.

Locations for what?

It was the same with all the pictures and sketches. His father had gone over the entire Monticello building room by room, even inch by inch, looking in hundreds of places marked with a circle. Each and every one was the same; crossed out, just like all the other buildings his dad had obsessed about.

His hopeful solution would have to wait until his dad got home. He had hoped to find a correlation between what he saw that day and his father's notes. Before he left, he decided to leave a few pages out of place, just to see if his dad would detect his intrusion. All part of the game.

He back tracked his steps, relocked the door, and returned the keys to their hiding place. It was nearly four o'clock and his father didn't usually get home until six-thirty. Thwarted for the time being, he headed into the kitchen and had his snack while doing his homework at the kitchen breakfast bar.

It was now 6:45. *Where is he. He's always home on time.* James kept looking towards the front entry. Anxiety shuttered through his body.

Susan had prepared dinner, which was now getting cold.

The home phone rang. Susan answered. "Hello?"

She hung up after a short conversation. "That was your dad and he wants us to get started so come to the table and let's eat."

James left his books at the kitchen counter and sat down with Susan at the table.

As she served up his plate she asked. "So, tell me, James, how did your field trip go?"

He didn't look up. "Oh, it was okay, I guess. I've been there so many times. A little more boring this time, actually." He was trying to downplay the nagging feeling he had about the South Dependency.

"Well, your father will want to know all the details as he always does," Susan said, smiling.

He continued to eat without acknowledging her, but did glance up to see her shrug it off and continued eating.

Richard Yates arrived home at seven. After he finished dinner, he headed upstairs. James had finished his homework and was waiting patiently for his dad to recover t

he key, come back down, and go into his study.

A few moments later, his dad called out, "James, please come in here."

Knowing he had left those few papers out of place, he expected to be called, of course. He walked into the study and closed the door.

"James, come here and sit with me."

He went and sat in his favorite chair. His father looked curiously at him from behind the desk.

"Now you know that I know you were in here today. I noticed several of my papers have been moved. Haven't I taught you to make sure everything is as it was prior to your visits?" He was of course reminding him of all the research trips they'd been on together and how many times they needed to be extra careful about disturbing the surroundings. "So I assume you wanted me to find something amiss?"

"Yes, sir," he responded quietly.

"Well, then, you have succeeded in arousing my curiosity. I know you had another trip to Monticello today, and I see the lower level sketches are now on the top of the stack, so you think you might have found something there?"

"Well, I'm not exactly sure. Something just didn't seem right in the South Dependency. I can't figure it out."

"I have taught you quite well, haven't I?" he said with a glint in his eye.

"Yes, sir. I mean, I'm not sure it was anything."

"But it was enough for you to come in here and look?"

"Yes, sir. I was hoping to find a clue in your papers about the location." James loved this interaction with his father. Even more so after his mom had been killed in a car accident three years earlier.

"I'll tell you what. Why don't we go out tomorrow morning and check it out? Then I'll bring you to school."

James had a broad smile on his face. He always loved these adventures.

Chapter 3

September 1772 - Boston, Massachusetts

A young boy was watching as the ship he was on entered Boston harbor. He was amazed at all the buildings, the bustle going on about the docks. There were people everywhere, more than he'd ever seen in one place. The ship docked and he went below to gather his things.

Once he collected his belongings, he returned to the deck and stood near the gangplank.

◊ ◊ ◊

A harbor officer stood at the bottom of the plank alongside Mr. Livingston, a stout man, dressed in semi-formal ware.

"You understand this boy is in my charge? Further, no mention of who he is to anyone, understand?" Livingston handed the officer paper currency. "For that price, I expect your silence in perpetuity."

"Yes, Sir." The officer nodded as he pocketed the money.

As Livingston waited, he thought, *how important could this fifteen-year old boy be? He's had no formal schooling. Was he to be enrolled right off the boat?*

He was yet to be convinced just what this boy would be able to accomplish.

Finally the boy reappeared. He stood a slender lad, yet tall for his age. He had a smooth-skinned face with a larger-than-life nose, narrow and protruding more than it should. His clothes were ordinary, shirt, pants, shoes. Blonde locks were mid-length and parted on the right. He had papers in one hand and a travel bag in the other as he stopped at the top of the plank and gazed, entranced at the harbor.

"Hey you boy!" the officer shouted. "Let's make some time here."

The boy gave him a wave when his gaze reached the officer. He smiled and proceeded down the plank.

The officer asked to see the boy's *Letters of Introduction.* "Well, everything seems to be in order here," He had a bit of trepidation in his voice. "Young Master, you are placed into the service of the good Mr. Livingston,"

"Yes Sir," the boy answered politely.

"Our carriage is over here," Livingston said, pointing the way for the young lad.

As they were walking towards a carriage, the boy continued to look around, astonished by everything he saw. A full harbor it was, bustling with commerce. There were many more buildings than his harbor at home. Warehouses abounded and goods were being loaded and offloaded from many of the ships. At least a dozen ships were docked with many moored in the harbor; tall ships with great masts and smaller vessels for fishing and trapping.

"So, this is America," the boy said softly.

"Well, actually, this is Boston and the Colony of Massachusetts," responded Livingston. "There are thirteen Colonies in all."

"Yes, yes, I know all about the Colonies. I've been studying your history for some time now," he remarked, showing a brash side.

Livingston thought for a moment and decided not to start off on the wrong foot. He would give this a chance to play out and there were several day's trip ahead. "Anyway, welcome to the Colonies. How shall I address you?" There was an uneasiness in Livingston's voice.

"Alex" he said as they both got up into the carriage. "You know, like Alexander the Great."

Livingston smiled to himself as he got into the carriage. *Perhaps he is the one.*

The carriage headed for New Jersey.

September 1772 - Monticello, Virginia

The carriage was slowly heading towards their new home; Monticello.

"This is fabulous," Martha Jefferson said excitedly as she saw the building resting up on the hill. "All your work can now shows its splendor."

"It will if I can ever get it finished. For now, this one small building will have to suffice, though we shall have no room for guests or family," Thomas responded, with a smile.

"Yes, but now we are really going to live here. It is a new chapter in our lives. You can rest now and enjoy your agrarian passions as our home gets built."

"Yes, I hope to rest. Political life does not suit me even at the local level, though you know I am a man of standing in the community. I shall always be available to represent them should they ask. If we can find a way to live in peace, I hope for that more than anything else."

They reached the summit and stepped down from the carriage. As it moved off they stood together looking westward as the sun set. It was a beautiful evening and the land all around was a wonderful vista of rolling green hills and rock walls lining the properties going this way and that.

"I am home," Thomas said softly.

And he was. It was being built from his own drawings and plans, Monticello, a two-story grand house with pillars and balconies. The only section completed was a small brick structure with a single room above for living quarters while below was a small kitchen. The land itself still needed much tending as trees, grass, and weeds covered most of the hill.

A fourth generation Virginian, Jefferson knew what the land felt like; it was part of his soul. The challenges of generations had made this moment possible. It was now part of the great works of his elders, and their communities, as they built their small spaces in the wilderness that was America. They had been driven out of England all those years ago and chose to start anew, risking everything.

Many generations had made it to this point. Many had not. But the one thing that held them all together was their faith and the potential to give better lives to their children. It drove each generation to the next. Jefferson's father had willed this land to him. While many settlements faltered from disease and hardships, others had prospered for over one hundred and thirty years since the first settlers came. While the Crown always held the power of ownership, they were self-sufficient. They had established independent communities, Colonies all along the eastern seaboard.

They were free Englishmen and reserved all the rites that free Englishmen held and believed in. For, by 1772, all of the Colonies had established governments of their own, though many had yet to write their Constitutions. They were set up as republics and each had its own measures and laws. The English-appointed governors by now were more like figureheads rather than drafters of laws for the communities, yet they had the power to dissolve colonial government, if needed. They kept the presence of the King and the English Parliament in plain view, yet allowed the people to set up both single level and double level representation within their own Colonies. This was the very heart of their republics for their local representatives were now the minds and will of the people.

Yet now, these free Englishmen, women and children, were facing increasing difficulty with the Crown. The King had already started imposing taxes and duties upon the people yet offered them no representation in England where these laws were enacted. A resistance because of non-representation began to swell. There were enactments made to challenge the authority of making laws with no representation even though the *Declaratory Act* passed by Parliament gave itself these powers. Some resisted altogether while others paid the fees. Most did not want to break away from their English heritage.

Over the next few years, acts of resistance started showing clear signs of things to come. Finally, one act seemed to strike the beginning of actions over the next eight years. Citizens of the Colony of Massachusetts, clothed in Indian disguises went aboard three East India Trading Company vessels and proceeded to dump several hundred boxes of East India Company tea overboard. The company demanded compensation and the King was committed to oblige. And so began the great war to secede from the English empire.

May 1777 - Pennsylvania State House

Agreed to by Congress 15 November, the *Articles of Confederation and Perpetual Union*, the first ratified alliance of the American Republic was also their first Constitution.

James Madison was engaged with Jefferson and James Wilson during a congressional break outside of Independence Hall in Philadelphia. The air was crisp and a bit cold for this time of year. "I am glad you have come to visit with me. Tell me Thomas, what do you think of our Constitution, or I should say, our Confederation."

Jefferson looked at him intently. "Perhaps it is better if you told me your thoughts on the matter."

"I am quite satisfied with the alliance. How often do thirteen independent countries join in partnership for the protection of all from foreign influences and wars? We have formed a Perpetual Union in our Federal Republic Government and we have successfully seceded from the English Empire, that is, so long as we win the war."

"This has been done before, all through history. So long as each colony, meaning each state, is treated on equal terms and control their own destinies, then I approve," Jefferson responded.

"And you, Mr. Wilson?" Madison asked.

"I believe this alliance is not nearly strong enough to protect the parts. We must coalesce into a more centralized unit, giving equal power to both the states individually and the central government."

"I believe the Articles will do just that," Madison answered.

They both looked at Jefferson; waiting for what they knew was a contrast in style. "I believe giving too much power to a central government will eventually destroy the states. What happens when there is a conflict between the two?"

Madison answered "The state, any state has the right to nullify a central policy. That is the protection in place. A state may also secede from the Union if they believe the central government is acting against their wishes."

"So New Jersey can stop a central government edict from applying to their state?" Jefferson asked.

"Yes. It can be stopped in their state or if a policy will be applied to all, they can veto it in Congress and stop it from ratification."

"And there lies the weakness of the accord," Wilson chimed in.

"I consider that a strength," Jefferson quipped.

"Then you have a paradox on your hands. On the one side, you have an alliance that bonds the states in a Perpetual Union, but on the other, any state can block the wishes of all the others, even to the point of secession. This is a serious flaw that must be explored further," Wilson concluded.

"Believe me, I have tried over and over again. The small states believe they will be overruled and overrun by the larger states if the rules are for a majority in the vote. I have tried to convince them they have nothing to worry about. State's rights, after all, are foremost in everything we do," Madison answered.

Jefferson responded "I am cautiously optimistic, however, there must be a check on the central government by the states otherwise tyranny will surely show its face and we will lose everything we have fought for," On this they all agreed. "If Virginia is on equal terms not only with the other states, but also with the State of France or the State of England, then I'm sure we can work through this paradox. We must always remember that the central government is not an entity unto itself, but rather a branch of each state allied together and must never be used to force the states or the people to comply with what it thinks is the betterment for all. Keeping government decentralized so as to protect our way of life is the only way to check power and possible corruption."

Madison was eager to satisfy Jefferson. "Most everything is governed at the local level where the people fiercely protect their community's rights to self-govern and practice their faiths. Why even the states themselves have little power over the towns and villages. Generations of our forefathers formed what they believed was the best governments within the colonies they could, allowing the most freedoms and liberties of any colonies, countries, or states before them. There are no monarchies, no dictators, and no supreme elitists or judges here and we will make sure it never happens."

Jefferson still looked concerned. "We had been loyal to the crown of England, but then we saw how subjects and slaves are bound to the monarchy. There is a great evil abroad and the Colonies were right to determine their own destinies and break away from the motherland. To self-govern on all levels, foreign, domestic, and local, just as we have been for over one hundred years. We have been using this structure for so long, it is as if we were already independent states, even with English loyalists appointed as governors and judges within each state. They have allowed us leave to self-govern."

Wilson nodded politely.

Madison still saw concern. "So we have formed an imperfect partnership made by imperfect men to protect their own state's interests. If men were angels, there would be no need for government at all. Since this is not the case, we must be willing to compromise for the good of all."

Madison paused for a minute to grasp the moment. "This dual federal republic can break the mold of all the republics that ever were. Having republic-style governments in the states with a central republic where they can have an alliance in regards to foreign affairs, leaving domestic affairs to the states is a master stroke. The checks and balances can be the best of both worlds. This is the key difference from every other attempt to form a republic since the beginning of time. We will have no standing Imperial American army to go abroad and conquer, and especially not to be used to invade a fellow state, no aristocracy ruling from on high. Keeping full government power within each state as it has been for each colony is our foremost goal."

"Just the same, I will give nothing away. Not to a central authority, a centralized judiciary, or a foreign country. Yes, you call this a Perpetual Union, yet each state will retain full sovereignty as bound in the Articles, and each must be able to nullify central government laws or even secede from this Union if they feel those laws infringe on their states' rights," Jefferson retorted. He too was wise with thought and concept beyond his years. "I see this as a constant conflict. But perhaps a constant conflict will indeed keep all parties in check. The first signs of trouble will be when the republic starts to slip into a democracy. If that happens, then this new alliance will follow all the others in history in spite of this dual effort. And how can we be a Perpetual Union if any state can secede? These are contradictory positions, the two are incompatible. Perhaps more thought needs to go into this relationship.

"Oh, there's one more thing. You mentioned compromise. That word is the death knell for any people beyond the local level. Once you give up your own rights in order to compromise, you become less free and give more power to any government you compromise with. And, if your representative votes away your freedom, then it is even worse, because now they no longer represent you. Perhaps a better phrase would be to allow all the freedoms associated with a person and his property.

"Government cannot give people freedom; they can only compromise or take it away, giving it to others or themselves. This was why we needed all thirteen Colonies to vote unanimously for our secession from the English empire. Had any one colony voted against it wanting to keep their loyalty to the Crown, then they would have been forced to accept whatever outcome the war has. Either win or lose, it would diminish their freedom to interact with each side. The Colonies would have thought twice before allowing one of their own to fight against them."

Chapter 4

<u>May 1997 - Monticello, Virginia</u>

Richard and James arrived at Monticello about 9:15 the next morning. There were already several tours going. His dad spoke briefly with the curator and soon they were heading to the Southern Pavilion through the all-weather passage below. They walked around and up to the Pavilion entrance on the main level.

James felt anxious and exited at the same time. His breath quickened.

Richard took a key out of his pocket and showed it to his son. "The privilege of working in historical records. The curator has allowed us to go into the Pavilion."

They entered the upper room. James stood in the middle of the room and spied around at the walls and the floor.

"What do you see?" Richard asked, motioning to speak softly.

"I'm puzzled about this room."

His dad looked but indicated he didn't noticed anything unusual.

James slipped under the rope at the top of the staircase and headed down. It abruptly ended before reaching the lower level.

"Careful there, son."

"This staircase is blocked off here below."

"Yes. There's a door in the men's room below to access the stairs, but it's locked. I have looked there and found nothing."

He came back up the stairs. "Let's go back down to the lower level."

They walked back around the outside. James eyed the south wall as they descended the grass slope to the lower level. "Something's wrong."

Richard looked intently at the wall. "What is it?"

"Why was Jefferson so careful about the use of space below all the upper rooms, except this one? The whole house is laid out in such detail. Every room has a room below it with a specific purpose except this one."

"Well, the Pavilion was initially two-stories tall. He moved in here in 1772 with his wife, Martha. They lived here while the other areas of the house were being built or renovated. The room below was the kitchen until they moved the kitchen to the first room in the South Dependency."

"So what did they do with the room below?" James asked.

As they came around the side of the building, they both examined the south wall thoroughly which had a centered window.

"They actually raised the grounds around the building some four feet. There was a door where the window is now." Richard surmised.

His dad grabbed him by the shoulder and suddenly said. "James, we need to leave right now. You're already late for school, and we can't have that," His voice was a lot louder than before.

"What? Why?"

"No time to explain. Let's go."

Father and son went back up the hill, around the Pavilion, and made their way through the house. As they were walking through the main lobby, James looked up at the Great Clock above the front door. It was just after ten when they left.

◊ ◊ ◊

Praetorian agent William Trumbull watched them leave. What had been a mission to observe and backup the agent sent by the Society, he now was genuinely intrigued by the Yates' actions. The other agent sent by the Praetorians was also watching them.

Trumbull shook his head and smiled, looking at the agent. *This agent has no idea I'm here, even though I just revealed myself to Yates.*

For two years, he had been the backup in stealth on several missions. He'd shown himself to Yates many times before even while keeping this knowledge from the many agents that had been sent to spy Yates out.

It was a cat and mouse game between him and Yates. He knew Richard was aware of his presence on many occasions, yet the societies were not at war, so Yates would do his research knowing Trumbull was there.

He saw the other agent calling in and decided to get close enough to listen without being seen.

"Sir, I'm not sure if they found something but they left in a hurry…well, they left unexpectedly. What should I do? Yes, sir. He should be dropping the boy at school. I'll nab him after that," he said with the hint of a British accent.

◊ ◊ ◊

On the ride to school, James asked, "What do you think, Dad?"

"I think you found something that needs further investigation. This corner section of the Pavilion does not show anything special on any of my notes or sketches. In fact, there are no records showing anything unusual, even in the archives." Richard kept watching his rearview mirror as he was talking.

"I know," James answered.

Richard looked at him and smiled. Then his smile slowly faded and a genuine concern grew on his face. "James, did you notice the man in the black shirt at the house?"

"No, sir. Was he watching us?"

"I think so. Listen, I'm going to drop you at school and head home. Remember what we talked about when there are others watching me?"

"Yes, sir."

"Good, son. Good. You remember what you need to do in case something happens?"

◊ ◊ ◊

"Yes, sir." His mind flashed back to the many times he was instructed on how to contact his dad's associate and the secret he held. "Do you think something is going to happen?"

"I don't know, son. I don't know." His voice trailed off. His dad called his contact on his car phone which was hardwired in between the front seats. "I'm dropping James off at school. Meet me there."

James sat silently in his seat and focused on the protocol he was given.

Richard stopped in front of the school. "Remember the key, the diary, and the code. Remember to pass them along to my contact if something happens, and remember, son, that I love you."

As James was getting out, he looked back and saw his dad react to something behind them. He grabbed James and pulled him back into the car.

They drove off with tires screeching. The chase was on.

His dad made a call. "Where are you? There's trouble. We're being followed."

James could hear the voice on the other end as it yelled. "Yes, I see them!" He turned to look as two cars now followed.

Facing front again, James closed his eyes and focused on remembering;

Look up, then down, walk long, follow sound
Look sharp, no fear, eagle's eye, shows it's here
Iron fist, moves the wall, follow hall, do not fall
Iron Gate, blocks the way, with the key, it will sway
Use the rules; take it slow, mark your way, or you will stray
Even in, to begin, odd it is, to show what 'tis
Up or down, you will go, choices sound, you're center bound
Don't go back, for it's a trap, move ahead, or you'll be dead
Iron Gate, blocks the way, with the key, it will sway.

They chased around several streets in downtown Staunton. James was lurching side to side as they weaved around traffic.

He hung on for dear life. Looking back again he saw they were leaving accidents in their wake.

In a brief strait-away Richard made another call. "Call Susan and have her get everything together!"

They lurched to the left again around another car.

"Doing it now!" yelled the contact through the phone.

James continued reciting:

Once you're there, the truth lays bare, read and see, our great folly
Take it up, take it out, use the rules, or you'll be fools
Never safe, never seen, show the truth, to all foreseen
Use the rules, to escape, find the light, or doomed to fate
Don't go back, for it's a trap, move ahead, or you'll be dead
Use the rules; find your way, the Iron fist, will show the day.

◊ ◊ ◊

Richard headed through another intersection, now at high speed. This one he didn't get through. A car smashed into the passenger side door, crushing it inward enough to smash against James, leaving him unconscious. The impact pushed Richard's car into the oncoming traffic and they were hit head on by a large pickup truck on the driver's side, causing the engine to crush Richard in his seat.

He somehow managed to looked at the rear view mirror.

The car chasing them swerved, avoiding them but smashing into cars parked on the side of the street right next to his car.

He looked at the agent slumped over his steering wheel, not moving.

He looked at his side view mirror and saw his contact stopped behind them and rushed to the car.

He cringed as pain shot down his legs.

"Take him. Take the diary, and here's the key," Richard said as he opened his sport jacket and exposed an inside pocket. "I'm trapped. Get him and the diary to safety. Go! Now!" He felt himself slipping into unconsciousness.

"Richard, I need the code. You're the only one who has it." The contact reached into Richard's jacket and retrieved his diary, now soaked with blood, and the key.

There was another car approaching. "I need the code," was the last thing Richard heard.

◊ ◊ ◊

"Richard!" the Contact yelled at him.

Richard didn't respond.

The Contact was out of time. He carried the unconscious boy over to his car and they left the scene. On the way, he made a phone call. "Susan, there's been an accident. Richard didn't make it. I have James. Break into the study and get all the papers and bring them to the safe house." There was silence on the other end. Susan was shocked and shaken. "Susan! Do as I say now!"

"Yes Sir." was all she could get out as she ran towards the study crying.

The contact looked at the unconscious boy in his passenger seat as they sped away.

◊ ◊ ◊

Trumbull stopped at the scene. He heard emergency vehicle sirens and knew he had a small window of time. He checked the Society's agent, who was just regaining consciousness.

"You idiot." He pulled his gun with a silencer attached and, making sure not to be observed, shot him through the head. Then he removed a small pin from underneath his shirt collar.

He approached Richard and saw he was regaining consciousness and crushed in his seat. "Richard, you're not going to make it."

Richard looked up. "Looks like our game of cat and mouse has finally ended." He cringed as blood soaked his shirt around the engine that impaled his gut. "Please leave my son out of this. He doesn't know anything."

Trumbull was watching him die. All this wasted time following him. He knew Richard had spent his entire adult life searching for something. Something he never believed existed yet the Society was bent on finding whatever it was. He returned to his car and sped away just as the emergency vehicles arrived.

I must find that boy. I have to find out what he knows.

<u>*May 1997 - Safe House; Texas*</u>

James slowly woke up. The nurse took immediate notice and headed out of the room.

"He's waking," she said, outside the door.

He looked around and saw he was in a bedroom. His head

was still throbbing and he was groggy. It looked like a twelve-year old's room filled with posters, shelves, and collectibles, but he didn't recognize anything familiar. A woman came into the room and approached the bed.

"How are you feeling?" she asked.

He looked at her still dazed.

"Dear boy, tell me how you feel?"

He didn't answer. He felt dizzy.

"Oh son, you gave us such a scare. Thank God you're alright."

He looked at her, confused. He didn't recognize the woman and started to get scared.

"There, there now, it's alright son. You're at home, in your own room."

"Who are you?" James asked quietly, then flinched as he realized his right arm was in a cast. His side hurt too.

"Oh dear, you hit your head harder than we thought. The doctor said you might not remember what happened."

James was scared and dizzy.

"Son, you were in a car crash. Your arm and three ribs are broken. You also hit your head pretty hard."

James tried fighting through the fog in his head.

Who is this? Where am I?

Then he realized the worst.

Who am I? What's my name? What happened? I can't…I can't…remember.

Dizziness overtook him as he passed out.

Chapter 5

January 1783 - Eastern Long Island, New York

The room was dark and damp, with only a few lit candles on the walls. A large round oak table, strong and sturdy, was set in the center of the room. Ten hand crafted chairs of wood were set around it with all the chairs occupied except one. One chair was fashioned differently than the others. It had a high back and was ornate, with many carvings.

For ten years they had worked independently, though they were in constant contact to coordinate their efforts.

Several servants were going about their business, including bringing meals and attending to the needs of the group. The Praetor, their leader, was in the main chair. He was young, yet dark and brooding. He wore a hooded cloak to conceal himself. All there knew who he was, yet no one dare reveal him or speak his name. Now that the war had ended and they awaited the peace treaty, he felt the need to bring them all together. There was one in their Society that had recruited these men. It took years to form the organization and their leadership. They were the Society of Praetorians, part of his personal army. He had nine other Council members. Behind him were two Praetorian bodyguards. One other, his lieutenant, stood by him.

Now, this was not the first group known as Praetorians. The Roman Empire was filled with these ruling elitists. They were the power…that kept Caesar in power. Most controlled vast areas of the Empire as they carried out Caesar's edicts and the Roman Senate's rules and laws. Some had their own small armies to rule with an iron fist. This is what the American Society of Praetorians was fashioned after, an elite and sometimes vicious group of citizens and the military. They had a secret allegiance with King George, looking to return the American colonies to the control of the King and the Imperial British Empire. They were enemies of the United States yet they were spread throughout America undermining all they could in the young Republic.

The door at the front of the room, a large wooden one with great metal strappings that were bolted in place, unlatched and a man walked in. He was tall, slender and had graying hair. He was dressed in a colonial uniform, clean and neatly worn with all the accoutrements of a general. He stood in front as the door closed behind him.

"May I come forward, Praetor?"

"Yes, come here before us and sit," the Praetor pointed to the open chair.

The General handed his coat and hat to a servant, approached the table, nodded politely to all there, and sat in the last chair. He was directly opposite the Praetor.

"What news have you, McDougall, and why are you wearing that uniform to my chamber, General?"

"My apologies Praetor. I'm just from a meeting with all the officers. I came here straight away as you requested."

"You shall do better in the future. Exposing our situation and location is all that uniform will do."

"Yes Sir," He paused for a moment but received no response. "The British have been beaten Praetor. A peace treaty will be worked out in France."

"Yes, we know…I'm sorry gentlemen, this is General Alexander McDougall. He has been working for me for some time now. He is now a Praetorian, replacing General Arnold and we have a task for him to perform to prove his loyalty."

General Benedict Arnold appeared next to the Praetor.

The Praetor continued. "McDougall has already taken the oath of loyalty like the rest of you. Let me remind you that any betrayals will be met with severe punishment not only for you, but for all your relations. This is a dangerous task we have agreed to undertake and we each risk as much as the one next to him in the name of the King." He looked to his side. "Lieutenant, if you please."

"Now each of you will be in charge of certain tasks in addition to working together. I have orders for all. Read them well. Each is expected to carry out these orders to the letter. Failure will not be tolerated. Is this understood?" asked the lieutenant.

"Yes Sir," all answered.

"These are your Society pins. Wear them concealed under your right shirt collar at all times so that other Praetorians will know you are part of our Society."

The pins were crafted in solid gold and shaped into the form of an eagle, proud in its splendor. They were given to all present and they pinned them on.

The lieutenant looked at the Praetor and gave him a nod.

The Praetor continued. "And what of the Royal Army, General Arnold?"

"Stationed in New York City at the present time. They will not depart until the treaty has been signed and delivered to the Commander."

"Good, good. And the Colonial Army?"

"Up the Hudson, keeping a watchful eye on the British," McDougall responded.

"Then plans are proceeding as expected." The Praetor looked to another man at the table. "Tell me Mr. Morris, what is the state of finances in the Congress?"

"The Congress is broke. It cannot pay most in the army. This Federation we have with the other states is inadequate to performing almost any actions," Robert Morris, a powerful and influential congressman in charge of all government financing, answered.

"Sir, there is a lot of anger up in Newburgh." McDougall added.

The Praetor smiled. "Excellent. McDougall, you will go to Newburgh and start to unfold our devices. Mr. Arnold, you shall meet with the British Commander and our New York alliance. Tell them we are starting our plans. Give this to the Commander."

The General received a satchel from the lieutenant.

"Praetor, many of the officers are already on board," said McDougall.

"And many allies in Congress are now eager to set everything in motion," said Morris.

The Praetor rose and the men did as well. "Then let us concentrate on the months ahead. That is all gentlemen. General…a moment if you would."

The men filed out of the chamber, each with orders in hand.

"General Arnold, I wish you could stay and continue our plans, but you are too great a risk for the Society. Committing treason and changing sides during the war has made you a great liability to us. You must leave the country when you have finished our business in New York. One of our ships will take you to London."

"Yes Praetor. I know the risk I am to the Society if I stay. I can be your emissary in England."

"You shall be. Oh, and I wanted to personally thank you for the trouble you raised in Virginia. Jefferson's ego took quite a beating and the ordeal has lessened his standing in government."

Benedict Arnold nodded and withdrew.

The lieutenant pulled back his cloak. He looked like an ordinary man casually dressed, but was set in a tone of English aristocracy. "Can we trust them?" Lord North asked.

"They are mine. They are broken, and will do my bidding. Otherwise, the strength of my secret army and resources from the King will rein down on them and everything they hold dear. If they want power, they must be willing to risk all."

North glanced out towards the door.

"Perhaps it is you that still needs to be broken," the Praetor said.

"No. I assure you, your will is done through your humble servant."

"I hope so. Having lost your standing in the Royal Ministry, you have lost much power. The King and I are only so tolerant. Your demotion to being my second does not sit well with me. The King will never forgive you for joining forces with his opposition, and your standing shall not shield you from my wrath. One more thing, you shall also address me properly, North. Your Lordship has no authority here. My authority is absolute in the American colonies, understand,"

"Yes Praetor."

"If it was not for your bumbling of this war, we would already be in power. Since the King has already replaced you and you have little value here other than to serve me, I suggest you focus on just that, serving me. Your job now is to oversee all importing and exporting of American and British goods. Stansbury is in charge of this. It is his job to make sure trade with the King's European enemies is disrupted as much as possible. Too many in the American states have an unplaced friendship with the French. That will change. Our trading exclusivity with the British Empire shall keep both nations strong and powerful. We will break this Perpetual Union these fools have created and form a central *Nation State*. Mr. Morris still has a lot of work to do in the Congress. Make sure you keep pressure on him for all the debt he has amassed. It gives us great leverage."

The Praetor turned to leave. "Come, we have much to plan. Gather your papers and bring them to my anti-chamber."

"Yes Praetor."

Late January 1783 - Secret Meeting, New York City

The room was well lit and private in the back of the building. Benedict Arnold was dressed in casual clothing and hooded to prevent anyone from recognizing him other than the men at the meeting. There were several men in the room all standing around a large rectangular table. The first was the Commander of the British forces, dressed in uniform. Two more officers were by his side. Four others were dressed in civilian clothes.

"General Arnold, you finally made it. Gentlemen, please take your seats," said the Commander, standing in proper military form.

Arnold sat facing the Commander.

"Now, we must start the next phase of our operations. General, I trust you have news?" the Commander asked, still standing as he leaned over the table.

"Yes I have news," he looked around at each of the men. "We will be changing the command structure of the American Army. General McDougall is on his way to Newburgh even as we meet."

"So this is it?" said one of the plain-clothed men, he was a banker in the city.

"Yes" replied the General. "Everything is now in motion. Each of us must now follow our part. Just so you all know, the Praetor will not take any excuses if any of you fail. Your loyalty and oaths will be put to the test,"

"And our reward?" asked another, a merchant with a large shipping interest.

"You will all be rewarded in the coming years. Nothing will happen overnight. You must remain true to the cause. Only then will the King and the Praetor reward you for all your efforts."

The third, a city politician, smiled as he looked at the General. "Well then, it seems this new western power will surely not survive. Men are destined to be controlled by the elite, whether be it a King or the aristocrats."

"No, it will not survive. But don't count them out just yet. They just defeated the greatest army in the world," The General, looked squarely at the British commander, then continued. "Taking their leaders too lightly will doom our purpose. The Praetor is already seething over this setback. Had the British been able to hold their own, we would already be enjoying our higher places in American society."

"Perhaps if we were better informed during the campaign, this might have gone differently." responded the Commander.

Arnold's rage came though. "I could not have drawn you a better map to success! For over two years I supplied you with valuable information. Troop strengths, storage depot sites, even plans Washington himself prepared. Between those and others within the command structure sending you almost daily reports, it's amazing you didn't win. Your bumbling incompetence is beyond measure. The King certainly lacks the judgment of choosing military leaders wisely. I warn you now, if you fail the Praetor in this new campaign, you will not survive long. His reach is more than you know."

He watched as the Commander retreated to his chair.

"But we have many allies in both the state and central governments. Won't this be enough?" the politician asked.

"Yes, we have many loyalists and the Praetor has made sure they are neither punished nor deported because of their positions during the war. Some have been exposed as you know and were forced to relocate. The rest are at his command."

"Quite a lot of power for one man," responded the Commander. He quickly changed the subject when the General glared at him.

"So tell me General, just how do you expect to bring down Washington? Now that he was able to turn the tide of the war, he is surely revered by all those who fought with him."

"I am disinclined to tell you how this will unfold. Just know that he has more enemies within the ranks than you could possibly realize. Make sure all is ready when it unfolds. Remember, any betrayal will not be tolerated."

February 1783 - Mount Vernon, Virginia

Alexander Hamilton was Washington's most trusted aide-de-camp during the Revolutionary War. His closest confidant. He genuinely liked him, even if they had not always agreed on positions during the war. He had given Hamilton unfettered access to all his correspondences, even personal ones. The only exception was the intelligence spy ring Washington formed during the war. On this he trusted no one outside the ring itself.

They continued corresponding and held a close bond throughout the rest of Washington's life. Hamilton was instrumental in keeping the Congress at bay during the war, and in the success of Washington's Presidency decades later.

Hamilton was an unexpected guest on this late evening. Washington welcomed him with a warm handshake.

"Tell me, Alexander, what brings you here? Have we heard news yet from Paris?"

"No Sir, I'm here because there is unrest in Newburgh. Many of the men, especially many of the officers, have become disenchanted waiting not only to go home, but especially for their pay. Congress does not have the capacity to raise enough money. I believe we should use this opportunity to strengthen the central government. The military can be a powerful persuader."

A grave looked appeared on Washington's face. "No, using the military to make governmental change is fundamentally against the principles of our Republic."

He reached into his pocket and pulled out a letter. "I just received this letter from a Colonel Nicola. I've never met the man, but this letter is un-quieting. I will share it with you, but this must stay confidential."

He handed Hamilton the letter. As he finished reading it, he knew his position was compromised.

"You know what this means don't you? The army or at least many in it are looking for a military coup. While my suggestion before was in this vain, you must understand I'm not involved with this Nicola."

"Yes, I know you're not, but the army is a dangerous instrument to play with, Hamilton." He gave him a hard look but then softened his tone. "I will find a way to deal with this issue, but I need you to go to Congress and figure out a way to compensate the men. Unless they can do so, we'll lose everything we just fought for."

"I will Sir."

Washington's trust in Hamilton trumped the circumstances. "Thank you Alexander. Your loyalty towards me has been far more than I ever expected, from anyone. Now join me for a late supper, won't you?"

"Thank you sir. As always I am your humble servant."

The two retired to the kitchen and had their fill.

The Praetorians were unfolding their plans to grab control of the young Republic even as they ate.

Chapter 6

February 2013 - Manhattan, New York City

Trumbull was a specialist. His combination of chiseled body and finely honed skills were what most men only dream of. He stood just shy of six feet tall, muscular and toned.

He had neatly cut dark hair and a particular shine in his eyes. *Always* dressed in black, he stood intimidating to those around him. If Jason Bourne or James Bond were real, they'd be William Trumbull.

Yet he could blend in with the crowd if he needed to become invisible to his adversaries. Strike with stealth, quick and deadly.

This was the first time he would see the people who hired him twenty two-years ago: the Praetorian Council. He knew who they were, but never actually met them in person. They never wanted to be seen by anyone other than their closest associates. They kept to themselves, using technology to communicate outside of their inner circle. Most had a public persona.

But now, he had forced their hand with an act of defiance. He had refused the last assignment he was given. Even worse, he killed the two agents they sent in his place. He was sick of killing innocent people. His world had grown hollow, empty. Yet he knew the consequences of trying to leave. No one left, ever.

He parked in the garage below the building and was met by two body building armed guards. They walked to the elevator. One stepped in with him and pressed the button for the penthouse. The guard looked at him as they ascended and gave him a 'what a pathetic little shrimp' smile.

Trumbull cracked a small smile of his own. "Do you ever actually use those muscles? I mean, besides at the gym?"

His remarks were met with a cold stare and a grunt.

"No? Pity, seems an awful lot of effort for a look that no woman would ever want."

The guard grunted again, as the elevator reached the top floor. The doors opened and the guard stuck his hand out for Trumbull's gun.

"I wouldn't do that if I were you." He smirked.

The guard grunted again, and reached for his own gun, holstered under his jacket. Trumbull stepped back, grabbed the guards wrist, and twisted. The guard let out a groan as he fell to his knees, still locked in Trumbull's grip.

Trumbull quipped, "If you want, I'll put in a word to your boss about getting you speech classes. Oh, and spend some time strengthening that wrist."

He smiled again and stepped out into a dimly lit, spacious room. Shadows were cast in all directions. There were ceiling-to-floor windows at the back of the room. Several bookshelves lined the side walls, filled with legal books of all shapes and sizes.

Two more equally large guards met him and walked him to the center of the room. Neither made an attempt to disarm him.

There were two things about Trumbull that stood out. His overt arrogance and dry, demeaning sense of humor.

He knew just how important this meeting was, as the Council almost never met in full. He recognized most of the men he was now looking as several had public persona's.

Wow. The Praetorians have infiltrated a lot of the government and must wield tremendous power worldwide.

The Praetor he did not know, however he did know the leader in the world banking industry, FED executive, General and Admiral, Senator and Congressman, FBI Director, and an Interpol Agent he'd had run-ins with. The tenth one he didn't know. They wore the finest suits money can buy, except for the military men, dressed in their uniforms.

They were all there, all the leaders of the Society in one room at the same time, to talk to him.

I'm the best they have and they know it. Now it's my will against theirs.

In front of him stood a large curved table forming an arc with its front ends or tips pointed towards the elevator. The surface was smooth and polished, hand crafted in wood, mahogany perhaps. It was some thirty feet from end to end. They stopped him some five feet from the table, front and center.

Behind the table sat ten men. They were old, some in their

sixties and others past seventy, perhaps past eighty. Most were bald and bent. Each had computers and other electronic devices in front of them.

"Well, so this is the famous Mr. Trumbull," said one near the middle, directly in front of him. He was the Praetor, the leader, and the rest were Praetorian Council members. The men looked dispassionate, as if the life was sucked out of them.

He smirked and gave a slight nod. "I'm flattered you know who I am."

"Don't play the fool to us Trumbull," the Senator said, his raspy tone not so nice.

The General looked at him hard. "You've disobeyed a direct order. Not only did you refuse your assignment, but you prevented the assassination of a prime target. Tell me, how was it killing two of your own kind?"

It seemed as if this old man wanted to feel the exhilaration he desperately missed.

"Too easy." Trumbull was cool and calm. "And before we go any further, the guards need to move behind you to the windows, and they need to leave their guns on the front of this table where I can see them."

A few murmured to each other before the Praetor nodded to the guards. These men needed Trumbull more than even he knew.

He scanned the room. "There are no video cameras in here. I guess you prefer privacy."

"So what are we supposed to do with you?" the World Bank Executive said, as if he didn't hear his remark. "You're the best we have. You know that. Now it seems you wish to withdraw your services."

"I'm sure you can find a replacement. Someone better than those last two I hope?" He eyed the guards carefully. "Well, perhaps not," and he smiled again. "I did you a favor, reduced your overhead."

"Perhaps we should be making those decisions," the Praetor said. "Here's the offer, Mr. Trumbull. We'll overlook this incident so long as you're willing to reaffirm yourself to the Society and continue what has been excellent work until now."

He looked at them all. So much power sat in front of him.

He smiled. "I'm just not interested in killing innocent people anymore."

The General responded. "Mr. Trumbull, surely you know they are not innocent. They represent a grave threat to our Society and to the *Nation State*. Were they to find the evidence now hidden, they could change the very fabric of the Federal Government,"

Trumbull glared at him. "I really don't care. All your conspiracy leads have run cold, and I'm tired of watching this latest target. There's no reason to kill him. Whoever he is, he has no desire to even leave his house, let alone try to find those documents. Personally, you're all fools to even think there are hidden papers that could undo your power. With the information you gave me, there aren't any traces left."

The Praetor looked hard at his best assassin. He crinkled his brow. "We know they exist, Mr. Trumbull. Our intelligence shows very clearly they still exist."

He was unfazed by the challenge. "You hired me all those years ago and set me to task. I've done everything you ordered me to do. Yet all this time I've seen nothing that would represent a threat to your authority or the government's, for that matter. All those people I've assassinated-school teachers, firemen, painters, office workers-they were all just regular people. That organization you think they all belonged to has been powerless my entire lifetime. The only remnants are fools that are grasping at straws and protecting those they feel are important. They keep to themselves. They're not dangerous. They're not revolutionaries.

"You, meanwhile, have been searching for those documents and that diary your whole lives. Even many of your old alliances have died off. You and your geriatric ward are all that remains of this Society." He knew his life was threatened even as he said this. His eyes scanned the room again. There was no one else besides the old men and the three guards. At least no one he could detect, yet he felt something, or someone, was out of place. This wasn't his element, out in the open and exposed. Stealth was his strength.

The Interpol Agent, who kept taking his glasses off to clean them, spoke. "Mr. Trumbull, good to see you again. Do you remember me?"

"Can't say I do." He answered in his trademark voice and smirk. Of course he knew him. They had encounters on at least three occasions. Trumbull was getting under his skin the best he could, and loving every minute of it.

The Agent grumbled and said. "We know your ways, Trumbull. Your insults show us your strength. We hired you for your strengths, yet you must realize we can kill you right now. But it is our hope that you will reconsider. You need us as much as we need you. You have over two hundred kills. The only other place you'll be is dead. So I would assess your options and hold your foul tongue."

Trumbull ramped up his sarcastic tone. "Please. Don't bother threatening me. For two months I've watched this one man, waiting for something, anything, to happen. He doesn't even leave his house. It's been twenty years now that I've been working for you. You've been wasting my talents for over a decade. Not one challenge have I found."

"You've done plenty of killing over the years," the Congressman, who was on and off his phone, replied.

"But it's empty. The challenge is gone. Most of my targets have not even been able to defend themselves. They're not soldiers, assassins, or even with any government. There's no honor in these tasks. The only fun I've had is killing your agents last week. At least they put up a fight. I need to move on."

"What you're asking for can't be done. You're too great a risk if we let you walk away," the Praetor responded.

Trumbull started pacing side to side, eying up each of the Council members. It was as if he was watching a ping pong match, the questions bouncing from the right, then the left, then the right again.

Some were clearly distracted with their electronics, as if they weren't even listening. He took a breath. "Why? What are the chances that any of the information was even passed forward from their ancestors or anyone else for that matter? The guy I'm shadowing clearly has given up looking for something he never found, and never will."

Trumbull was as skilled in historical knowledge as he was an assassin. He started animating his speech with his arms and hands, pointing each time he referenced the Council.

"History's already been written. Even if someone like him did come forward, they wouldn't be able to prove anything and the media would paint them as extremists. You've made sure of that. Discounting information that just surfaces has never been easier. Your sideshow of political chaos is entrenched in partisanship. The media feeds the frenzy and the people just eat it up for their own purposes." If there was one thing Trumbull did know about these leaders, it was their passion for power and control. He was feeding them vocal candy and he watched as they ate it up."

He paused for a moment, waiting for a response. Not getting one, he continued. "The religious and secular zealots insure instability for all mankind. Most of the people are now addicted to technology. They live in virtual worlds with no accountability. Pathetic creatures created by the partisanship of the elite. Don't you have enough control already? I mean, the people are like cattle, just as you wanted them, except for a very few who actually do educate themselves. But even then, they're looking at the materials you and your Society have written all through the years. You really don't need me."

The Congressman looked up from his computer. "We must insist that you reconsider. Your assignment is more important than you know. You can't just leave." He said cold and sternly. "You're told all that you need to know, and you know much less than you think."

Trumbull was still unmoved. He'd had enough. The old men, while not alone, were powerless to do anything. They could kill him, but he was too valuable. He stared at them with the cold look of a hired gun, a killer. For that was Trumbull's purpose. He was hired for his unique abilities, but those abilities were not being used. Not by these men. He was eager to move on. The thrill, the danger, the satisfaction were all gone now and he wanted them back.

He watched as several of the old men looked like they were unsettled by his glares and animation. He was getting under their skin and he knew it.

The FBI Director settled back into his chair and in a quiet tone said. "Tell me, Mr. Trumbull, do you really think truthful information will always be cast off?"

Trumbull lowed his voice and minimized his animation. "All I know is for hundreds of years the truth, that is the truth you think is out there, has been hidden. The internet has thousands of pages of history at everyone's fingertips, yet no one is doing anything about it. People cherry pick whatever they think fits their perception of times past. They refuse to actually take the time to find out. No one has the time anymore. People are engrossed in their own small worlds."

He took a moment to motions towards a few of the members on the right, staring at their computers, validating his point. He continued, but shifted more towards the right side of the table, eying the tenth man at the end.

"Only professors and Think Tanks spend any real time on all this and even then they write their findings in pure partisan politicking. The system you now have is so entrenched, it will never be overturned. The people are addicted to it. Even the crazy ones on both sides have no foundation to build a resistance. Sure, they will pick off a few issues and politicians here and there, but this Colossus you have amassed will never be stopped. You already have everything you wanted, power, control, wealth, and mankind under your whip. Not just here, but all over the world." As he finished he was directly in front of the tenth man, watching him dawdle on his computer.

The FBI Director raised his arm towards Trumbull, as if to point at him, but didn't. "Yes, and we intend to keep it that way. Where the others in history have failed, ours is the greatest achievement ever made. You are right. We do have almost total control now, but we must make sure we keep it. Like it or not, if those documents come out, it could spell trouble for us." He finished with a matter-of-fact look.

"Not anymore. The people have no stomach for it. They will continue to follow your Nation State just as it has been for a very long time. *The American people will never take back their own government.* They lost it before it even started. Following the partisan leaders is all they can do, and they have been doing that for over a hundred years."

The Admiral stared at Trumbull. "You've been doing quite a lot of investigating on your own."

Trumbull could tell more and more of them were becoming curious about his knowledge, as they abandoned their electronics to engage in the discussion. A few even started conversing with the counterparts sitting next to them.

"What about these Libertarians and other Constitutional groups?" the Admiral asked, trying to get his attention.

Trumbull knew they were testing him. His research was the only thing keeping him going. He was stuck in this nightmare so he became as much interested in finding the lost documents, if there even were any, as those who had become his prey.

He now stood directly in front of the ninth man to answer. "They are just more groups unable to coalesce around anything. Their very message is individual expression and protection of personal property above all else. That's been the weakness of the other side forever, the same as the Jeffersonians' before them. As long as you keep them looking like radicals, they'll never garner a majority on anything. Your two-party system destroyed the Republic and has controlled everything from the bottom up since its inception."

Trumbull glared at the tenth man, who had not joined the conversation.

Something about him is not right. What is it?

He slowly walked back to the center of the table, finishing his thought.

"Democrats in power, Republicans in power, it doesn't matter. You own both sides. The machinery is so complex, that the ability to have another faction move in is simply not even in the equation. In fact, half the other fledgling political parties are bent on going back to the Constitution! And therein lays your control. The circle is closed and they're making sure of it."

"You sound as if we no longer need to worry at all. So very sure of yourself. However, we're not convinced, so we must continue to look. Will you reconsider?" the Praetor asked, just as Trumbull was now directly in front of him.

He stood motionless. He could tell they were not going to let him go.

I need to figure out how to placate these guys.

He shook his head. "The endless search for the Holy Grail of the Republic."

The Praetor pressed. "Nonetheless, we do need you."

"No, you don't need me. I'm sick of watching and waiting. I could kill all their leaders and end this once and for all."

All ten men were now fixated on Trumbull. He sensed they were waiting for his capitulation.

The Interpol Agent, now fully engaged in the discussion, chimed in. "Ah, yes, kill them all. We have thought about that long and hard, however one holds the key, if there is a key, to all this. We also believe that several splinter groups are somehow connected to them, though we don't have all the information we need on those groups. So killing who we can might, in fact, backfire in media exposure. And what would happen if someone else just came forth with the information? Perhaps one of them has already shared what they know with their own organization or others."

He looked at them, hardening his tone. "This is pathetic. The Society of Praetorians quaking in their boots. You hold all the power on the planet and you sit there like scared little school girls. Where am I, at a Brownie convention?"

"Always the jokester, Trumbull," the Praetor responded.

Trumbull was losing patience and could tell they were as well.

He raised his hand as if to include them all in his next diatribe.

"Okay, now listen and learn what you should know already. The perpetual partisanship and the media would never allow the change. You could go on TV tomorrow and say you have conclusive evidence that a great conspiracy had taken place and you could even show documents to back up your claims. It wouldn't matter. The people are not listening and the tale would be so far-fetched that the person coming forward would be labeled a nut. You and your organization have total control. You don't need me anymore. Have one of your minions watch this old fool until he dies. I'm not doing it anymore." He turned to leave.

Two agents came out of the elevator blocking his exit. Someone in the room had signaled for help. He turned and glared at them. He was a dead man and he knew it. He needed to make a play now, either fighting his way out, or talking his way out.

"The first one that gets killed is you." His gun was already trained on the Praetor. "So have the goons put their weapons on the table."

The Praetor motioned and they complied.

I've overplayed my hand. Satisfy them now and worry about it later.

"Okay, here's the deal…I'll consider staying on, but no more babysitting. I need a lot more intensity. You do understand, right?" He smiled and lowered his gun.

He could see the collective sigh of relief in the room. His word had always been good with the Council.

The Praetor took a deep breath. "Oh, and Mr. Trumbull, I believe you have something of ours?"

Trumbull walked back to the table, took out two small gold eagle pins, and slid them to the leader. "You know what my abilities are. If you cross me, every one of you shall meet a horrible death. Think of Jack the Ripper if you need a visual."

"And yours?" the Senator asked, stumbling over his words after the gruesome threat just made.

Trumbull lifted his collar to show the gold eagle pinned underneath. He turned, walked into the elevator, and waved.

"Sorry, I must be on the wrong floor." He smirked as the door closed.

◊ ◊ ◊

The Praetor gazed at the elevator. *Is he really going to stay with us? Maybe I should incarcerate him for now. We need to keep this quiet. I need to stay in control.*

Council members got on phones, computers, tablets, corresponding with their underlings. Most were in a state of anxiety and stress. These types of encounters with their assassins were few and far between.. None of them cared for the exposure and possible leaks to the media. The room was filled with chatter.

The Senator looked at the elevator, then the Praetor. "Well…can we trust him?"

The Praetor, who was now on his computer, grabbed his phone and called down to security on the main floor. "He's heading down. Hold him. I don't want him killed. And he's still armed."

"Yes, Sir," the guard on the other end replied.

"Do you think he has information about the documents?" the General asked.

"We'll find out," the Praetor regained his composure.

Several members were now pacing the floor, some on their phones, others just stressed out.

◊ ◊ ◊

The head guard stood directly in front of the elevator, holding an Ruger SR9c pistol. All the guards were armed with the same weapon.

He was flanked by two other guards.

They held their breath, guns ready, as the doors opened.

It was empty. He wasn't there. On the back panel was a small note: Sorry, you missed me.

The head guard went in and looked up at the escape hatch on top.

"Get me that stool." He pointed to one by a desk. He climbed up and opened the hatch, then called in. "He's gone."

◊ ◊ ◊

The Praetor ended the call. He looked at the tenth man at the end of the table, the only one who hadn't spoken. "He's yours."

The tenth man smiled and went to the elevator.

The Praetor slammed his phone down on the desktop, shattering it. "Damn it!"

He looked at the tenth man. "His job is now yours. I want him alive, do you understand? We must find out what he knows."

◊ ◊ ◊

The elevator reached the top floor again and opened. The tenth man entered and hit the button for the parking garage below the main floor. On his ride down, he reached to the side of his face and removed what had been a clever face mask. He was in fact quite younger than the mask showed, mid-thirties.

He readied himself as the doors opened, pistol pointed out into the garage. *I'll show him what a real assassin can do.*

◊ ◊ ◊

Trumbull was there all right and was waiting for him as he stepped into the open. Trumbull fired a single shot, hitting him in the shoulder. He wanted him wounded and disarmed, not dead. Not until he had a chance to grill him.

The assassin recoiled slightly but kept coming and was already returning fire. It was all Trumbull could do to get to cover. One bullet grazed his right hand, his shooting hand, creating a long slice across the back of it. He found a safe spot behind a Jersey barrier.

"Kevlar," Trumbull said softly to himself. "Let's find out where that vest ends."

"Trumbull! They just want to question you. I'm not here to kill you or you'd already be dead. That flesh wound was nothing more than a show of strength. You and I are cut from the same cloth."

Trumbull didn't respond. He peaked around the side of the barrier to see the elevator doors were closed. The assassin was to the left of the elevator standing in front of a parked car. His pistol pointing at the Jersey barrier.

Trumbull smiled to himself. *This guy thinks he's better than me. He has nowhere to go…standing in the open.*

"I beg to differ." Trumbull offered.

He rose to fire just as the elevator opened and three agents ran out.

They were directly in his line of sight.

Three kill shots and they were down, but now the assassin had his weapon trained on Trumbull's head.

"You're the best they've got?" the assassin said in an arrogant tone. "Place your gun on the ground and slide it towards me."

It was the same sarcastic tone Trumbull was famous for.

"Victor Shaw?" Trumbull replied, sizing up his competition.

"I'm surprised you know me." Shaw moved a little to his left, then his right, keeping his weapon trained on Trumbull.

"Well, one does keep up with their competition. I do hear you're quite good." As he answered, he slipped his right hand in his pocket.

"Hey! Keep those hands where I can see them!" He raised his gun and moved a step closer to Trumbull.

He complied but kept his right hand closed.

With distain, Shaw answered. "I had heard the same about you. This is a disappointment." He motioned with his gun as he said. "Now if you please, your weapon."

Trumbull paused. Then he squatted and slid the gun to Shaw across the concrete floor.

Shaw picked up the gun. "The Praetor wants you alive. Get into the elevator." He motioned with his gun hand again.

Trumbull cracked a small smile and opened his cut hand to expose a devise.

Shaw's eyes narrowed at him in slight confusion. "What's that supposed to be?"

"The best of the best doesn't have one of these? Huh." In quintessential Get Smart-alecky voice. He paused as the anger grew in Shaw's eyes. "It's a detonator linked to that gun you're now holding."

Shaw looked at the gun, now in his non shooting hand, turning it. "I don't see anything here."

"Nevertheless, it is."

"I'm supposed to believe you? What a weak attempt at trickery."

Trumbull shrugged with a grin from the corners of his mouth. "Either way, your funeral."

Shaw saw the seriousness in Trumbull's eyes and attempted to throw the gun, but not in time. It exploded from inside the handle, covering his face with fragments of metal.

He screamed and fell backwards.

"I hate losing a good weapon," Trumbull quipped to himself as he made his way to his car, but not before he heard Shaw yelling.

"Damn you, Trumbull! I'll return the favor the next time we meet."

Trumbull backed his car out of a parking space and looked in his rear view mirror. Shaw was some fifty feet away holding the left side of his bloodied face. It looked like there were left several slices and one bad injury. His eye appeared to be gone.

"Running are we, Trumbull? You're pathetic!" Was the last thing Trumbull heard as he saw Shaw stagger to the elevator.

Trumbull had indeed met his equal that day and he was sure they would cross paths again, but not this day. This day was about staying alive. This day was now about revenge. What the Society had claimed was their best weapon, their best resource, was now their worst nightmare.

Chapter 7

February 1783 – Newburgh, New York

McDougall entered the command quarters dressed in common clothes. General Gates, bored going through paperwork on his desk, was talking quietly with a dispatcher standing before him.

There were several other officers and aides in the large room, at desks or standing near them. All seemed to have independent conversations going on in all manner of subjects.

Gates signed and handed the dispatcher some papers. "See to it these get out immediately."

"Yes Sir. Will there be anything else Sir?"

"Not at the moment, thank you."

"Yes Sir," the dispatcher stood for a moment.

Gates paused, and then said "Well, go on. You're dismissed Corporal."

The Corporal nodded politely and exited past McDougall standing at the door. Gates looked at him and gave a disgruntled sound. The General's aide went over and met him.

Gates watched the two men until his aide returned.

"General, McDougall asks to see you right away."

Gates gave him a quiet unrecognizable response. The aide then motioned for McDougall to go into the Gate's private room.

He soon joined him. "Well, sit down then," Gates grumbled as he went behind his desk and sat. He clearly did not want to hear or see anything to his disliking, but knew it was coming.

"General, I have instructions for you to carry out," he said under his breath.

This was the last thing the General wanted to hear. He knew this day would come but dreaded it. "Give them to me."

McDougall pulled out the concealed satchel and handed it to the General. Gates looked at it for a moment. "Well, wait for me outside until I have a chance to go over these."

"Sir, the Praetor demands that you carry these orders out immediately."

Gates gave him a snarl. "Perhaps you should spend less

time meddling and more time just doing your job. Do you understand me? Now go and wait for my orders and send in my aide."

"Yes Sir," McDougall said, playing to the part. He left for the other room. No one, save Lord North, knew just how close General McDougall now was to the Praetor.

A few moments passed and the aide entered.

"Get Commander Bishop."

"Yes Sir."

Bishop entered the room, closing the door behind him.

Gates was sitting with the satchel, in a light trance. Bishop stood uneasily in front of him. "Well then, those are the orders?" he said quietly.

Gates looked up at him, said nothing and then opened the satchel and removed the papers.

"What are they this time?"

Gates read the first page and handed it to Bishop, then the second and finally the third.

"Can this be right?" Bishop asked.

Gates sat back in his chair and was in deep thought.

"Sir, how can we possibly do this?"

"The instructions are plain enough." Gates confirmed.

"Yes, but to do this now? It will ruin him."

Gates paused before he answered. "Yes it will ruin him." The General then wrote a quick note and handed it to Bishop along with the satchel and the documents. "Give this to McDougall. Tell him to leave at once. No need to tell you how private these materials are and he must show them to our associates in Congress."

Commander Bishop took the satchel and left the room. Gates' mind was racing as he stood and went to the window. He didn't see the beautiful landscape of rolling hills with a great river in the distance. All he saw were army tents surrounded by angry soldiers who had yet to be paid.

Bishop gave McDougall the satchel. "You must leave at once."

"I know what to do," he snapped "Just make sure you're ready when the time comes. He expects it to be done by May. I'd hate to have to tell him you were not prepared." A devious smile came across McDougall's face.

Commander Bishop stood his ground but was clearly dismayed as McDougall left. He re-entered the Generals room. “Sir, I just don’t understand why he chose McDougall. Having a general running around meeting people in the open is dangerous to everyone.”

“General McDougall has been playing an important role in all of this from the beginning. His ties to the army and Congress make him uniquely qualified. He can make arguments to Congress directly. Besides, he’s meeting Robert Morris and they are both going to Congress to demand action in getting the men paid. Helping in the matter is Gouverneur Morris. He has written a private coded letter to Congress saying that the army may very well march on Congress and a military coup could take place.”

“But the Praetor…this is what troubles me. How can all these representatives follow a bastard immigrant with no ties here?”

“I would take care how you speak, Bishop. There are spies everywhere.”

“Surely many will resist and simply ignore him. Do you really think we are going to change this new country with him at the helm?”

“It does not matter what I think. King George chose him many years ago. Washington does not deserve this, but only through his removal and disgrace can we hope to achieve our purpose,” The General turned again and looked out the window. “Tyranny seems to be the only real power in government no matter what the people want.”

Commander Bishop paused in thought; realizing Gates was no longer interested in discussing the topic, he left.

◊ ◊ ◊

It had been eighteen months since the victory at Yorktown, which ended active combat. The British still occupied New York City, so Washington had the army station near Newburgh to keep a wary eye on the British until a peace treaty was signed. This took much longer than expected. Already broke and with ever-dwindling supplies, many in the army became restless and angry. Most had spent their own money on food and supplies and were now broke. Congress did not have enough money to pay them.

These eighteen months had been especially hard as the weather broke the spirits of most of the men. Still owed most of their back pay, an officer wrote a letter to Washington concerning the state of affairs they were in, suggesting for him to become king and allow military officers the chance to create their own state in the west by taking control of the government. It was written by a field officer, a Colonel Lewis Nicola. While this letter was independent of other attempts to force Congress to pay, it greatly distressed Washington that some in the ranks would consider such a mutiny.

Meanwhile, a military coup was now being considered by at least some of the officers. They asked Washington to at least threaten Congress for redress. Several of them also wanted him to be made king of America. Others wanted to destroy him. Washington responded to the letter and rejected the entire premise.

Soon after, a flyer had been distributed to all the officers in camp. They were to hold a secret meeting to decide what to do next. Washington found out and canceled the meeting, asking the men for more time to respond to their plans. This was not the first time a conspiracy had occurred to remove him as Commander in Chief. They rescheduled a few days later.

◊ ◊ ◊

It was late morning yet the grass was still damp with the morning dew. He strode towards the rectangular building that was forty feet wide by seventy feet long with a small dais at one end, known as the Public Building, dressed in his best uniform. His boots were muddy from the trip, the frantic trip to get there. As he approached a side entrance, he heard the commotion from inside. Things were clearly degenerating into chaos. He heard anger, disgust, disdain and a call to arms.

As he stopped at the side entrance, he realized this was the most pivotal moment of his career. With all the battles lost and won, this battle would decide the fate of the new Confederation. He listened as the Chair of the meeting started, gave him a moment to settle the crowd, and then he entered the building. As he did, the chatter stopped.

There was genuine shock on General Gate's face. He stood as if turned to stone. This was more than unexpected; it was totally uncalculated in Gates' mind. The secret meeting had been breached, a meeting that could spell the end for all of them as traitors to their own cause.

"General, with your permission I would like to speak to the officers."

Gates stammered. He look at the men and then back at the uninvited guest. "I,I…well, yes Sir of course," was all he could get out. He stumbled, backing off of the speaking podium as he allowed the uninvited guest to approach.

Standing before the group behind the podium he looked at all the officers. One was missing, Colonel Nicola, though Washington probably would not have recognized him. He drew some papers from his pocket, unfolded them and began to read.

"Gentlemen, by an anonymous summons, an attempt has been made to convene you together. How inconsistent with the rules of propriety! — How unmilitary! — And how subversive of all order and discipline, let the good sense of the army decide. In the moment of this summons, another anonymous production was sent into circulation; addressed more to the feelings of passions, than to the reason and judgment of the army. The author of the piece, is entitled to much credit for the goodness of his pen: — and I could wish he had as much credit for the rectitude of his heart for, as men we see thro' different optics, and are induced by the reflecting faculties of the mind, to use different means to attain the same end: — the author of the address, should have had more charity, than to mark for suspicion, the man who should recommend moderation and longer forbearance or, in others words, who should not think as he thinks, and act as he advises. But he had another plan in view, in which candor and liberality of sentiment, regard to justice, and love of country, have no part, and he was right, to insinuate the darkest suspicion, to effect the blackest designs.

"That the address is drawn with great art, and is designed to answer the most insidious purposes. That it is calculated to impress the mind, with an idea of premeditated injustice in the sovereign power of the United States, and rouse all those resentments which must unavoidably flow from such a belief. That the secret mover of this scheme, whoever he may be, intended to take advantage of the passions, while they were warmed by the recollection of mind which is so necessary to give dignity and stability to measures, is rendered too obvious, by the mode of conducting the business to need other proof than a reference to the proceeding."

He continued on for some time with his prepared speech.

The military coup had been exposed. The army was to march on Congress and take it by force if need be. They would install selected officers and elite aristocrats to run the new government. The Confederation would melt away and an empire would replace it….an American Imperial Empire.

It would start with General Gates replacing Washington as Commander and Chief. This was Gates' second involvement in an attempt to oust Washington. The man behind the scenes and pulling the strings was, of course, the Praetor. He again set the entire plan in motion and promised Gates he would be able to march on Congress and take control.

Washington paused when he had finished his speech. He looked at the officers. Their expressions had not changed. Anger was still playing its evil upon them. They were unmoved by his words. Washington had lost his chance to purge their actions. Despondently, he took another letter out of his pocket to read. A low murmur of discontent started in the crowd. They were still fixated on his face. They had heard these types of impassioned remarks from him before to push them, ever push them. They were past the breaking point.

This second letter was from a member of Congress pleading for the military to allow them more time to compensate them properly. As Washington went to read the letter, he realized the penmanship was much smaller than his own and he could not see it to read. He fumbled in his pocket for a moment and then pulled out a pair of reading spectacles and put them on. "Please forgive me as the war and my efforts have made me more fragile than my years."

The men were stunned. Most had never seen Washington with glasses on and only now realized just how much he had suffered with them. Many were brought to tears as Washington read and by the time he was done, the entire room had abandoned their conspiracy attempt. It was an impossible turn of events, but one that happened all the same.

Now Washington focused on the source of the original pamphlet. He had been tipped off as to who was behind this attempt, officers under the command of General Gates. It was only because he managed to get a copy of the pamphlet that he was able to hurry along and stop that fateful meeting.

But the failed attempt hit its mark. There would now be a call to give Congress more power so it could fulfill its obligations.

The Praetor's plans were unfolding even in this setback. It was now only a matter of time before he could rule as the omnipotent emperor of America he so longed for.

◊ ◊ ◊

Washington returned to his headquarters outside of Newburgh. It was a large home just north of the city. An old friend was there to meet him at the door.

"Hello Mr. Hamilton. I am happy to see you."

"Thank you General, you are most kind."

"Nonsense, in fact I have a tale to tell you that you will find extremely troubling. Please let us sit and talk." Washington motioned for them to go into the drawing room. There was a large lit fireplace centered on the outside wall. Washington welcomed the warmth as he approached and stood at the hearth. "It seems a large conspiracy was in full swing over the last few months. I am grateful for your correspondence exposing the plot."

Hamilton joined him. "Yes, I had heard rumors while at Congress that this conspiracy was being put together and I thought it wise to alert you of its intent, especially after that Nicola letter you showed me last month. You know who your enemies are, and you know to what lengths they will go to have you discredited. Who was it this time?"

"This time it was almost my entire core of officers. I believe the Nicola letter was unrelated to the coup attempt, but it certainly was in the same vein."

"You can't be serious."

"Oh yes…and it gets even better. It seems General Gates was ready to step in to take my place."

"Gates again Sir?"

"Yes. It seems he was given another opportunity after the Conway Cabal attempt failed five years ago. Poor Gates, I know him to be a good officer, but it seems he has a weak constitution." Washington looked at Hamilton and the two chuckled.

"He does have a place in his heart for the men though. I think he would do anything for the men. Perhaps that was part of his failing."

"Yes Alexander, you are right about that."

"Are you going to take any measures against him?"

"No. Poor fellow has enough on his plate now." They chuckled again. This was Washington's character. Such a serious situation and he could laugh about it soon afterward. He seldom held grudges if at all. "So tell me Alexander, what cause do you have to be here?"

"Well, with what you have told me, perhaps my efforts are misplaced."

"Oh come now. You know you can talk to me. No one knows me better than you, save Martha."

Hamilton smiled. "You astound me like no other. Our country will forever be in your debt," The two paused a moment as they warmed by the fire. "Actually, I am here on an errand of mercy. I have been talking with Congress and they do want to compensate the men as best they can. I was instructed to put together a meeting of all the officers, including General Gates. It seems my timing is a bit off."

"Don't worry. I will write Gates and the top officers. What are your plans?"

"I mean to establish a…*Society*, for the officers. One that will help them -and- have clout with Congress."

"To what end?"

"To secure fair compensation for all the veterans, for both their time served and a pension for their coming years."

"Yes, I have been thinking the very same thing. These men have given everything to join the cause and most could use a voice and organization to work things out with Congress."

"Well Sir, Major General Knox had the initial idea. I was hoping you would join us. The problem now is General Gates. It might seem rather odd after what has happened."

"Nonsense, this is for the men and I have already told you we can move past the recent events."

Hamilton was relieved to hear this. "Then I will prepare the meeting."

"Yes by all means. Let me know. I will tell my officers to make ready."

"Thank you Sir, and as always I am in your debt."

Chapter 8

May 2018 - Bogata, Texas

Emily Miller's world collapsed in an instant. She heard the words, knew what each word meant, repeating them in her head as Betty, the school secretary, spoke. She felt her body go numb as her brain only began to process it all. Betty's voice grew slow, muffled even, her words dragged out.

Emily felt her mind fade into darkness as her thoughts intensified. All at once, as if life sped up to meet her in that moment, she felt one thing…anger. Through the anger her adrenaline rose, creating panic. Out of panic came fear…terror. It shadowed the anger as she suddenly spoke into the phone.

"What? What?" she stammered. "My girls! Betty!" she cried out. "What happened?"

"They took your girls." Betty cried into the phone.

Emily's world ceased to exist. Her heart was pounding as if to leap out of her chest. She stumbled, grasping at the countertop. She felt her pulse beating through her temples, getting louder and louder inside her head. She tried to talk into the phone clutched in her hand, nothing came out but air. In her mind she heard her girls, their voices, as they played in the backyard singing and giggling on the swings. Then silence and darkness.

When she opened her eyes she was curled up on the on the floor of her kitchen with the phone laying on top of her open hand.

"Emily… Emily, are you there? Can you hear me?" a familiar voice in the phone persisted. For a moment, she didn't understand why she was laying on the floor.

Then realization came rushing back to her… *my girls! Who took my girls? Why would someone take my girls?* Her mind reeled with these questions, her pulse started to pound again and her vision became blurry. She grabbed the phone and was able to push past the lump in her throat to verbalize the thoughts swirling around in her head. She brought the phone to her ear and with a shaky voice, that seemed too high pitched to be her own, she stammered, "Who… who took my girls?"

"Emily, two men made Gus stop the school bus after the last pickup at the Keller's house." Sheriff Pete Lucas calmly told her. "They were armed. They got on the bus and asked for Sara. Gus said a few of the other children looked at her instinctively, not realizing it would give her away. They took the girls, smashed Gus' radio, and forced all the kids to give up their electronics. With no other houses around, he had to get the bus to the school before we found out. I've already called the FBI."

"My Girls Pete! Oh, my God." Emily choked on her words.

Emily attempted to accept the information she had just heard. *Taken!* The one thing every mother fears… *someone taking my children. No… not my girls!* "Pete, did you say they were armed? Who are these men and what do they want? We're not rich. Why would they choose my girls, by name, and take them away?"

"Emily, we'll talk at the station. I've already sent Mike over to pick you up. I haven't talked to Thomas yet, but I'm calling him now. Just hang on, okay?" Pete's voice broke a little at the last.

Emily finally sat up on her knees and wiped the tears off her cheeks. "Pete.......Pete did they hurt them? Did they hurt my girls? I have to know." Did she really want to know? What if they were hurt? How would she go on?

"Gus says one of the men walked them out of the bus and put them in their car. He said they didn't hurt them. I'm bringing Gus to the station."

Emily tried to pull herself together with thoughts she had been taught from childhood. *'Things aren't as bad as they appear,' 'God protects children,' 'everything will turn out alright.'*

Nothing was working. Images of her daughters' smiling faces danced in her mind. Their innocent laughter as they played a game of tag in the back yard with Deputy Mike. Amanda squealing with delight as Thomas pushed her on the swing, 'Push me higher Daddy, push me higher' she would yell out with a laugh. Sara smiling as she ate one of Sheriff Pete's famous Lucas burgers with everything on it.

Just this morning, making the silver dollar sized pancakes that Sara loved for breakfast and seeing the joy on her eight-year-old face as she came into the kitchen. Amanda following right behind her, a very precocious ten, stating, "Oatmeal would be healthier for you Sara, but I love pancakes too!" Amanda always enjoyed helping out with her little sister as they selected their clothes in the morning, helping her on and off the bus, walking Sara to her class room in school and making sure she was there to walk her to the bus when school was over. Emily and Thomas had taught her well.

Emily loved the morning ritual of getting the girls ready for school. The hustle of selecting 'just the right outfit to fit my mood' as Amanda would say. Sara grinning in the mirror as Emily brushed her long blonde hair. Packing lunches, not forgetting to add little notes to make the girls smile, and know their mommy and daddy cherished them.

She had waved as they climbed on the bus this morning and smiled at Gus the bus driver. He smiled back and closed the doors. Gus had been driving the girls' bus since the time Amanda first started going to school, six years had gone by in a flash. The bus moved along towards the next stop, kicking up dust from a drier than usual spring, as it drew out of sight.

Why my girls? Emily broke down again and sobbed uncontrollably. The tears coming too fast to bother trying to wipe them away. Leaning forward with her forehead touching the floor Emily heard Deputy Wilson knocking on the front door. Not being able to respond to him, she heard the screen door opening and closing as Mike came in.

"Emily…Emily?" Mike asked so softly, Emily almost missed it.

She looked up and grabbed his hand as he helped her up.

"We need to go. Pete got a hold of Thomas and he's on his way to the station."

She stood on unsteady legs and buried her face into Mike's side as he led her out to his cruiser.

Emily's mind was still racing, *I need Thomas!*

◊ ◊ ◊

Thomas was rushing out of his office, his mind on overdrive, when his cell phone rang for the second time within a minute. His heart was racing and he really didn't want to take the time to answer. Anything that would take time away from getting to the sheriff's office should be ignored. He looked down at the screen of his phone as he ran across the full parking lot to his dark grey Lexus. On most days he would spend a moment smiling at his prized possession that held lots of fond memories. Now the car didn't even register in his mind. Unlisted number flashed on the screen. As he neared his car, winded from running, he answered the call.

"Mr. Miller?" a man's voice on the other end asked.

"Yes?" Thomas stopped in his tracks a few feet from his car, confused.

"Mr. Miller, we can clear this all up very quickly. Just give us what we want, and your girls will be back home in no time." The voice was quiet yet threatening.

"What? Wait…wait…who are you?" Thomas physically shook his head trying to clear his mind, and started walking.

"You know exactly who we are. Please don't make this any harder than it has to be. Make yourself ready to comply with what we want, or you'll never see your girls again. Do you understand?" his malicious tone no longer veiled.

As Thomas reached the car he pleaded into the phone, "Okay…okay…" he gasped. "Just don't hurt my girls. *Please*, please don't hurt them."

"We'll call with further instructions." The caller hung up.

Thomas looked down as if there would be more information showing on his iPhone screen. His hands started to shake and he had to blink several times to keep the tears at bay.

Who was that?? This isn't happening. What's going on? My girls!

He managed to get himself together enough to start the car and head out of the parking lot towards downtown Bogata, Texas, and the Sheriff's office. On the way, his phone rang once more. Unlisted showing on the car radio screen. Anxiety overwhelmed him as he pushed the answer button on the steering wheel. His voice shook with nervousness and his knuckles turned white from gripping the steering wheel as he answered.

"Mr. Miller?" This was not the same voice from the last call, this voice was smooth and polished.

"Yes?"

"Mr. Miller, listen very carefully. I know your girls have been taken. I'm going to explain what this is about. Don't tell anyone, save one, what I'm about to tell you. Are we clear?" The voice was calm but persuasive and not to be argued with.

Thomas was having trouble keeping his car on the road as he drifted into the wrong lane. He pulled the wheel to get back to the right.

"Yes, please tell me what's going on." He listened for several minutes as the voice continued to bounce off the leather seats of the car with information and instructions for him to carry out.

After hearing more than he could possibly process, Thomas practically whined to the voice on the other end, "But I need to talk with someone. You said there are two groups, what are they? Who's involved? Why is my family being targeted? Who are you?"

"Talk to the Sheriff, and only the Sheriff. Don't reveal anything other than I called you. If you do, your girls might be hurt."

"You're one of them aren't you, the kidnappers? This is just some ploy, some trick." His voice was shaking. He wasn't processing the information as it pulled his mind in different directions.

The car skidded along the shoulder of the road as he drifted again. He yanked the steering wheel to regain control. His heavy breathing could be heard through the Bluetooth.

"No, it's no trick. This is as real as it gets. Talk to no one but the Sheriff, understand?"

"I don't understand, who are you?"

"You will understand once you talk to the Sheriff," the calm voice said, a little more forcefully.

He shook his head. "Okay…"

The caller hung up before Thomas could asked another question, so he sped up toward the station.

◊ ◊ ◊

Harry Matthews drew in a deep breath and exhaled slowly. He was a pro at taking what didn't belong to him, but deep down he felt he had just crossed some imaginary line that will follow him the rest of his life. He ran his hand down his face as he turned around and looked into the frightened blue eyes of the young girl. This one must be Amanda, older of the two, and by the looks of it growing up way to fast. He was impressed by the stubborn uplifted tilt of her chin as she looked at him while trying to comfort her younger sister. He could see she was frightened by the tears that made tracks down her cheeks and yet what captivated him was how she tried to steel her resolve and overcome her fear.

Facing forward again, Harry smiled to himself. At the same moment, he realized how low he'd sunk in his own life. Her innocent courage made him despise his participation in this latest scheme of the Society, and he hated himself a little for not standing up to them when he had the chance.

It was not the first time he and his cohort, Cliff Barden, had done this. Adults young or old, it didn't matter. Yes, he and Cliff were getting well paid for their certain expertise. This was the seventh time. In fact, they were getting good at finding spots and places with which to waylay unsuspecting innocents. Neither cared about the underlying reason behind the scenes.

This one felt different though, as it was the first time they'd taken kids. This time he didn't have the same feeling of success and satisfaction. It couldn't be guilt he felt, yet what else could it be?

The plan was flawless so far. They were both dressed in black business suits, and they had pulled masks over their heads as the bus approached. The bus driver never had a chance to get a good look at them. It seemed easy to force their way onto the bus and simply ask for the girls.

Their masks were now off. They weren't concerned about the girls seeing their faces.

Harry was tall, lean, and well-muscled. Not the bulky muscles of a body builder but the sleek build of a runner. He had dark brown hair he kept short and darker brown, almost black, eyes. Cliff by contrast was a shorter, stockier build, blonde hair, blue eyes, and a tan that said he had too much time on his hands.

Turning around one more time looking into the wide blue eyes of Amanda, Harry was surprised when she summoned the courage to ask a question.

"Where are we going?" Amanda asked and he heard her voice shake a bit.

"Someplace safe," Harry answered. "Don't worry, we won't hurt you…so long as you listen to us and do as you're told. Soon you'll be back with your parents. You just stay buckled up and scrunch down in your seats. If you don't, I'll have to tie you up and that'll make for an uncomfortable ride." He presented a low and scary voice, and saw the girls shudder with fear.

The girls did as he asked and both lay down as best they could, with the seat belts digging into their shoulders and stomachs.

Chapter 9

May 1783 - Fishkill, New York

Two months after the attempted coup, Major General Henry Knox and Hamilton, who had written to all the officers in the army and navy who had served at least three years, asked them to attend a special meeting in Fishkill. The British were still in New York City as the peace negotiations were going on in Paris, but military engagements had long since stopped.

"I call this meeting to order" Hamilton said. He was the organizer, chair, and speaker at the meeting.

"Our first order of business is to name this new Society. With that in mind, I recommend the Society of the Cincinnati. As many of my learned colleagues know, Cincinnatus was a Roman farmer who was called on to become dictator and save the Roman state from destruction. The main reason I selected his name was because once the task was successful, he returned to his farming. '*Omnia relinquit servare Republicam*'…he relinquished everything to save the Republic. He in fact did this twice."

"I move for this name to be so given to our group," shouted one of the officers.

"I second," another said.

The vote was unanimous.

"I further propose our Society be based on pure honest intentions for three purposes that we will call the Immutable Principles:

To preserve the rights so dearly won;
to promote the continuing union of the states;
to assist members in need, their widows, and orphans."

Again the motion was passed.

"Officers who have served three or more years are allowed to join the Society, including some French officers who have helped our cause in the war." Hamilton had captured the hearts of the men.

"I would like to propose General Washington be the president of our Society. Now, we all know what happened a few months ago in Newburgh. Voicing your support now will indeed be welcome as we move forward."

"Yea," was heard from all corners of the room.

"The motion is passed. Congratulations General."

Washington nodded in approval.

Hamilton continued. "I also have some good news from the Congress. They have agreed to many of the terms requested by the army including back pay and pensions for the officers. They are putting this measure out to the states for approval. The money will be raised by Congress somehow. We will also see a strengthening of our central government, for it has to be stronger in order to satisfy its obligations."

An agreeing approval sounded throughout the room.

The meeting took some two hours as they went through an extensive list of priorities the officers had regarding additional compensations for those who had spent most of their own money. They broke out into groups, mostly by state, to discuss how they could convince Congress to fund all they asked for.

Hamilton motioned a close to the meeting. "Now I must ask you all to go back to your states and press them for this proposition. It is only through the strength of our newly formed Society that we can receive the restitution we are all due."

During the next year they, recruited others from the military and those sympathetic to their cause in all the states and effectively had the largest organization in the country.

May 1784 - Eastern Long Island, New York

The Society of Praetorians gathered for another important meeting. As before, all ten Council members were there as was Lord North.

"Now gentlemen, we have been pressing for some time now to increase the power of the central government so we can step in at the right moment. While we have been making progress to this end, two individuals have been able to thwart some of our efforts. We must now decide on our future course. Do we take over through force? Do we eliminate these two individuals? But before we decide this matter I need to hear someone's report." The Praetor looked directly at him. "Let us start with you, Stansbury."

Joseph Stansbury nervously stood. "Praetor, gentlemen…I have been using all our means to disrupt trade with France. I believe we have been effective in doing so as I hear from many of my contacts to this effect."

"That's very interesting Stansbury as I have heard different," the Praetor responded in a dissatisfied voice.

"Sir, you must understand. I cannot single handedly stop all trade. It is beyond the scope of anyone to do so unless it comes from Congress."

"Don't pass your failings off onto me," Robert Morris snapped. "The Congress is moving towards our goal. We cannot enact a law prohibiting trade with France. It would never pass."

"That's not true!" yelled Stansbury.

"Gentlemen, please. There is no need to quarrel here. Mr. Stansbury was given specific orders. He was given the resources to carry out those orders. He simply failed to do so." The Praetor seemed calm, almost too calm.

"Sir, even with your resources, I cannot stop pirates and illegal shipments. I need more help, additional men."

"I think not Mr. Stansbury. I have given you more than enough."

"Sir…please."

The Praetor pulled out a pistol. "This is what happens when you fail to carry out simple orders."

"No! Please!" Stansbury screamed raising his hands in an attempt to cover his face.

Bang!

The Praetor shot him through the head.

The Council members gasped, several ducking for cover, while others stood.

Lord North intervened. "Everyone!" he shouted. "Just calm down, and sit down!" he ordered.

He motioned to servants and they removed Stansbury's body.

The fear in the room was staggering. Some of the men were appalled at what they just witnessed, yet would not speak or challenge the Praetor.

The room fell silent for a moment.

The Praetor spoke evenly. "Now, is there anyone else who

cares to report falsely? Hmm…anyone? I thought not. Let this be a lesson to all of you. Some have done well. Others…well others need to pick up the slack. Am I clear?"

"Yes Praetor," they all responded, in low, subjugated voices.

"Good, then on to business. General McDougall,…excuse me, Congressmen McDougall, your report please."

McDougall rose. "Sir, by your orders, I met with many of the officers along with our alliance in New York City. We have covertly instituted the Society of Praetorians, within the Society of the Cincinnati, yet unknown and secret from most Cincinnati members. It includes not only officers, but business and political contacts. We are continuing plans for control of the government. While our last attempt failed, we are working our way into the hearts of those who wished for power and glory. The difference now is the additional resources of the military. Having merchants, bankers, shipping interests, politicians, creditors, land speculators, and most being lawyers, our plans are starting to materialize. A powerful military organization in the Society of the Cincinnati, augmented by our group in the private sector now gives us the strength we needed to take control."

McDougall nodded to the Praetor and sat.

"Now, that is the kind of report I was looking for." He turned his attention to Morris. "Tell me Morris, what can be done about those two flies in our soup?"

"Sir?"

"Oh come now Morris. Surely you can think of something?"

Morris felt his collar tighten. "Well…"

The Praetor gave him a moment to compose himself.

Morris was thinking hard. "We could…"

"Perhaps I can help Mr. Morris. Appoint them as diplomats."

Morris thought for a moment. "Yes, we can. I will have Congress take this up immediately."

"Good Mr. Morris."

Morris and the rest knew he was let off the hook for now. The Praetor needed his leadership in Congress. Killing him would only hurt their efforts whereas Stansbury had become a liability.

"And be sure to give each of them something they will enjoy. Adams fancies meeting King George and Jefferson will feel right at home with the riffraff in France. I wouldn't want to see either of them miserable in their new stations." He had a grin on his face.

"Anything else gentlemen?"

The rest of the Praetorian Council was perfectly happy to remain silent.

The war officially ended with the Treaty of Paris in 1784. General Washington retired and returned to Mount Vernon to run his several milling businesses. Jefferson was commissioned to delegate in Paris and arrived by mid-summer. Adams was again asked to stay abroad, though this time more to his liking, in London.

For the next two years the Praetorians enlisted hundreds more to their cause offering power to each. There were now dozens seated in the very heart of government controlling what they could.

July 1786 - Eastern Long Island, New York

General McDougall had died a month earlier so the Praetor elevated his most trusted spy as second in command. While the General's death was questioned, only a very few knew he was murdered by the Praetor. The Praetor would often kill a Council member if he felt they had become a liability. This was the case with McDougall.

A man by the name of Benjamin Church, a spy for England during the war, was introduced to the Council by Lord North. He'd been running most of the secret field work for the Society. He was thought lost at sea in 1778 and so it gave him freedom to infiltrate American society without the worry of name or rank. His loyalty to the king would finally pay off as he took his place in the leadership of Praetorians.

The Praetorian Council was meeting again in their dark stronghold.

"Tell me the news, Church," the Praetor asked.

"Sir, I have established leniency for many of our Society of Praetorians in Boston. The loyalists have re-established their former positions of wealth and power. They once again are the elite not only in Massachusetts, but throughout New England."

"Very good…you have done well. Now we must turn the tide. You are to start a rebellion in Massachusetts against the seat of government there. Once this is accomplished, the cries for a stronger central government will rise to a pitch not yet reached. Then we will be able to establish once and for all the central power we have worked for."

The Praetor had thought long and hard on this. It was a risky move that might expose them, but he had not been able to centralize power through the political channels yet and time was running out. He was also seeing his minions growing ever stronger with malice and lust for power. His plans were unfolding and his strength growing as more and more of the elite joined the dark Society of Praetorians.

◊ ◊ ◊

It was a month before Church returned with his report. He met privately with the Praetor in his chamber.

"I have contacted our English loyalists in Boston and have set them in motion to demand payments for debts owed from their loans to the soldiers during the war," Church said. "The soldiers, who are mostly farmers, are destitute having never gotten paid for their services in the war. Most were conscripted, having no choice. Now that they have not been able to sustain a living off the land, let alone pay the debts they owe, we can form a coalition and have them revolt against the state.

"Yes Church and this will force the Massachusetts' government to put down this rebellion," the Praetor said.

"Yes Sir." Church just realized they were not alone. Lord North was in the shadows of a corner window. He could just make out his silhouette.

The Praetor continued. "This is the linchpin we need to finally get most of the aristocracy in the north in agreement to govern as a central entity. They must be made to realize that the south has no positive attributes other than agrarian. They must become subservient to their counterparts in the north. We will use force of arms if necessary to extract their wealth. Meanwhile, the use of tariffs on imports can siphon funds from their agricultural exporting. It is the only use the south is to the northern states. But we must convince them that a strong central government is essential to their defense and insures free trade through strong treaties. Up until now, they have been resistant to such power centralized."

"I have already had correspondence with several delegates from many of the states and I have convinced them that we need more centralized power to secure the liberties of the states and their citizens," Church said. He seemed troubled. "Praetor, will they be willing to give up so much power?"

Now it was plain to see he was preoccupied with North's presence.

"They won't be," he responded. "They will have their power within the central government instead of the states and I will be their Caesar. A meeting in Annapolis has been scheduled for next month."

He opened a parchment.

"Commissioners appointed by the respective States in the Union, at such time and place, as should be agreed upon to take into consideration the trade and Commerce of the United States, to consider how far a uniform system in their commercial intercourse and regulations might be necessary to their common interest and permanent harmony, and to report to the several States such an Act, relative to this great object, as when unanimously ratified by them would enable the United States in Congress assembled effectually to provide for the same."

"We will feign a compromise to establish a larger central government, while at the same time convince the states that the power will remain within the states. This rebellion will be a great asset towards that goal. Many are looking forward to the new power they will receive as representatives of their states. They know once centralization takes place, it will be virtually impossible for the people to regain control of their own government."

"Yes Sir," Church answered.

"Go then. Rise them up into a fury and make sure they follow through," North said from the shadows.

"Sir, may I speak with you in private?" Church asked as North's blatant statement revealed him fully.

"Leave us North."

He did as requested and left the Praetor's chamber.

Once Church felt North was out of earshot, he spoke. "Sir, why is he hiding in the shadows? He has no authority here. I feel uneasy with him lurking about."

"Church, you must know I cannot have only one asset at my disposal, but many. Your role in this quest is but one small part. North is the King's emissary. For now I must endure his presence. Soon however, you and I shall discuss a resolution to this predicament. But for now you shall see developments moving towards our position that you did not initiate. Focus on your tasks and leave the rest to me."

"Yes Praetor." Church now knew his position in the conspiracy had lessened. He hoped he was still to be rewarded as well as he had previously thought.

Chapter 10

<u>May 2018 - Bogata, Texas</u>

"Any contact with the FBI yet?" Pete looked over to Daniela, one of the secretaries, as he was unsuccessfully trying to control his frustration. He berated himself, this was unacceptable. No one in the office understood how deep his anger at himself went. This was more than just a kidnapping of a close friend's children to him. He was not doing his job. How could he have been so negligent in his primary purpose, the Miller's safety?

The Sheriff's office was buzzing with activity, even though it was a rather small facility. There were four desks in the open room and several extra chairs lining the perimeter. Pete and Mike were at their desks. Emily was sitting at one of the chairs in front of Pete. She was shaking and quietly sobbing, continually wiping her tears with tissues he had given her. Unable to help herself, she started carefully straightening Pete's Desk. It was a lifelong OCD issue. Her eyes measured every centimeter on the desktop as she positioned objects squarely and spaced them evenly.

Pete watched silently. When she was finished, Pete followed Emily's gaze over to Gus, who was talking to Mike. Gus had a gauze patch taped to the side of his forehead and looked like he was in shock.

"Yes, Agent Johnson is waiting for you on line two," Daniela spoke quickly despite her deep southern drawl. Pete could feel the tension rolling off her with the same intensity as his own. Kidnapping was not the usual day to day crime they experienced in Bogata.

Picking up the phone Pete's spoke in a curt tone.

"This is Sheriff Lucas in Bogata. I need to know when you're going to get here."

"Were on route and we'll be there in about fifteen minutes." Agent Johnson replied, "Make sure the bus driver is there, as well as Mr. and Mrs. Miller." Johnson's authoritative tone actually set Pete at ease, sensing that Johnson knew his business and what needed to be done. Hopefully Pete could trust him.

"Mr. Miller's on his way and the other two are already here." Pete responded looking over at Emily to check on her once again.

Johnson grunted in reply adding, "We're sending another unit to the crime scene."

"Good," Pete answered. "My secretary, Daniela, will fill you in on the location, and I'm sending Deputy Wilson out to meet your team." Transferring the call back to Daniela and turning to Mike he added. "I need you to get out to the crime scene right away."

Mike nodded and immediately headed out of the station.

◊ ◊ ◊

Emily's breath hitched as she watched Thomas, his face ashen, walk in at the same time Mike was leaving. After the men gave a quick greeting, Thomas rushed across the office approaching her and Pete. Emily stood and hugged him sinking into his embrace. She could feel the tension in Thomas and couldn't tell if she was shaking or he was.

"Are you okay?" Thomas asked her softly.

"No…no…I'm not okay." Emily stuttered. Taking in a shaky breath she asked. "Thomas what happened?" Once again the overpowering sensation of helplessness overcame her and her eyes filled with tears. She didn't even bother to wipe them as they fell down her face. "Why would anyone want to take our girls?"

"I don't know." Thomas replied quietly, hugging her a little tighter.

Emily looked up at Thomas and could see the tears in his worried brown eyes, his voice shook as he repeated. "I don't know…I don't know."

Emily opened her mouth to ask another question when she noticed Thomas looking over her head behind her. She turned her head and caught Pete giving Thomas a confirming look. It was written all over Pete's face. *Did he know what was going on*? She needed to press him to find out.

"Em, I need to speak with Pete. I need to find out what happened. Please give us a minute." Thomas gave her a sincere look, rubbing his hands up and down her arms.

"No!" She was surprised at the force of her declaration.

They started walking towards Pete's desk.

"Whatever's happening I need to know." she said and sat down in front of Pete.

After a moment's hesitation, both Pete and Thomas took their seats.

"Umm…" Pete looked uncomfortable, but Emily couldn't imagine why. "Did anyone call either of you?"

"Yes." Thomas spoke up. "I got a call as I was coming over. They said they would call me back with instructions."

Emily was shocked. Rationally, she knew that they hadn't had time to talk, but this was so important. *Why did he wait until he was asked before offering this information?*

Suddenly Thomas swayed in his seat and Pete jumped up out of his chair to help steady him. Emily's breath caught, and she wanted to reach out to help, but she was unable to move.

"Easy Thomas," Pete said quietly, "We'll get through this. You need to be strong. You need to pull yourself together for your girls."

After several deep breaths Thomas slowly sat up once again. And although he was still pale and his brow was damp from sweating, he had more color in his cheeks than before. Emily reached over, grabbed his hand, and gave it a squeeze. When they made eye contact, she knew Thomas was feeling a bit better.

A moment later Thomas asked. "Pete, I don't understand. Who is he? He said I knew who it was, and what he wanted. I don't. Do you?"

◊ ◊ ◊

Thomas' question startled Pete and he had to pause.

Should I tell them? Why hasn't my contact called?

Pete decided Emily and Thomas had the right to know at least something. He would give them as much information as he felt he could, at least for now.

"Thomas…Emily, we can't talk here. Let's go in the back."

Pete led them to a room in the back used for interrogation. They entered, and Pete moved to the corner and unplugged the video camera. He motioned for them to sit on the other side of the table in the middle of the room.

Pete sat facing them, and started immediately, "Listen, I need to tell you something that will sound…well, crazy, but it will make sense once you understand what's happening."

Both Emily and Thomas looked anxious.

"I think the girls are alright, for now." Pete leaned back in his chair and gazed at the wall thoughtfully, "If the people who took them, hurt them, it would change the balance of power."

"Balance of power? What balance of power?" Emily almost shouted, her mother-scolding-the-kids-voice echoed off the walls, her eyes flashed with anger. "What on God's green earth are you talking about?"

The wrath of motherly instinct Pete saw took him off guard, not that he blamed her. He needed to give them information that would help them understand why he thought the girls were not in any immediate danger. But how?

He hesitated again. *If I give more information about the secret societies than I should, it'll start trouble. Yet Thomas and Emily should know their part in this war between the societies that has quietly gone on for centuries. The Absconditus Verum, the group I was raised in, seeking the truth, and The Society of the Praetorians, trying at all costs to stop the Verum from discovering the truth. How much would be too much? How much will they even believe at this point? I really need to figure out what to do. Perhaps just enough to help them understand.*

"You guys need to listen carefully. Please let me explain." Pete began. "There are two organizations involved in this and Thomas, you're a member of one."

Emily's head snapped to Thomas, her jaw clenched.

"I don't understand," Thomas answered, looking at Emily and shrugging his shoulders. "How can I be a member of an organization and not know anything about it?"

"Let me ask you this," Pete continued, sitting forward in his chair, placing his palms on the table. "Thomas, have you been able to remember anything from your childhood?"

Thomas shook his head. Pete knew he was asked this question most of his life. Thomas sat back in his chair running his hands through his hair. "Not much…I mean I had the concussion when I was twelve. I still don't remember anything before that. Why do you ask?"

Pete ignored Thomas' question for the moment and turned to Emily instead. "Emily, have you heard any rumors or stories that seemed to be odd or curious."

Emily's patience snapped as she sat forward in her chair. "No, Pete, now get to the point," she growled.

Pete flushed from the neck up as he realized he was botching the explanation.

Taking a deep breath, he began. "Okay, your part in this started twenty-five years ago. Thomas, you were brought here after an accident. You didn't remember the accident or anything that happened before it, and it was thought that your amnesia would protect you. They obviously have found out who you are. I can't believe they've continued to search for you all this time. Perhaps something or someone has been pushing them."

Before Thomas answered he rubbed his hands up and down his face several times and released an exasperated sigh. "Come on, Pete, this isn't making any sense, just tell us." His voice had an edge to it that Pete wasn't use to.

Usually, his friend was calm and relaxed. Pete understood Thomas had a reason to be on edge, but it was something Pete hadn't seen in the nine years they'd known each other.

Pete look directly at him, "You're not Thomas Miller, at least you're not Miller, anyway. Your name is Yates. James Thomas Yates. Your father was Richard Yates, a direct descendant of Robert Yates."

There was stunned silence in the room, then Thomas and Emily started talking at the same time.

"Robert Yates, one of the Founding Fathers?" Thomas's expression changed from anxiousness to dumbfound.

"Who is Robert Yates?" Emily asked.

"The very same." Pete directed his answer to Thomas.

"So, if I was in an accident, why didn't my father disappear with me? Are you're telling me my father abandoned me?" Thomas asked.

"No. Your father was killed in that auto accident when you were twelve. You were in the car with him. One of our operatives got you out and safely to the Millers' in Bogata. Your mother died some years earlier also in a car accident. At the time it wasn't suspicious but after your father's death, her accident had more questions than answers as well."

Emily stood, the legs of her chair scraping on the concrete floor. Clearly agitated she nearly shouted "But that doesn't make any sense. Are you telling us that Thomas' parents are not his real ones?"

"That's exactly what I'm telling you. They're part of an organization we all belong to. Their job was to be your parents and protect you while you were a child. Once you grew old enough and got married, we thought the past wouldn't catch up to any of us unless you started to remember your childhood in Staunton, Virginia."

"Virginia?" Thomas repeated softly.

"What organization?" Emily asked.

Pete answered Thomas' question first, it was the more direct of the two. "Yes, Virginia, and since you didn't remember anything, we thought the ruse would never be seen through. But obviously we were wrong."

"What organization?" Emily repeated a bit louder, exasperated.

"Yes, the organization. Now I must bring you both into the fold. I'll give you a quick explanation now, but I want to focus on getting the girls back. There are two societies that have been at war with each other for over two hundred years and unfortunately, your family is caught right in the middle of this. Once we have the girls back, I'll give you a detailed explanation."

"What two societies, who are these people?" Emily's mounting frustration was evident in her rising voice and the fact that she started pacing around the room, only stopping to talk.

"Emily." Pete and Thomas said together trying to get her to calm down. Thomas rose from his chair and crossed to her taking her hands in his.

"We've trusted Pete for years, let's continue to trust him through this, okay?" Thomas was quiet and back to the controlled, tranquil man Pete was used to.

"Thomas," Pete softened his voice as well. "You need to act as if you know who these people are so you can negotiate for the girl's release. Find out exactly what they want from you. They will call you again and you need to be ready. I can't say any more. I've probably told you too much already."

"You still haven't told us what this is all about, Pete." Thomas persisted, walking back to the table and bringing

Emily with him. Once they sat he continued. "Who are these people? How was Richard Yates involved? What did he do?"

"Your father was a member of…" Pete stopped and looked at both of them as they were hanging on his every word.

"Well?" Emily asked, raising her eyebrow, clearly daring him not to go on.

Pete realized he was giving them information that might be compromised once the FBI got involved. He wanted to make sure the Miller's didn't accidentally give out information that was sensitive to an agent for the Praetorians. "I think we need to step back for the protection of everyone."

"What? Wait a minute. What were you going to tell us?" It was Thomas' turn to jump up, overturning his chair with the swift rise to his feet. "You have more information that could get our girls back! You have to tell us!" Thomas was practically vibrating with anger, his hands were clenched in fists and his eyes were fierce.

"I have to talk to my contact before I can reveal any more information. This is too important to get out." Pete knew his defense was paltry, but that was all he could give.

"Are you out of your mind?" Emily shouted also jumping out of her chair. "Our girls have been kidnapped! I want to know what the hell is going on!"

Pete felt awful. *How could I have made such a mess of this?*

"I can't tell you any more right now. Just know that we'll do everything in our power to get the girls back." He placated the couple. "The FBI will be here shortly, and we need to be able to play this through as best we can until I can reach my contact. I shouldn't have told you this much. The less you know now, the better it is when you talk to the FBI. Can you do that?"

Pete looked at Thomas intently, finally seeing him calm down enough to give a nod. Thomas put his arm around Emily once again leading her back to her seat.

Emily sat down in a huff. "Are you saying we can't trust the FBI?"

"I honestly don't know. Right now we just need to keep it together. Thomas, is the item I gave you safe?" Pete relaxed a bit as his friends calmed down.

"What item?" Emily asked.

"The old fashioned key I gave Thomas about eight years ago," Pete nodded towards Thomas.

"Yes, well for the moment. It's hidden in our house, however, if the FBI is going to our house…" Thomas paused letting the sentence hang.

Emily's jaw dropped and she started to rise out of the chair again. "Wait a minute. What are you two talking about?" She asked through gritted teeth, her mouth barely opening to get the sound of her words out.

"Ok, good," Pete said, ignoring Emily for the moment. "We still have the upper hand no matter what. My instincts are telling me this is just a scare tactic. I can't believe they would actually hurt the girls. No…no way they would do that, okay?" Pete knew he sounded like he was trying to convince himself and well as the others, but from everything he had learned about the evil Society, he believed this was true. He was well versed in their schemes, even though he had never actually come in direct contact with them. "They'll never compromise their superior position on a cruel stunt. Especially one they can't control when it's made public."

Pete stood and walked to the door, putting his hand on the door knob. "Once I make contact with my associate, we'll have help working through this. Let's go back out and see where we are." He stopped and looked back at the couple. "Just one more thing, don't let on that you know anything about our organization."

"You haven't told me anything!" Emily yelled with an expression of rage.

Pete gave Emily a stern look to quiet her. "I shouldn't have told you yet. And don't mention the key. In fact, try not to talk about anything except the kidnapping. I don't know who we can trust, including the FBI. Emily, please, say nothing, or we cannot hope for the girls." Pete warned as he opened the door.

He could hear commotion in the office area. He watched Emily bite her lower lip as they exited the room to walk down the hall toward the front room.

Thomas stopped Pete before they made it into the hallway. "Pete. I got a second call in the car on the way over. Some guy saying he's involved. I don't know who that was either. He said not to talk to anyone but you. Do you have any idea who that could be? He mentioned the two societies to me, it sounded like what you are trying to explain to us."

Pete was now doubly concerned. "That might have been my contact. Right now we need to talk to the FBI. Say nothing about this second call or anything we've talked about, understand?"

Emily pulled upright and in a hushed voice she spit out. "I'm going to beat the living crap out of both of you for keeping these secrets from me!"

Pete began to feel the sweat trickle down the side of his forehead as he thought. *This could end very badly…for all of us.*

May 2018 - Northeast Texas

"You gonna call in?"

Harry nodded, pulled out his cell phone, and placed the call.

"We got them," he said with no greeting.

Harry never felt comfortable talking to his superior and the voice gave him an uneasy feeling. He listened for a moment then gave the curt reply.

"Yeah, okay. I'll call when we get to our first stop."

He ended the call and nodded to Cliff, signaling to continue as planned. They traveled a few more miles, then turned off the road and stopped in a remote area where there was plenty of shade from the trees, and the scrub brush hid the empty car parked out of sight to anyone.

"Time to change cars," Harry said to the girls as the cloud of dust created by the car settled around them.

Cliff got out and opened the back door to get the girls moving. Sara couldn't remove the seat belt and started to sob again. Amanda reached over and unbuckled her. She held her hand until Sara sobs quieted and she was able to get out of the car.

Harry uncovered the brush from the second car and tossed the keys he removed from the front wheel-well to Cliff. He took over escorting the girls to the back seat and belted them in as Cliff started up the car. He was taking his time, making sure they were sitting comfortably. As he was about to close the door Amanda caught his eye. Her innocence coming across loudly. He paused as a feeling of remorse rose to the surface. A small smile grew on his face. *I will make sure these two get back home safe.*

He got in the car and it was only a few minutes before they reached a main paved road and headed northeast.

Harry called in. "We're on our way again." He said to his superior.

"Good. Looks like this'll be wrapped up before long, so go to the house as planned," the authoritative voice on the other end commanded.

"I'm not so sure," Harry hesitated, running his free hand through his hair. He had a bad feeling about this part of the plan. "It's closer than I'd like to be. Are you positive this'll be resolved quickly?"

"Just leave the thinking to us and do as you're told. I'll contact you when we've arranged the drop." Three beeps in his ear indicated his superior ended the call

Harry wasn't pleased. He knew he, Cliff, and the girls were still way too close for a sure getaway. They had only gotten about ten miles out. He had argued this part of the plan when it was first explained to him. The same uneasiness was pulling at his insides. The Society had a habit of killing the innocent they abducted while negotiating their release. In one instance he was the one killing a fellow agent along with those taken. *This situation is all too familiar. They intend to kill us. We need to change locations.*

He'd been in situations like this many times in the past and he knew the best way to insure a successful 'grab and run'. If he was truly going to be able to let the girls go, he needed space between him, the Society, and the FBI. Enough space to vanish into the night. The more Harry thought about the next segment of the plan the more he confirmed it was a set up to take a fall, a permanent one. It was one thing to placate his superiors but another to willingly walk into a trap.

"Well?" Cliff asked. "What's going on?"

Harry decided. "We're taking them to the house in the woods."

"Are you sure? You want to go to Horatio?" Cliff look over at Harry, squeezing the steering wheel a bit tighter, clearly nervous at the last minute change of plans. "That's across the state line. What was he saying to you?"

Harry shook his head, "Never mind. I'm making sure we don't get caught, so just drive. Too many of our agents have been killed recently. Something doesn't add up, and I'm not taking any chances. We've both been in this line of work too long to make stupid mistakes."

Cliff nodded in agreement.

The next call came in fifteen minutes later.

"Are you all set?" His superior demanded.

"No…we're going to a secondary location. I'll not be the fall guy in this. We'll call you when we get there." Harry hung up knowing he was caught between the FBI and the Society. The second location was secret and safe, known only to him and Cliff. At least he thought so.

In his gut he believed the Society was going to offer them up to the FBI, no doubt a shootout, ending in the death of the four of them. If they did manage to escape, he and Cliff would have to disappear, and it wouldn't be easy to hide. The Society had eyes and ears everywhere. These last several months there had been too many 'accidents' and 'coincidences', too many agents mysteriously ended up dead and he didn't want to be one of them. Cliff would hang with him on this. They knew each other well enough.

Yet what if the Society did know about their secret location?

Chapter 11

February 1787 - Mount Vernon, Virginia

Alexander Hamilton had just arrived with a guest.

"General. I fear the worst has happened. Many of the men who served with honor have been pressed by the State of Massachusetts to fulfill tax obligations on their properties. Most were not paid as you know and many spent their own wealth, what little they had, to support themselves during the war. Congress has not been able to fulfill its financial obligations to the men as they promised. Now, the state means to confiscate their lands and property as compensation for back taxes and debt to creditors. And if those confiscations are not enough to pay off the debts, then any who still owe are being thrown into debtor's prison.

"Sir, I also believe there is some dark purpose behind this. I felt its presence during the Newburgh conspiracy and now I'm feeling the same. Someone or something is driving this force. To what end I do not know, but I do know that the soldiers are caught in a no win situation. Even now they are banding together to stop the courts from processing the legal suits to have them imprisoned. I have brought one such farmer with me. May I have him join us?"

"Yes please, Alexander. Have him come in."

The farmer entered the room. He was wearing old torn clothing, barely enough to cover himself. "Sir, I did ask him to wear clothing I have provided, but he insisted that you see how they are living up there,"

Washington nodded. "Tell me son, what is your name?"

"Plough Jogger Sir."

"No doubt named for your profession."

"Yes Sir and I was a corporal in your army."

"So Corporal, what have you seen or what do you know of this trouble in Massachusetts."

The farmer was overwhelmed to even be in the presence of the General. He saluted and bowed.

"At ease Master Jogger. Come and sit with me and Mr. Hamilton."

They sat together in a meeting room in the front of the

General's house. He ordered food and drink to be brought in. While they were waiting Washington started. "So tell me what is happening."

"Well Sir, I have been greatly abused, having been obliged to do more than my part in the war, been loaded with class rates, town rates, province rates, continental rates and all rates, been pulled and hauled by Sheriffs, constables and collectors, and had my cattle sold for less than they were worth. The great men are going to get all we have and I think it is time for us to rise and put a stop to it, and have no more courts, nor Sheriffs, nor collectors, nor lawyers."

Washington was aghast to hear this news. "Son, are you suggesting that the government of Massachusetts is treating you in such a manner?"

"Yes Sir, and not just the politicians, but the judges, the aristocrats, and the merchants. Even some who spoke strongly against the English crown have now taken the Crown's place."

Washington and Hamilton were deeply troubled by this remark.

"How can this be?" Washington asked. "Don't they know that most were not paid for their services during the war? Don't they know all must be set at compromise so that those who gave them their very freedoms must be protected and allowed to live what lives they have? Tell me Master Jogger, do you know who is behind this madness?"

"I know of one besides the Governor, Sir. One who was with us in the beginning, when it all started. One who tarred and feathered tax collectors of the Crown."

Both Washington and Hamilton were bracing themselves for the name.

"General, Mr. Hamilton, Sir…it's Samuel Adams. He has betrayed the very cause we fought for. For the very liberties and freedoms we earned in victory."

"How is this possible?" Washington asked incredulous about what he was hearing.

"Well Sir, he has helped to establish a law to act upon our resistance. It is called the Riot Act. It suspends Habeas Corpus, denying our rights to defend ourselves. They keep us in prison without a trial. And now he has proposed a new legal distinction: that rebellion in our Republic should be punished by execution. He then proceeded to condone his own actions against the crown as patriotic and justified even though they too were also against unfair laws at the time."

Washington and Hamilton sat motionless. Finally Washington asked, "Do you know who is leading the patriots against the State?"

"Yes General, he is Daniel Shays, Sir. Served in the Continental Army, same as myself. He has given us hope against a new tyrant, against Samuel Adams and the elitists in Massachusetts. Most of them are English and were loyal to the Crown during the war. Now they mean to destroy us from within."

Washington looked at Hamilton and then back to Jogger. It was some time before Washington spoke and the food had not arrived from the kitchen yet. "Master Jogger, please, go to the kitchen and have a meal."

"Yes Sir, thank you Sir."

They were quiet for several minutes until the General spoke. "Alexander…This is a grave threat to the very fabric of our new alliance. We cannot just sit idly by and watch a fellow state abuse its own people. We must act. You need to help me secure the freedom and safety for the people once more. We can press our Society of the Cincinnati to step in and put a stop to all this. This whole affair is in violation of the very principles we have established."

"Yes Sir…you're right of course. I will help you and we will put a stop to this insanity. It seems the more the aristocrats gain in position, the more they lust for everything the people hold dear."

"And we cannot stop there. We must strengthen the central government. It must have the authority to step in and stop a state from abusing its own citizens." Washington replied.

He thought for a moment and decided it was time to clear the air. "Mr. Hamilton, tell me now if you are someway involved in all this. A very intricate web is being weaved and it seems this dark force you mentioned is looking to increase centralized power just as we are. The problem is this Society is bent on tyranny, not freedom and liberty. Tell me what you know of this."

Hamilton looked astonished. "Sir, my goal is the same as

yours, to protect the freedom and liberty of the people and the states. I assure you, General, that I have nothing to do with this other faction…I'm sorry, what did you call it?"

"It's a society, just like the Society of the Cincinnati but with ulterior motives."

Hamilton paused. "Do you know who they are?"

"They are called the Society of Praetorians. They are using the Roman Republic model of a *Nation State* society and it seems they are looking to take central power as soon as we develop it. There is a fascination, almost obsession about this group. I've heard they have already infiltrated several of the state governments as well as Congress."

"General, I'm sure this cannot be true. For this to happen, someone with extraordinary power and ability would be in charge. A conspiracy this deep would be impossible to keep hidden, keep secret."

"Which is what I have heard. Now, on your honor Alexander, tell me what you know."

"I know nothing Sir, I'm sorry." He paused. "However, I can start an investigation and we can get to the bottom of all this."

Washington still had suspicions, but they had to remain as they were. "Then I'm telling you to investigate, but for God's sake keep it quiet. I want regular reports. There have been too many grabs for power already. I will make sure our states do come together and fend off this new threat. I'll be damned if anyone destroys what we have fought for."

◊ ◊ ◊

Once Jefferson heard the news about the Shays Rebellion, he responded in a letter to a close friend. Part of it read;

'The tree of liberty must be refreshed from time to time with the blood of patriots and tyrants. It is its natural manure.'

He was of course referring to his own words in the Declaration of Independence. A little revolution now and then was wise if the government overstepped its boundaries.

Chapter 12

<u>*May 2018 - Bogata, Texas*</u>

The three of them were sitting at Pete's desk again when two FBI Agents arrived.

Finally, Emily thought. *The FBI showed up!* At least now they can move forward and find her girls. Emily didn't think she could take more waiting. She tried to sort through the jumble of thoughts in her head. Keys, phone calls, 'don't talk about any of that'. Every minute wasted was another minute for the kidnappers to escape. Emily forced herself to take a deep breath and count to 10. It wouldn't help for her completely loose it.

The Agents stopped by Daniela's desk in the front of the office and she pointed over to her, Thomas, and Pete. Emily stood up to meet them as they approached.

"Mr. and Mrs. Miller?" the older of the two started. "I'm Agent Ben Johnson, the agent in charge, and this is Agent Timothy Dean." Indicating the younger man standing slightly behind him. As they shook hands Emily thought Agent Dean was much too young to be an FBI agent. He couldn't be more than 25, whereas Agent Johnson was probably closer to 50.

Pete pointed to Gus, "that's the bus driver."

Emily realized Gus hadn't moved from the chair next to Deputy Wilson's desk.

Johnson nodded to Dean and he went over to meet Gus.

She and Thomas sat down as Pete brought another chair to his desk for Johnson.

Emily knew nothing like this had ever happened to Gus before. He'd spent his whole life in this community. He and Dean were conversing quietly and while Emily could hear their voices she couldn't make out their words. Gus was shaking his head slowly and wringing his hands. He kept wiping his eyes and Emily's heart went out to him.

"Do you know anyone who might have done this?" Agent Johnson asked, startling Emily back into focus.

"No…No," Emily answered.

Thomas just shook his head without saying a word.

"We have a field team already heading to the site where the bus stopped. We'll get to the bottom of this, don't worry," Johnson said with a convincing assurance. "We have an all-points bulletin out including the make and model of the car Gus gave to the Sheriff so whoever this is, we'll find them."

Emily nodded and looked up at Pete, but he seemed to be watching Thomas. Turning to him, she noticed he was much calmer than before.

Dean joined them. "The bus driver gave me a more detailed description of these two guys and I think we may be able to identify them."

"Yes, we already have that," Pete said as he grabbed the notes and went over to Daniela's desk.

"Make sure our team has all that information, as well. We have a short window here and we need to make sure we know what we're dealing with." Johnson directed Dean and then turned his attention to the Millers.

Emily could feel her blood pressure rise and she watch this exchange between the men as if they were ordering their lunches. *Maybe they face this type of thing every day, but these are MY girls missing! Why couldn't they be more frantic like I am?* She knew that wouldn't help any, but the thought was there.

As if Agent Johnson could read her mind he said in a calm voice. "Mr. and Mrs. Miller, I have several questions I'd like to ask. If you can give me some answers we can form a plan and work to get your girls back."

"Okay," Pete cut in, returning from Daniella's desk, "We're doing everything we can right now. In the meantime, you two need to stay here."

Getting a little frustrated that no one was doing anything, Emily found herself looking over at Gus again.

He was slumped over, crying into his hands. Emily rose out of her chair and went over to him.

"Gus." she said softly as she laid her hand gently on his shoulder. "Gus, what happened?"

He shook his head and started, "these guys had their car right in the road. I thought maybe they'd broke down. Then one of them pointed a gun at me as I was slowing down." He continued with more emphasis. "I had to stop…I had to or he woulda shot me. I was scared, Mrs. Miller. He woulda shot me." Slumping further into the seat Gus covered his eyes with his hands.

"Gus, my girls. Did they hurt them?" She tried to hide her anguish.

She could see Gus trying to compose himself.

He looked up at her. "No. The kids said they just took them off the bus and put them in the back of their car. I'm sorry, Mrs. Miller. I'm so sorry." He broke down again. There was so much pain in his voice.

"Why didn't you use one of the kid's cell phones?"

"They took them…" His voice trailed off into sobs.

Struggling with her own tears, she looked at the patch on the side of his face. "Are you alright? Shouldn't you go to the hospital?"

"Oh, I'm alright. One of them hit me with his gun. Knocked me out. Some of the kids were pulling at me when I woke up. They were scared to get off the bus. They musta been told not to move. I didn't know how long I was out until I got to school. I was 'bout fifteen minutes late."

Above his soft crying, she could hear the agents talking to each other.

"Make sure Agent Hill's team gets to the Miller's house and I want a report from the school as soon as they can. Perhaps one of the other kids has some information that will help," Johnson said.

"Agent Brooks is already at the crime scene, and Agent Hill just got to the Millers," Dean responded, flipping through his note pad.

"Good. I'm going out to the Millers. Have Brooks make sure he gets me his preliminary analysis as quick as he can." Agent Johnson rose out of his chair as he spoke.

"Yes, Sir." Dean answered almost militarily.

"We have a short time window here. Make sure the Sheriff's office knows that as well. Those girls are our number one priority." Johnson was getting louder and louder with each command

"Yes, Sir." Dean answer again.

Johnson looked at Emily and Thomas, "Mr. and Mrs. Miller, please come with me."

◊ ◊ ◊

Watching Agent Johnson talk to Emily and Thomas, Pete sucked in a shaky breath. He was clearly concerned he couldn't control the situation. The FBI was literally taking over. *How can I contain this with so many outsiders? The Millers are my responsibility and have been for years. Why hasn't my contact called?*

"Look, Agent Johnson, I think the Millers should stay here, or if not, at least let me bring them back to the house." Pete attempted to gain some of the control that so easily slipped out of his grasp. He needed time to talk to Thomas and get the hidden key to safety.

"No, Sheriff, you need to stay here and let us do our job. Your office can help by getting ahold of all the other parents not yet contacted and interviewing them. For right now, I'm in charge Sheriff, is that clear?" Johnson emphatically stated.

Pete didn't answer, he just clenched his teeth and kept his mouth firmly closed. Agent Johnson was clear and he wasn't happy about this at all.

He turned to Daniela, his secretary. "Mike should be at the crime scene soon. Have him call me with any information as soon as possible."

She gave him a nod.

Still grinding his teeth, Pete watched out the window as the Millers got into Agent Johnson's car and sped away. Then he went right to his desk and called his contact, breaking established protocol.

"It's Pete. Why didn't you alert me? Agent Johnson of the FBI has the Millers and he's bringing them back to their house. What the hell am I supposed to do?"

"The first thing is to calm down," the voice on the phone responded. "Unless you stay focused, we'll lose everything, do you understand?"

"Yes, I understand, but we weren't ready for anything like this!" Pete's fist was clenched so tightly his nails were biting into his palm. He took a deep breath and tried to sound more rational. "How could they know about Thomas? I never signed on for something like this!"

"I know. This wasn't foreseen. The Society must've decided we're too close to finding the documents. Somehow they found out who Mr. Miller is. It's a panic move. Someone must have snapped or felt things were going to collapse. That's the only reason for this crazy action."

Pete took another deep breath, not that it helped. "Okay, but what am I supposed to do? And who the hell is on our side that I can trust?"

"You know I can't divulge any others. It could jeopardize everyone." The voice sounded like a scolding father.

"This is one time we need to break secrecy. For God's sake, it's their children!" Pete's anger shot through the roof again.

His contact paused and then spoke calmly. "Johnson is a neutral. He has no idea what this whole thing is about except that it's a kidnapping. Just stay where you are for right now. I'll contact you shortly. Can you get a hold of Mr. Miller?"

"Well, I can call him on his cell, but he's with Johnson so he can't talk openly." Pete replied.

"Give them time to get to the house and then call him. Find out if he can get the key and get it to you, so you can give it to me."

His contact hung up. Then he realized. *Dam. I forgot to ask if he called Thomas. Should I call him back?*

"Sir." Daniela called across the room. "I have the school on the phone."

Calling his contact would have to wait.

◊ ◊ ◊

Emily stared out the car window of Agent Johnson sedan, nothing really registering in her mind. They were on the way home, a path she'd traveled countless times before, and yet everything looked different to her today.

Bogata was a typical small Texas town. It had one gas station, several churches, a school district that served several towns, and other small local shops, not more than a quarter of a mile from one end to the other. That was what Thomas and Emily liked about it. She could remember how they spent weeks looking for just the right small, homey community to live in. The Sheriff's office was down and across the street some 1500 feet from the local hotel. The Miller's house was only ten minutes from town, to the north.

The town was going about its usual business. People were walking and talking. Some dropped into shops out of sight, while others were coming out of shops. It just didn't seem real, almost like she was outside looking into another world.

"Don't they know what's happening?" she asked sadly.

"Yes Em, everyone knows. Pete let the word out just in case someone sees those guys. But people have to keep going." Thomas replied quietly stroking the back of her hand with his thumb.

"Thomas, I'm so scared. What if…what if?" Emily whispered as if someone was listening.

"Let's keep praying they'll be all right. We need to pray for them, Em." Thomas' voice broke on the last word and when Emily tried to look at him he held her even closer. She knew it was so she wouldn't see the tears rolling down his cheeks.

He rocked her in his arms. "Rest for a bit, Em. Try to close your eyes for a few minutes."

Everything seemed surreal. She kept thinking she would wake up from this nightmare. She'd had wild dreams before, but this didn't feel the same. She wasn't going to wake up. She was awake and in the biggest nightmare of her life!

◊ ◊ ◊

It was ninety minutes since the abduction when they arrived at the Miller's house. Several government cars were in the driveway so they parked on the street. The scene was buzzing with activity. Special agents were setting up a command center in the living room and others were securing the surroundings.

"Anything?" Johnson asked Agent Aaron Hill as they were getting out of the car.

"No, Sir, no calls and nothing found so far." He answered.

Johnson turned to the Millers. "Let's go inside and get you guys ready for the next step."

Emily got out of the car and looked at her home of the last nine years. A well-built forty-year old ranch that had been updated with a nice contemporary flair. The edges of the front walkway were planted with a variety of different colored flowers. The yellow daffodils were always Emily's favorite as they heralded in the spring. Today her thoughts were of the key Thomas never told her he had. She needed to get him alone and find out what the key was and more importantly where he hid it.

They entered the house through the front door. The living room furniture had been pushed to the side to make room for a folding table and chairs. Agent Johnson indicated for Emily and Thomas to take a seat, then pulled out a chair across from them.

"Okay, Thomas. Can I call you Thomas?" Johnson asked

Thomas nodded. "Yes, and Emily."

"Okay, Thomas, Emily, is there anything unusual that you might have seen in the last few days? Anything at all?"

Emily was searching her mind. They both looked around, trying to see something out of place or somehow different.

"No," Emily finally said. "No, nothing."

Thomas shook his head. "No."

Another agent, tall, slicked back hair, and a dark suit approached Johnson and whispered something in his ear.

"Well," Johnson started. "This is Agent Hill, he's heading up the team here so if you need anything, please let him know. I'll be back when I can. I'm going to check on a lead.

Hill, took a seat with Thomas and Emily and nodded. "We've swept the house and haven't found anything unusual. No bugging devices or anything that looks tampered with."

Emily gave him a perplexed look. *Bugging devices?* She kept close lipped.

"I'm heading to the crime scene. Keep me posted," Johnson said.

Agent Hill nodded and Johnson headed out. He peppered them with questions for the next several minutes, none of which resulted in anything useful.

Emily looked around her lovely home again, and realized how their lives would never be the same. She didn't want to think about the worst case outcome, the one thought that solidified in her mind was a prayer, *'God, please help'!*

Five minutes passed, then another five. Agent Hill continued asking questions and they continued to answer what they could.

Thomas stood up abruptly. "I need to get some air." He crossed to the back door and walked out of the house.

Emily watched Thomas walk out to the swing set, sit down with his back to the house, and bury his face in his hands. She looked at Agent Hill who nodded, and she went out to Thomas.

"I'm sorry, Thomas. I'm sorry." Emily's voice broke. Reaching out to put her hand on his shoulder giving him a slight squeeze.

◊ ◊ ◊

Thomas was slightly startled when Emily came up behind him and put her hand on his shoulder. Her reached up with one hand and laid it on top of hers.

No…no," Thomas said softly not knowing what to say. "This isn't your fault. This…this…is my fault. Sit down. I need to tell you why."

She sat down on the swing next to him.

He reached out and took her hand, clasping it in both of his.

"Em, I have to tell you something, something that you must not repeat. It involves more than just us and the girls."

She looked at him intently. He glanced back at the house. Agent Hill stood at the back door looking at them. Thomas knew he was out of ear-shot and they had a private moment.

"The girls will be okay," he started. "They won't dare do anything to them."

Emily eyes opened wide. "How do you know that?"

"Because if they do, they'll lose everything they've done…everything." He leaned over past the chain that held up the swing and spoke softly to her. His face only inches from hers.

"The second call I had on my way to Pete's office was a man who said he knew about the kidnapping, even though he couldn't stop it. He knew it was the society that kidnapped the girls and said I needed to talk to Pete. He told me there was two societies and I was directly involved with one of them, even though I didn't' know it. That I should work this through with the Sheriff." Thomas thought for a moment, trying to remember exactly what the polished voice on the phone said. "The guy said they won't hurt our girls because what they want is too valuable to chance not getting it. He said 'It's critical you don't give them what they want, or I can't guarantee the girls will be safe.' I couldn't get his name, or how he knew all this. Honestly, I was so upset I don't remember any more."

"How do you know you can trust him? What is it they want?"

"The key. This may sound weird, but I just feel like we can trust him. He seemed to have a certain command about the situation. Something Pete doesn't have. Maybe I'm just hoping because it's what I want."

Thomas turned to look at the house and saw Agent Hill approaching. He looked at Emily and shook his head, indicating she not say anything.

"Are you folks alright?" Hill asked.

"Yes, just needed some air, a little space," Thomas said.

"I think perhaps we need to get back to the house in case they try to contact you." Agent Hill was definitely suspicious.

"Yes, you're right, of course. We'll be there in just a minute." Thomas replied

Hill paused and looked at Thomas. Then he nodded and went back to the house.

"We can't talk now, but just know the girls will be alright." He paused. "There is one thing. I need to get to our bedroom alone. The key is in there. I also need to talk to Pete. This whole thing is much more elaborate than we were told, so I need answers too."

They got up from the swings and started walking to the house. Thomas's cell phone rang. They both stopped short and realized Agent Hill heard the ring from the back door and was waving for them to come in. Thomas looked at the number. It was Pete.

"It's okay, just a friend from work calling." Thomas motioned for Emily keep going. "Keep Agent Hill busy." He turned and walked back to the swing set as he answered the call.

"Can you talk?" Pete asked.

"Yes, but I only have a moment." Thomas turned to see Agent Hill in conversation with Emily.

"Thomas, you need to get the key to me any way you can. Will you be able to?"

"I don't know. We only got here a little while ago, and I'm not sure if they'll give us any room inside the house. For all I know, they've found it already."

"I'm coming over. Perhaps with the two of us there you might have an opportunity."

"No, Pete. Stay at the station. We can't afford to bring even more attention to this. And now it's the three of us."

"You told Emily?"

"Well, yes. She knows this is more than just us. Pete, I know more than you think. That second call I got?"

"The kidnappers?"

"No…well, someone else, I guess. He seemed to know just what was happening. He told me things that I don't understand, things about me being involved."

"It might have been my contact, but until we know, stay silent on this."

"Okay. Emily knows to keep quiet, and this other guy said not talk to anyone but you."

"Then it must have been my contact," Pete responded.

Agent Hill was moving towards him.

"I have to go." Thomas hung up abruptly and starting walking to the house. "It's okay, Mr. Hill. Just a good friend of ours and he's worried, trying to help."

"I understand, Mr. Miller, but we really need to know everything that's going on, and right now that's every conversation taking place. We need all the information available to help us out. Okay?"

"Yes, Sir, I do. I don't have any more information." Thomas gave Agent Hill a bit of a hard look. "And I would appreciate some latitude here. It's my daughters that have been taken."

Agent Hill quickly backed off. "Mr. Miller. I'm just trying to do my job. I apologize if I seemed insensitive. I certainly didn't mean to."

Thomas took the edge off his look and they went back into the house. *I have to find a way to get that key. The girl's lives depend on it!*

Chapter 13

May 1787 - Pennsylvania State House, Philadelphia

The Constitutional Convention.

"John Lansing, Jr," said a loud voice over the noise in the room. No one answered. Only three and one half days had passed since they started and things were not going well, not at all. It was just after lunch.

"John, are you here?" Again no answer. "John!"

"Yes, yes, I'm here!" John finally shouted. "You know damn well I'm here…I was just talking with you not five minutes ago!"

Even with the unexpected strain of the moment, the group broke out in laughter. William Jackson was not amused. It was his job as secretary of the Convention to make sure the roll call was done in the morning and again after lunch.

"Let's get the roll call done!" He shouted back.

The crowd simmered down and started to settle into their familiar chairs behind their small tables.

Secretary Jackson looked around the room while taking the roll; he could see how all the delegates were dressed in proper attire for the assembly, some more formal than others, but not much. They were all divided up into states with a small table in front of each group and a wooden chair for everyone. They all jockeyed their chairs behind or to the sides of their tables so everyone was facing the front of the room. The tables had papers scattered on them in no specific piles, mostly notes taken by delegates for their own purpose.

Virginia had submitted a new plan earlier in the day designed to be a total replacement to the Articles of Confederation and Perpetual Union.

"I would like to make a statement," said Robert Yates, a delegate from New York.

"The chair recognizes Mr. Yates from New York." It was the voice from the front of the room, George Washington from Virginia.

The Philadelphia Convention for amending the Articles of Confederation was underway having started four days earlier. Some state delegates had not yet arrived, but there was enough for a quorum.

The delegates in attendance were to make necessary changes to the Articles to help establish Congressional authority without going too far. Now it seemed something else was afoot.

Mr. Yates started and was passionate in his delivery. "I apologize in advance for the length of my remarks, whose body is necessary to define the moment.

"First off, I would like to clarify something that many are confused about. Others here however, are purposely confusing this for improper reasons. It is the essence of who we are. Gentlemen, I think we can all agree that we are no longer colonies. We are, in fact, states. But just what does the word state mean? Some think it is merely an extension of some central government like a province or district with little or no sovereignty. Others, and I would say correctly, know the word state is, in fact, equal to the word country with all the sovereignty a country and its people hold. When we say the State of New York, we are talking about the Country of New York. Yes gentlemen, most Americans hold their own state as their own country, not a piece of some central government, some *Nation State.*

"A person, on the other hand, is a citizen of their respective state. They hold fundamental rights of property. Until we can decide on these most critical issues, we have an impasse that cannot be broached. It seems we have a plethora of meanings for state's rights in this very room.

"Therefore, I make a motion to determine that our states are thirteen independent countries, like the State of France or the State of England, and each holds full sovereignty of itself and its citizens. This is in the treaty we signed with King George and he listed us out as thirteen independent states with each having its own full sovereignty.

"I bring this exhibit as further evidence of this fact. Article 1 of the Treaty of Paris:

"His Brittanic Majesty acknowledges the said United States, viz., New Hampshire, Massachusetts Bay, Rhode Island and Providence Plantations, Connecticut, New York, New Jersey, Pennsylvania, Delaware, Maryland, Virginia, North Carolina, South Carolina and Georgia, to be free sovereign and independent states, that he treats with them as such, and for himself, his heirs, and successors, relinquishes all claims to the government, propriety, and territorial rights of the same and every part thereof."

"Now, while we are united as states, it does not mean any state has given up any sovereignty except those limited enumerated powers vested in Congress by the Articles of Confederation and Perpetual Union. This treaty clearly states that England can treat with any state individually. Now while it is important to have unified foreign relations and we have given Congress the power to act as representatives of all the states collectively, it does not mean the states no longer have a say in foreign matters. Our representatives in Congress give each state their own unique voice.

"So, I ask for each state to put forth just what they believe regarding the issue of sovereignty."

"Motion for clarification of our current government is asked. Second?" asked Jackson.

"Excuse me Mr. Jackson, I want to add further that state sovereignty includes the right to nullify central government laws if they feel they are adverse to the state, and finally if any state so chooses, it can secede from the Union. These rights, while not explicitly written within the Articles are nevertheless critical to any further discussions regarding central government."

"Second," answered Gunning Bedford of Delaware. "And I will add the five delegates from Delaware are prohibited from changing central government, meaning the Articles of Confederation and Perpetual Union cannot be changed without going through the amendment process. They also cannot be set aside to form some new government. I happen to know firsthand that Rhode Island is in complete agreement with Delaware."

The vote was taken and the motion indeed clarified that all the states considered themselves to be free and independent with full sovereignty. There were, however, several individuals who believed the states had little or no sovereignty at all. This was a most troublesome position.

Yates continued. "There are several here including myself who have grave concerns with where this convention is going.

We were sent here to amend the Articles of Confederation, and with the exception of Rhode Island, who has not even sent delegates; we all realize some improvement is needed.

"However, it now seems that a number of you are looking to abandon the Articles totally and form a new government. What part of Perpetual Union do those delegates fail to understand? This Virginia Plan submitted by Mr. Randolph is well beyond the scope of our task and something we are not given permission or authority to do," Yates was now pointing the blame, and change, of the convention's purpose squarely on Edmond Randolph's Virginia coalition. Randolph was a delegate from Virginia and Governor of the state. While Randolph had submitted the plan, it was conceived and written mostly by delegate James Madison also of Virginia.

"Had we known up front that the intentions from some present, to have a *Nation State* superseding state's rights, sovereignty, and the state's rights to nullify central government laws and secede from the Union, this Convention would not even be taking place.

"And part of this new proposal, that we have affirmation from only nine states, is totally unacceptable. The Articles call for a unanimous vote. What will you do if one or more states do not go along? Will you force them to? Will some central *Nation State* now invade and occupy a state, an independent American country, or as some prefer an independent state? Just where will they get a standing army that will enforce this plan? Will it be made up of Americans, our own brothers in arms? It is listed right here in your plan. This is inconceivable.

"Think about this, gentlemen. Didn't we just win independence from the very same thing; our brothers being our English brothers?"

The Articles of Confederation and Perpetual Union Yates was referring to were the ones now in place for the central government which was essentially just Congress, no executive branch, or judicial branch. They had been put together both during and after the war ended and ratified by all the states to allow Congress the voice of foreign affairs. They did not give much power to the fledgling central government and that was the way the states wanted to keep things.

"We are thirteen different countries with a loose

partnership, an alliance, as a dual system of republics being the states as one part with each its own, and a central republic being nothing more than a representative of our countries, or states, to handle our foreign affairs. Loose in affiliation though, not in how it issues its authority. This new Virginia Plan is just the opposite. It would give far too much power to the central government and would set up a *Nation State*, exactly what we don't want.

"We must be very careful here and tread lightly, gentlemen. Simply disbanding our current Congress, one that all thirteen states signed on for is rash and irresponsible to say the least! We are a Perpetual Union, with an unbreakable bond, are we not? And now you want to just dissolve this unbreakable Union and form a new government that is an unbreakable Union?"

There was quite a bit of murmuring from the group, both affirmative and not. Heads were shaking in agreement while others were shaking their heads no.

Yates continued. "This was the hardest type of system to set up and protect. It has never been done before. It requires a constant vigilance to keep evil at bay. To keep evil from corrupting yet more government. Having the most freedoms also means being the most vigilant, for this dual republic we have formed is an easy target to many who wished to rule and obtain power. We have all heard about this dark Society of Praetorians who mean to take power once we strengthen Congress to be more efficient. Power corrupts gentlemen, and we all know how it can consume those who we give this power to. So we must make sure we have checks and balances in place for, if we do not, then we are condemning ourselves from the start.

"This Republic will stand challenges of corruption, no doubt, and evil would find great allies to help in the unmaking. We think we know what to do and how to do it. We have learned our lessons from history and the classics of the past. We have seen government rule in every conceivable form and we have a will to change it for the better. We have set up a new system, taking from the good pieces of the past and removing the oppressive ones.

"We are all committed to our own countries gentlemen,

mine being the Country of New York. We are no longer part of the English Crown. Yes, we are a Union, but only insofar as a defensive posture and foreign relations. We fought for our independence from the tyranny of the English Empire even while others plotted, still loyal to the Crown, still fixated on the perfect government the English thought they had created, still convinced this is the only way to form government and rule. Yes to rule, not govern. This is always a fine line, and finding the right sort of dedicated representatives to stay true to the purpose is the hardest part of all in this dual republic.

"In that regard, the State of England has suffered the most horrible defeat imaginable. The State of France aided us in the defeat of their mortal enemy. The fight between the English and ourselves could not have gone better for France. England is weakened and now France wants us to ally with them against England.

"Yet we resist the failed trappings of any other alliances save to ourselves. We have learned from history that today's enemy can one day be tomorrow's friend, and we also know the reverse is true. Americans are set in their desire to remain neutral, even while many of the elite here want us to choose this side or that side. We still consider many Englishmen our brothers even though we fought them for our very freedom. We can see reconciliation even now, now when some want to ally with France who came to our aide at the most dire time. I tell you evils are still at work and we must recognize them and defeat them at every corner. If we do not, if we lose the will to fight, fight for the very freedoms we have just won, then I fear we shall slip back into evil. We shall wallow under another taskmaster, another *Nation State*, another tyranny. These Praetorians will wait until we have become weak. Then they will strike. They will strike as surely as an eagle strikes its prey.

"Tyranny comes in many forms and we have seen them. Some are dictatorial and so oppressive the people are strangled under the pressures and so are oppressed. Yet other forms seem fair to the eye and to the ear. They promise to protect us and help us to be a better, fairer society. They offer democracy as a better form than our republic. They offer kindness in the form of help that most see as noble and true.

They trick us with their false veil. They demonize some to show favor to others. For when the truth is revealed, they really cannot just give out freedom. No government can. No government ever has, even as they tell you they can and will. My example is this very city of Philadelphia, the largest of cities in all the states. They enacted a redistribution scheme during the war and the city dictated pricing structures to ensure everyone had an equal share. And what happened? The war did not kill the city. The politicians did. The wealthy left in droves rather than have their money, their personal property, confiscated and redistributed. The system collapsed from its own weight. No such system can ever succeed. God help us if we turn into a democracy with entitlements and redistribution. Then all will be truly lost. Philadelphia was once the largest city, and now look at it. I shall say now that if anyone here has visions of socializing a centralized *Nation State*, then it will become a tyranny worse than that of England.

"So the question is what shall we make of a powerful centralized government? For the worst tyranny of all is one shrouded in the disguise of good. It rules over us and promises of things it could never deliver save unless it takes them from others, your fellow Americans. That is a true tyranny and we must be watchful of this. The taking from the fruits of one's labor, his own earned property, to give to another without his approval whether by force or through taxation is inherently evil, yet it seems every central government conceived ends up using this device to its own destruction and the destruction of the very people it is supposed to represent.

"Man was given free will and ownership of himself. This is the first most important and perhaps the only right a person holds. It is also the right through which all other rights are derived. Government cannot give rights to people; they can only restrict rights through compromises, bad laws, and even worse legislation.

"This Virginia Plan you have devised is madness. We must make sure our central government has only the most limited of powers to allow the people to live free, whether in local, state, or national forms. The fundamental style of government in this plan has seen its rise and fall through all the ages. It has never ever been able to sustain itself. For at some point, the ones being taken from say enough, or the ones needing the help are so many that the system that must ultimately fail, does fail.

"Sometimes the few can stop the thieves from robbing them in the name of government. They rise up and cast off these thieves. Sometimes the many, wanting more and more will cast off the thieves, realizing the tyrannical system the thieves set up can no longer give them all they want, or better yet they recognize how the thieves give them just enough to keep them enslaved."

"That's enough!" shouted Randolph. "You go too far!"

"Do I? Do I?" Yates countered with a glare. "Is it going too far to demand protection for the states and the people? There are ample protections here for the states in our current Articles. We're not some power hungry coalition looking to prey on the people, are we? No. We're here to strengthen a weak fledgling Confederation, nothing more.

"And why is it weak? Because it must go to the states to fund itself? No Sir. You are wrong. It must go to the states for authority in what it does. Otherwise, if given the chance, a central power, one *Nation State*, whose only restriction is itself, will corrupt itself wholly and usurp power in every venue it can. History has shown this to be true in every instance."

Randolph again interrupted. "History, Mr. Yates, has not been written yet for our republic. Your claims are based on weaker countries and weaker people. We have just defeated the greatest war power in the world. We can certainly make sure a strong central body of government remains in check by the states. History indeed. Have we not shown in our own history a radical change from the monarchial system to our own self-governing structures in place? Each state has its own republic. Why would I want my own state to be under the whip of tyranny again? Your claims are unfounded and unjustified. Everyone here is bound to state sovereignty and the people to decide how they are governed."

"Thank you Mr. Randolph for proving my point. You just said it. We defeated the greatest war machine in our day with the Articles we now have. And you want to junk it and start another? I know there are places for improvement, and that is why we are here. What we are not here for is to undermine this very government we have. No Sir. We shall not usurp power from the states."

"Mr. Chairman?" Benjamin Franklin had now stood up. Yates gave him a glare. Franklin simply smiled. "Mr. President, I think it might be wise to have a pause in the discussions."

Washington nodded to Jackson.

"We will recess until after lunch…that would be one o'clock gentlemen. Please make all efforts to return on time."

Chapter 14

<u>May 1012 - Horatio, Arkansas</u>

Another hour passed before Harry had Cliff turned off the main road. They were now almost ninety miles away in Horatio, Arkansas. There were no signs of pursuit from any direction, so Harry knew their escape had worked. The area they were in was mostly dry and barren except for a heavily treed spot. They turned onto a dirt road and entered the woods. About two minutes later, Harry pointed to the left. Cliff pulled into a driveway, or at least it looked like a driveway. They were again on a dirt road, but it was little more than a path with tire gullies marking the way. Some five hundred feet or so through the trees, they emerged in an opening. A small house, old and un-kept, sat in the middle of the clearing.

Harry was uneasy. “Keep your eyes open. We’re caught in the middle of this, and I’m not sure what they’ll do. It seems they’ve been in panic mode the last few weeks with all the killings. Perhaps things are getting ready to explode in their faces.” He looked at Cliff. “So just be alert.”

Cliff pulled the car up to the front corner of the house. The driveway continued on by the house and passed a small garage in the back.

Harry scanned the area. The little hairs stood on the back of his neck. He’d directly disobeyed his boss so he knew he had to be extremely cautious. *Did they know about this secret hideaway?* Since they hadn't called back, he had a feeling someone might be waiting to meet them. His experience was telling him to trust those twists in his gut.

He was on alert, trying to see and hear everything around him. He looked at the house again. Overgrown shrubs covered much of the windows. The lawn grass was tall and brown. There were no broken windows, and the old curtains inside were still and fell down straight. He felt the presence of something. Yes, that was it… in the house. Someone was waiting in the house. He looked at the girls in the back. They were quiet and still, their eyes closed. *They must have fallen asleep along the way.*

"Cliff," he whispered, "check it out." He nodded toward the worn down house.

Cliff pulled his gun from a shoulder holster and smiled. "Sure, you got it."

As Cliff went in to investigate, Harry continued to spy the surroundings from the passenger seat. The girls were motionless with their seat belts on.

After a few moments, Cliff called out from inside house. "It's clear!"

"Okay, girls." Harry started as he woke them, "We're going to get out of the car and go into the house. Don't worry, we're not going to hurt you. Just a little while longer, and you'll be back with your mom and dad."

Amanda looked at him, but didn't answer or react. Sara stared ahead at the house. Her look turned to horror. Amanda gently took her hand, but she recoiled as if surprised.

She started crying. "No! No! I don't want to go in there."

Amanda held her hand, facing her. "Just stay with me Sara. It'll be okay."

Once out of the car, they slowly crept to the house with Harry behind them. He wanted to check things out for himself before he went in with the girls, but Cliff's assessment had to do for now.

The house was small, single floor, and they entered into the living room. There was a kitchen in the back with an eat-in area, old and worn, with several cabinets missing their doors. To the right was a hall that had a bathroom and two small bedrooms at the end, one in front of the house, the other in the back corner. The living room had an old dusty couch. A broken end table was below a front picture window. Two pictures lay on the floor, their frames broken. The kitchen had two chairs from a dining set that was once there. The house was otherwise empty of furnishings.

Harry guided the girls to the couch as Cliff grabbed a kitchen chair and brought it into the living room. He kicked aside the end table, sending dust up and around the room, and put his chair in front of the window, facing the girls. Cliff sat down. Harry remained standing by the front door.

"Now, girls, you just be still. Don't give us any trouble." Cliff said firmly

They looked at him without answering.

An hour passed, then another. Sara cried now and then as Amanda did her best to keep her calm. Harry sensed Amanda was crying on the inside. A curious feeling was coming to the surface. One he had not experienced in a long time. He tried to determine what it was. *Compassion?* This little girl was effecting him more than he wanted.

"Can we use the bathroom?" Amanda asked.

Harry went to the bath to see if it was working. There was water still coming into the house, probably from a well which seemed to have enough natural pressure to keep the plumbing working. He stepped out and motioned for the girls to go ahead. Amanda took Sara by the hand and into the bathroom. Harry remained outside the door to discourage a possible escape attempt through a small window in the bath. He'd hear any such attempt.

◊ ◊ ◊

Emily paced anxiously from her living room, down the hall, and back. It was mid-afternoon and they hadn't heard a word. She wore a heavy burden on her face, drained by the entire ordeal. *Why haven't we heard anything? This can't be good. Why doesn't the FBI have any better answers?*

With every moment that ticked away, the feeling of ultimate dread grew in her soul.

Where can they be? What if the girls are hurt or worse? How can I go on without them? No. We'll find them and they'll be all right. She could picture Amanda holding on to Sara and quieting her fears. *'Now don't you worry any Sara, she would say. 'Mommy and Daddy will find us and we'll be okay and back at home in no time, you'll see.'*

Amanda was always so brave. Sara, Amanda, and Thomas were her whole life.

Each time she returned to the living room, she looked at Thomas. She could see the anguish on his face. The feeling of helplessness she shared with him. He was staring out the front window.

"Why haven't they called?" she finally asked. "I think they would have called by now, don't you?"

"Mrs. Miller, these things can take some time to develop. We just need to be ready when they do," Agent Hill said.

"Our teams are out looking for them. They'll only call when they believe they're safe to do so."

"Meanwhile, can we rest for a while? And a little privacy?" she asked as she stopped pacing.

"Sure. Feel free to use your room," Hill responded. "We'll be right here if you need us."

Emily approached Thomas and rested a hand on his shoulder, bringing him back from an almost trance like state. They slowly walked to their room. He closed and locked the door, then sighed deeply. Emily went over and sat on the end of the bed. He joined her.

"Where's the key?" she asked quietly.

He looked at the closet door in the room.

"So get it," she encouraged.

"I don't dare. Not with them in the house. If they take it, we lose any leverage we might have."

"I don't understand." Emily asked.

"That other caller I spoke with said not to trust anyone except Pete. Not even the Feds."

Emily gave him a confused look.

"That's all I know." he said choking on the words.

He was wearing his emotions on his sleeve. She leaned over and rested her head on his shoulder as he wrapped his arms around her and held her. She began weeping quietly as he stared at their image in the mirror over the dresser.

Can we get the key to Pete without the FBI knowing? What if they catch us? My girls. What will happen to them if we lose our leverage?

◊ ◊ ◊

As darkness fell on the old house, Harry couldn't wait any longer. It was nearly nine o'clock. He had to call in even though he had disobeyed his orders. Since the Society never called him about the *negotiations*, he knew he was right, going to Horatio. It was a secret hideaway he and Cliff had not used for decades. He went outside to call.

"We've been here long enough. What's going on?" he asked his superior.

"You were right. You would've been caught had you gone to the original hideout," the voice said. "Just hang on. Arrangements have been made for us to get the key. Where are you?"

"Somewhere safe. Make it happen in the next hour or we're gone and the kids are returned. I know what you planned on doing. These kids are much more important than you let on."

"You must wait until we call you. Then you can let the girls go and be on your way. Just stay put until we call." He hung up.

This had to play out real soon. Harry looked around the yard, and then left towards the car. Nothing seemed amiss that he could see or hear. No sign of recent activity. The only tire tracks in the dirt were theirs. Everything looked untouched. Then what was nagging at him? There was something wrong. Suddenly he could hear the faint wail of sirens in the distance, probably several miles off. He drew his gun and listened intently. They were slowly getting closer.

He started back towards the house. Then he heard it. Several soft sounds coming from inside brought him to a stop. He almost missed them as he was listening to the sirens. He recognized the sound though. A silencer had just gone off. The girls started screaming.

Harry threw himself against the house, trying to cut down any angle the shooter might have against him out in the open. *The Society sent a hit man! How did they find us!* He quickly slid back to the corner where the car was to gain some level of protection. He knew Cliff was dead and he had to kill the assassin in this broken down house in order to save the girls. He was solely and utterly on his own.

The girls kept screaming.

He made his way cautiously around the side of the house. He knew the assassin could hear the sirens coming closer just as easily as he could and would be making his escape out the back. He knew what he would do in this situation and that was to protect himself from capture first and then try to fulfill the mission at another time.

Harry looked around the back corner of the house. Nothing. Yet he felt a presence. He had to move, and move quickly. He turned and headed to the back door. He went about twenty feet across the back grass towards the back door, then stopped. His instinct told him he'd made a fatal error. This guy was an expert, better than himself. Harry straightened up. He sensed someone behind him.

"Drop it." the assassin said calmly.

Instead, Harry turned to shoot.

The assassin was leaning out the back window of the bedroom. He shot Harry in the right arm and his gun dropped.

Pain seared up his arm and he bent forward.

"Easy Harry. No sudden moves. Move to the back door, slowly." The assassin climbed out the window.

I have to stop him. Do something! He stumbled towards the door and fell. His gun was now under his body. He tried to reach for it but his arm seized from the wound.

"Harry, Harry, you know I'm better than that." the voice was almost a taunt.

Harry was puzzled and in pain. "From the Society are you?" He tried to focus.

"No, Harry."

"Then how do you know who I am?"

"Because it's my business to know. I missed you in Zurich two years ago. And remember that couple you killed last year in Colorado?"

Harry didn't answer. He was shifting his left hand underneath him in a desperate attempt to grab his gun. *How could he know these events? He's monologuing. Maybe the chance I need.* His figures touched the gun handle.

"I was late in getting there and you were early in doing your work. Well, this time I'm on-time. Tell me what plans the Society has and this can all be over. You're going to die either way, so why not help me out? Tell me what they're doing."

Harry recognized the arrogance, the dry wit in his voice. *It can't be!*

He rolled over with the gun in his left hand. The assassin's shot tore through Harry's wrist. He dropped the gun, wincing as the pain was intense, closing his eyes. It took him a moment to collect himself. He managed to open his eyes enough to see who it was. *No, it can't be.*

"But you're dead. The Society killed you."

"Not yet," the assassin said with a wry smile. "Tell me what their plans are."

He was standing next to Harry, gun pointed at his head. Harry was helpless, both arms immobile.

"You know I can't."

"Then there's no point in talking. I'll take it from here." He shot Harry square between the eyes.

◊ ◊ ◊

The sirens were getting closer. The assassin knelt next to Harry and searched him. Harry was carrying Euros, and his wallet had an Interpol ID. No surprise there. The Society had indeed expanded its operations. *Pawning himself off as an Interpol agent? The war has indeed begun, finally.*

He smiled, and, almost out of time, needed to make sure the girls would be safe. He took the items and started to get up. Something under the front corner collar on Harry's jacket caught his eye. He flipped the collar up to reveal a small golden eagle pinned under the collar.

"I almost forgot." He took it and went back into the house.

The girls were still in the living room standing in front of the couch, looking at Cliff's dead body on the floor. A large pool of blood surrounded Cliff's head.

"Amanda, hold your sister's hand. We need to go outside and the police are coming to get you. I won't hurt you. Please come with me."

She looked at him but didn't move.

He knelt beside her. "Amanda." he whispered.

His deep brown eyes looking straight into her own blue ones. "Take Sara and very quietly go out and into the woods and hide."

"What's happening?" Amanda managed to ask. "Who are you?"

"Shh…don't talk just listen. Do you hear the sirens?"

Amanda nodded.

"That's the police. They'll be here in a few minutes. I'm going to leave, but you and Sara need to stay hidden in the woods until the police get here."

Harry watched as Amanda turned with Sara's hand held gently in her own and headed out the front door, into the woods past the car. Sara stumbled as they went, staring blindly ahead.

He checked to make sure the girls had reached the relative safety of the trees. He started searching Cliff but was out of time, though he took Cliff's eagle pin as well. He needed to leave in a hurry or he would be wearing cuffs or worse, a toe tag. He wouldn't allow that to happen. There was too much to do. The sirens were close now. He headed out the back and disappeared into the woods.

The war had indeed started.

Chapter 15

May 1787 - Pennsylvania State House

It was just after one o'clock, and amazingly, all the delegates had returned from lunch on time. Yates still held the floor and was standing at the New York table.

"Would the good Mr. Yates yield the floor for an organized response? Surely we have not digressed into a shouting match." Franklin queried.

George Washington had been elected as the President of the Convention. It was his job to see proper decorum and gentlemanly behavior was held. He himself was not directly involved in the discussions. In fact, he seldom even spoke unless it was as part of his assignment. "Mr. Yates, will you yield the floor to Mr. Franklin?"

Robert Yates shook his head no while sitting down, indicating he was reluctantly yielding.

"My dear colleague, Mr. Yates does have a point, but let's not be overly dramatic about the process. We are all here in good faith to deliver our country a better, more balanced approach, between our fledgling central government and our great states. No one here is suggesting one all powerful *Nation State*. Well, almost no one." The smile on Franklin's face was evident as was his remark intended for one individual in the room.

A good round of laughter followed. Everyone knew Franklin was picking on Alexander Hamilton also of New York and his notion of a monarchy with no states at all. He took it in stride with a gentle smirk of a smile. He had seen the Virginia Plan now and it served his purpose quite well. No, it did not totally destroy the states, but he felt Madison had reached far beyond the middle ground and he approved. Now was not the time to suggest going even farther. He would bide his time. He saw how England had broadened its central power over time even from their own revolution which was meant to give Englishmen their rights as individuals to govern themselves. He saw history repeating itself as it had always done. He also knew Yates and the state's rights advocates realized it, so he had to work his way into the hearts of both sides of the debate.

Franklin was also one of the diffusers of the two sides aiming to bring consensus to the group. This was his specialty and one of the reasons he was invited to partake in the exercise, being now quite old and not having any state as his passion, though he was a delegate from Pennsylvania.

"Let us for now think about our purpose here. Why did we all come here? Was it to try to fix the Articles?"

There were a few answers of yes from the room even though Franklin was not really asking the question. Since a few did answer, he nodded approvingly. "Yes it was, initially. Now, however, we all realize we need to be looking past our Articles."

"I'm not!" William Patterson from New Jersey replied, rather forcefully. "Not unless each state continues to have equal share," He was sitting behind their state table and had not even risen to respond.

"Yes, Yes, Mr. Patterson. I understand the concerns of the smaller states here. This is precisely why we must come to an agreement on how to proceed. Unless we are all working together towards a common purpose, and we can all agree about just how much power the central government should have, then and only then will we be able to produce a solution worthy of all."

It was another stroke by Franklin to attempt to disarm either side. This was his strength and many there knew it and were respectful of his approach.

Most were now nodding their heads approvingly for this new purpose. Franklin knew Madison's idea of a sweeping change was more than many had hoped for and as soon as they saw it that morning there had been strong words on both sides.

The Virginia Plan was a big step, but perhaps too big and his little speech was a warning of trying to give too much power away. He paused for a moment and continued.

"I believe we all see the weakness built into our current Articles and the need to find a solution to satisfy both the large and small states. Those who wish strong centralization and those who wish to keep the power of government in the hands of the states. Why do you think the Articles were written as they are? Isn't it because we all believe that our great states are truly independent countries?"

Now there was a much larger answer of yes in the room.

"So gentlemen, it seems we must make sure we codify this central government in such a way as to not be a threat to the sovereignty of any of our states, and to make sure each state reserves their rights to nullify or secede if they feel central government has reached too far. But we must be realistic. How can we defend our states if the central government cannot even pay for that defense?"

"Well then, what do you propose, Doctor Franklin?" Yates said, now willing to hear an alternative, any alternative to the Virginia Plan.

"I propose we create a heading in the direction of strengthening the central government without it becoming more powerful than any one state and continue to allow the states total sovereignty including everything that implies. So we should not look to take away each state's right to nullify both central government legislation and judicial decisions that would look to supersede state laws. I did notice these powers of superiority for central government are included in the Virginia Plan and I agree with Mr. Yates, on the risks of allowing a central government to become too strong. I will add further that any state must retain the right to secede should they determine the central government has broached the very purposes on which it was called into existence. In fact, every state here will be seceding from our first government based on the Articles of Confederation and Perpetual Union in order to now form a new government."

"I'm sorry Doctor and excuse me for interrupting, but how can a state secede from a Perpetual Union?" asked Lansing.

"I believe because if the central government is abusive for its own ends, the states and the people should have the right to abolish such government in favor of a new one."

"I'm sorry Doctor; I'm still at a loss. Are you saying that a Perpetual Union which is defined as not allowing a state to secede can be dissolved by a state or states in order to secede and form a new government?"

"No, a state must be bound by the Union so long as the central government has not abused its power." replied

Franklin.

"Then please explain to us how the central government, who has not abused its power, is using this Convention to usurp power from the states and start a new government?"

"Perhaps we should look to our Declaration of Independence for clarity;

"*When in the Course of human events, it becomes necessary for one people to dissolve the political bands which have connected them with another, and to assume among the powers of the earth, the separate and equal station to which the Laws of Nature and of Nature's God entitle them, a decent respect to the opinions of mankind requires that they should declare the causes which impel them to the separation.*

"*We hold these truths to be self-evident, that all men are created equal, that they are endowed by their Creator with certain unalienable Rights, that among these are Life, Liberty and the pursuit of Happiness. That to secure these rights, Governments are instituted among Men, deriving their just powers from the consent of the governed, That whenever any Form of Government becomes destructive of these ends, it is the Right of the People to alter or to abolish it, and to institute new Government, laying its foundation on such principles and organizing its powers in such form, as to them shall seem most likely to effect their Safety and Happiness. Prudence, indeed, will dictate that Governments long established should not be changed for light and transient causes; and accordingly all experience hath shown, that mankind are more disposed to suffer, while evils are sufferable, than to right themselves by abolishing the forms to which they are accustomed. But when a long train of abuses and usurpations, pursuing invariably the same Object evinces a design to reduce them under absolute Despotism, it is their right, it is their duty, to throw off such Government, and to provide new Guards for their future security.*

"So gentlemen, although we are throwing off our weak government instead of a tyranny, it is for the same purpose, and that is to provide a better government, but still based in whole by the governed and not by its own ends. Now, knowing our boundaries, and if this body is in agreement with this course of action, let us move forward and resolve our differences in a way to satisfy all."

Gouverneur Morris stood up. "I second the motion."

"All in favor?" Washington asked. A light majority of states carried.

Lansing turned to Yates and whispered. "Did he even answer my question?"

"Of course not. This has nothing to do with the states, it's a power grab, clear and simple," Yates replied.

And so the purpose was drawn to allow the states to secede from their Perpetual Union, which made no sense at all, and the limits set about it were well defined in favor of a new *Nation State*. They were agreeing on something that none of them were given the authority to do.

Franklin continued. "I suggest perhaps we take a vote and see just where we are with this plan proposed by Virginia."

The central theme of the Virginia Plan was establishing a new broadly reaching national government or *Nation State* with sweeping authority over the states, giving a huge advantage to the larger states in proportion to the number of legislatures in the new body, as well as giving the central government the ability to supersede state laws for the good of the union, or in this case the good of the central government at the expense of the states. The smaller states immediately saw through this and were now objecting.

"What about the suggestion you just made?" Yates said. "You no sooner say we must be careful where we tread, and then you propose a solution just the opposite."

Several were now standing in objection to the swing Franklin had just tried.

Franklin responded. "Okay, yes. We all know the body of the proposal is rather in favor of the central government and the larger states, but we must start somewhere. Can we not at least look at the proposal before we dismiss it out of hand entirely?"

"I say no," Lansing answered. "And Mr. Franklin, please have the decency to call the proposal what it actually is. You say central government, but what does that mean? To some it means an alliance of states. To others it means the consolidation of power into an elite group who will govern at their own whim. Let's be clear. We have two choices. To strengthen what we have, which is our purpose and the only authority we have, or to create a *Nation State*. We all know a *Nation State* with sweeping powers will devour everything in its path. Just look at the Roman *Nation State*. It became one of the greatest tyrannies in the history of the world."

He paused for a response, but his explanation was clear to Franklin and everyone else in the room.

"Why aren't we starting with the government we already have in place? We are here to amend the Articles of Confederation and Perpetual Union, nothing more. And those changes must be ratified by every state. That is our purpose. That is our job. That is why we have an amendment procedure spelled out in the Articles. What you are asking us to do is ignore our states, our constituents, the people we represent, and just set up a whole new government. You may do well with convincing Doctor, but our Articles are hardly a long train of abuses you refer to in the Declaration. I know Jefferson would be appalled if he knew the real intent of his own Virginia, his own country represented here, to destroy the states and our alliance."

Mr. Randolph stood up. "I ask for opening the Convention up to consider the Virginia Plan so we can move on to discussing it instead of wasting time trying to amend an unamendable set of Articles that we all agree are totally inadequate for our central government.

"No Mr. Randolph, we don't all agree," William Patterson of New Jersey said.

"Okay," Washington said. "Although we do not all agree that the Articles should be totally abandoned, we must find a way through this process. So I ask for a second to Mr. Randolph's motion."

"Second." It was Madison. Being the chief architect of the Virginia Plan, he was very set on putting it into play, though now he was seeing some use his well-intended device for more powerful purposes.

"Ah…pardon me Mr. Madison, but wouldn't it seem more toward decorum if more than one state decides on the acceptance of a motion!" Yates voiced, angrily. "I mean, Virginia has seven delegates in attendance. New York, an equal in Congress, has only three. If we are to go by these rules, then the states with more delegates will control every issue, every motion."

"Gentlemen, I expect you all to be instrumental in our greatest time of need. Mr. Yates' point is valid." Washington said.

"I second," Gouverneur Morris of Pennsylvania said.

The motion carried.

"Okay, this motion is carried and the Virginia Plan shall now be part of the discussions. Let me make clear, however, that this is not the abandonment of our Articles. I agree with the delegates from New York. We do not have the authority to just setup a whole new structure. However, all sides need to be heard."

This was the most Washington had spoken since his arrival. He knew and did not want to make the smaller states just roll over. He also knew they needed a strong majority to make this work, especially after the Shay Rebellion in Massachusetts.

And where was Rhode Island? Had they been there they might have effectively voted down the Virginia Plan at the outset. A strategic mistake by the small state who did not want any changes to the Articles. They had a very prosperous shipping trade. It was perhaps one of the largest of that trade in the states.

For Robert Yates however, this was untenable. You could see it in his face. Yes, he was from New York and they would greatly benefit from the Virginia Plan. But that was not why he was there. He was there for their original purpose and now it was compromised.

"I would like to say gentlemen, that if we do indeed scrap our Articles, our Perpetual Union, then we must realize that any further recognition of any perpetual unbreakable *Nation State* or union is mute. Indeed we will be establishing that there never can be an unbreakable union for we are now doing exactly that," Yates said.

"Gentlemen, it is time to adjourn for the day," Jackson interjected, happy to break up the now escalating debate. This and other issues could wait until tomorrow.

Randolph had one more item on his agenda however.

"Before we break, gentlemen, I would like to have one more vote. These proceedings must be kept secret, and I would like to add to the request that for the protection and safety of all involved, these proceedings and their contents should be sealed until the last member of these proceedings has passed. This is for the protection of all and their families should there be any resistance from the people,"

There was an immediate outcry.

"Secret?" Yates asked. "Are you making jokes? We're here for a specific purpose, to represent the will of the people. How can we possibly keep all that is done a secret? This flies in the face of common sense. Unless you mean to create an oligarchy for the elite to rule, being similar to the one we just cast off, it is our duty to detail all that is done out in the open so the people can see and trust in our actions. Secrecy in the acts of government towards its own people is nothing less than a usurpation of authority not granted!"

Yates stormed out along with many others to the dismay of Washington, Franklin, and Madison. There was a brief pause from everyone.

"Well now, since we still have a quorum, I ask for my motion of secrecy to be voted on."

"Second." Gouverneur Morris said, the strong central government advocate from Pennsylvania.

Franklin quickly responded.

"Wait a minute gentlemen. We must be careful here. Voting on this issue now with fully one half of the delegates protesting will surely make a compromise all the more difficult."

"Thank you Mr. Franklin, but we are within the bounds of precedent to hold a vote so long as there is a quorum. Should we stop every time either side is at odds with any issue, we would never get anything done. Now then General Washington, can we have a vote on the second?"

Washington was quite alarmed at what he was seeing, but feeling he himself was in favor of a stronger central government, meant to protect the people, he granted the request.

"Yes. Please continue."

Jackson called for the count. "All those in favor?"

The motion carried easily with the delegates still in the room.

"Then the motion is passed. All members including those not currently in attendance will comply with the rule of secrecy on all that is said and done within this Convention. I will draw up the paperwork for tomorrow's session so all the delegates can sign them."

Washington felt a strong urge to appear compassionate for the others who had left.

"I am compelled to ask that a member keep a detailed account of all that is said and done, so that when these proceedings do come to light, it will show our honest efforts to do the will of the people."

"I agree Sir." James Wilson said, lawyer and delegate from Pennsylvania.

"And since the Virginia Plan is now part of the discussion, I nominate Mr. Madison to take the notes."

"Second." It was Hamilton. The vote was unanimous and they adjourned for the day.

The stage was now set for the central government *Nation State* faction to move their agenda forward no matter what the people wanted, even though the delegates knew they had no authority to abandon the Articles; a perpetual, unbreakable union. The nationalists also knew they were in the minority with their own constituents.

It seemed there were several different groups pressing for centralization, though they were independent of each other, and for different purposes.

Washington and Madison were playing into the hands of the Society of Praetorians, though not willingly.

The news traveled to the Praetor quickly. A devilish smile crossed his face. "It seems we have many others helping us fulfill our goals, even if they don't know it. Let them fight for centralization and then we will take it from them."

Chapter 16

May 2018 - Bogata, Texas

Night had fallen. Thomas woke with a start as his cell phone rang. He had forgotten to put it on vibrate. *Did the FBI agents hear the ring?*

He and Emily had both fallen asleep from mental exhaustion.

The phone rang again and he answered.

"Okay, you've had time enough. We want the key now," said the same voice he had heard before, yet now it was much more sinister.

"Okay, Okay. Just give me a little more time."

"You're out of time."

Emily woke as he continued. He decided to put it on speaker.

"But I have a house full of FBI agents thanks to you. How am I supposed to get it to you?"

"Where is it?"

"I won't tell you. I want to talk to my girls."

"Perhaps we've not been clear enough for you." A gunshot went off in the phone.

"My, God! Oh, my God!" Emily grabbed for the phone.

Thomas, shocked, raised his arm and blocked her from taking it.

"That was just a warning shot." the man said in a tone of complete control.

Thomas panicked while still warding off Emily. They were both now standing.

"It's here at the house!"

"At the house? Are you sure?"

"Yes, I'm sure," Thomas said resigned to defeat.

"Well, then, just leave the rest to me." The caller hung up.

"Give me the phone!" screamed Emily as she grabbed his arm.

"He hung up!" Thomas yelled back. "It's over! They've won!"

"No! It's not over!" Her emotions turned to rage. "The girls!"

"Em, the FBI has to do this. They don't get the key until we get the girls back."

He gave her as much of a sincere look as he could. She was hyperventilating.

"You need to calm down. I need you." he said as they both heard a thud against the locked bedroom door.

Emily looked at Thomas just as Agent Hill's leg came crashing through the door. He reached in and up, unlocking it.

She screamed as they both backed towards the far corner of the room. Hill's gun was still holstered as he entered.

"What's going on in here? Are you two alright?" Hill asked.

Thomas managed to catch his breath. "The kidnappers just called. They want it." He paused. *Is Agent Hill a part of Pete's organization? What should I do?*

"Do you have it?" he asked calmly as he shook off the impact of breaking in.

Both Thomas and Emily were startled. They'd only met Agent Hill that day. He was an FBI agent, yet now busting in on them?

Thomas was taken aback. "What do you mean?"

"The item, the key," Hill responded.

Thomas looked at Emily who was suddenly sizing up Agent Hill.

"How do you know it's a key? We didn't tell you." Emily interjected. "Who are you and what do you know about this?" she asked sternly.

"I'm working with your organization, of course," Hill responded.

"Busting down our door?" Emily shot back.

"I heard a phone ring and yelling. I thought you might be in danger," Hill responded, though not very convincingly.

"Then you know we must get the key to the kidnappers so they'll release the girls."

Thomas, stunned, had never seen this side of Emily. She was playing out the scene, a scene she had no idea about, and had Agent Hill on the defensive.

"Yes," Hill said. "I'll take it for safe keeping. Your sheriff is working with us. You know. Your organization."

Thomas looked long and hard at Agent Hill. "How is it we haven't been made aware of your presence in our organization until now?"

"Protocol," Hill responded, as his eyes moved from the Miller's to the glass slider on the back wall of the room.

Thomas glanced to see an outline of a figure standing outside the door in the dark.

Agent Hill went for his gun.

Pete's gun was already drawn and he fired two shots through the glass door, spraying glass everywhere.

Hill reeled back against the broken door behind him and dropped to the floor.

Thomas flinched at the encounter as he pulled Emily to the floor.

There was shattered glass flying everywhere.

When he looked up, Pete came through the broken slider.

"Pete. What's going on?" He asked, distraught.

"He's not with us," Pete said as he moved to check on Agent Hill, kneeling beside him.

"He's a Praetorian agent. A plant in the FBI, I would guess. Thank your wife for seeing me outside and turning Hill's attention to you guys."

Agent Hill was dead. Pete had hit him with both shots, one in the center of his chest. He unhooked an eagle pin under his collar.

"What about the other agents inside?" Thomas asked, puzzled.

Pete stood up. "Gone, and we must be gone now! Pack what you can and let's go!"

"Wait a minute," Emily said "What the hell is a Praetorian?"

Pete motioned for them to get packing. As they were, he started.

"Remember the two Societies I said were involved? One of them is called the Praetorians. The other is the Verum."

Thomas went to the closet. It was small with a hanger pole and shelf, not large enough to walk into. He reached up above the trim on the inside of the door opening and felt around, until he found it. He grasped hold and slid it off the picture hook he had fastened above the molding and put it in his pocket.

Emily was frantically packing.

Once they finished, they rushed out to Pete's cruiser. The Millers sat in the back as they headed into town.

Pete continued. "Agent Hill sent his team out on a wild goose chase about an hour ago. Gave them information, thinking the girls were being kept close by. I got a call from Agent Brooks telling me to get here as fast as possible."

"The agent from the crime scene?" Thomas asked.

"Yes. He'd come into town and talked to me earlier. He's my contact. You know what? I forgot to ask him if he called you earlier. Was it Brooks?"

"I don't know. He never identified himself, though he said he wasn't with any law enforcement."

"Brooks had to go along with Agent Hill's game and was involved in playing the hoax to draw Hill out. Actually he didn't know who it was until Hill got everyone running. Agent Johnson is a neutral, as far as we know, as are all the other FBI agents now in Bogata. With so much going on, we aren't really sure who is who. Johnson is out following another lead."

"What's a neutral?" Emily asked.

"Just a normal FBI agent doing his job and not affiliated with either group. He's going to want answers for this, and I'm leaving it up to Brooks to supply them."

"And you, Pete?" Emily asked.

"I'm also with Brooks' organization. I was sent here nine years ago to watch over you guys. Keep you safe. Right now I'm thinking of the lousy job I'm doing."

"Are you kidding?" Thomas said. "None of us saw this coming."

Emily interrupted. "What about our girls, Pete? If you just killed one of their agents, how will they respond?"

Thomas could see her heightened alarm.

"I honestly don't know. I wish I could've done something else. I had to take him down or he would've killed both of you once he had the key. Brooks told me the Society of Praetorians killed four of our members in the last week."

Thomas gasped. Emily looked blindsided by another event.

"Killing other members?" Thomas asked.

"Yes, but you won't hear about them. The Praetorians control the media and can keep these things from coming out. Even the local media and communities don't know. Cover stories have been planted, like gone on vacation or visiting relatives. It'll be some time before anyone who knows our members will start asking more questions," Pete said. "Brooks is meeting us in town in front of the hotel. The station is no longer safe."

"That means the girls are no longer safe!" Emily shouted.

"The girls are safe, Emily. They are because we have the key. We still have the leverage." Pete said. "But as for everyone else, who knows? I don't know any more than that and only because Agent Brooks took me into his confidence."

◊ ◊ ◊

A cloaked figure entered the Miller's house and soon found Agent Hill's body. He called in. "Hill is down. Looks like they had help before I could get here. I told you I should've handled this! And from now on, I will." He hung up and checked Hill's collar, but the eagle pin was gone. "Damn bureaucrats!"

He headed to his car while making another call. "It's me. They're probably heading east with the sheriff. Intercept them at all costs. We need to stop this right now."

◊ ◊ ◊

Pete watched the Miller's in his rearview mirror as he drove.

"And what about that key?" Emily asked as she looked at Thomas.

Thomas's cell phone rang before he could answer her question, just as they were coming up to the hotel. "This is the same guy that called us in our bedroom."

Pete motioned for him to answer and put it on speaker.

"You shouldn't have killed Agent Hill."

"Listen, I've got the key, but I'm not giving it to you until my girls are safe." Thomas answered.

Pete slammed on the brakes and the cruiser skidded to a stop just before the hotel.

"You have no choice in the matter," the man responded. There seemed to be a change in tone with the voice on the other end. The man was now a little unsure of himself.

Pete motioned Thomas to stop agitating the caller. Emily watched Pete's action while in disbelief.

Thomas ignored him. "If you do anything to my girls, I'll make sure your entire Society comes crashing down and everything it's connected to!" Thomas looked emboldened now. However, he had no idea just how big this whole operation was.

The man on the other end hung up. Clearly he wasn't prepared for this type of resistance, especially when he seemed to have all the cards. Pete moved the car forward towards the front of the hotel.

"My God, Thomas, you just gave him a choice of the key or the girls!" Emily yelled as she burst into tears. She started hitting him.

"Emily!" Pete shouted. "It's not his fault! Look up ahead, that's Agent Brooks."

Agent Brooks hurried from his car parked in front of them.

"Did they call you?" Brooks asked as Pete and Thomas were getting out of the car.

"Yes," Thomas said, as he flexed the arm Emily had been hitting. He turned to Emily who hadn't move and reached out his hand. "Come on, Em, we need to go."

Pete took their bags out of the trunk and put them in Brooks' trunk. Emily finally got out of the back seat, still in tears. Thomas helped her to Brooks' car and they sat in the back. As Brooks was getting in, he looked back at Pete.

The sheriff locked eyes with him. "Did you call Mr. Miller earlier?" Pete asked.

"No."

"Well, someone did. He said he wasn't with either Society."

"I'll find out who it was." Brooks looked puzzled.

They gave each other an affirming nod. Brooks got in his car and Pete watched them head out of town. He saw Emily look at him through the back window.

Sheriff Peter Lucas was now fixed on finding the truth behind the kidnappings as he got into his cruiser. He pulled back in the street and caught sight of a car heading east into town at high speed. Instinctively he swerved, blocking its path as it attempted to pass him. The dark sedan clipped his rear bumper and crashed into a group of parked cars on the side of the road.

Pete was shaken but otherwise okay. He got out and approached the car, gun drawn. "Come out with your hands up!"

He stood for a moment, trying to see through the tinted windows. There was no movement. A few seconds passed, and Pete crept near the driver's door. He reached down and swung it open, pivoted and had his gun set with both hands. The car was empty. He made his way around to the other side and saw the passenger door was slightly open. Whoever had been here, was gone.

◊ ◊ ◊

The shadowy figure staggered down an alley, making his way back around to a building corner behind his wrecked car. He watched the sheriff searching eastwards and knew he'd successfully eluded him.

He took out his phone. "They're heading east out of Bogota. They're now in a grey sedan. I can't pursue. What's your ETA?"

"We should intercept in the next ten minutes." an associate responded.

"Take them out, then meet me on the west side of town. Don't use the main road." He walked slowly westward and out of sight.

◊ ◊ ◊

Pete called Brooks. "I stopped someone from pursuing you here in town. Whoever it was, he got away. I'm calling ahead to the nearest safe house. You should stop there for the night until this blows over."

Pete wondered. *There are too many players in this. I need to find out what's happened to the girls. I have to save them. Save them before…*

Chapter 17

May 2018 - Horatio, Arkansas

Deputy Wilson arrived at the house with a dozen other agents, including Johnson and Dean. He'd joined the FBI in the pursuit, hoping to do what he could to help find the girls. There were no less than six cars on the scene. As they pulled into the driveway, he saw them huddled together behind a large tree.

Amanda saw Mike as he stepped out of the car. She glanced down at her sister, giving her a reassuring smile. Cautiously she stepped out from behind a large pine tree, one foot after another, working her way through the darkness.

Mike saw the movement from the corner of his eye and turned quickly, hand moving to his side arm.

Amanda froze at Mike's reflexive motion to pull his gun.

Mike eyes narrowed as he pierced the darkness. "Amanda?" he whispered, taking his hand off his weapon. He reached out. "Amanda." He said just loud enough for her to hear.

She smiled and ran towards him.

Sara, who was watching the events unfold in the dark, hesitated, and sunk herself in a soft bed of leaves behind the tree.

Amanda collapsed into Mike's waiting arms. He shushed her sobs as he squeezed her to him. "Where's Sara?" he whispered.

She turned around and looked at the tree line, sniffling, rubbing her eyes. Grabbing Mike's hand, she walked him to the large Pine on the edge of the woods. "Sara!" she called out.

Sara didn't answer so they walked around the tree to find her sitting, face tucked to her knees, hands over her ears.

"Hi, Sara." Mike said softly. "It's Deputy Mike. It's okay to come out now, you're safe."

She looked up at him, tears streaming down her face. She saw her sister next to Mike.

Amanda nodded. "Come on Sara. Let's go home."

Sara hesitantly got up and took Sara and Mike's hands. They walked out of the woods to the cruiser, her eyes glazed over.

He knelt down and pulled both of them to him. His expression was one of relief and heartbreak. He was very fond of these two girls, as if they were his own kids. He had spent many weekend afternoons playing with them in between hot dogs on the grill in the back yard. They were holding on to him just as tightly.

"Are you alright?" he said, trying to keep his emotions in check.

"Yes," Amanda said. "They didn't hurt us."

Sara burst out crying as Mike tried his best to comfort her. He touched the back of her head and stroked her hair gently. "Shh, now, now, it's ok. I've got you. No one will hurt you now. Uncle Mike will never let anyone hurt you again.

Though he wasn't really their uncle, he was treated as one of the family for years. They had always called him uncle in the most affectionate way.

◊ ◊ ◊

Agent Timothy Dean was a young FBI agent who joined the force soon after high school. He was highly skilled in gathering information and tracking persons of interest. He tended to be a bit rash when it came to engaging difficult situations. This was one of the reasons Agent Ben Johnson took him on all his assignments. Johnsons calm demeanor and professionalism kept Dean grounded.

Johnson had been with the force for almost thirty years. He was a high level commander who directed other agents during extremely stressful events, such as kidnappings. Though in his fifties, he had a keen grasp on technology and was a wiz at electronics.

◊ ◊ ◊

Once the house was secure, Agent Johnson went inside. A man lay dead on the floor in a pool of blood. From the descriptions they had, this was one of the kidnappers. He looked familiar. He'd seen his mug shot somewhere. He wondered what happened. Something didn't add up even though he'd been tipped off. He knew there were two of them from Gus the bus driver.

Agent Dean called from the backyard, "Sir! I found the other guy."

Johnson went out the back door, joining Dean. Now something really didn't add up.

Both men killed? Shot in the head?

He examined the clothing. His FBI training recognized the European cut of the suits.

"I know this guy, both of them. They work together. This is Harry Matthews, which means that's Cliff Barden inside." A chill ran up his spine as grave concern showed on his face.

"Dean, you need to call this in right away."

Dean got on his cell. "We found the girls, and I have two dead bodies here. I need forensics right away. Alert the rest of our teams that two men are down and we think they're the kidnappers. And send me the dossiers of Harry Mathews and Cliff Barden."

Not knowing how long ago the events took place, Johnson wasn't sure these were indeed the two kidnappers they were looking for. There was more at play here with the killings. He had to make sure and he had to do it quickly. He looked through Harry's pockets but came up empty.

Agent Kelly Waxman came out of the house with some items carefully taken off the body inside. She showed them to Johnson who's look indicated this was not protocol. "Don't worry, I made sure not to contaminate the evidence. From the guy inside. Cliff Barden. He has an Interpol ID."

This confirmed Johnsons assessment. "And this is Harry Mathews. These guys always worked together, but Interpol? We need to get the CIA involved. They're Americans dressed up to look European."

Johnson had already encountered the work of these two thugs when he was working with NSA, but never a kidnapping of children. He turned to Waxman. "Call Agent Brooks and have him tell the Millers we've got the girls and they're not hurt. Deputy Wilson will be bringing them to the hospital in Clarksville, but before he leaves, he needs to bring the oldest one back here."

"Sir? Isn't it too traumatic right now?" She asked.

"Yes, but I need to know something right now. Have him bring her."

Agent Waxman disappeared around the house. A few moments passed and he couldn't wait any longer. He came around the side of the house and heard Wilson talking to the eldest, then the younger one, who was now crying.

Mike turned to Sara. "You stay right here with this nice police lady, and I'll be right back."

"No!" Sara continued crying.

"I'll take her," Waxman said.

Waxman led Amanda to the back corner of the house where they joined Johnson.

"Amanda, my name is Ben and I need you to help me. Can you be strong one more time for me?" Johnson asked.

Amanda looked at Waxman who had knelt down beside her. She looked into her eyes. Waxman looked back into hers and gave her a small nod.

"Amanda, was there anyone else here at the house? Any other person?" Johnson asked.

Amanda nodded.

"Was he the one who took you off the bus?"

She shook her head.

"Was he helping the other men?"

"No. He helped us," she said quietly.

Johnson paused for a moment. "He helped you?"

"Yes."

"How did he help you?"

"He shot the man in the house. He helped us go to the woods and hide."

Agent Johnson fears were now realized. He knew there was another killer on the loose. "Can you look at this other man and tell me if he was the one that took you?"

"Do I have to?" The break in her voice was evident as was her visible shuttering. She was scared more than he had seen any child.

"I'm sorry, Amanda, but I need to know who he is. Try to keep as calm as you can. It will only take a moment and then you can go with Deputy Wilson, okay?"

Amanda hesitated, then went over to the body with Johnson and Waxman. "Yes, that's the other man." She closed her eyes and hugged Waxman's leg. "I want Uncle Mike".

"Okay, Amanda," Waxman said. "You did great. We're all very proud of you. How strong you are. Let's go see Mike."

Johnson motioned for Waxman to bring her back to her sister as he followed.

"Waxman, there's another suspect on the loose, possibly responsible for these killings. Get our teams out. Capture alive if possible." Agent Johnson was troubled. "I have a feeling this is connected to all the other killings this past week."

Johnson watched as the Deputy's car left the driveway, kicking up dust and disappearing. The girls were saved and the case coming to a close, yet there were too many unanswered questions. *Who is this third man? Was he the one who tipped us off? Who else in involved?*

Johnson got in his cruiser and headed for Bogata. He needed to talk to the sheriff.

May 2018 - Bogata, Texas

There were a hundred questions bouncing around in Emily's head. Thomas sat quietly beside her in the back of Brooks' car. Brooks got in and started driving northeast. It was nine o'clock as they sped away.

"Agent Brooks, where are the girls?"

He looked at her through the rear view mirror. "We got a tip and agents we can trust are on their way now to get them. It seems one of the kidnappers called in although we can't be sure. He said he'd keep them safe until we could get there and that should be happening quite soon now."

Emily looked at Thomas. "What's happening?" She tempered her anger and frustration.

Thomas was seated behind Brooks and Emily caught his glance in the rearview mirror.

"How much do you know, Thomas?" Brooks asked.

Emily could see he was making eye contact with him.

"I need to know. Otherwise, I can't keep you guys safe."

"How can you help us?" Thomas looked frustrated. "Pete said members were being killed! And did you know Agent Hill was working for the Praetorians? And what the hell is this Society of Praetorians?" he ended in a loud exasperating tone.

"We've saved as many as we could," Brooks responded. "I didn't know Agent Hill was on the other side. I though he was a neutral, just doing his job. I only found out a few hours ago when he sent his team out to apprehend the kidnappers. It was a ruse so he could be alone in the house with you two. That's why I sent the Sheriff out to your house."

Thomas was visible shaking. "Yes, Pete told us. Agent Hill confronted us at the house and was going to take the key from me. Then I got a call on my cell from them on our way back into town. They knew we had escaped the house with the key and Agent Hill was dead. You still haven't told us what this is all about, and how'd they know what happened to Agent Hill?"

"They must of had someone else close by."

Emily watched as the two men were working their way through the events. Her focus was on the girls.

Why aren't they talking about the girls?

She was no longer hearing the conversation as visions of the girls bounced in her head. She finally broke. "Where are the girls!" she shouted over the men talking. Her emotions flooded out. "Where are my girls!"

◊ ◊ ◊

Agent Brooks was a leader in Pete's society and he now had to take full control of the Millers. It was time to break the chain of command and talk directly. There was no other choice. Everything had unraveled, and now Thomas and Emily needed to trust him as much as Pete.

Brooks already knew the events of the past week were far greater than he could share. His society had been compromised and several of his friends had disappeared, some had been killed. For his part, he couldn't act on those events without compromising his position and risking even more devastation to his group. The Millers were his responsibility.

"Mrs. Miller, I need to tell you and Thomas what's really going on. I'm sorry, for all this. For the last twenty-five years, the Society of Praetorians has been looking for Thomas and many others in our organization. Other than an occasional threat, nothing really materialized. However, over the last week, there've been four murders. Several of our key people have barely escaped. The others, well, some were taken. At least one was tortured. She managed to escape and contact us just before they caught her again and killed her. She said they didn't get any information to jeopardize our organization, but we just don't know. That's why we're moving everyone we can.

"Many in our group only know that our organization exists and even those only know of its existence through their families, and have no information about what is really at stake. Our hierarchy makes sure information is only given out on a need to know basis. You two were safe until today, and only through an outside contact were we able to mobilize as quickly as we did, though it wasn't fast enough to stop the kidnapping."

Brooks' phone rang and he answered. He listened while Pete explained the encounter in town.

"Got it." He hung up. "Seems whoever reached the house after we left was chasing us. Pete stopped him in town." He was looking at Emily through the mirror.

"I'm still waiting for you to tell us what's going on." She looked both scared and angry.

Agent Brooks paused and then started. "The only way for me to explain this is from the beginning. The Society of Praetorians has been in existence since 1783. Many of their first members were our country's Founding Fathers. They were brought together for one purpose to destroy our new republic. They are now comprised of the elite political and bureaucratic class that control most of our government and most of the country's wealth. Our organization is also a society that started soon after to thwart their efforts, and we too had many of the Founding Fathers."

Emily shook her head. "You mean to tell me that a Society over two hundred years old is still in existence and has kidnapped our daughters?"

"Yes, that's exactly what I'm telling you." He was doing his best to drive and make eye contact in the mirror. It was a challenge to say the least. He was keeping his speed about twenty miles an hour over the limit. "Other members in our organization have been tracked over time and, for many years, members needed to act to try to save their families and loved ones. Most were able to, but some were not. Some had already gone through threats, kidnappings, and murder. Some spouses were brought into the fold when they realized something was being kept from them. We share what we can to protect both the organization as well as it's families. It was the only way to keep hidden the secrets we had and keep the organization as safe as possible.

"We're not a consolidated unit. In fact, each of us only knows a few other members. That's what has kept the Praetorians from ravaging our ranks. So long as we stay apart from each other, it helps the protection of all. You must understand what's at stake. Our purpose is to keep the truth of what America is supposed to be. The Praetorians changed the course of America early on and have maintained a hold on power ever since. They have been trying to snuff out our society since the beginning. Yet after all these years, with all that has taken place, our members are still holding together… barely. It's never come this close to you and Thomas. The Praetorians have also been hit with several assassinations of their top operatives. We don't know who's doing it, but those assassinations may have forced their hand with this stunt."

"Now, however, it seems we are plunged into the center of it, though I have no idea what you're talking about." Emily said.

"Yes, and Thomas holds the *key* to everything, literally."

Thomas drew the old skeleton key from his pocket.

"I don't understand what this key has to do with anything," said Thomas.

Brooks watched as Thomas examined it.

"Pete just told me to keep it secret, to keep it safe. I thought it was his. I thought it was an heirloom from his family. And by the way I had no idea I was part of this Society you belong to. I was helping the local Historical Society in town, not some secret group."

"We were hoping your work in the local group would jar your memory. Anyway, that was your father's key. It's part of a puzzle we haven't been able to solve. We've been searching for locations where we believe several sets of documents have been hidden for a very long time. These documents are believed to hold many historical events that have never seen the light of day and are nowhere to be found in any records, history books, or family lineages since they were lost, or I should say hidden."

Emily looked puzzled. "I still don't understand. Why don't you just give them what they want. Wouldn't it end all this? Isn't it more important that everyone is safe instead of keeping this war going? What's the point?"

Brooks knew this would take some time to explain. The depth of what was happening was being lost in the moment. This couple just had their kids kidnapped. Why would they care about any of this? He had to press on. "The point is Emily, you and your family are in grave danger. We are here to keep you as safe as we can until we can unravel the mysteries before us. This may not mean much now, but what we do going forward will affect every single American and is the only way your family will be safe."

Brooks focused on Thomas again. "Now, we know there are three separate places where the documents are, but don't have their exact locations. We thought we found one of them when your father was alive, but we haven't been able to put it together. His notes don't have the code, which makes it even harder. You, Thomas, are the answer. In your memory lies the secret code. Since you haven't been able to remember anything, we haven't been able to search beyond the information we have. That's the downside of having such a loosely affiliated group. We didn't need the key because we haven't found any doors or locks it might fit. If we had, we would have asked for it."

"So you're saying that somehow Thomas has information about where these sites are?" asked Emily. He could still sense the sharp tone in her voice.

"Yes. This has been passed down through Thomas's ancestry since Robert Yates originally started our organization. You see, Thomas is a direct descendent of Robert Yates. Only two other members in our organization are direct descendants of the original founders."

"Pete said his name earlier. Who the hell is he?" Emily asked in an agitated tone. She looked at Thomas. "I don't understand! I thought we agreed years ago we wouldn't keep secrets from each other."

"I didn't have any secrets from you… just the key, really." Thomas sounded pretty ridiculous but Brooks knew it was the truth.

"It seems to be a pretty big secret Thomas, if our girls were kidnapped and our lives are now in danger. Why would you keep something this big from me?"

"Because he didn't know," Brooks said as he let out an exasperated breath. "We don't have time for this right now. Thomas didn't know any more other than the key was Pete's."

"Okay, Brooks. Get on with it," Emily said sternly.

As Brooks watched her in the mirror, she seemed to composed herself and was even able to look at Thomas without glaring.

"Go ahead, Brooks, tell us what this is all about."

"Thomas, you know you're James Yates. Pete said he told you."

"He did. The name means nothing to me."

"It's your real name. You were in a car accident with your father. Your father, Richard, didn't make it. After the accident, you went into hiding and we changed your name to protect you. Robert Yates, your ancestor, was one of the Founding Fathers. He was a delegate from New York attending the Constitutional Convention back in 1787.

"When the states gathered together after the Revolutionary War, they attempted to fix the fledgling government they had started. It was a mess. Yates was one of the delegates working towards a solution. He was there when it all started."

"When what all started?" Emily asked.

They were now about ten miles out of town when Brooks received another call. "Hold on, I need to take this," he answered the phone. "Yes?" He paused, listening.

He could see Thomas and Emily were straining to hear the conversation from the back seat.

"Okay, I'm getting the Millers to a safe house," he replied. "Keep me posted." He hung up.

"Well?" Emily raised her eyebrow.

"Deputy Wilson has just picked up the girls."

"Oh, my God…thank God." Emily grabbed Thomas and hugged him. "Are they all right?"

"Yes, only a few bumps." Brooks looked at Emily.

"When will we see them?" she asked.

"They're bringing them to…"

Glass sprayed everywhere as the sound of gunfire and ricocheting bullets filled the air. Someone had just passed them in the opposite direction, unloading a clip from a fully-automatic weapon. Brooks looked in the mirror at the Millers just as Thomas froze, his eyes widening before blood came spurting out of his neck all over Emily.

She lurched her upper body away from him, then looked at him with her mouth wide open. He fell into her lap.

"Oh, my God! Thomas!" she shouted hysterically, "Do something Brooks!"

Brooks twisted around and could see Thomas had been shot in the neck. "Hold pressure on that wound, pressure on both sides! The bullet went through. And…and you're bleeding too!"

He was right. A bullet had found its mark, coming through the left rear window where Thomas was sitting and exited through the window on the other side. *It must have grazed her cheek*. Emily hadn't realized she was hit. She reached up and felt her wound.

"It's only a flesh wound!" Brooks yelled. "Emily! Help Thomas!"

She put one hand on each side of Thomas's neck as his head was resting in her lap. He was dying.

"Hang on!" Brooks floored the gas pedal. "Keep pressure on the entry and exit wounds and slow the loss of blood," he barked out in a commanding tone.

The car that had passed them spun around, tires screeching, to pursue. Brooks continued on passing several cars while barely avoiding oncoming traffic. They almost hit head-on several times. The chase car was closing on them.

He had no choice. "Hang on!"

He got back in his lane and hit the brakes hard as the chase car smashed into them. Emily and Thomas were both whiplashed into the back of the front seats. She pulled him back up when they recoiled from the impact and held his neck. The car weaved back and forth as Brooks tried to regain control.

The chase car driver and the passenger, who was still holding the weapon, seemed to be caught off guard. Sparks flew from the impact and metal against the pavement. Their car flew to the right and down a steep embankment exploding as it flipped over several times. The sparks igniting a broken gas line.

Brooks made a call. "We need help! We were just ambushed and Yates was hit. We're on Route 37, about ten miles out of Clarksville. Meet us at the hospital!" Brooks hit the gas.

He pulled into the hospital emergency room parking lot and up to the double automatic doors. A team was there waiting for them. An orderly with a stretcher and a doctor stood ready.

They pulled Thomas from the car even as Emily was holding his wounds. Two large patch compresses were exchanged for her hands. Blood coated Emily's hands, her face, and her clothes. She even had streaks of red in her hair. She tried but Brooks could see she couldn't move.

He reached in and pulled her out. Her eyes were wide and round and she felt cool to the touch. She was limp in his arms.

"She has a wound on her cheek," Brooks said. "And she's in shock."

He carried her into the Emergency Room, and watched as she passed out. He placed her gently on a stretcher. She and Thomas were quickly taken into care.

He was waiting in the Emergency Room when his phone rang. Not bothering to check the ID, he answered. "Brooks."

"Agent Brooks?"

He recognized the voice but couldn't place it.

"Yes, who is this?"

"This is Agent Waxman, sir. I'm with Deputy Wilson. We're bringing the girls to the Clarksville Hospital."

Now he remembered. Agent Waxman was assigned to Agent Hill's team. Uneasiness crept up on him. "Good. I'm already at the hospital. Get them here as soon as you can."

"Yes, sir. We should be there in about forty minutes."

"How are the parents?" she asked.

"We were ambushed. Tell the girls their parents are here, but don't say anything else. I'll need you to stay with them. They won't be able to see either one for a while."

"Okay, sir," Waxman responded.

Brooks hung up. *I have to find a way to get this family to safety.* He made a call. "Yes, it's me. Meet me at the hospital and we need security here. Make sure they're neutrals. I'm counting on you. Don't talk to anyone else, especially your superior. Trust no one until we can sort this out."

The man on the other end responded. "Yes sir. I'm on my way."

Brooks had no choice. They might be safe for now, but he had a feeling this was going to get a lot worse before it got better.

Chapter 18

May 1787 - The Constitutional Convention

Nothing else got done that next day as the factions were starting to coalesce in the room and the arguing was continuous. Yates, Bedford, and others made the rounds in the room from group to group, pulling aside a delegate here and there for a quick private discussion. Randolph did the same.

That evening, Yates met with some of those delegates who were also against the new purpose that was presented the day before. They were dining at one of the local pubs. Joining him were John Lansing also of New York, William Patterson of New Jersey, Thomas Mifflin of Pennsylvania, Gunning Bedford of Delaware and Hugh Williamson of North Carolina.

They were sitting at a round table with wooden chairs. There were a half dozen or so of these tables. A few rectangular tables were up against the outer wall by the windows. The tavern had a bar, of course, with an assortment of spirits and beer. A large fire was burning in the fireplace.

The tavern had other people in it as well. About thirty or so, some at tables, some standing at the bar, most dressed very casually. They were casual as well to help 'blend in' with the other folks, which of course didn't help them become less conspicuous as the locals all knew they were there for the meetings. They each had a drink in hand along with his own plate of dinner. They were eating and talking about the day's events and what was to become of this mess. There were no other delegates in the pub, Yates made certain before he started to speak.

"I'll tell you this," Yates started in a rather low voice. "Virginia means to run our country and I will have none of it. Did you see Madison? He was quite pleased with himself during the proceedings. And why isn't Patrick Henry here or Richard Lee? Mason is the only one from Virginia on our side, yet there are hundreds of other Virginians that would oppose this Virginia Plan."

The entire delegation from Virginia except George Mason

was pressing for their plan and yet so many from Virginia had not come. Patrick Henry said he 'smelled a rat' when asked to attend.

He continued. "We must protect ourselves and the interests of our states and the people."

"What about their coalition?" Patterson asked quietly. "They control most of the committees and are pushing us around."

He was right of course. How else could anyone explain such a turn of events in just four days? They were all talking in a hushed tone to protect their conversation.

"And Hamilton." Lansing stated. "We all know his positions. He would like nothing more than to shove a British monarchial system down our throats."

"We also must assume that some here at the Convention may very well be part of the Society of Praetorians. If that is the case, it is even more imperative we stop them," Mifflin added.

Williamson interjected. "We must come up with another plan to counter this change in dialogue. Meanwhile, we must keep this group at bay. Let's keep pressing for a central government based on total state's sovereignty and equality so that the states can still maintain control."

"Now that they have forced us to use this Virginia Plan as the template while they trashed our Articles of Confederation, does anyone have any thoughts about an alternative plan?" Yates asked.

"We do," Patterson offered. "David Brearly and I have a good deal of information we are planning to discuss during the amending. Now that we're being pressed like this, we will put them into a proposal to submit."

"Very good," Yates answered. "Get to work on it when you can and we will all draw out the discussions and voting until we are ready to make the proposal for the plan. I know Sherman will be making a case for the states as well, but until then we must keep the discussion going. This will give us some cover and protection for a while anyway."

This was Roger Sherman of Connecticut. He had a history of looking out for the states although he was also too willing to compromise on many important issues.

Yates now put both hands on the table and leaned forward. He was looking at them all. He needed to express the conviction and seriousness of what he was going to say, a rallying cry for support.

The look in their eyes told him these were men who could be trusted. He had already started to take private notes at the Convention and he now saw his way to making a second set, different and apart, since the delegates, at least those left in the room after the walkout had decided to keep all the proceedings secret with only Madison taking official notes.

"I propose we take an oath gentleman, an oath of brotherhood to protect our own states and the others as well. This must be a secret oath and must bind each of us to the others. We cannot and must not lose our own states, our own countries, to an all-powerful central authority.

"The very uniqueness of each state is our strength as a group. We shall not be under the boot of tyranny again, only years after casting the British boot off. In order for this oath to supplant any unaccepting *Nation State*, bent on the state's destruction, we must act on it if or when the time ever comes. We are only six here, but I know of at least ten more who will readily join us at the Convention. That gives us sixteen at the start. Each of you needs to think of who else we can trust to our cause."

"This will be difficult at best," Williamson responded. "If even one member gives us up, we will be lost."

Yates continued. "Perhaps and we must have secrecy above all else, yet think about what we are taking an oath to? It is to our very own states. The very reason we're here, to amend the Articles, not to create some centralized super power. It is to our Republic form of government. We're taking an oath against tyranny and any central government that uses itself to expand and grow for its own power even while claiming it is working for the people. Too many times in world history have tyrannies been formed with the consent of the governed because they lacked the will to understand what was really happening.

"Yes we must be true to each other, but even more than that we must be true to our countries, our states, our neighbors. We are the ones in the right here. We are the ones now fighting to keep our Confederation, our Republic alive. It is the others, gentlemen, the others who want a national supreme authority, a *Nation State* run by the elite. They are the true enemies now. Yes they are Americans just like us, but now they speak of an oligarchy rule similar to England and most other forms of suppressive central governments.

"We are the nucleus now. The center of the American federal universe and we must be careful whom we trust to join us. If our group becomes compromised, then we might not have the authority over the outcome of this Convention should we need it."

"Well…we will be keeping the truth of all things done." Patterson said.

"Yes…yes, and it will be hidden," Yates said almost to himself. "The hidden truth."

"The Absconditus Verum," Bedford offered.

"Yes," Yates concluded. "The Absconditus Verum…the hidden truth."

They all took a moment and Yates could see it in their eyes as they each nodded with approval. They were all versed in Latin, they knew the meaning.

"Well done Gunning," Yates said. "The Absconditus Verum Society, and it is our goal to thwart this attempt to usurp power whether by some delegates who have taken the wrong path or the Praetorians."

They were all in agreement. There was nothing more to be done, at least not then. They would coalesce with their allies and moderates at the Convention and as a group they would keep a unified front, yet seem like they were working independently.

◊ ◊ ◊

There were too many state's rights advocates that did not come to the Convention. So many leading figures missing, leaders that had fought for state's rights against the British who were now not in attendance. Was this by chance? Thomas Jefferson of Virginia was in Europe as was John Adams of Massachusetts. Samuel Adams of Massachusetts was also not there nor Patrick Henry of Virginia. The Virginia Plan was what only half of Virginia's leading men wanted and the rest refused to be a party to it. Many more were missing as well and they were in a great majority, state's rights and state sovereignty advocates. The deck had been stacked from the beginning, stacked against the states in so many ways. A small faction had been pushing this for years; to assemble here was now becoming all too clear.

Yates asked, "William, while you're working on an official proposal for the convention, the rest of us will use your notes to form our covenant. The binding covenant we need for the authority we might have to use at a later time. Since the Convention seems to have abandoned its own purpose, our resolutions will be as binding as theirs, in fact so many of our supporters are not even here and will most assuredly join our cause. And remember above all else that each state's ability for nullification and secession must always be available to protect them from any new central authority. I fear those wanting centralized power also want to strip the states of their power, including nullification and secession. If that happens then the states will fall to mere provinces begging the central *Nation State* for funds."

The freedom fighters were finished for the evening. They each got up, said their goodnights, and left.

Only Yates remained. He was picking up the tab for the meal that night and pondered what they had just done. He knew they were right. In his gut he knew…the Absconditus Verum Society. The second battle for liberty and freedom had just begun. The difference now was that they were fighting their own countrymen.

◊ ◊ ◊

More than three weeks had now past since the Absconditus Verum Society first met. They had indeed brought eighteen more to their cause along with several from outside the Convention. They had been sending secret messages to the states, more specifically to certain individuals in the states who were aligned with their purpose.

Meanwhile, they had been chipping away at the Virginia Plan. Slowly but surely other delegates began to see the real purpose of the Virginia Plan to use central government to take control of the states and the people. Many were now moving to a more balanced approach, keeping state sovereignty and equality, as the most important decision they could make.

All of this was done in spite of the attempts of the nationalists to control the dialogue, the votes, and the actual writing of their new purpose.

William Patterson of New Jersey, Luther Martin of Maryland, along with others from the smaller states had finished the proposed New Jersey Plan now ready to be presented to the Convention.

It was now early summer as the Convention met.

"Yes, the floor recognizes the delegate from New Jersey." Washington pointed them out.

"Thank you General," Patterson responded.

"Since we have been here, we have seen many delegates propose a spectrum of ideas, from simply amending the Articles of Confederation and Perpetual Union, the job we were all selected for, to a central *Nation State* that is stronger than all the states combined.

"We all recognize the positions each side is taking as well as their intentions for implementation. So in order to present fairness in the debate, I would like to submit another plan. This plan has the honor of our purpose as delegates, as well as the protection of all the states from each other and especially from any new central government.

Patterson held up documents as he continued. "I ask the chamber to vote on allowing this New Jersey Plan into debate so as to balance the playing field, that being the Virginia Plan that favors the larger states, and our plan which protects the smaller states."

"The question of allowing the New Jersey Plan to be a part of the proceeding is now open. Do we have a second?" Washington asked.

"Second." A delegate yelled.

The motion passed.

"We shall now look at both plans," Washington responded. He believed this was the wise course to bring everyone to the table.

The New Jersey Plan was based on the original Articles and was aimed at keeping the states in charge, yet strengthening the central government for the purposes of foreign legislation and protection.

"Thank you General. I have copies for all the delegates."

"We'll take a short recess to examine the new plan. Debates shall continue after lunch and then both plans shall be put into our committees for further reviewing." Washington said.

This was the best Yates and the Absconditus Verum Society could hope for at this time. They knew the big states were now ready to use central government to disproportionately delegate power and control.

Yet as the Convention wore on, they were beginning to think perhaps they would not need the Absconditus Verum at all. Perhaps the others would come to their senses and realize the pro-British model they were acting on.

Yates and his secret organization now had over twenty delegates and hundreds of others in the states, so they still had a fall back if they needed. No one, including Yates, really wanted to have to act outside of the Convention proceedings if it could be avoided. Only time would tell now. The challenge still ahead was the minority of delegates for a *Nation State* still held a majority regarding actual state votes. This handful continued its march towards tyranny.

◊ ◊ ◊

For the next two days, the debate was reaching a crescendo, with each side unwilling to yield in almost all issues, yet again the Virginia Plan was slowly being undone. This kept happening because it kept pushing for too much central power. Everyone knew this, even Madison and Hamilton, though Hamilton was the only one still looking for absolute centralized power.

Madison, and others that wanted to strengthen the central government, also did not want to give it unlimited power. They still regarded their own states as sovereign countries.

This was a delicate balance they were trying to strike. How would it be seen afterwards? Frustrations were running high as Roger Sherman and the centrists tried their best to work out compromises. Those, of course, would mean each side had to give up freedoms and liberty and give them to the central government.

No one was in much of a mood to do anything at this point, yet there came another voice…

Chapter 19

<u>*May 2018 - Clarksville, Texas*</u>

Emily woke to see Agent Brooks nodding in a chair in the corner. Pete was sitting by the bed. She could tell she was in a hospital or clinic as the room had a sanitized white look about it.

"Well, good morning," Pete said softly.

"Pete." Emily shook off the drowsiness. "Where are the girls?"

"They're right outside. I'll get them."

He left and a few moments later the girls came rushing in with Pete in tow.

"Mommy! Mommy!" They flung themselves up on the bed and hugged her.

"Oh, my darlings. I'm here, I'm here, and we're safe now." She held them tightly and noticed Brooks stirring in the corner.

"Girls, where did you get those clothes?" Emily asked. They looked unfamiliar and new. Amanda had a cute plaid skirt and white top. Sara wore jeans and a button down shirt.

"Pete got them for us. They're brand new," Amanda answered.

Emily was smiling as she looked at Pete. Pete smiled back, though only for a moment before pain flashed in his eyes.

"Girls, I need to talk to Mr. Brooks for a few minutes but then we'll spend the entire day together," Emily did her best to sound calm and collected.

"Say, girls, let's go get some breakfast," Pete offered.

"Pancakes?" Sara asked.

"Sure, Sara…pancakes." Pete gave Emily one last look of anguish before he led them out of the room.

Agent Brooks stood and came to the bed.

Emily tried her best to stay calm. "So, Mr. Brooks, how is Thomas?"

"Emily, do you remember what happened last night?"

Tears formed in her eyes as she remembered what happened. "Yes," she reached up and touched her cheek.

"Yes, that's right, and you got hit too."

Emily realized she had a hand on a bandage on her cheek.

"The doctor says you'll be just fine."

"Mr. Brooks," Emily said, looking into his eyes. "What about Thomas?"

Brooks hesitated "He's in a coma. They were able to stop the bleeding, but he'd lost so much blood they had to induce a coma until he stabilizes. The doctor says it could be a few hours or a few days, they just don't know yet. They operated most of the night on him."

Emily shook her head. She started crying softly. "Agent Brooks, what is this all about?"

Brooks looked at her. "This is about something that started two hundred and thirty years ago and it's a very long story. We'll talk about it later. Let me just say for now that you, Thomas, and the girls are safe."

A woman in scrubs entered the room with a breakfast tray. She placed in on a swinging table attached to the bed.

"Have yourself some breakfast and then we can talk." Brooks said.

The nurse asked Brooks if he wanted breakfast, but he declined and sat in the corner chair again. Emily was hungrier than she thought she should be until she realized she hadn't eaten since the morning before. Even though the food looked bland, it didn't take her long to finish. Once she did she swung the table to the side of the bed.

"Agent Brooks, this is silly. What's your first name?"

"Joseph." He answered with a smile.

"Joseph, I only remember some of what you told me in the car. Let's see…Thomas is actually James Yates. His family are descendants of a Founding Father?"

"Yes, Robert Yates."

"And he was brought to Texas to hide from some organization, some Society. I know he has no memory of his youth…and something about a key."

A knock on the door brought Agent Dean into the room and he motioned to Brooks who stood up and joined him. They whispered to each other for a few moments before Brooks looked at Emily, and Agent Dean left the room.

"Now what?" Emily was agitated. "Oh, no! I'm not going anywhere until you tell me what this is all about!"

"Seems like I'll be telling you in the car. You need to get up, get dressed, and we need to leave immediately. The Praetorians now know we're here." Brooks motioned for her to start moving. He motioned again before leaving the room.

Emily was fuming as she got dressed.

Damn it! Tell me what's happening!

She was finishing up and walked out the door. "Brooks! Where are the girls?" she demanded.

"Pete has them. He's moving them to a safe house."

Emily started shaking her head. "No, no, no!"

"It's for their protection. You and I must get on the road. Dean, grab her bag."

"You have no right to treat us like this. It's unfair, cruel…cruel." She was on the verge of crying "I want to be with my girls."

Brooks put his arm around her shoulder and led her outside to the car. Dean put her bag in the car and handed him the keys.

"I'll follow, sir."

Brooks nodded as he helped Emily into the passenger seat. "Dean, have two agents that we can trust stay here to protect Mr. Miller.

"Yes, sir."

Emily looked back at the hospital's main doors.

Thomas. Oh, Thomas. Please come back to me.

Her heart was breaking. She hadn't had a chance to see him. To hold his hand. She wouldn't be there for the girls when they needed her most.

She didn't care about the mission. Brooks said they needed her. They said she had to go. But right now she couldn't see why. She just wanted to be left behind with Thomas and her girls. Would this be the last time she would ever she them?

This is wrong. Why me?

Soon she and Brooks were heading east on Route 30. They had to make their way as covertly as possible. It was not long before she composed herself enough to ask a question.

"How the hell did the…Society or whatever it is find out we were at the hospital?"

"I'm still working that out." He answered as she stared out the front window. "Dean is following us and will be until we get to Lexington and then it's on to Staunton."

"Virginia? We're driving to Virginia? Great, just great." she threw her arms up in exasperation. Then she looked at Brooks.

"No, Dean is not a double agent." He answered her unspoken question. "The fact is Dean is one of my closest confidantes in the Verum. You would not find a better agent or society member. He's a great kid who went through a terrible ordeal when he was younger. You see, the Praetorians murdered is parents. From that time, he has devoted himself to the Verum and became an FBI agent to help the cause. Once you get to know him, you'll see. I'd put my life in his hands if I had to."

"Well, that's a relief," she said sarcastically. "Seems now I'll finally get to hear what the hell is going on."

Brooks smiled at her. "Our organization is located all over the country, and some are overseas. There are several thousand members. Only a handful of the leaders are now helping us search for the hidden documents. The rest have all gone to safe houses. Just as your life is now changed forever, theirs have too. They've left their homes, their schools, their towns, their jobs, and must now live their lives under the radar similar to a witness protection program. It's not easy for any of us. Four members have been killed that we know of. None of them were leaders, but that doesn't mean they weren't important. They were. We all are."

"And that key?"

Brooks took it out of his pocket and handed it to her. It was dull and worn, though it had a unique shape and handle. It was made of iron. She could tell by the weight. The end of the handle was shaped into a solid flat oval with a raised outer rim. It had an inscription on it: *Absconditus Verum.*

Brooks watched her examine the key. "You know Pete was sent to Bogata to protect you and your family. Nine years of his life he gave to you and our cause. The same for the Miller family that adopted Thomas. They raised him as if he were their own son, knowing it was for one purpose - to protect him. We've all given our lives for this, something that may never be solved in our lifetime, maybe never." His voice trailed off.

Emily's face softened. She thought about how significant this whole quest must be for so many to live their lives in constant danger, all for no personal gain of any kind, other than to find some secret that was still hidden from them. "This sounds very heroic."

"You realize the importance of our mission don't you?" he asked.

"Well, not really…I mean why can't you do this and let me stay with Thomas and the girls?"

"Is that really what you want?"

"Of course it is. I'm no threat to anyone. Neither are the girls or Thomas."

"I wish it was that easy. You must understand that the Praetorians now know who you are. They will hunt you the rest of your lives. They will never stop until they have the key or you're all dead. Thomas' genealogy has brought you into this battle, a battle that we believe in, a battle that could change the future of all Americans now that it's spilled over into all our lives. This is a battle about freedom, American freedom. Not what you hear from our politicians, but what true freedom really is and how we have lost it over the years."

"I don't care. I just want my girls and Thomas." She was fighting herself, trying to rationalize her position. Trying not to think about what she should do, or had to do. But she did know. Deep down she knew what was happening. How others had sacrificed for her. How Thomas would be in her spot right now trying to help. But he wasn't. She was in his place. It was now her turn, her turn to do everything in her power to help Brooks discover the truth and find the lost documents. For she now knew the only way her family could live their lives without being hunted was by helping resolve this war. "Tell me everything."

"This goes back to the beginning. The beginning of our country, or what some called our united States. That's with a small u."

"Why was that?"

"Because the Colonies, the first states, were united. Not as a country, but as an alliance. Thomas knew his history well, even if he didn't know what drove him…How about you?"

"I know what I was taught in school. I know quite a bit," she said confidently.

Brooks continued. "Did Thomas share his knowledge of American history with you? Did he tell you why he studied so much?"

"Well, no, not exactly. I just thought it was a personal interest he had. A hobby, I guess. How do you know so much about his interests?"

"Because Thomas and Pete would talk about it. Pete was well versed in historical knowledge, though to look at him you wouldn't have suspected."

"He looks like a regular southern Sheriff, I guess."

"Meaning you wouldn't have thought he was well studied?"

"Well, yes…I guess."

"Thomas and Pete spent all those evenings together. All those nights Thomas went into town, to the Historical Society meetings."

She stared intently ahead. "I had no idea it was so important."

"You knew how interested he was with history. How driven and passionate he was. The whole purpose of the meetings was to help jar his memory. He didn't choose to do this. It was his destiny…and now it is your destiny."

This grabbed Emily's attention. She knew how fascinated Thomas was with American history and the Founding Fathers in particular. He was always reading something about the beginnings of the country and the start of the government, and he attended the Historical Society meetings with Pete. She had a sudden understanding that whatever Brooks was about to explain would also explain Thomas's passion about the early Americans forming the new government. Thomas had told her how his foster parents encouraged him to learn these events. Now she knew it was in the hopes that his memory would come back with the secrets he held.

Emily sat silent for several miles, absorbing the information.

How can this possibly be true? Why my family?

She kept her emotions in check. "Tell me more."

"Brace yourself because this is going to sound like the biggest conspiracy theory you've ever heard, and it'll take time to understand it all. Right now we're headed for Kentucky, and as we are, there are others also on the road with similar missions to other places."

Emily studied Brooks' face.

This is some extreme group bent on Armageddon.

"So you're part of some group from the far right or the far left, certainly not associated with the centered principles of our country. I've heard about plenty of radical government conspiracies, from the WMDs in Iraq, to how we bombed our own World Trade Center, to turning the country into some socialist utopia. I sure hope Thomas was involved in something a lot more grounded than those."

Brooks broke into a small smile. "It's more grounded then you might ever believe. You see, our society has passed down many events that happened through many generations. Events you will never see in current history books. Events we believe happened over time that have been hidden from the people. Erased from American history as we know it today. We believe they, in fact, took place and our mission has been to keep these memories alive. Keep hope in restoring the truth and liberty to every American."

"I don't understand. I have freedom and liberty now. What would you look to change?"

"Your paradigm. You believe the limited freedoms and liberty you have now are in fact total freedom and liberty. Once you open yourself up to what liberty really is, you'll have a whole new perspective on just what many of our Founders really meant. They fashioned our organization on the very foundation of what they believed in the beginning. That the truth was being kept from the people during the formation of the country. They were witness to these events and recorded everything that happened."

Emily tried to picture some of the Founders in her mind. The glimpses of photos and artwork she saw over the years. She never really thought about the interactions of the men who formed the country. It was all just a snippet of history for her, something that had been taught and long forgotten with no meaning now.

"Well, then, fire away," she said "With all we've been through in the last twenty-four hours, I doubt anything you tell me will surprise me."

The composure she had back in the house with Agent Hill returned. She was ready, at least ready for what she thought Brooks was going to talk about. She envisioned the men of the past going through the motions of what she was taught.

"The best place to start is answering the questions you now have."

"You're kidding, right? Fine…Okay, why were our girls' taken?"

"For leverage to get your husband to bow to their demands. I'm quite sure they would have released them had your husband complied."

"Who are they?"

"It's a hidden Society, draped behind many layers of other groups not so hidden, but known by few. Their name is the Society of Praetorians. They have one purpose. To control every western civilized country on the planet. This wasn't their original purpose, but it's grown since its inception."

"That sounds like radical Islam or some right-wing neo-Roman group."

"No, this is far more dangerous than any theological war. This is being perpetrated by Westerners on Westerners. The fact that America and some other countries are involved in a war on terror simply gives the Praetorians cover for their operations. It's actually quite clever. They make a point of using religion, any religion, and class warfare to meet their ends, for only with the willing participation of the people, keeping them divided with partisan politics, ignorant of the truth, can they achieve their goals."

"Don't the people know what they're doing? Can't the people stop them?"

"They could if they understood just what it was they were up against. You must understand the scope of this conspiracy is beyond what most people, including educated ones, can possibly perceive. Most people believe the America they know is exactly the one that was set up in the beginning. That nothing other than what they were taught happened, so in their reality, America today is as it should be, even with all the gridlock and partisanship. They think that's normal. They think limited liberty is normal liberty."

Emily was fidgeting with the key in her hand as she talked. "Does this have anything to do with the Tea Party movement?"

"If that movement knew just what it was they were fighting against, it might, in some small way, affect the Society. The same goes for the movement on the left and the Libertarian movement for that matter. None of these groups know how deep this goes. They're all just barking at the moon. That's the extent of their influence."

"But I heard the Tea Party was helping to throw out the incumbents and making inroads into the Republican Party. That would seem to present a push by the people for a return of their freedoms, wouldn't it?"

"It would if they were negatively affecting the plans of the Society. But they're not. In fact, the Praetorians are happy they're using the government system in place to try to change it. The Praetorians control the very system the people are trying to change. The government will never restrain itself, you must know that. This Colossus of a central *Nation State* and the elitists we now have was not the intent of many Founders in the beginning. The central government has given itself omnipotent power to do almost anything they want. Sure, a few righteous politicians might get into the system, but they will never change it.

"Look at Ron Paul as the perfect example. He might have had some small influence, but he couldn't change the very fabric the government is using. You could vote out every incumbent in the system every year we have elections, but it still won't change the system. The system is entrenched and reaches far beyond our shores. It's a global system now, just as it was meant to be from the beginning, although back then it was to be a glorious Imperial American Empire that ruled the western world."

Emily paused for a moment and tried to absorb the inordinate amount of information Brooks was giving her.

"Okay, let me backtrack for a minute. What has this Society of Praetorians got to do with Thomas?"

"Thomas is a direct descendent of Robert Yates."

"That's what you keep saying." The car scene flooded back into her mind, and she started getting upset again.

"Yes, Thomas is involved because of his genealogy. So are most of the others in our Society."

Emily looked at the key. "Can you tell me more about this group you're a member of?"

"Our organization is called the Absconditus Verum Society."

"The hidden truth." Emily said almost immediately. She held up the key with the inscription on it.

"Yes. That's right. You see why we believe a truth is out there. Our ancestors named our society the very thing they wanted to protect."

Emily pondered the reasoning. *What if there is some truth out there that I don't know about? Would it make any difference in today's society?*

"Did you study Latin? You know the translation." He pointed to the key.

"Yes. As a specialized architect, my field of study is historical architecture from the Greek and Roman Empires through the age of Enlightenment. The structures and how they were built using the tools and mathematics of their day."

"Really, now that is coincidental and perhaps beneficial to our plans."

"Why?" she asked as she just noticed how much Brooks was checking his rearview mirror. She turned and looked behind them but there were no cars following as far as she could see.

"Because, if you're good at interpreting puzzles, then you can help me put together the pieces now in play."

"Pieces?"

"Yes. We are just one of the three prongs that must be combined if we are to find the truth." He glanced at Emily. "My apologies. While I'm well versed in our mission and hold many of the hidden truths, I'm really not much of a story teller and there's only one who knows the entire tale. Perhaps we should take a short break. This is a lot of information."

"Before we do, tell me what pieces we have."

"The key you hold now, the code buried in your husband memory, and the secret encrypted diary of Robert and Richard Yates. We also know that the Society of Praetorians is a secret offshoot of the original Society of the Cincinnati. This group formed after the Revolution to help military widows and their families, as well as pensions for retired officers. In fact, I doubt any current members of the Cincinnati are even aware they exist. They used the Cincinnati as cover when they first organized. There were only a few in the beginning. The war was winding down, the fighting had stopped, and the conspiracy was just forming."

"Okay, before we get into this Cincinnati, why the name Praetorians? I mean that's a Roman Empire title."

"Because the group that first formed the Praetorian Society was drunk with an obsession of Roman history. They wanted the same form of Republic to rise once again within the American states. The Roman Republic was a republic in name only. The Praetorians or magistrates of Roman society wielded great power. They were the upper class known as Patricians. Caesar himself had Praetorian guards. Later it was a reference towards the English aristocrats, though only in secret, because this secret Society was made up of several elitists of the time. They formed the Society of Praetorians sometime around 1783, though we don't have an exact date. Officers from the war, bankers, politicians, mercantilists, lawyers, and a whole coalition bent on ruling the new states, the new central government. They were King George's pawns and he used them to create as much chaos as they could after the colonies won the war."

Emily was in deep thought. So much she had never known or even heard of. This was not in the history books. "How do you know all this if all the documents are lost?"

"These stories have been handed down from parents to children for all these years. The ones who were witness to the events are long gone, but their tale is alive and well in the Absconditus Verum Society. I also have the diary."

"You were able to decipher the diary? You said it was encrypted."

"Most of it is encrypted, but some parts we have been able to use. Several entries have helped us piece together parts of the past, our true history. Still, most of it we haven't been able to figure out, but we will over time once opportunities present themselves that the diary will solve. Those are mostly the encrypted pages."

"So why is all this happening now?"

"Because the Praetorians must believe they're in some way gravely threatened. I would guess someone is going after them. It's not anyone in the Absconditus Verum, at least none that I know of, but someone has their attention and they know that we hold the answer to all this." He looked down at the key when he said this, and Emily looked as well.

"So I have the fate of the country in the palm of my hand?" she asked.

"Not only our country, but the fate of western civilization. That's how important that key and this mission are. We've been forced from the shadows to combat the Praetorians in the open now. The reason why doesn't matter. We must defend ourselves and hope we uncover the truth in time to save who we can and restore the true intent of the Federal Government."

"I thought you said this was a secret society?"

"It is, and it has total control over our political system. I told you this would sound radical."

They were now in eastern Texas heading to Lexington Kentucky.

"Let's stop for something to eat," Brooks said

Her head was swimming with all this new information.

They stopped at a diner, had a quick bite, and were on their way again. Emily heard Brooks instruct Dean to stay a few miles behind them on lookout for possible pursuit.

She was envisioning a revolution was about to take place and her family was right in the middle of it as she fell asleep in the back seat almost as soon as they left the parking lot.

Chapter 20

June 1787 - The Constitutional Convention

Hamilton stood up and requested some time to speak. Everyone else had put their cards on the table, so he decided to do the same. He'd watched the early successes of the Nationalists being chipped away. The Virginia Plan was now not the only plan. The New Jersey Plan had been proposed and was gaining momentum and a Connecticut Compromise Plan put together by Roger Sherman and Judge Oliver Ellsworth was blending both sides. This went even further against what he hoped for. It was no surprise, of course, as the small states were trying desperately to position themselves to have equal influence. It was time to put a stop to this and he needed to act.

He'd not been sitting idly by, but had been busy himself and was now proposing his own plan, called later the Hamilton Plan or the British Plan, due to its resemblance to the British system of strong centralized government. It was a four-hour speech, which for Hamilton, was moderate. His skill of the pen and the ability to write extremely lengthy papers as well as bloviating were his strong points.

"I propose a permanent lifetime appointment of a King or President who would have the authority to pick and seat the governors of all the states, as well as veto power over any and all state laws. Our central government will set up and run a mercantilist economy through regulatory constraints on independent businesses while holding interests, or shares, in many large corporations. It will set up corporate welfare subsidies to fund internal improvements and it will have the right to hand pick selected businesses for success based on their competency.

"We must look gentlemen, to only have those few companies that can produce superior goods. So how do we fund all this? We must create a large public debt to show our credit worthiness to the world. Protectionist tariffs that will aid and protect our infant industries and commercial businesses.

"We should establish a central banking system so that the

central government can control all money both in coining and in determining value through interest rates to inflate and deflate the values as to what we deem appropriate to stabilize monetary policy for swings in domestic issues. We cannot depend on a free market philosophy.

"Having the states each with their own currencies has plagued interstate commerce. And regarding the states, ***we must annihilate them***. They must become provinces, or districts, of the central government. They should not be recognized as countries, or even states.

"A central government must be strong enough to enact laws and spending. To help create balance for the people of all the states, for we all know that the people, given the chance to self-govern, would destroy themselves. We must protect them not only from foreign influences, but from each other.

"We will become *one Nation State*, and our power and influence shall be the envy of the world. As far as I'm concerned, the states are merely artificial beings. Only a central *Nation State* that is indivisible can be sovereign. The states never really existed and never shall. Oh sure we had different named Colonies, but only as a convenience for local communities. It's time to end this separation.

"Religion is the main cause for the divisions that created the Colonies which were not thought to be states. The states were made from the central government, weak as it is through their delegates. It is foolish to think otherwise. How else can you explain the Perpetual Union of the states?

"Nullification of central government laws needs to also stop as does the ridiculous notion of secession. We must have order and balance. We must have a Central Supreme Judiciary that shall decide all the laws within the states. How can one state have a law that is different than another? No gentlemen. We have seen democracy in action. We have seen Republics come and go.

"We must use the English system. Yes it has its corruption, but I believe corruption is acceptable so long as the results are favorable to the *Nation State*. Only through the nobles, the aristocrats can a nation be successfully run. And we need to pledge our allegiance to the central *Nation State*. Having this notion of representation for the people is insane. The people cannot govern themselves. We must govern for them, for their own good. The Shays Rebellion is the perfect example."

He continued on with his diatribe for four hours until he finally finished, thanked his fellow delegates, and retired from the chamber.

"Thank God that's over with," Yates said to his fellow Verum members. Most of the delegates were exhausted just listening to Hamilton's Plan.

"I must give him credit. He's more than willing to share his conceptions of government out in the open, no matter how misplaced they may be. He may well just tell us to allow the Society of Praetorians to move right in and start ruling on high."

It was after lunchtime with more meetings set up and everyone was showing the wear of the days and the debates. While issues had been slowly moving back towards a state style instead of a national style, Hamilton completely upset the donkey cart that fateful day.

He was personally put off that no one in attendance would even consider any part of his proposal. Surely his plan would be taken up with the others to stop the hemorrhaging of the strong central government proposed. He joined the others in the afternoon session.

Yates, Lansing, and others were so offended by the Hamilton Plan; they decided it was time to draw a line in the sand. They knew this was coming and they were ready for it.

Lansing stood. "Mr. President, since there seems to be such a divide regarding the central government's role and what rights the states actually have, I believe we should reaffirm our loyalty to our individual states.

"Many here look for centralized power, yet they are here because their own states believe they act as state representatives. It's time we find out just who is true to their states and who is looking to destroy their own states sovereignty.

"Since these proceedings will be kept secret until the last delegate dies; you do remember that vote for secrecy being taken when almost one half of the delegates left in protest on the fourth day; I think there is little danger to advocating one way or the other. You want us to trust strong national government being set up in secret, then I ask for this protection for the states."

He paused for a moment as Abraham Baldwin, a delegate from Georgia handed him several documents.

"What's all this about?" asked Wilson.

"Well, Mr. Wilson, several delegates here believe there is an attempt by the Society of Praetorians to influence this Convention. And since their desire is to rule as dictators, we must all affirm our loyalty to state sovereignty. That is the only way the people can keep control of their own government."

"This is absurd," Gouverneur Morris answered. "Of course we all agree on full state sovereignty."

"The trouble Mr. Morris is in what we just heard. Mr. Hamilton's position was just made very clear, 'Annihilation of the States'. That sounds to me like a plan to destroy the states, unless I misunderstand the meaning."

Hamilton stood. "Forgive me gentlemen. In my exuberance, I simply meant that no small state need fear a large one, just as no small county in a state fear a large one."

"I certainly interpreted the word annihilation differently," Yates responded. "If you say now that the states still hold their sovereignty, then you will have no trouble affirming this in writing."

"I see no need for that. Since we vote here as states and not individuals, state sovereignty is obviously kept."

"Except that you, Mr. Hamilton, have continuously split the New York vote with Mr. Lansing and myself. The other states seem to find unity in their votes. You have been undermining our state's input on almost every motion put forth. This obvious ploy does exactly what you want. Render the vote of New York State less than it should be. If you believe differently, then signing an affirmation should not be an issue."

Yates had him. Hamilton's ability to entwine and deflect any and all issues was now laid bare.

"So Mr. Hamilton?" asked Bedford.

Hamilton looked around the room and realized what he had done. The strong nationalists showed in their faces his critical error. They now knew the hope to wrest power and control of government totally from the states was lost.

"Mr. Yates," Washington said.

"Yes Sir."

"Please bring the document to me." Washington looked it over very carefully.

"Mr. Jackson, please read this document to the delegates."

The secretary stood next to Washington's desk and read the affirmation.

"*Agreed to this 19th day of June 1787,*

We, the delegates of this Constitutional Convention, do hereby affirm our loyalty to the sovereignty of our own states. That it is our intentions to strengthen central government as needs be without compromising any states right of sovereignty. These rights include the right to nullify central government laws any state believes acts detrimentally to their own state.

"*Further, we affirm that any states may, at any time, secede from any central government of the United States, being from our Articles of Confederation and Perpetual Union where that right currently exists, or any new Constitution drawn up at any time in the future. We further agree that any disputes between states, while having input from a central authority, can decide on their own a due course in remedy.*

"*The states can, do, and will always have the power to run their own governments without central government interference, laws, or edicts. That any commerce between states shall be settled, with the central government and the states, having equal say. That any state in the minority of any said settlement retains the rights to nullify such settlement or laws pertaining to their own state so long as they do not impede others states with their decision.*

That the central government will not be allowed to raise and hold standing armies at any time other than for defensive measures.

"*That the states may, in addition to the covenant of any Constitution, form alliances separate and apart to their own benefit. This shall not, however, override the central government's representative duties to manage foreign affairs.*"

The room fell silent. This was an astonishing attack against the nationalists and power hungry men in the room.

"Mr. Jackson, if you would." Washington held out his hand.

Jackson handed him the document and he signed it.

"Mr. Jackson, please have all the delegates sign this

affirmation. Mr. Yates, I expect you have copies for all the states?"

"Yes Sir including Rhode Island."

"Why does Rhode Island need a copy?" Robert asked Morris.

"To show that the acts done in this Convention are done with their state sovereignty protected."

Baldwin brought all the copies to Washington who looked over each one and then signed. Jackson brought them around to all the state tables for all who were present to sign.

This was Washington's moment to solidify his standing in what would be the new Federal Government. "I want to make this clear to all. If you do not hold your state's sovereignty above the central government's authority, then do not sign these documents. However, you must understand the ramifications in your position. History will show your actions for what you are. Tread carefully your decision as it weights against your commitment to represent your state at this Convention and the authority by which you are here."

None of the *Nation State* advocates were pleased by this requirement, however none of them were willing to go out on such a limb in defiance of their own state.

There was a collection of documents now forming a pile on the New York table. Everyone in attendance had signed except one.

"Alexander?" Washington asked.

He didn't respond as he looked at the pile of documents.

"Mr. Hamilton," Washington pressed.

"Sir? Yes Sir."

"What say you? Will you sign the affirmation?"

"Sir, I…I…" He looked at the papers on the table. He looked around the room and saw many delegates in a state of shock. He realized his speech was a huge setback for the central government nationalists.

He had no choice as he sat down and signed each and every one.

His diatribe that day would put off what he hoped would be instituted immediately. While his positions weren't taken into consideration at the time, they did indeed stop some of the hemorrhaging. Many advocates of a strong central government found some of his ideas to be beneficial to their cause even if they had signed. Hamilton ended up leaving the Convention on June 30th, disgusted with the lack of interest in his English alternative to become one nation, indivisible.

◊ ◊ ◊

It was two days later in the afternoon and the delegates were deliberating in earnest. Oliver Ellsworth and Roger Sherman continued working towards a compromise of the two plans submitted. There were two major issues still to be decided. It would determine the future course of the young states.

"Mr. President, with your permission?" Ellsworth asked.

"You have the floor," Washington answered.

"Sir, fellow colleagues, we have two main issues left before we can move forward. The good Mr. Randolph has proposed that the structure of the government be changed from a federation to a *Nation State*. Mr. Hamilton did him one better and suggested; I believe it was an indivisible *Nation State*. While nation is just one word, it is perhaps the most important of all. It is the fundamental difference in the room. Just because we have moved forward without the Articles of Confederation and Perpetual Union, it does not mean we must change everything. In fact, I still don't understand how a Perpetual Union can allow all the states to secede from it.

"Anyhow, Mr. Sherman, and I are working on many compromises as you know, but this cannot be compromised. We are either a federation of states, those being independent countries, or we become a centralized *Nation State*. I believe in the interest of the people we represent, that we must remain a federation. A *Nation State* as we have seen in history will ultimately become a centralized tyranny. This is a proven fact. Now I know all here want to amend the central government so we can govern effectively. This is both in the desire to amend the Articles as well those who want a totally new system. But we must make a decision as to which direction we go." he nodded to Washington.

"Mr. Randolph?"

Randolph stood for his response. "Thank you Sir. I believe we already determined this three weeks ago. We have been using the words 'National Government' since then and this is the direction we are moving towards."

Ellsworth was quick to answer. "Yes, I understand the change you made in the title, but we did not vote on this change, and you must understand that this is perhaps the most important issue we have. You have indeed changed the government title from United States to 'National Government'.

"The Declaration of Independence defines us as United States. So does the Articles of Confederation and Perpetual Union. The people have agreed to a Republic form of government. A *Nation State* will eventually strip the Republic and state's rights. It will either turn into a democracy, an oligarchy of elitists, or, God forbid, both."

"I disagree Sir. A 'National Government' will protect the states and their rights. That is why we are here, to provide protection for the states."

Ellsworth turned to Washington. "Mr. President, I would like to have a vote on this change. Unless we do vote, the change becomes a unilateral decision and no one man should be deciding what kind of government we have."

Washington nodded to Secretary Jackson.

"The motion for…what is it exactly?" Jackson asked. He was only half listening at the time. Having the duty of secretary was a tremendous task. His duties included keeping the minutes, maintaining secrecy, and destroying many of the records after the convention. While he had applied for this task, it was proving quite burdensome.

"I propose a motion to strike the word National, eliminating the possibility of a *Nation State*, and reinstitute the correct federation term United States," Ellsworth clarified.

"We have a motion to change the term of National introduced by Mr. Randolph some three weeks ago and restore United States keeping the style of a state alliance."

"I second the motion," Yates answered.

"Okay, okay…I withdraw the word *National* from the text," conceded Randolph.

"Mr. Jackson, will you please see to it that any words about Nation or National be struck from the text and the United States is inserted in all instances," Washington said. "The words Nation and National shall not appear anywhere within any final Constitutional document. All here have agreed to keep our Confederation of states."

The push that had continued even after the affirmation vote on state's rights took another blow and a National Government was soundly defeated. The states would retain full sovereignty with the exception of certain powers they gave the central government.

"Thank you Mr. President," Ellsworth acknowledged.

"You mentioned two issues judge. What was the second?"

Roger Sherman looked at Ellsworth who nodded. "Sir, as you know, the judge and I have been working together on these issues. I can answer. It concerns nullification and secession."

"Not again," Gouverneur Morris voiced.

Washington needed to clear this up once and for all. "Gentlemen, we have already affirmed our commitment to our states in the protections of their sovereignty, their ability to nullify, and the right to secede. What else are you looking for Mr. Sherman?"

"I believe if we do not put it into the Constitutional text, it will be ignored and the central government will try to influence all matters regarding the states."

"I disagree," Morris said. "The new text will be the limited enumerated power of central government. It is not a text about state rights. If the states do not give the power to the central government regarding these issues, then the central government will not have any authority in this area."

"I must agree with Mr. Morris," Washington answered.

"Nonetheless Sir, I believe the text is needed in some form."

"If this is the case, then you can make it during the state ratifying conventions or as an amendment. For now, the affirmation is binding in all matters here. We shall move on. This subject is resolved."

July 1787 - The Constitutional Convention

Today was the day of the long awaited compromise. Roger Sherman had just proposed it and a majority had now voted to move forward. This was a big blow to both sides. They each were now forced to give up their very liberty's to secure a compromise.

This was the death knell for the states. Hamilton, Madison, and the others who had wanted a National Government to rule above the states now had to contend with equal representation in the Senate.

Yates and Lansing were gone, as was the central part of their coalition other than the delegates from New Jersey and a few others. The affirmation was the protection they could not secure in the new text. They only had the authority to amend the Articles. They had done all they could.

The Connecticut Compromise was now in play. The state's rights activists had to allow a House of Representatives based on population. This meant a minority voice for all the small states. It seemed no one was happy at this point. Both sides felt they had given in too much. It was now a government of compromises and they all knew both sides had to give up freedoms to form this coalition.

Hamilton was the most put out. His dream of an American king and monarchy were fast slipping away. He left the room in a huff. Not one person had supported his plan, let alone any states. The rest continued on as they had now for weeks. Committees broke out in sessions for the rest of the day.

The great compromise as it was called was more of a melding of the two sides together, giving each only a part of what they wanted in the central government. It was blended into the Virginia Plan with portions of the New Jersey Plan. So both sides had a victory and a defeat. Most of the work was now done. It was now up to the several committees to pull together everything they had worked on.

The key factor that kept them all going was this was the makeup of the central government and the states would not be subjugated to Federal authority. It was still considered an alliance. The states still retained all their governmental powers and sovereignty. The central alliance was still to be used for foreign affairs, but not for controlling the states or taking power from them. It would help settle disputes between the states, had the power to collect tariffs to fund itself, and other restricted enumerated powers. The states and the people still controlled their own government.

"General, I would like a moment to voice some concerns."

It was Elbridge Gerry of Massachusetts. "Several of the delegates here are concerned about state ratifications of the new government. All the states don't need to vote to ratify. Only nine out of thirteen could form this new union. The others, well, let's just say they will be forced into joining. This has been the main concern for all the small states. The point is there is one organization represented in all the states that could greatly influence the results. I'm not talking about the Praetorians because I believe their numbers are too few. I am however talking about the influence of the Society of the Cincinnati. A popular election, in this case, is radically vicious. The ignorance of the people would put the power of one set of men dispersed through the Union and acting in concert to delude the people into voting for a pro-Cincinnati candidate.

"While we all appreciate such a society of men, we must understand that, in fact, this small minority banded together can deliver the results as they want. Yes they are respectable, united, and influential, but they will, in fact, elect the chief magistrate in every election, if the people vote based on the Cincinnati's power to convince. My respect for the characters composing this Society cannot blind me to the danger and impropriety of throwing such a power into their hands."

This was a troubling matter for everyone. It would serve the purpose of the few, especially the Praetorians, and nothing could now prevent it.

Chapter 21

May 2018 - Traveling

Brooks drove a few miles when Agent Johnson called.

"You need to fill me in with what you're doing. Agent Hill had me running around on false leads until I got the tip on where the girls were. Why have you taken Mrs. Miller? Where are the children? Where are Agents Dean and Waxman? And why the hell is Agent Hill dead?"

Brook attempted damage control. "Sir, the Millers are in grave danger. The children have been brought somewhere safe, and Mrs. Miller is with me. Agent Dean is also with us. Waxman is with the children. Mr. Miller was shot and is at the Clarksville Hospital."

"I know that. We have two agents protecting him. And Agent Hill? Does this have to do with that organization you're associated with? I've had suspicions about several underground groups within the government. I know you're involved."

Brooks now had a decision to make. Dean and Waxman were indeed with the Absconditus Verum even though he had said they weren't. Agent Ben Johnson however, was a neutral so far as Brooks knew.

"Yes, sir. I need you to meet us in Lexington, Kentucky. We'll be there tomorrow afternoon. And I need you to keep this to yourself. This war, which has now started, will explode in the next few days. There are several key people in our government who are involved. Ben, meet with me. You need to make a choice. Give me a chance to explain all this."

There was a long silence on the phone. Had Brooks made a calculated error?

"Ben?"

"I'll meet you at the plaza. I'll be in the food court."

"Ben, this is much larger than you or me, so again, please keep this to yourself."

"Just so you know, the entire Federal Government has been affected. Joe, we have already lost two FBI agents. I heard five government agents have been killed globally and it extends into several government departments. I have no idea who's behind this, but apparently these Societies are involved. And the kidnappers were from Interpol, at least their IDs indicated it so this is a worldwide event."

He had hoped to contain the situation, but now it was completely out of control. "Okay, Ben, we'll meet you there."

He hung up, looked in his rearview mirror and then called Dean. "Where are you?"

"I'm about a mile behind you."

"Have you heard?"

"I just did on the radio."

Brooks hadn't even realized they had the radio off in the car.

"Brooks, what are we going to do?"

"We're meeting Johnson in Lexington. You need to close in behind us so we can protect Mrs. Miller."

"Yes, sir what's going to happen?"

"Well, it's started. The war is spreading all over the world. No one is safe or immune. Contact everyone associated with our Society that you know. We need to make sure everyone is at a safe house. It's now only a matter of time as to who will survive. The odds against us are very long, you know that. The Praetorians control almost every government agency and almost all the media outlets. Only time will tell."

He saw Emily sitting up in the back seat.

"I've got to go. Get up here now." Brooks ordered.

"Yes, sir, I'm almost there."

Brooks could now see Dean's car in his mirror.

"Well?" Emily said.

"How much did you hear?"

"All of it."

"Then you know that life as we have known it will change...forever."

Emily climbed up front. "Can you trust Agent Johnson?"

"Yes, I believe so. Johnson will join us now that events have unfolded. In any event, I must sort him out when we meet. He'll have to take sides and my bet is he'll join us. I've known Ben for over twenty years. He's a straight shooter, no nonsense guy. He moved up the ranks same as me. I've never taken pause with his actions.

"The most troubling thing is there are far more agents and officials involved than we knew. The Praetorians have been very careful to conceal so much involvement. Up until now we've had only a few hundred on either side actually involved in day to day operations. It's been, more or less, a standoff. Now, the scale is tipping heavily in their favor."

"And what about Thomas?"

"I have two trusted agents protecting him at the hospital, but perhaps we need to move him."

Brooks placed a call. "Dean, get hold of Agent Grant at the hospital and have Mr. Miller moved to one of our secure facilities."

"Yes, sir."

"What makes you think he's still safe after all that's happened?" Emily asked in a nervous tone.

Brooks hung up, but didn't answer her.

A few moments passed, and Dean called back. "Sir, I can't get hold of Grant or Agent Tillman. What should I do?"

"I'll take care of it." Brooks called the Sheriff. "Pete, what's your status?"

"I'm on my way to the hospital. There was a shooting...several shootings."

"Find out the status of Mr. Miller."

"I'll be at the hospital in another minute."

"Call me with what you find out. He's the most important link we have."

◊ ◊ ◊

Emily stared out the front window. Her mind was racing.

Great, as soon as the girls are safe Thomas isn't. This nightmare will never end.

She blurted out, "Call Waxman and make sure the girls are safe!"

She caught Brooks off guard as he flinched at her directive and tone. He made the call.

"Yes, Brooks, I have the girls and we're at the safe house," Waxman said.

"Good. How many of you are there?"

"I've got seventeen here. All the other houses have about the same, just like we planned in case of this scenario."

"Ok. Any other news about the rest?" Brooks asked.

"Reports have been coming in. I believe four members have been killed, though we can't be sure."

"And I know of two more now so that's six, just in our area. Jesus, keep me updated," Brooks said. His expression changed to serious concern as he ended the call. He looked in his mirror again.

"Well?" Emily asked as she turned to look as well. It was Dean's car, now right behind them.

"We've taken a big hit. We've lost six Verum members in the last week that I know of which means a lot more around the world."

"My God." Emily sat back, not knowing how to react other than shock.

Brook's phone rang. He put it on speaker. It was Pete. "Brooks, Thomas is gone and your two agents are dead. Security here says someone came in and shot the agents and was going to kill Thomas but someone else, I don't know who, shot the assassin. He took Thomas and an ambulance. I have no idea where they went. We've called for a helicopter but it seems they're all in use by the Federal Government."

"Pete, get Agent Waxman and find him. She's at the safe house."

"Mike's there as well. I'll call him. What do we…" The phone went dead.

"Pete? Pete?" Frustrated, Brooks put his phone down.

"What is it?' Emily asked.

"No signal."

"So we don't know what's happening?"

Brooks turned on the radio. It was buzzing with reports on every channel about the killings.

"*Reports are coming in from Europe. There have been several terrorist killings. It seems some of these happened during the last few months and were kept secret for security reasons. We don't yet know who is behind this…*"

He turned off the radio.

"Shouldn't we go back to the safe house and help find Thomas?" Emily asked.

"No. Waxman and Pete need to handle that. We have to keep going."

Emily felt anxiety creep over her. *I have to get back. I have to find Thomas.*

Agent Dean had been behind them for some time now. He came up beside them as the road widened to two lanes each way.

"Brooks!" he yelled out his passenger window. "The phones are dead."

"I know. Pull off at the next exit." Brooks pointed to a large green road sign they were just passing. It was for an upcoming exit.

They took the ramp off the highway and stopped their cars in a commuter lot. Dean parked in a far corner near a dumpster, hiding most of his car from the rest of the lot, and joined them, sitting in the back behind Emily.

"Mrs. Miller, you remember Agent Dean? You met at the Sheriff's office and the hospital."

She nodded. "Hello, Mr. Dean. I hope you have some good news for us." She turned in her seat to see both men.

"Ma'am." He answered, ignoring her request, and turned to Brooks. "Sir, what are we supposed to do?"

"All we can do is press forward. Unless we can find all the documents, the country, and it seems the world, will collapse into anarchy, or worse, military control." Brooks stated.

"From what I could gather on the radio, most of the western countries are on high alert, looking to crush any rebellions or terrorist acts." Dean surmised.

"Then it'll be a military takeover. If that's the case, we can expect Praetorian members will gain even more power throughout the western world."

Emily was fidgeting with the key as her hands started to sweat. "We already have several tyrannies abroad, don't we?"

"Yes, we do, but now it will include most of Europe and the United States." Brooks answered.

"How can something as insignificant as this key be the linchpin to restore order?" she asked.

"Well, it wasn't intended to stop this type of crisis, only to bring light on the truth. Now…I don't know and we won't know until we get a look at all that is hidden." Brooks looked very troubled.

"What about Mr. Miller?" Dean asked.

Emily could see the raw look of a new recruit in young Dean and it wasn't making her feel any better.

"That, right now, is a mystery we must also solve. Any ideas?" Brooks queried.

"Well, I know the Praetorians have been mobilized," Dean offered.

"Yes, and our two agents at the hospital are dead. The Sheriff said there was a second shooting at the scene. It seems someone killed the Praetorian hit man and took Mr. Miller away in an ambulance."

Dean thought for a moment. "It must be one of our operatives. Someone we haven't heard from yet."

"And we won't hear from anyone now with communications down." Brooks looked at his cell phone. "Now we're in one of those stupid dead zones, or the government has taken over the system."

"Then we can't complete our mission until we have more information from Mr. Miller, if he can even give it to us," Dean answered.

"So our goal now is to get to Lexington. But how will Agent Johnson get there?" Emily asked in a calm, more engaging voice.

"Good question," Brooks answered. "I have to assume air traffic's been shut down. He'll need to come by car. That means he's several hours behind us."

Dean interjected. "And we don't even know if he'll join us, though I've been working with him for some time now and I believe he will." He gave a confirming look to Brooks in the rearview mirror. "But with all that's going on, should we take the chance?"

"We have to. He has much higher Federal Government clearance than I do, and I think he can infiltrate deep enough to help us. And we have another problem at the moment. The main roads are no longer safe. You know the Feds will start setting up roadblocks to keep us from getting to the east. We must proceed cautiously."

The importance of the mission continued to rise in Emily's mind. *How can all this be happening? So much to do and under constant threat? I must be in some sort of parallel universe!*

◊ ◊ ◊

Thomas slowly opened his eyes. He looked around to see he was on an ambulance stretcher with an intravenous line in his arm. He tried to talk and immediately stopped with terrible pain in his throat.

He noticed a man in the shadows on the far side of the room. The man approached. "Easy. You're lucky to be alive. Take it slow. You'll be able to talk soon enough, but you need to whisper or you'll keep hurting yourself. Now, do you remember what happened?"

Thomas thought for a moment, then nodded to the stranger.

"Do you think you can tell me?"

Thomas nodded again. The stranger sat in a chair next to the stretcher. They were in a small room with windows boarded up on the inside. The lighting was dim. There was something familiar about the stranger, but he didn't know what it was.

"I…I remember being in a car." Thomas started in a whisper. "I remember it was traveling at a very high speed…and then it crashed. Where are we?" He grabbed the bandage on his neck.

The stranger gave him an odd look. "Easy does it there. Are you sure you remember it that way?"

"Yes, although I can't remember if I was in the back or front, and I heard glass shatter and I choked." He grabbed his right arm as if it had been struck.

The stranger thought for a moment. "We're safe for now."

"Where are my wife and girls?"

"They're all safe. Your girls are with Deputy Wilson. Your wife is with Agent Brooks. I've asked the sheriff to join us."

Thomas looked perplexed. "Where are we? Who are you?"

"We're safe for the moment. I'm here to help. I know Agent Brooks. His Society is compromised and there have been killings all over the country."

"How can all this be?" Thomas asked as he was overcome with dizziness.

The stranger stood and started pacing from the bed to the opposite wall. "It's because the Praetorians, Brooks' enemy, are pressing for some information they think you and others have."

"Information?"

"Yes. You have a key, a diary, and several documents that the Praetorians want to get their hands on. It seems if they don't, they think it can ruin them and all they control. Can you tell me anything that might help?" The stranger said in an even, approachable voice, with a hint of arrogance.

"I don't even know who you are. You could be a Praetorian or whatever you called them. How do I know you won't kill me after I give you the information?" Thomas continued to struggle with his neck pain and dizziness as he tried to focus.

"Well, you don't…seems I'll need to prove to you that I can be trusted."

"That would be a good start."

The stranger smiled. "I'm the one who called you yesterday with all that information. I also saved your children. I'll tell you what, take some time to clear your head and we'll talk some more later."

Thomas tried to grasp what the stranger said. "You saved the girls?" he asked just before passing out.

◊ ◊ ◊

The stranger walked to the front door of the house and made a call.

"What's your status?" the voice on the other end asked.

"I have Yates."

"Is he talking?"

"No, I don't have any information yet. I'll call you when I do. See if you can catch them in Lexington. We need to act quickly."

"I'm on my way…"

Looking at his phone, he realized there was no signal. He walked through several rooms and out the front door.

Still no signal. *Unless a satellite is down, the Federal Government is interrupting the whole system. Could they have acted this quickly?*

He went back inside and sat, waiting for Thomas to wake up again. Patience was a difficult virtue. He was one of action, not patience.

◊ ◊ ◊

Brooks, Dean, and Emily, drove through the night and most of Sunday on secondary roads to go undetected. It was difficult, as they no longer had GPS to map the route.

They finally stopped for gas and picked up several maps. Brooks had decided to ditch Dean's car so they could strategize since the phones were out. The men took turns driving. Emily slept most of the way.

They finally arrived in Lexington close to four o'clock in the afternoon. Brooks drove into the plaza shopping center and parked.

"Dean, check into that hotel across the street."

"Yes sir. Should I get a separate room for Mrs. Miller?"

"No, get a suite."

Dean nodded and Emily went with him.

Brooks' phone started to buzz. It was for text and voice messages. *Seems the lines are working again. They must feel comfortable enough to bring them back online. The challenge now is not to get traced. I'll buy some burn phones so we can communicate in private.*

His phone buzzed again. He didn't attempt to use the phone, figuring it was probably tapped.

While Brooks milled around the shopping plaza, he thought back to how he became involved in this saga. It was his senior year in college. He was a good student, though not high honors. His major was criminal justice. He landed a job as an intern for a Federal Judge in Massachusetts. It wasn't long before he gained recognition within the ranks and was accepted into the FBI two years later.

He worked his way up to the Criminal Investigative Division, where Agent Ben Johnson was his superior. They've worked together over twenty years now, and have become close friends. He was counting on this friendship now more than ever.

He was also a leader in the Absconditus Verum, in secret of course. His charge was to oversee James Thomas Miller and his wife Emily. Sheriff Pete Lucas was the go between and would report directly to him. It was critical each level of the organization stayed independent for the protection of all. Most members only knew their superior, not the chain of command heading upward.

His link to the Verum was through his mother's side of the family dating back to the Civil War. His distant relatives fought for the Confederates, though now family members lived all across the country.

Brooks was in his mid-fifties, with salt and pepper hair, and stood five foot ten. At 170 pounds, he was in relatively good shape. He always dressed in a suit, even on casual occasions. He wore a neat goatee and kept himself well-manicured.

He had good moral bearings and believed strongly in the Constitution and individual liberty. This was what held the Verum together through the years, for it was destiny to bring the truth to light.

The plaza was packed with people. There was no panic, just people looking to stock up on things they might need after hearing the terrorist news from the previous day. Johnson still hadn't shown up. *We can't wait anymore. I have to get to Staunton.*

He headed out of the plaza with new phones in hand when he spotted Johnson just getting out of his parked car. Johnson looked around and saw Brooks as he approached.

"Thanks for coming, Ben." Brooks started. "I wasn't sure you had deciphered all the events from the last few days."

Johnson seemed receptive. "I have. You know, you took a big chance asking me here. Not knowing where my alliances are."

Brooks gave him a small smile. "Well, it was a risk, but I knew you'd come our way."

"So I'm here and I'm in, now you just have to tell me what's going on."

"Let's talk in the car." Brooks motioned and they both got in Johnson's car.

Brooks went on to explain all about the two Societies and their quest for the hidden truth. Johnson didn't seem too shocked about any of it.

"So what's the plan now?" Johnson asked.

"We need to get information here in Lexington and then head for Monticello. It's all we can do until we hear from Mr. Miller," Brooks said as he got out. "Meet us over at the hotel." He pointed to the hotel across the street.

They drove their cars to the hotel parking and headed to the lobby. It was a nice four-star establishment and rather pricy. Brooks checked the front desk for the room and they took the elevator up to the tenth floor.

Dean had gotten a suite in the hotel. He'd ordered some food from room service for all of them. Brooks and Johnson joined Dean in the main room.

"Mrs. Miller's in the other room sleeping." Dean pointed towards one of the bedrooms.

"Seems like we've gotten into a lot more than a kidnapping," Johnson said, looking at Dean.

"Yes, Sir," Dean answered. "I knew you'd join us."

Brooks caught Johnson eying Dean rather curiously, but decided not to act on it, at least for the moment. "Ben, can you forward my phone to one of these?" he asked as he handed the new cell phones to Johnson.

"Yes, I'll do it now." Johnson spent the next ten minutes setting up the phones Brooks bought.

They decided to let Emily sleep for now as they took time to eat at a dining table in the main room. They discussed the mission ahead and who they could trust in Federal Government while they ate. Brooks and Dean did most of the talking as Johnson listened intently.

They were just finishing up their plans when Brooks new phone rang. It was an unlisted number.

"What do you think…our side or theirs?" Dean asked.

Johnson was calm, but Dean looked both anxious and attentive. They were still seated at the table in the main room.

"Is this traceable?" Brooks asked.

"No, it's a secure line now," Johnson assured.

Brooks answered the phone.

"Agent Brooks?" asked a strange voice.

"Yes, who am I speaking with?"

"I can't tell you at this time." The stranger sounded sincere, yet a little brash.

Brooks was a bit unsure how to respond. Perhaps a direct approach would work best. "Then this conversation is over."

"No, Brooks…wait. I have James Yates."

Brooks was flabbergasted. "Who is this?"

"I told you not to ask."

"Where are you?"

"In Texas. I know you're going to Monticello. I also know you need information from Yates."

"Why would you think that?"

"I just know. Tell his wife he's out of his coma. I spoke with him briefly. He's still quite disoriented, though I think some of his old memories are starting to return."

"Hold on a moment." Brooks covered the phone. "Whoever this is has Yates and seems to know what we're doing," he whispered to Dean and Johnson as he covered the mouthpiece. He got back on the phone. "Okay, I'm listening."

"I'll call you back when I get some more information from him. My suggestion would be to finish your business in Lexington and get to Monticello as fast as you can. The window of opportunity will close very quickly. I've bought you some time, but not much I'm afraid." He hung up.

"Well?" Dean asked in an excited tone.

Brooks was troubled. "Seems we have an unknown player involved, and he's very well versed in our operations. Dean, go get Mrs. Miller."

◊ ◊ ◊

As she came into the room she could tell there was news.

Brooks approached and stood in front of her. "Thomas is out of his coma. He's been speaking."

Emily's emotions surfaced again and try as she might a tear rolled down her cheek.

The other men were speaking softly at the table as Brooks continued. "We don't know where he is or who he's with. It seems to be someone either in our organization or someone in the Society of Praetorians who has possibly defected. We don't have any other information…but we do need to finish our business here tomorrow and get to Monticello."

"Move again already? We just got here." She said with a resigned sigh. *Here we go again.*

She managed to eat some dinner as the men relaxed in the T.V. area of the main room. They watched the news for the rest of the evening as Dean switched channels continuously. Emily joined them when she finished eating.

The news was awash in Federal Government activity; what they were doing in response to all the killings and terrorist actions. Pundits were arguing about the way the government was reacting as they ever did, in constant partisanship, laying blame on this department or that person.

◊ ◊ ◊

Brooks called the safe house they were headed for and let them know they would be there the next day.

The group went to bed around midnight and did manage some sleep as Brooks was reluctant to share any more information with Dean and Johnson just yet. Not until he was confident they were indeed allies.

In the morning, they ordered some breakfast to the room, ate, and were ready to go by nine. The men dressed in suits as always, Emily in a smart blouse and pants.

At the car, Brooks directed them, "Dean, you ride with Johnson. You'll head east on Route 64. Emily and I will meet up with you at the next rest stop. Then we must get off the main roads again."

Each team went their respective ways. Brooks headed for the Eastern Savings Bank in downtown Lexington.

Once they got there and parked, they went inside and proceeded down a wide flight of stairs to the vault and safe deposit boxes. Meeting a guard at the desk Brooks asked. "I'd like to get into my box, please."

"I can help you with that. Do you have your key?"

Brooks took his safety deposit key out of his pocket and handed it to the guard. They all went into the box area and once the guard identified the correct one, inserted them, turned them, retrieved his box.

"There you are, sir." He handed Brooks the box and motioned towards the private viewing rooms.

"Thank you." Brooks headed towards a room with Emily in tow.

Once inside the private room, he opened it. There was nothing inside except for an old piece of paper and a blood stained diary. He took them out, returned the box, and they made their way out to the car.

As they were driving away, Brooks handed the paper and diary to Emily. He turned the radio on low to a news station.

A quizzical look crossed her face. "What does this mean? Wednesday is Saturday…ten is eight." she said as she looked at the hand written note on the paper.

"That's what we need to find out from your husband. The paper is his…or rather the paper is mine but the code is his."

"How do you know?" Emily asked as she started flipping through the diary.

"Because he was mumbling it over and over when I took him out of the car. The problem is I have no idea what it refers to."

Emily looked confused. "I don't understand. When we got to the hospital he was talking?"

"No. Back in 1987, when I took a twelve-year old out of the car his father was driving and took him to safety. That's what he kept repeating over and over." Brooks thought back to the accident that killed Richard and left a young James with no memory. He was part of the chase and remembered Richard's car getting hit broadside, forcing it into oncoming traffic. He tried to save Richard but it was no good.

He took the diary and the key along with the unconscious boy to safety.

"Brooks? Are you saying Thomas was the boy?" Emily asked.

He nodded to her and continued. "I took the paper and the diary to the safest place I could. The Absconditus Verum leaders examined both. They brought in trusted experts, but they haven't been able to crack the entire cypher in the diary all these years. The problem is it's also encrypted, so we've only broken part of it. Until we get some more information, we can't tell what the rest of the secrets in the diary hold. The code on the paper is where we'll find the secret to the door that the key goes to. At least that's our belief."

They headed east out of the city. The car radio suddenly got Brooks' attention. He turned it up.

"*It seems the terrorist killing spree is over. Officials state that this was a global terrorist plot to take over power in many western countries. The terrorists were not - I repeat, were not - from the Middle East. It seems these were all home grown terrorists as one hundred and fourteen people have been killed and identified so far. The military of most of the countries affected have returned power to their governments. This is breaking news. We will update our listeners as soon as we receive more information, but for now the crisis is over.*"

Brooks turned the radio down again. "So the cover story is already being put out. Seems you and I are now terrorists."

"How would they know this so quickly?"

"They wouldn't. This is all preplanned for the media from the government. Radicalize the threat and we become the bad guys."

Brooks could see Emily was trying to work her way through the information.

"What can we do now…now that we're marginalized?" she asked.

"We can only do what we planned to do. Find the documents and find a way to get the truth out to the public."

She sat silent for several minutes as she continued to flip through the diary, though not focusing on any one page. "I know now you think that some kind of truth is out there. But it's been my understanding through life that there are many who believe their ideology is the real and only truth. Which of course means that there are always several *truths* at the same time, many being at complete odds with other so called truths. What truth are you talking about?"

Brooks knew this would take some time. He had to be patient with a woman whose life was just ripped apart. "My father told me long ago that many historical events were written down and kept hidden in the beginning. These events somehow paint a different picture of American history; one the Praetorians do not want public. To protect their friends and families, the Verum decided to keep these events secret until it was safer to make them public."

"But how do you know these are true events and not someone's fictional story?" she said as she closed the diary and examined the dark blood stain on the cover.

"We know because the Praetorians have desperately been trying to find them first. If they posed no real threat to their power, they wouldn't care if the documents came out. It's their pursuit of us and the papers that gives legitimacy to the documents more than anything else. Consider the elitist now in power. Do you think they will willingly allow the people to take back their government? They are in power and control our lives more than you think."

As Brooks was finishing his explanation, he turned off the road into a rest stop on Route 64, where they met up with Johnson and Dean. The men got out to talk. Emily stayed in the car and continued to examine the diary.

"Looks like the odds are stacked against you, my old friend," Johnson said to Brooks.

While Brooks was committed to their plans, he still felt uneasy with Johnson. "Yes, they are. Remember, stay on the back roads."

Yes, he had invited him to join the cause, but he really didn't know the man's politics or ideological stance on anything. They were good friends for many years, but he was friends with others he found out were Praetorians.

Was he risking too much? The entire plan was based on trust. Now there was a wild card which could undermine everything they believed in. Perhaps a call to the head of their society was warranted, but not just yet.

He decided to ride it out for now. Take one step at a time and measure Johnson's responses.

Chapter 22

Safe House - Staunton, Virginia

It was late evening when their cars pulled into the driveway of a safe house, located on a farm on the eastern outskirts of Staunton, Virginia.

Brooks, Emily, Johnson, and Dean, all grabbed their travel gear out of the cars. They were now less than an hour away from Monticello.

As they approached the house, the owner, Ms. Pamela Sanders, met them at the front door.

"Ms. Sanders, I'm Joseph Brooks. This is FBI agent Ben Johnson, agent Timothy Dean, and this is Emily Yates."

"Can I see some identification?" she asked.

The men showed her their credentials.

"Ok, we can never be too careful these days, with all that's happened. Come in please."

She was a lovely woman, in her mid-fifties with graying hair, and a soft look about her face.

A homemade southern dinner of ribs, potatoes, and greens was served, which was something they all enjoyed thoroughly. Conversation was at a minimum during dinner. Emily spent time carefully arranging her utensils, lining them up at equal spacing.

When they finished, they retired to a large sitting room. It was in the front right corner of the house with a large open hearth fireplace. There were several wing backed chairs, a small couch, and a recliner. An area rug covered the hardwood floor near the fireplace. It was almost eleven o'clock.

Emily was restless. "I want to call Pete and talk to the girls."

Brooks was just about to make the call when his burn phone rang. "Yes?"

"Is the line safe? You must keep this between us and the Millers." It was the same mystery man he had spoken to the day before. The one who had James Thomas.

"Hold on." Brooks motioned Emily to step outside with him onto the front yard. Once they were alone, he turned his attention back to the phone. "It is now."

"Okay, Yates is awake. He wants to speak to his wife."

"Hold on." He held the phone out with the mute button on. "It's the guy who has your husband."

"Can I talk to Thomas?" she asked.

"Put him on." Brooks said and handed her the phone.

Emily took a moment to gather herself. "Thomas? Thomas? Are you there?"

"Hello?" It was a very soft voice.

"Thomas? Is that you?" she asked.

"Yes, Emily. I here. You're alright and safe with Agent Brooks?"

"Yes…oh, Thomas…what about you?"

"It seems my new *friend* here has some knowledge of patching up someone who's in pretty bad shape."

"Oh, Thomas…The girls are safe, too."

"Yes, I heard. They're with Mike. In fact, Pete is on his way to meet me."

"Oh Thomas, you have no idea the day I've had. All this cloak and dagger business. I'm not cut out for this. Where are you?" she queried.

"We're near Clarksville. My new *friend* says this was one place they would never look. I'm not sure who to trust. Does Brooks know?"

Brooks broke in. "Emily, I need to talk to Thomas."

She nodded. "Thomas…I'm giving the phone to Agent Brooks. I love you." She started crying again as she went to the front porch and sat on an old rocking chair. Her thoughts flooded with the desire to be with Thomas and the girls. She wanted to go back to before all this happened. Her life, the life she loved so much. Her girls. She wanted to hold them, hug them. She buried her head in her hands.

◊ ◊ ◊

"Thomas, this is Brooks. Are you in any danger with this new friend of yours? Has he given you an idea of who he is?" Brooks was pacing as he talked. He knew the gravity of Thomas-James' situation. If he was prevented from helping them, the quest would fail.

"No. It seems like we're not new friends but old ones. He knows all about me."

This was very disquieting to Brooks. "Really? Well, first thing's first. We're in Virginia. Can you give us any information?"

"Yes, it seems my childhood memories are returning, though a bit convoluted. Bits and pieces for now. One thing I remember is being at Monticello. The other is an odd phrase. Wednesday is Saturday and ten is eight. At least I think that's the phrase."

"It is. Anything else?" Brooks hung on every word, waiting, hoping for a breakthrough.

"No. Not yet, anyway. Only that those two are connected in some way. Oh, wait…I do remember one other thing. I remember seeing drawings and sketches. Lots of them. Buildings. They had notes and x's all over them."

"Yes, they were your father's. We have them and all the rest of your father's research."

"Yes, my real father…Yates. Richard Yates."

"That's right." Brooks held out a glimmer of hope. *He's starting to remember!*

"Well, that's all I remember right now, and I have someone that wants to talk to you."

Brooks didn't like the situation at all. He had no control and whoever was holding James was calling the shots. "Okay, James, get well fast. We need you."

The stranger took the phone. "So Brooks, what do you think?"

"I know two things. One is you're not there to kill him, and two is I have no idea who you are."

"Yes, you do actually."

Brooks thought hard on who this could be but came up empty. *Who the hell is this guy?*

"Well, since I'm not able to place you, who are you?"

"Let's just say I'm the man in black."

A flood of memories came back to Brooks. "My God…Trumbull?" he answered in a hushed voice. Alarm bells rang in his head.

Brooks knew this man since the encounter that took Richard's life. He was a cold blooded killer, a deadly assassin, who worked for the Praetorians. Many times in the past, Brooks would show up at a homicide scene only to realize it was yet another mark left by the man they knew as Trumbull.

"Yes."

"I heard you were dead a long time ago." He was trying his best not to convey panic in his voice.

"That does seem to be the rumor going around." Trumbull said in an arrogant self-indulged tone.

"So tell me how you're fitting into this whole drama. Looking to trap us and get information to your bosses?"

"Well, I'm part of the reason for some of these killings in the last week, though this isn't the outcome I had hoped for."

His lack of emotions towards the killings only heightened Brooks' already high anxiety.

"Christ! Do you know how many people have died in the last week? How do I know you didn't orchestrate all this?"

"You'll just have to trust me. I wasn't able to stem the tide once it broke."

"And how did you manage starting the tide?" His resolve returned, Brooks worked on getting information. He continued pacing across the front lawn of the farmhouse.

"I've been taking out many of their top agents. What do you think I've been doing these years after I was dead?"

"It's been you all along?" Brooks was torn now between trust and deception. So much bloodshed caused by this man he now had to trust if they had any chance of success. He had no choice. Trumbull had James. He needed the riddle solved before they could attempt to continue their quest. He was at the mercy of this assassin.

"Yes, well, I'm only responsible for some. The last one was at the hospital. Got there just in time too or you wouldn't have much to go on. Too late to save your agents, I'm afraid."

"I'll bet." was all Brooks managed to get out.

"Oh please." Trumbull said in the same sarcastic tone. "The Praetorians are in panic mode. I called them with the agent's phone and told them Yates was dead and you were close by so they'll be tied up in Texas for a while, giving you some time. Anyway, I have Yates and he's doing quite well for a man just out of a coma. So are you going to invite me to this party? I mean after all they still think I'm dead. I'd say I'm a pretty good asset to have at such a crucial time."

Brooks now had a decision to make. *Either I trust him or not. I have to decide.* "My God…you're the same old arrogant bastard, aren't you?"

"Why, of course I am. But now I've had over twenty years to learn everything about you and the Absconditus Verum. While I've enjoyed killing many Praetorian agents, and made them raging mad, it's time we end this, don't you think?"

With all this new information, Brooks decided.

"How soon can you get here?" Brooks made his play. He needed James. It was no use resisting as he figured Trumbull would just kill James once he had the information if indeed he was still a Praetorian.

"Now that the airlines are back up and running and the Sheriff should be here any time now, I would guess about ten hours."

This made his decision a bit easier. *There's no way he would let James go with the sheriff unless he does mean to help.* "Meet us at Monticello."

"So it was there all the time?" Trumbull asked in a somewhat surprised tone.

"Actually we still don't know, but I aim to find out."

"I'll see you there. Hopefully, Yates can give me more information. Oh, by the way, the sheriff finger-printed the agent I killed at the hospital and it was the same guy he intercepted in town when you left Bogata," Trumbull said

Brooks hung up.

I can't believe it. Trumbull…after all these years.

He had to call in to the Verum central command. There was too much at stake now and he wanted them to sign off on his decision.

"Sir? It's Brooks. I've just had a conversation with William Trumbull. Yes, sir. He wants to join us at Monticello… Are you sure? Yes, sir. Oh and we need all the Monticello notes, sketches, and pictures, to be brought over to the safe house in Staunton. They're already here? I haven't had time to talk to our contact. Yes, sir."

Having the approval of his superior was reassuring, but he was still extremely leery of getting Trumbull involved. He gathered Emily on his way back into the house. "Did you hear?"

She nodded.

Brooks said quietly. "Emily. Don't let anyone know about Trumbull. I'd rather keep this under wraps until we actually need him. I'm not sure how Johnson or Dean will react to a Praetorian helping us. Ok?"

Emily nodded and they went back inside.

◊ ◊ ◊

Unbeknownst to Brooks, Ms. Sanders was listening from the kitchen window and heard all that was said.

◊ ◊ ◊

Brooks and Emily rejoined Dean and Johnson in the Sitting Room. Now that she had talked to Thomas, she was eager for Brooks to share more history. She wanted to know every detail, every nuance. She believed it would help her with the upcoming mission.

"Tell me more. What happened at the Convention." Emily was tired, but not enough to stop Brooks from explaining those fateful events in history.

It was now nearing midnight and they had a small fire burning in the fireplace. No one would sleep much that night as they knew the importance of the next day's events. Brooks had almost finished the history of the Convention.

"Some delegates were never coming back. Others returned to sign the new Constitution. Madison, who realized the power he helped create would destroy the states, reluctantly signed. Fifteen delegates didn't sign it. They felt either it was too weak as the Articles had been, or too strong and would absorb the states. The moderates carried the day though, and for the most part they had managed to defeat the strong central government that some of the delegate's planned for total control.

"The new government was to be no stronger than any single state. This they had all agreed to. The chance to create a *Nation State* by the few had past. It was utterly rejected. In fact, the word nation was removed and the words United States in the plural were inserted in its place. A Federal Democracy was also rejected. Mob rule would never last and that is what a true democracy is. They chose a Republic, similar to the state

Republics that were set up.

"The moderates made sure that even the words 'democracy' and 'nation' were not used in any instance of any portion of the new Constitution.

Here's the crux. In drafting the actual document, Gouverneur Morris, a strong nationalist, was at the helm. His specific wording was used for a reason. No matter how several of the parts were written, he made sure they could be 'interpreted' to fit the needs of the nationalists even after nation had been specifically crossed out and replaced. That's why we have the oligarchy elitist government running the indivisible nation of today. It was secretly set up during the Convention."

"I don't understand," Dean said. "I thought we're using the Constitution as our guiding document."

"Well we are, sort of. But think of it as a terribly corrupt interpretation, one that ultimately gives power to the few to control the many. Think of the Roman Republic style. That's the government we have today."

"So that's why the two parties have total control?" Emily asked.

"Yes, and also why judges have supreme power over everyone. They were never intended to write laws from the bench. They were the weakest part of the three branches and were meant to strictly interpret the laws congress created.

"Today, their decisions can be interpreted as changing the laws they don't like. This is completely the opposite of their real role in government."

"Waite a minute," Emily interjected. "That's not right. The Supreme Court can change any law they want with a simple majority. I remember when they took up abortion in the 1970s. All the states had their own laws restricting abortion in some way. The Supreme Court determined abortion was legal in all the states."

"You're correct," Brooks answered. "They forced all the states to comply with the Federal Courts decision, but they were never given that power in the Constitution. In fact the Constitution doesn't even define their enumerated powers. Once the Constitution was written, The Judges in office in the Senate wrote the Judicial Act, giving themselves the power to use Judicial Review.

"Now this power still did not give them the legal right to change laws, but they used it as a way around the laws of Congress if they wanted to and now the people just accept this a real powers granted to them.

"Anyway, getting back to history, you must realize there were more than one group working against the government. There were, in fact, several groups. Some even interacted with others.

"Now here's the most important part and the reason we're here. When Gouverneur Morris drafted the wording he purposely left out two other words. The moderates and state advocates didn't take note of this emission for they had voted and agreed they were to be instituted no matter what the final draft was.

"Most held them to be their most precious rights, with no need to write them in. It wasn't even part of the argument after they voted to secure them. They were state nullification and secession.

"By purposely, not restricting the central government from usurping these two fundamental rights from the states, and leaving them out of the Constitution, they became the two issues that brought the states to their knees and stripped them of almost all the power they had left. This was the underlying cause of the Civil War, though other issues did become very important.

"It next went out to the states for ratification."

Dean looked perplexed. "I'm a bit confused. If the Constitution was written as a restriction on central government power and authority, why would they have included nullification and secession? Didn't the states hold all the power not specifically enumerated to the central government?"

"Yes. However, you must realize that the 10th Amendment was added after the Convention to further define the small amount of power the central government had. But it made no difference. Once everything was finalized, the nationalists simply ignored what was written or how it was written."

"Time for a break…I made some tea for everyone." It was Ms. Sanders that interrupted Brooks for a moment. "Now everyone needs to get some sleep. Chamomile tea will help." She gave them each a cup.

It was quiet for some time before Emily pressed to go on.

Brooks continued. "Well, the Society of the Cincinnati did indeed deliver nine states in such a quick timeline, there was no doubt any more about their influence. They had elected the majority of ratification delegates in almost all the states within a few months, while blocking nominations of state rights advocates, a timeline almost unheard of in those days. This was the first subversive act against the states, but by far, not the last. Virginia was the tenth state to ratify and there was such heated debate, a fight almost broke out. Many of the Founding Fathers who had not attended the Convention realized this was a solid move for power hungry individuals to rule on high. It did pass although the vote was very close. There was a call for specific amendments immediately, to protect the people's rights."

"So the Bill of Rights was written for the people?" Dean asked.

"No, not really. It was written as a document to restrict the central government, the same as the Constitution. So, in essence, it was not written as rights for the people. A government cannot give natural rights to people; it can only take them away through laws and legislation. The 10th Amendment was written for this expressed purpose, protecting the rights the states and the people already had by keeping a check on the central government."

"I never knew that. We were taught they were rights given to the people," Emily responded.

"And therein lies the root of our problem. The people have been taught the wrong information. This was the intent of the Federalists as well as the Praetorians. While not working together in a direct sense, they both created their own version of history that was different from our actual history, and then passed the fraud down through the generations so that, what was actually falsehoods, became reality."

"And the documents we are seeking?" Dean asked.

"The documents we are seeking are some of the real history lost as well as many truths that lie hidden. That's been the mission of the Absconditus Verum Society from the start; to record all that happened because they saw firsthand the deceit and injustice being forced on the people. We believe documents exist that specifically show all the Convention delegates were agreed on state's rights. This has been one of the many tales passed down through the years. Up until now, there are no records showing this most important issue."

"This is incredible if indeed it's true," Dean said with an astonished look.

"Indeed," chimed in Emily, taken aback by all these accounts.

"This was just the start. New York was the next state and the ratification was ready to be rejected. Too many now knew what was going on and they were determined to stop it. If New York refused, it would effectively cut off the New England states from the south as to a connected land mass. They would be forced to the sea for travel. This threatened to undo all that was done and most in New York were ready to do so."

"So that would have stopped the new government with a new Constitution?" Emily asked.

"Yes. By splitting the states and forcing them to negotiate travel through New York, they held a trump card."

"I thought you said all the states would be forced to join?" Dean asked. It seemed like he who could hardly contain himself.

"That's true; at least it was for the small states. No one expected a large state to resist even though two of the three New York delegates had abandoned the Convention,"

"I know one was Yates, who were the other two?" Emily asked

"Lansing and Hamilton."

This was a shock to both Emily and Dean. "You mean Hamilton and Yates were there proposing two totally different structures?" Emily asked.

"Yes. Even though the three were from the same state, two were for state's rights and Hamilton was for extermination of the states. It turned out during the convention, that when all three were present, the New York vote was constantly split. This effectively removed any influence from New York either way, but it also negated two of the strongest state's rights advocates."

"How come we never heard about all this in school, I mean they couldn't have kept this from coming out?" Dean asked.

"Well, who runs the schools in the country?" Brooks asked.

"The Federal and state governments," Emily said.

"Yes, the government. Now, think about this. Would the Federal Government want everyone to know how much of a fraudulent exercise took place to form our new government? And today, since the states are simply an extension of the central government, they are party to the corruption and the people no longer have any representation, even though they vote the politicians in."

Dean didn't answer but Emily could see he was just realizing the scope of the deceit. Emily was as well. "You mean all the teachers are in on this?"

"No. I mean all the approved teaching materials are carefully crafted to present our history the way the government wants it to be taught. In fact, many teachers really do know the truth, but the system they're in is so far removed, they'll lose their jobs and tenure if they speak out, now that the unions are so strong. Some will anyway, but not to the extent of challenging the entire system.

"And here is the other part of the puzzle they give us. The politicians call our country a Democratic Republic, an American Nation, an Indivisible Union, or in most cases, just a Democracy. These are just different names for the elitists to rule, but we're taught that these names, in fact, represent our true government and country. It could not be farther from the truth.

"Another problem is most elected officials are voted in by the majority. They believe this gives all the people true representation but it doesn't. Who represents all those who voted for the other candidates?"

"They say the winners write the history and get to make all the decisions," Dean answered.

"That's what they say, but there are two problems with that. Number one is, politicians who win elections don't represent their constituents once in office. They join the entrenched coalitions already in place and become part of a voting block formed with other elected officials, mostly in their own party.

So they're not really representing the people who voted them in at all.

"While some of the votes do end up giving the majority voice some small pieces of their ideology, the politicians could care less, so most of the people are not represented.

"The politicians are in power and the only job they have to do is get reelected, and 90% of them do. You'd think that's because they actually do represent their constituents, but in reality, it's because the two-party system is set up to give the people no other choice. If they vote in the other party, the same thing happens. The people are left with almost no representation at all.

"The two-party system is, in fact, a one-party system just as Hamilton wanted in a monarchy. We have an elitist style now, though not a king, and a structure based on the old British model. They pretend to show us a difference. But their actions show how corrupt both sides are and to what lengths they'll go to maintain power. You can't have the debt load and deficits the country has without both sides being in league with each other.

"The people vote and the politicians just move around the chess board. The game is being played by one person; big corrupt government. It owns the chess board. We're the pawns that are sacrificed during the game. They are the aristocrats in the back row and barely get scratched because they only move the pawns and then replace them. Not quite the game of chess we know.

"The second reason is; not one of the Founders ever wanted a democracy in any form at all, neither the nationalists nor the state's rights advocates.

"Democracy is a fraud. It's majority rule or what many call mob rule. The minority voice is totally snuffed out and they have no representation at all. Sure parlor tricks they show us can prevent votes on this or that, but they have no desire to give up their power. On top of that, the majority also has no power to stop the corruption. They say to vote out the bad politicians, but because of the system, the corruption continues."

Emily thought for a moment. "So how do we get all this information out? If most of it is already out there and no one is listening, how can we make a difference? It's like much of the truth is hidden in plain sight."

"What if someone collects all the information and presents it all together?" Dean asked.

"That's part of our mission. To find some way to get the information out and have the people start to regain their former freedoms and government," Brooks answered.

"Actually, now that I think about it..," Emily said. "Someone in our organization needs to collect everything including what we're searching for and write a book, or have it become a movie like *The DaVinci Code*. That way millions will get the message. The key though is to present it without all the partisan ideologies, because it's the partisans that truly keep us divided."

"That would be the only way to get the quickest response, and I'll leave that up to you Emily." Brooks concluded.

"I'm not a writer."

"Which is why it's perfect; an unknown regular middle class American capturing the essence of everything done and being done." Brooks said.

Emily smiled as she thought about it. "Perhaps I need to strengthen my writing skills."

"This would be incredible," Dean said. "I know lots of people my age would take notice."

"Mine too," Brooks said.

"Anyway, where were we?" Emily asked. "Brooks you have an annoying habit of going off on a tangent."

"Because it's all connected," he responded.

"I know, but my head is spinning," Dean said.

Brooks smiled as he looked at the two of them.

"So what happened in New York?" Emily asked.

"They initially rejected the ratification. They were going to force any centralized *Nation State* government to do what it was supposed to do and that was to amend the Articles of Confederation and Perpetual Union. That was the whole purpose of the Convention. Realizing what had been done; several states were now reluctant to join. Two more demanded the Bill of Rights to further restrict central authority."

"Okay, so here you go again." Emily was now used to

Brooks going off on a tangent.

Brooks smiled. "I know, I know. Anyway the delegates from the New York ratification met behind closed doors. Governor Clinton was the leader of the resistance and Hamilton was for ratification. He knew his side would lose so he pressured the Clinton coalition. He told them that New York City, which was his power base, would secede from New York and become its own state unless Clinton agreed to ratify."

"Secede? I thought Hamilton didn't believe in those powers?" Dean asked.

"That's true, but if Hamilton and the others did indeed sign affirmation documents, then the point was moot. Hamilton and a handful of others wanted the state to be annihilated, but their view was utterly rejected at the Convention even if it was not within the Constitution. Remember, if it was not specifically delegated in the Constitution, then the central government had no authority to act. And even though, the central government's third branch, the judiciary, had no authority at all in even determining Constitutionality of issues. Yet after the Convention, Judges Ellsworth and Wilson wrote a Judicial Act the next year that gave judges omnipotent power to shape our society in any way they wanted. Justice Marshall followed in their footsteps and judicial review was embedded into our society even though it's not in the Constitution,"

"Wait a minute. I thought Ellsworth was the one who pushed for the affirmation? Now I'm totally confused."

"You're right, he did. At the time, he was representing Connecticut. Once the new Federal Government started and he was chosen as a Senator, he switched sides. His reward years later was being selected as the Chief Justice to the Supreme Court."

"Okay, let's skip that for a moment and get back to New York," Emily said. "So now Hamilton was using secession, one of the devices that protected the states, against the state?"

"That's right. His threat forced Clinton and enough of his group to acquiesce to the demand to ratify, though we believe Clinton was rewarded with a guarantee of personal wealth. After that it was only a matter of time before the remaining states had to join. Rhode Island was, of course, the last to hold out. They kept postponing ratification well into Washington's first term as President. They finally did ratify 34 votes to 32 votes, and only because several non-nationalists abstained. They were also under threat from Providence. The town threatened to secede from the state, just another example of the right to nullify or secede."

"So it was by fake and fraud the United States was formed?" Emily said.

"That is the real truth. The one our Federal government will keep hidden at all costs, using the Society of Praetorians to do all their dirty work. If the people find out what really happened, they would abandon the current political system and every politician would be kicked out. Think of it. Delegates are selected to amend central government to help defend the states and strengthen it though only to a point where it did not supersede any state authority. What they did was to secede from the original government completely which was the Articles, and set up their own new government. None of them had the authority to do this, yet they did it anyway. The Articles were a perpetual unbreakable Union of the states, yet they did break this everlasting Union with only a handful of carefully selected men. They threw the Articles into the trash can and just made up a new structure. The United States was anything but united. It was now the states against the central government. What does that remind you of?"

"The Colonies against King George and Parliament," Emily said almost under her breath.

"Exactly," Brooks said. "We no sooner win independence from the English Empire, now this elite group granted themselves parliamentary power and a powerful executive as well as a judiciary bend on total control over the people. Not all of them mind you. There were still many Founders that wanted the government to stay decentralized and the power of government to stay with the states. But it didn't matter. The Hamilton Plan that was utterly rejected at the Convention would now be enacted in the new government and he would have almost total control through the Treasury Department.

"Then they used a military society, the Cincinnati, which was the largest organization in the states, to get the new government ratified. Does that sound like the America you were taught existed?"

"No," Dean said.

Emily was shaking her head. "How could this possibly be true? How could this not be known by all the people?"

"Well, first, because all this was done in secret behind closed doors. It was decades later before the notes even became public. Almost everything that was done back then was done in secret and then the people were only told about the results and they were expected to obey without question. By the time the truth came out, the lie had been told over and over for decades until it became the truth, though it was not. A Founder by the name of Noah Webster was one such individual making speeches and telling the people that the central government set up the states instead of the reverse."

"But that's what is going on even today!" Dean was almost shouting.

"You mean back room deals in committees and ramming legislation through no matter what the people say or want?" Brooks asked.

"Yes. It happened only recently with healthcare, stimulus money, bailouts, ever-increasing government debt, and policing the world." answered Dean.

"Be careful, Mr. Dean. You'll be called a radical for even questioning these decisions," Brooks answered with a wry grin.

"Now, they worded the new Constitution to seem like it was protecting the people; *We the People.* On top of that they called it a Federal Government, which means it's nothing more than a coalition of states and not a central entity of its own, to fool the people yet again. They actually created a very different meaning of the word Federal to attach it to the central entity, just as the Romans did with their Republic. That's why Jefferson formed the anti-Federalists. Not because they were anti-alliance of the states, but because the Federal term was being misused by the nationalists to further fool the people.

"What many came to believe through political propaganda was that a great American nation was set up at the Convention even though nation was specifically removed.

Over the years, this lie was told and was taught to such a degree that it became the truth, though it was not.

"Lincoln used this same mantra to try to stop secession by the southern states. He called it an unbreakable Union, just as the Articles of Confederation and Perpetual Union were all those years earlier. That story is for a later time.

"So, it no longer mattered what was put into the Constitution because the power hungry made sure it could be interpreted into whatever meaning they wanted, to grow power and centralize government. People back then called it an energetic central government. People now call it a living Constitution. It doesn't matter which phrase you use, they both mean that the central government can and will do anything it wants and use political smoke screens through partisanship to grow stronger and bigger.

"Our organization, the Absconditus Verum, knows the real truth and this is only one small piece of it."

"Seems like a pretty big piece to me," Emily said.

"You're right, it is. The catch is that almost all this information is already out in the open. The Madison and Yates notes on what happened at the Convention are in the public records. You can go online and read them right now. The challenge is re-educating the people. So long as the government has control of the education system, they can teach whatever they want whether true or untrue. They write history to their own ideology. Some have recently come out with books exposing some of the true information, but they are attacked by the academic sect of the government. That keeps them marginalized. So most of the hidden truth is in plain sight, but not many are seeing it."

Emily yawned. "I know it's late, but I need to ask a few more questions. I thought the Federalist Papers were written by Hamilton. I seem to remember that those papers were meant to show the people of New York that they would retain all state's rights and the central government would only have a few powers."

"You're right. Madison and John Jay also helped write them. Jay was a nationalist and Madison believed what they were writing. Hamilton used the Papers to mislead the people."

"So Hamilton was openly lying about what the new Constitution was about?" Dean asked.

"Yes. Almost everything he wrote in the Federalist Papers was distorted to satisfy the people that no central government power would ever threaten the states and the people's rights. Since everything at the Convention was unpublished and kept secret, save for the Constitution itself, the people would not realize the scope of the corruption until far too late. The only information they were given was the ideological views of the framers themselves. The very ones not willing to show transparency of the process for fear they would be exposed as traitors by ripping down the only government they represented, the Articles of Confederation and Perpetual Union.

"The rather odd thing is Hamilton did slip in some glimpses about central authority that contradicted his own writings. He was able to so confuse a reader as to somehow convince them of something with no basis in truth."

"But Washington trusted Hamilton," Emily said.

"Yes, he did. In fact, Washington believed much of Hamilton's ideas were indeed his own. That was Hamilton's intent and his ability to use others to move his own will. He never realized that Hamilton was using him to rewrite the new Federal Government into an English style monarchy run by the elitists. Or, perhaps he knew but never stopped him. Here's a perfect example. When Hamilton became Treasury Secretary in Washington's cabinet, he changed the meaning of the Constitution almost immediately. He said the Federal Government not only had enumerated powers as in the 10th Amendment, but it had *Implied Powers* that weren't written. His reasoning was that the states retained all the other powers, but the Federal Government was equal to the states and therefore had the same powers as the states, and so he decided the Federal Government could give itself any powers it wanted. This was his convoluted resolution to everything he wanted to do, to twist any meaning he wanted, and to increase central power. He really believed the states had no power or authority so he managed the Federal Government based on his own views.

"When one thinks of representative government, they

believe elected officials are the extension of the people's will, doing only what their constituents want, voting by what the people say. Only through the Jeffersonian decentralized government could the people maintain control of their own government. Now you know why the anti-Federalists no longer exist.

"The Democrats represent big government, entitlement addiction, internal improvements, and huge spending. The Republicans represent Imperial America which is big government, entitlement addiction, huge spending, and forcing the world to be democratic in the name of our defense.

"Right now, our own government spouts the lies every day. The President and Congress say we're a democracy over and over because they want the people to believe that's what our government is. Liberty and freedom are not built into a democracy which is why you need a few elitists running everything. It's to take away liberty and freedoms.

"This *American System* Hamilton created out of thin air, that so many are so proud of now, is the exact opposite of what a Federal Republic is supposed to be. It is central government run amok with total control over the people. Hamilton and his Federalist party established an unlimited accumulation of debt, corruption, protectionist tariff laws, and mercantilism. And most importantly they gave the government the power to take personal property, which at that time hurt the southern states and helped the northern states' industrial machine. These are anti-capitalist positions. Then we have judicial review that was never a power given to the judiciary, it was just totally made up by judges appointed by Washington and confirmed by Congress. Next is corporate welfare, which is taxation of the people to give free money or tax breaks to preferred corporations. Another is internal improvements to again take even more money from the people and send it to lobbyists of the railroads and ports. The Federal Government was never given the power to make internal improvements. They even created politically controlled banks.

"Basically Hamilton wanted a glorious Imperial American Empire to rival England and France, and based on England's model of government above all else. He nearly accomplished this feat in the four years he was running the Treasury Department. His cronies and followers over the years went even further and now we live in Hamilton's Republic. It's not a Republic at all but everything we fought against in the Revolution…an indivisible *Nation State.* Centralized Government out of control, destroying everything most Americans hold dear."

Emily started shaking her head. "I just can't believe Hamilton, considered an American icon and father of our great capitalistic system was at the root of all this manipulation. I always believed the Founders were men of great honor and integrity and beyond reproach. How is it they were not? And what type of people were they?"

"Ah, now you're starting to understand. You might think they were the representatives of the people. A few were, but only a very few. You see having government decentralized and kept within the states and communities allowed the people to control local politicians, their own government. To have those selected to protect and vote for them as they would themselves.

"Massive Federal Government is the opposite. It will almost always attract the very ones we don't want in government, the power' hungry elitists who want to rule on high. The basic characteristics of a politician now must be the willingness to spend other people's money, use corruption, deceit, make back room deals, pay off lobbying interests, and have no remorse at doing any of it. The very people we don't want to represent us are the very people we elect.

"Every day regular people, those who are supposed to get elected to represent their communities, can't get elected. The two-party system prevents it. The two parties have all the power, all the money, and all the partisanship to keep the people at each other's throats."

"And the Founders at the Constitutional Convention?" Dean asked.

"Most had economic interests in a centralized government. Eighty percent were public creditors who loaned money, 33% were land speculators, 20% had shipping interests, manufacturing, and most were lawyers. The most important group, the ones protecting the producers which represented over 80% of the people, being farmers at the time, whether a small farm or large were not even selected to be representatives. So the deck was heavily stacked in the favor of the National Elitists and northern state mercantile interests from the start, and they wasted no time in consolidating power and removing the voice of the very ones they were there to represent; the people."

Emily and Dean both sat in deep thought by all they were told.

◊ ◊ ◊

Brooks needed them to know, to know the hidden truth. "This is our purpose. This is why the Absconditus Verum Society was formed. All because of what happened in 1787 through 1800. In fact, we believe there are even more secret documents that show conclusive evidence of exactly what happened. Two other Verum teams are now looking for those in two other locations. We hope to hear from them soon.

"Now you must understand that our Verum Society has the utmost respect for many of the Founding Fathers and everyone who, over the years, has risen to protect our freedoms; our very lives. We respect the rule of law, the rights of individuals, and the rights of free choice. We are patriots like most Americans. The difference is we are not nationalists. Most pledge allegiance to the flag of an indivisible *Nation State* every day.

"We are not on a crusade. We're not some ideological movement bent on forcing others to our will. In fact we're the opposite. We believe that each and every person has innate freedom and liberty. This sets us apart from the left and the right, from the liberals and the conservatives. This sets us apart from the Democrats and the Republicans, from the Tea Party and the Libertarians, even from the Occupy Wall Street groups.

"It even sets us apart from the Constitutionalists and the Socialists. We stand apart from all those current and past ideologies, save one. Our message is simple. Keep government close to the people where they can run it themselves, and every single persons is equally endowed with Liberty and Justice. This is the fundamental form of government we were supposed to have, and indeed did have for over one hundred years until the Constitutional Convention.

"Now we have the opposite. A colossus bloated Federal Government who every day strips the people of the Liberty. And it employs over two million! Does it take two million people to run the Federal Government and the states?"

Brooks could see Emily and Dean now understood more and just how important this mission was.

Brooks stopped. He knew this was a lot of information for any of them to process, it would take time. And one thing made him uneasy during the night. Johnson had not said a word. He quietly listened to the story. He never seemed surprised or upset by anything they were talking about.

*Was I wrong about Johnson?...*was all he could think about the rest of the evening.

Finally, they all got up and retired to bed. It was now nearly three in the morning, and daylight would soon be upon them. Needless to say, no one got much sleep.

Chapter 23

June 1788 - Federal Hall, New York City – U.S. Capital

"Mr. President. I have not been able to glean much information concerning the Society of Praetorians," Hamilton said.

"That's very troubling Alexander. I must tell you how concerned I am regarding their intentions. They are aligning themselves with many of our positions. While our intentions are pure, theirs is the opposite. Soon I will have to explain why we are governing as they might, but without the tyrannical dictatorship they would impose," responded Washington. "Have you been able to find out where they meet?"

"No Sir, not yet, and I fear they are gathering many of our wealthy to their cause."

Washington shook his head. "Then we must do what we can to connect the people to our Federal Government. We must entice the wealthy to join us. This will undo the Praetorians' plans."

"Very good Sir. Once the Praetorians realize there are so many to contend with, they'll think twice about making a move."

"I want you to strengthen our relationship with the people."

"Leave it to me Sir."

Washington thought for a moment. "Alexander. I will need your close help in forming and protecting our new government based on the Constitution. Now, I know your position on setting up a monarchy, but you must forego that for the sake of the people. Will you help me?"

"Nothing would give me greater pleasure than to give the people the government they truly deserve. I shall forgo my earlier positions for the sake of them."

"This will be hard. Jefferson and many others are adamant about keeping government decentralized and closer to the people. We must show them that the new Federal Government can and will be just as effective, if not more so. While local government is important, we must also have enough strength here. We cannot protect the people unless they have faith in us.

"Each member of Congress has taken an oath to uphold the Constitution. They are to be the people's representatives, nothing more. Anyone looking first at their own ambitions must be dealt with aggressively. I will not have usurpation of power on my watch. You must be my eyes and ears. My trust is in your loyalty and honor."

"And I shall fulfill that duty…but in order to do so, I will need some latitude to create the proper structure. You do realize we will need to have at least the same authority as the states and more on foreign affairs. Will you allow me to propose measures to Congress that shall protect the people?"

"That is what I want you to do."

"Then we shall lead them into a new prosperity like none before."

January 1790 - New York City

Jefferson was now the Secretary of State and Madison was the leader in the House of Representatives. They were having breakfast.

Madison was leafing through some papers. "Hamilton submitted his report today. I have a copy for you."

"Any surprises?" Jefferson asked.

"Yes. He went far beyond his authority. The Federal Government debt from the war is included as we knew, but he also included all the state war debt and all foreign debt."

"We can't do that," Jefferson said. "We shall go bankrupt like every foreign power that has set this system up. The only way to cover all this debt is through high taxation of the people. You know that, and Washington must know. Why is Hamilton in charge? He will do everything in his power to duplicate the Imperial English model of government."

"It comes to some eighty million plus all told," responded Madison with a look of depression on his face.

"I understand buying back the war bonds, many veterans bought those to help in addition to their sacrifice in blood. They do deserve a fair compensation, but all this other debt? It is more than we can possibly handle. "How will the central government cover the money for the bonds?"

"You know how. Hamilton will simply print more securities and bonds. It's fiat money, not backed by anything other than the promise of central government to pay interest. We have no money or specie to make money yet. This is just like the Continentals that were printed before and during the war, worthless."

"Then how the hell can you run a government on debt and printing worthless money to pay the debt?" Jefferson asked.

"That is his scheme. As long as he offers interest on the loans, it keeps the wealthy invested. They bring in a $100 bond and he gives them a new one for $106, essentially adding the interest to the new bonds so it seems like they are more valuable. No real gold or silver changes hands to renew securities, although many of the wealthy are now buying bonds with gold and silver. It seems the Treasury is starting to hoard specie.

"Then the bondholder can use the bonds as collateral and make purchases. So a retailer gets nothing for his goods except the promise to get paid at a later date. So that just exacerbates the problem."

"This is the bank trickery used in Europe over the last thousand years. Create value out of nothing, just print money and claim it has value. As long as people exchange it for goods, then it has perceived value. But when you bring it to the bank for specie, either gold or silver, the bank doesn't have any, or holds only one-tenth the amount needed to pay off all note holders. That is why a run on the banks destroys the economy. Everyone realizes the money they are holding has no value," Jefferson was frustrated.

He wasn't finished as he read more of the report. "Why is Virginia included as owing one full share of all state debt? Virginia has already paid off a large portion of its debt. Now we must pay part of Massachusetts? In fact, the northern states owe much more than the southern. Now they look to pawn debt off on us. This is the epitome of what is wrong with centralizing government. The will of the people is crushed. Now our young country is in the hands of the aristocrats." fumed Jefferson.

"I don't understand why Washington would allow this. He knows this won't work," Madison said.

"It is because he has put too much faith in allowing Hamilton to structure everything and, even worse, to do it all behind closed doors without the consent of the people." Jefferson was angry. "Well. James, you wanted to strengthen central government. I hope you're happy, your Federalist Papers," Jefferson gave him a look.

"You know my intentions were for the betterment of the states. Now I look like an idiot. I didn't know Hamilton was playing us when I agreed to help write them. You know I was against the final version of the Constitution. It made a mockery of all who acted in honor on behalf of their states."

"Then why did you push for its ratification? If Virginia rejected it, we would not be under the whip of tyranny."

"I feared Federal Government would raise an army and invade Virginia."

Jefferson looked at him incredulously. "They don't have the power to raise an army and invade our Country of Virginia. Washington is a Virginian. He would never allow it."

"It does not matter what he wants, or what we want. Hamilton's Federalists are the majority in both Houses of Congress. It will be all I can do to hold this legislation off."

"So how will this affect the states?"

"They will turn over all outstanding debts to the Federal Government, who, in turn, will pay each state interest each month while changing the debt over to new centralized securities and bonds. The problem is, now the states will become dependent on the central government for up to 20% of their own budgets."

"Of course they will. That's Hamilton's plan. Make the states dependent on his Treasury Department. This will greatly diminish a state's ability to balance the state budgets. It does lower the tax burden on the citizens for the moment. A lot of the state debt was borrowed from their own citizens, but they too will now deal directly with central government. Hamilton's new Centralized Tax and Tariff schemes simply shift the taxes from going to each state to going to him.

"And having the Capital up here in New York is totally unacceptable. The south refuses to accept this location. Unless Hamilton and Washington agree to a more southern location, the south will indeed secede. Then let them try and run a Federal Government without money coming from the south. They can't compete with European imports as it is. New England will simply become a satellite of the English Empire and we will be forever threatened from the northern states."

Madison knew where this was going. "This is what keeps us attached to the northern states and central government. The northern states know they now have the power to make the south subservient. The choice is united and under the whip of tyranny from the north, or divided with England on our doorstep. The chasm between north and south is already great. Hamilton is making sure it continues to grow. They need our agrarian southern economy and we need goods made from the north and imports. We are tied together for now because we need each other. However, I fear it will not be long before this chasm opens so wide that it will indeed undo the states united."

"It has already started. The north owns Congress and is forcing the south to pay an unfair additional amount due by the states. The damage has already been done. I warned you about central government control. Our course now is to minimize the damage."

Madison knew he had made a great error in trusting the nationalists at the Convention and compounded it by working with Hamilton and John Jay on the Federalist Papers to have the states ratify. All he had warned against in his writings was now ready to swallow everything they had worked for. Everything the people had demanded of their delegates, their representatives, that they be held accountable for their actions.

The battle for the Republic had begun.

Madison had to do something. "I will do all I can to block this legislation from ever seeing the light of day, but I fear in the end it will get passed.

"Hamilton has moved away from the central government that was set up at the Convention. He has already built the Treasury into the largest and most important department in the entire Federal Government. He is building an army of tax agents to be in every corner of every state. He means to bind the people directly to central government and obliterate the states completely. If he pulls this off, most of the rich will be holding Federal Government bonds instead of state bonds. They will be more interested in the success of the central government than that of their own states."

"It says here that he means to pay the full 100% value on the war bonds. This is the one item I agree with," responded Jefferson as he was looking over the report.

Madison knew it was time to tell Jefferson everything. "I have already found out his intentions. Since he submitted this report, I have seen many in Congress and business people associated with Hamilton already sending out their minions, scouring the countryside looking to buy bonds from unsuspecting veterans. Right now they are only worth 10 to 25% of face value. If this legislation goes through, people now owning bonds will get scammed out of full face value."

"What can you do?" Jefferson asked with a tone of resignation.

"I can offer legislation to compensate the original bond holders at full face value in the House. Then the government will be forced to pay double for the same bonds. It seems I must try and stop everything Hamilton is setting up. It is a monarchy just like England's. Even though his ideas of government were rejected at the Convention, and the Constitution was set up to protect the states and the people, he is doing the opposite."

"How does he plan on covering all the foreign debt?"

"He'll issue new securities with a very attractive interest rate. Basically, foreign countries will receive American central government securities to pay off the debt. Foreign countries can also buy bonds."

"So our Federal Government will be funded by foreign countries?"

"Yes, at least part of it."

"What happened to our independence?" Jefferson asked, understanding how much damage Hamilton was creating.

"He's killing it as fast as he can. Can you talk to Washington? You must still have some influence with him."

"I have tried already. He sees Hamilton's vision and our decentralized vision and he leans towards Hamilton. So far, he has rejected every argument I make to stay Hamilton's plan. You must keep blocking legislation submitted by his

Congressional minions. Meanwhile, our new Anti-Administration Party, must grow its ranks in the states. It's now our only way to resist our fall into an Imperial English clone."

"How could this have gone so wrong so fast?" Madison asked.

Jefferson thought for a moment, understanding Madison was not expecting an answer. "Tell me what you know of the Society of Praetorians."

"Mostly that they mean to take our central government once it is established, through a coup, I would think."

"Then tell me what the difference is between Hamilton and the Praetorians?"

"What are you getting at? Are you suggesting Hamilton might be affiliated with them?"

"Well, think about it. They have basically the same plans for central government. He suddenly has an army of tax agents ready to enforce any new laws regarding Federal taxation." He couldn't believe what he was saying. "This can't be happening. He fought against this very thing in the war. Why would he now try to impose the same thing?"

"I don't think he has the same ambitions as the Praetorians. He wishes to strengthen our resolve, not destroy it."

"Perhaps," Jefferson answered.

◊ ◊ ◊

Hamilton was visiting with Congress in New York City on the day of the vote. Once it was approved he met down the street with several business associates and Congressmen who had just voted for the measure.

"I suggest any of you who have not already bought up bonds, to do so immediately. Make your way to all corners of the country. If you can beat the news of the vote, you can buy all you can. I would suggest no more than ten percent face value.

"Oh, and I know you will all thank me for this opportunity. Not so much in monetary reward, but your loyalty to vote for all my recommendations. Remember, the more we are tied to the government, the harder it will be for the Praetorians to interfere." He paused and looked at them. "Well, that's it. Be on your way while you can still stay ahead of the news."

July 1790 - Eastern Long Island, New York

One month after the Bond scheme was struck; Church met with the Praetorian leaders in their stronghold. "I have sent as many of our coalition as possible to buy bonds. This free money shall improve our ability to leverage our positions in the government."

"And what of the President?" the Praetor asked.

"He's supporting Hamilton's positions on everything. He has become quite an asset for us, though it seems to others that the Praetorians are still looking to take hold of central government." Church replied.

The Praetor smiled. "Deceptions can be very useful, but we must be careful. Guard your tongue. Now, since Hamilton is doing all the leg work for us, our allies in Congress can help to make it all happen.

"We need to gain access into all the state governments. I want all those affirmation documents recovered and brought to me. While those exist, our power in Federal Government will be forever challenged by the states.

"Now, once we are strong enough to withstand any resistance from the people, then I shall be declared King."

"But what of General Washington?" Robert Morris asked.

Church watched as the Praetor gave Morris a cold stare. "You idiot. I will not actually become King. I have no aspirations for such a position. Look at King George. His political influence becomes less by the day…I shall always be behind the scenes, where the real power is.

"Washington is the puppet and he needs a good puppet master." he stopped and looked at Church.

"Church, I need you to accompany Lord North back to England to see the King. I no longer trust some of the couriers. You both must see him and coordinate our efforts. Bring me back support and aid from him."

Lord North stepped forward into the light next to Hamilton's chair.

"Yes Praetor," Church answered. He always hated knowing North was lurking about.

"I have a coach waiting Church," North said.

"As you wish Mr. North." Church was fuming inside. He'd

lost his favorite son status with the Praetor.

The Praetor cut in. "North, please go to the coach. Gentlemen, you have your orders. I want those documents. Church and I have some discussions which do not concern the rest of you so leave us."

"Yes Sir." North did as he asked and left for the coach.

The others left as well.

"Now, Church. I have another task that you must carry out before you see the King. I do not want any of North's allies interrupting this mission. Here are you orders." He handed him a satchel with several items in it. Do not open these orders until you are docked in London. Now go."

"Yes Praetor." Church turn and left with a hint of a smile on his face. He had a feeling he would enjoy this trip with North.

Yet he was starting to feel uneasy about the mission the Praetorians were implementing. He was starting to doubt his involvement. *Is being a* Praetorian *worth it? I've not been paid for any of this.* He started questioning his role between the Praetorian's goals and his own future.

Church gathered his things and heading toward the coach where North was waiting. Soon they boarded a ship headed for London.

Chapter 24

<u>*2018 - Staunton, Virginia*</u>

Brooks was up early and the first of the guests to head downstairs at the Staunton farmhouse. He decided not to share his conversation with Trumbull just yet.

Ms. Sanders had breakfast ready for the new arrivals.

"Let's go everyone!" he shouted up the stairwell. Ms. Sanders handed him a cup of coffee in the front hall. He went outside on the porch. The porch swing looked inviting enough to sit. It was a bright crisp Tuesday morning. He was in deep thought about the mission.

Do we bring Emily? Is Johnson really on our side? Can I trust Trumbull? What happens if the Praetorians know what we're doing?

He continued bouncing thoughts about until he heard the rest of his team coming down the stairs.

He returned inside as everyone was now in the dining room. The maps and notes of Richard Yates had been delivered early that morning.

Nothing beat a farm fresh breakfast. They studied what they could until everyone was finished and readied to leave. Ms. Sanders supplied them with a few tools they thought they might need for the trip.

They were about forty-five minutes from Monticello.

"Tell us more about what happened back then" Dean asked, as they started out the driveway.

Emily eagerly nodded.

Johnson seemed indifferent about it.

"What happened after the bonds vote?" Emily asked.

Brooks looked at Johnson, who was driving. He gave Brooks a shrug.

"Well, the race was on. Congress had approved the bond measure. The bonds were nearly worthless before the vote due to the failed inflationary tactics of the Continental Congress. The currency called continentals were printed by the central government and were worthless during the war due to the inability of the government to back them with any specie-gold or silver. Ever hear the phrase 'as worthless as a continental?'

"Now, however, the bonds could be exchanged for new ones at face value. Congressmen were now in a competition with their own passage of the law, as were all of Hamilton's coalition and the Praetorians. If they were to outrun the news, which many of them could, they'd buy the bonds from unsuspecting veterans who still thought they had no value. Ten to 25% of face value was more than they ever expected, so they gladly sold them to any who offered to buy, especially since most of them were poor, having given everything to the cause.

"And buy they did. Many of the corrupt made millions once the government paid them off. Congressman Robert Wilson, part of Hamilton's coalition, pocketed some eighteen million. Today that would be over three hundred million, preying on the poor. Oh, and Governor Clinton also had the advance notice and gained tremendous wealth with the insider information. This was the payback to Clinton from the state ratifying convention."

"That's just horrible!" Emily said. "Hamilton was pure evil."

"Most think it was just his maniacal ego to make his mark in history in a blaze of glory. I do think he was in competition with King George. Each knew more than most about the other.

"It seems Aaron Burr found out about their allegiance as well as an affair Hamilton had. These became some of the reasons for the dual they had later on, though no documents found yet support this theory. Those papers are also part of what we're searching for."

Dean shook his head as in disbelief. Brooks smiled at him. "Oh, this was one of his more subtle actions. Once his coalition was wealthy beyond measure, he started rewriting the structure of the Constitution and the central government."

"But why didn't Washington stop him?" Emily asked. "Most think Washington was the greatest man that ever lived."

"Because while Washington was well versed in war, he was not in the political arena. He truly believed Hamilton was doing what he asked of him, protecting the people. He also was concerned about his own social standing. It seemed no matter how well the people admired him; he was always looking for more ways to improve himself to the socialites of the day."

"This is just incredible," Dean said softly.

"Perhaps that's enough for now," Brooks said.

"Are you kidding?" responded Dean. "I can't wait for more."

"But I just don't understand how Congress was allowing Hamilton to do these things without consequences," Emily said.

"You would think that Emily, and some did try. Madison who was leading the House of Representative at the time put forth a measure to have the Federal Government pay all the previous bond holders full value to compensate those who were preyed upon."

"So what happened?" she asked.

"The measure was soundly defeated. You must understand that what you see today in the Federal Government was also happening back then, even more so. His measure never stood a chance because there were twenty-nine bond holders in the Congress out of a total of sixty-five members. They didn't want their names coming to light as thieves and con artists.

"This also was part of a growing rift between north and south. Many of the original bond holders were from the south and most who had advanced knowledge of the scam were northerners."

"So Madison had now moved to Jefferson's position of decentralization?" Dean asked.

"Yes, though the two of them shared in this debacle. Madison had initially defeated the Debt Assumption Report, which was the central government assuming all the state war debts and paying 100% face value on the bonds.

"It was some time later that Jefferson saw Hamilton walking down the street in New York City. They had rooms nearby as that was where Congress was stationed. Madison also was staying there.

"When Jefferson saw Hamilton's depressive state, he invited him to dinner. The three met and another back room deal was struck. Hamilton's measure would pass the Congress with Madison's support, but only if Hamilton agreed to move the Federal Government capital down to the Potomac River so the Virginians could keep a watchful eye on it. The other provision was to relieve Virginia of a large portion of debt that was assigned to them. They all agreed to this. It was known as the Dinner Table Compromise.

"They also had the backing of Washington to do this. He had a stake in it as well. The land chosen on the Potomac was near land that Washington owned, thereby greatly increasing Washington's land values and essentially guaranteeing the stability of his financial future."

"Where were the people during all this?" Emily asked.

"Oh the people were there. They listened to the propaganda put out by the local medias, who were in league with the politicians. You must remember, back then, a printing press was a powerful tool. The politicians owned or were allied with the Press, so they could print their ideology and use it as fact or news."

Emily interjected. "That sounds awfully familiar. Isn't that what's going on today?"

"It's exactly what is going on today, though more indirectly." Brooks responded. "And the people supported the measure, even though this one compromise was a larger rift between the north and south. The northern mercantile interests, bankers, and lawyers would lose some of their stronghold having the capital move south and even worse, move to an area donated by two slave states. The southerners were angered because the capital had been set up in New York City instead of Philadelphia as they thought it would after the war.

"The state debt deal of full portions was totally unfair. Most of the states in the south had paid down large portions of their debt, though I believe Georgia had not, while many of the northern states had not. It was a clear case of leverage and power by the north. The measure did pass though, but the key to how this rift was unfolding was in the vote. The northern states voted almost unanimously for the measure, while only six southerners voted in favor. And that was because Madison convinced them to switch their votes. The measure passed by four votes."

"Okay, so I don't understand something," Dean said. "I

thought the politicians elected to represent their constituents actually did so once they went to Congress."

"That was the theory," Brooks answered. "In reality, once they did get to Congress, they formed powerful coalitions to further their own careers and wealth.

"Samuel Adams said 'Nothing is more essential to the establishment of manners in a state than that all persons employed in places of power and trust must be men of unexceptionable characters."

"You mean the same Sam Adams that wanted to execute war veterans resisting unfair taxation in Massachusetts?" Dean asked.

"The very one. Sounds like a contradiction in terms doesn't it? Many of the Founders used opposite views depending on who their audience was. Later on, Lincoln became the master at catering to the locals and the press in his speeches.

"Anyway, the exact opposite happened and it's still going on today. The corruption we all see started at the very beginning and that's why most politicians in office now feel they have every right to usurp power and abuse the people.

"They also know how to play the game of politics. Offer the people enough to buy their votes and once elected, use every means possible to keep getting re-elected.

"Now this is the most important part of Hamilton's scheme. The plan created an army of Treasury agents across the country that would be tied to the Federal Government instead of any individual state. Assuming the debts of the states would also tie the financial elites in those states to the central government and less so to state governments, thereby reducing the risk of secession. Hamilton's scheme was called the First Report of the Public Credit."

Emily and Dean sat silent in the car for the rest of the ride. This was some story they were hearing. Neither of them had known the extent of debauchery that was part of American political history.

They arrived before eight in the morning. The building wasn't open to the public yet. In fact, no one was there.

They decided to walk the grounds to familiarize themselves with the layout. Being that it was a large expanse of property, they kept to the top of the hill where the main house was located. While the property itself was steep in some places, there were several small roads and paths around the hill allowing for a gradual incline on the estate. Apart for the main house were several small buildings, some from the time that Jefferson had lived there being refurbished. Houses for the servants and slaves, a smoke house, and a small barn. The visitors center was about halfway down the hill. Most of the grounds looked as they always had.

Once the house was open, the team entered. Johnson spoke with the curator and soon there was a closed sign down the road at the main entrance. No specific reason, just closed. They also posted the closure on their website.

"We have the entire day to look around. I suggest we do so in pairs in the hope that someone will spot something. As far as the curators know, this is a security matter. With all that's happened, it wasn't a hard sell. They're not to speak with anyone unless they go through me," Johnson instructed in an authoritative tone.

Brooks was still uncertain about him, but it was too late now, so he broke out the maps and pictures they had gotten in Staunton. Emily joined Brooks, and Dean teamed with Johnson. They spent the entire morning going over the whole house, including the lower rooms and hallway areas below ground. They found nothing.

"Well, until we hear from James, we have nothing more to go on. This place has been searched for decades with no findings of any kind," Brooks was frustrated and still a little wary of Johnson, though he hid it well.

Brooks looked at the Great Clock over the front entrance and wondered how long it would be before they got a call from Trumbull. They took out a lunch that had been prepared for them by the good Ms. Sanders and ate in the backyard among the many plantings that graced the circling walkway. The day stayed chilly and grew damp as the hours passed.

They searched all afternoon with no luck. It was now almost seven in the evening.

"I think we need to leave. This is just a waste of time. Until we hear from James again, we can't hope to find anything of importance," Brooks said.

They locked up and headed back to the farm. Johnson drove with Brooks in front. Emily and Dean were in the back.

On the way Brooks decided to let them know who to expect. "The man who saved James Yates as well as the children of James and Emily will be meeting us at the farm. Hopefully he has information that will help us solve this riddle at Monticello. Just so you know…he's a Praetorian."

"What?" Dean asked incredulously. "Since when are we working with any Praetorians?"

"I know, I know. All I can say is we have to trust him. He has done too much for us to ignore. And I don't want any escalation in this. Is it understood?" Brooks looked directly at Dean.

"Agreed." Johnson added for emphasis.

They drove in silence the rest of the way back to the farm.

◊ ◊ ◊

There was someone else waiting for them inside.

"Mr. Brooks, there's a man here to see you. He's in the sitting room. He gave me a detailed account of the Verum Society and your mission before I allowed him in," Ms. Sanders told them as they approached the front door of the ranch.

Brooks walked into the sitting room, followed by the others. There was indeed a man in one of the high back chairs. He couldn't see him upon entering as the chair was facing away from them, towards the fireplace, which had a nice fire going.

"Please, everyone, sit," he said as Brooks gave him a hard look.

"Trumbull." Brooks noticed a suitcase and duffle bag on the floor next to Trumbull's chair.

"Yes. I told you I'd get here. I thought it best not to meet you at Monticello for security reasons. Anyway, we can't do anything until tomorrow.

◊ ◊ ◊

Timothy Dean was dumbstruck. He stood as if lightning just hit him.

Emily, who was following him into the room bumped into him. "I'm sorry Mr. Dean."

Dean was motionless, staring at Trumbull. *It's not possible! It can't be him! I don't understand. What are we doing?*

"Perhaps introductions are in order?" Trumbull asked.

Dean had to shake his head to clear his thoughts. He still didn't speak.

No one else spoke up.

"Ah, then allow me. Mrs. Yates, I'm William Trumbull. I was an associate of your father-in-law for some time before he was killed. I saved your girls and helped your husband get out of the hospital."

Dean watched as Emily stared at him and then softened her tone. She went over and gave him a big hug. "Thank you for helping Thomas. Is he alright?"

"Yes. Sheriff Peter Lucas has taken him to a Verum Society safe house. He's recovering nicely. I believe your girls are also safe at the same house, though I didn't go with them."

"Oh, thank you, Mr. Trumbull. Thank you."

Dean watched Trumbull, whose body language showed he was uneasy about being hugged. What was happening before him was surreal.

"It's okay." The assassin managed to get out.

Emily went and sat down in one of the chairs.

Trumbull looked directly at Dean. "This must be Agent Dean. My God, Brooks, have we gotten this old? He's no more than a kid. Twenty-three I would say?"

Dean didn't answer, giving Johnson a grave, conflicted look.

"It's okay, Tim. Mr. Trumbull is working with us now." Johnson responded to his look.

Brooks looked shocked by this comment. "What do you mean?"

"Joe, I'm Trumbull's contact. I was the one he sent ahead to meet you. I know you were worried about my involvement. Well, I'm a Verum Society member too. We never had reason to share this until now. I'm sorry for waiting to let you know. I had no choice."

Brooks glared at Johnson for a moment, then turned his attention to Dean. "Why didn't you just tell me?"

"Because up until now, it was best we all had limited exposure," Johnson interjected.

"Dinner is ready, everyone," Ms. Sanders said from the dining room.

"Well, I for one am looking forward to a nice home-cooked meal," Trumbull responded in an upbeat tone.

Dean watched as the others went into the dining room, then followed. It was a table for six with two on each side and one on each end. Trumbull sat at one end. Next to him was Johnson, then Emily. Brooks sat opposite Johnson, leaving the chair opposite Emily empty as was the one on the other end of the table. He decided to sit in the open chair opposite Trumbull. He watched as Emily lined up her utensils.

"Are you joining us Ms. Sanders?" Brooks queried.

"No Mr. Brooks, I've already eaten." was all they heard from the kitchen.

They passed the dishes of food on the table to each other and once they started eating, the conversation began to flow. Dean was slow and deliberate in everything he did, watching Trumbull the entire time.

Brooks started. "So, Trumbull, what have you been doing all these years?"

"Mostly disrupting my old organization. They're quite angry with me," he said with an arrogant smile as he looked at Emily. "Please, my regrets that you've fallen in with a professional hit man."

She didn't return the smile.

"Anyway, I've been living all over the world. I'm very resourceful, you know. The Praetorians have been so kind to fund my travels. Their agents have access to a lot of things, most of all money."

"Are they looking for you now?" Brooks asked.

"Oh, yes. But they just don't seem to have very good help these days, except for one. Victor Shaw," he smiled, looking rather proud of himself. "And besides, they don't even know it's me. They think I'm dead, just as you did. That's why they started killing members of your organization. They think one, or more, of your members have been killing off their agents. In fact, they're meeting right now in some secret hideaway trying to figure this all out."

Dean cut in. "You seem to know an awful lot about everything." His voice was curt. An inner anger just below the surface was evident. A man in deep distress.

Trumbull gave him a smile and laughed. "You're much too young to have such a sour look on your face. This has been my full-time job for the last twenty-seven years. I certainly hope I've gotten well versed." He paused. "Anyway, I have information from James that will help us tomorrow."

"And what's that?" Brooks asked.

"Wednesday is Saturday and ten is eight."

"That's nothing new. I already have that."

"Yes, but do you know what it pertains to?"

Brooks didn't answer.

"Well…I didn't think you knew. I'll tell you when we get to Monticello. No sense spilling the beans until the last moment." He looked at Emily. "Less chance of prying eyes and ears," he said softly and motioned to the kitchen.

"Anyway, I have a present that will help the Verum." He reached into his pocket and pulled out a bag. He opened it and poured at least fifty small gold eagle pins onto the table.

"Good God!" Emily exclaimed. "I saw one of these when Pete took it off of Agent Hill's collar!"

"Those were made by the first Praetor, the King's Pawn, and given to his Society of Praetorians members," Brooks explained. He looked at Trumbull. "You've been busy."

"Yes, the Society gives them to all their members during their sworn allegiance and as a way to identify themselves to other members. These are over two hundred years old."

"What did you mean when you said the King's Pawn?" Emily asked.

"King George of England funded the start of the Praetorian Society after the Revolutionary War." Brooks answered. "He had hoped they would undermine the new American Republic enough to retake the colonies."

They were just finishing dinner and were about ready to move to the sitting room.

Dean simply couldn't take it anymore as his emotions sprang to the forefront. He stood up abruptly and pulled his gun, pointing it directly at Trumbull.

Emily gasped, holding her hands to her face.

"Tim…Agent Dean," Johnson countered with a firm voice. "Holster your weapon."

Dean stood motionless, eying Trumbull.

"Mr. Dean, What's going on?" Brooks asked in a commanding tone as they were all now standing. He corralled Emily with his left arm and slowly pulled her behind him.

There was a brief moment of silence before Dean spoke. "Sir, he killed my parents, he shot them, in our house. He knocked on the door and they thought he was with us, the Verum Society. He came in and they talked. He was trying to get information from them…"

"Tim," Johnson looked at Dean as his superior. "Tim, you need to put the gun away."

"He killed them." Dean responded in an angry voice. "They didn't know anything. He shot them, right there, right in our living room. I know…I know because I was there. I…I was home…upstairs. He didn't know I was there. They didn't give him information so he shot them. They were defenseless."

◊ ◊ ◊

Trumbull stood motionless. Brooks could see he had a gun in his right hand, just below the tabletop, but visible from his position.

He focused on the young man. "Agent Dean. Look at me," he insisted.

Dean continued to stare at Trumbull, ignoring Brooks.

"Agent Dean." Brooks was a bit louder and more forceful as one of authority. "Tim!"

Dean finally broke his stare and looked at Brooks.

"Give your gun to Johnson." Brooks motioned towards his mentor.

Agent Johnson moved slowly towards him and held out his hand. Dean resisted, still pointing the gun at Trumbull.

Brooks watched as Johnson got close enough to put his hand on the weapon. The two made eye contact.

"No Tim. Not like this." Johnson sounded like a father figure now, trying to convince a son to stop what he was about to do.

Dean relented and let Johnson take his gun. His head was hung as he looked down.

Emily let out a sigh, and Ms. Sanders did as well. She had been peeking from the kitchen doorway.

"Tim. I know this is hard, but that was ten years ago. Things are different now. Trumbull is here to help. We need him. You need to trust me on this," Johnson did his best to sound convincing.

Dean glanced up at Johnson and nodded.

"Okay." he said quietly. His body language was saying the opposite. His faced showed pain.

"We all need some rest. Agent Dean, we need to know this won't happen again." Brooks directed.

Dean nodded but Brooks could tell this wasn't over.

Brooks scanned the room. First at Johnson, then Trumbull, and Ms. Sanders, who had quietly entered the room. He turned and looked at Emily, who was behind him the entire time. Both women were clearly shaken by the encounter.

It was a moment of silence.

"Let's get some sleep." Brooks finally said.

Brooks nodded to Johnson, who escorted Dean upstairs. There was no need to scold him even though he had resisted their commands. Reacting to his parent's killer in a negative way was certainly expected so Brooks decided to show some empathy.

He went out into the entry and watched them go up the stairs and around the corner of the hallway out of sight.

"I'll meet you at Monticello tomorrow," Trumbull said as he walked by Brooks heading towards the sitting room. "It's the only way to diffuse this for now. Better if I'm not here." He gathered his belongings and hurried out the door.

◊ ◊ ◊

Trumbull left soon after dinner and was to meet Brooks, Johnson, Dean, and Emily the next morning at Monticello.

Keeping his distance was important to remove the emotional escalations of Dean. He had killed his parents and was paying his penance the best way he could, by trying to reveal the truth and destroy his old employers any way possible.

Killing Dean's parents was probably the first time he actually felt some remorse about harming innocent people. The guilt had increased as the years went on. He continued killing, but had finally decided to quit. It was a hollow existence with no challenge. That was when he met with the Praetorian Council.

◊ ◊ ◊

Brooks watched from the front door as Trumbull drove down the driveway. Then he returned to the dining room. "Are you two alright?"

The women nodded, though he could see they were both still shaken by the events.

"Trumbull's gone so let's all calm down. We need to get some rest. Tomorrow is a big day. Ms. Sanders, is there a spot downstairs Emily could sleep?"

"Why, yes. I have a small room off the master bedroom. She'll be safe there."

Brooks nodded to Ms. Sanders who hurried off to setup the room. He stood in front of Emily. "Are you ok?"

"I'll be fine. Let's get this done so I can get back home." Her voice was calm and determined.

Brooks was surprised at her resolve as she headed toward the master suite.

As he headed upstairs, he thought. *This is a powder keg, just waiting to explode tomorrow.*

Chapter 25

May 2018 - Southern France

A Secret Meeting in Southern France.

The Praetor's lieutenant, The Senator on the Council, was in no mood to argue. He was quite angry at everyone in the room.

"So gentlemen. Have you been able to find anything out?"

One of the men in the front row responded. "Sir, we interrogated quite a few of the Absconditus Verum members, but they don't seem to know much about the inner workings of their own Verum Society. Most are just average people. Several were killed as they fled from our organization affiliates all over the world. We did kill dozens of them as of a few moments ago."

"Yes, and with those went any chance of finding out more. Isn't it clear to you by now that only a few leaders have the real information we're looking for? These other killings have only brought more attention to us. It seems the Praetorians simply cannot get competent help." He paused "How is it you so-called leaders, from every single western country, are no closer to the truth than we were twenty-five-years ago? And why is it we have lost ten Praetorian agents over the past week in addition to the forty from the last several years?"

The men in attendance were from over fifty western countries. They were all seated in an amphitheater. It was a small venue and the Senator was on the stage sitting in a comfortable chair. Next to him; their top assassin Victor Shaw.

He wore a hooded cloak concealing most of his scarred face, now half covered with a metal mask thanks to that fateful day in the parking garage.

There were over one hundred seats in the gallery gradually rising from row to row so all could have a clear view. Sconces on the walls produced the lighting.

Another member from the front row spoke. "Sir, we have total control of all the western economic systems as well as all the monetary exchanges. Does it really matter what this other organization has?"

"Well, now, let me think," he said in a dark brooding voice. "I believe we've heard this argument before. Yes, and the last time we heard it was when we made some changes within the Society. This is an old story indeed."

He glanced up at Shaw. A lightning draw and the last member to speak was shot through the head. The bullet ricocheting off a member's seat behind him.

The others gasped as both leaders watched them writhe.

"Now, are there any volunteers who want to rise up to a command level?" Shaw quipped. "We just now have an opening," he finished with a devilish smirk.

The Senator smiled as he looked at the rest of the room. "This is what happens when you fail to do your jobs. The rest of you can take this as a warning. Perhaps it is the motivation you need."

The amount of fear in the room was staggering.

"So, do I have any volunteers to step forward and lead?"

No one answered.

"Perhaps the rest of you need a little time to reflect on your commitment and purpose here."

He rose, turned, and left the stage by a side exit, followed by Shaw. They went to a small room in the back. This was, in fact, one of many strongholds the Praetorians had used through the years.

"I'm wondering if that was really necessary." the Senator asked as he sat behind a small desk.

Shaw started pacing. "It was. The only way you're going to control the world is through fear."

"Well, my young student, our plans go far deeper than that. Only through total global conquest can we truly have all men bent to our will and live under Praetorian rule. Fear alone will not accomplish this. These leaders are mostly looking to rule in their pitiful little domains. Not unlike the United Nations, they come looking for power, not realizing they have none, even in their own countries. They're impotent, unable to see just how important they can be in the new Empire. We need leaders, ones who can rule and keep their people, their thralls, in place. I don't think anyone but you really understands just how much power they can have."

"I know how much power I can have and I must say you don't have very good executive skills."

"And you do? Watch your mouth. I knew it was a mistake to put you on the Praetorian Council. Assassins are brawn, not brain. You shall only keep your place so long as you can find me competent leaders. I'm sick of looking for help. You're now charged with building our Society leaders. Let's see if that brain of yours can handle such a simple task. Don't disappoint us like so many others."

"Yes, sir, and I think we'll start with the second in command." He pulled his gun and pointed it at the lieutenant.

The Senator glared. "How dare you threaten me. Put that weapon away. I'm in no mood to banter with you."

"Too bad, because I'm in the mood to start making changes. You old men no longer have control of your own Praetorians. You've all held onto your stations too long. You should have retired and enjoyed your old age. Being complacent in power has made you all weak. I have a new order that will take over." Shaw gave him a cold stare.

"I will not have this conversation with you again. There's a chain of command and you continue to threaten me and others on the Council."

This was one of many times Shaw had approached a Council member to betray the rest.

The Senator continued. "I'm tired of this action. Now put that gun away. We have lots to do."

◊ ◊ ◊

Shaw was tired of these feeble fools, just like Trumbull before him. Unlike Trumbull however, he was bent on retooling the Society. He kept his weapon pointed at the Senator.

"What are your intentions?" the Senator asked impatiently. "Are you really going to shoot me? The council will never allow it. You're a dead man of you do." He paused. "Well?"

"I've already told you. Now is the time for a new order. I will be Praetor and a new younger generation will lead us into world domination. And the first thing we're going to do is find out what's going on with that Verum Society, and once and for all crush them, and the truth they still might find."

Unbeknownst to the Council, Shaw had been recruiting loyal followers from the assassin ranks. He was finally ready to make his play.

Shaw could see the Senator finally understood his position.

"Let me talk to the Praetor. I'm sure we can work something out that will be mutually bene…"

Shaw shot him at point-blank range.

"A new order is rising and you're not included." he said to the dead Senator, with a sinister smile as he left the room.

Chapter 26

September 1790 - New York City

Hamilton's coalition met on a beautiful evening in one of the best restaurants in the city. They were all in a cheerful mood having successfully duped the southern states as well as many of the poor who had held war bonds.

"I must say Hamilton, you are a schemer," James Wilson said.

"I will take that as a compliment, Mr. Wilson. As you know, the north needs the southerner's cash crops to keep the economy running. All the new tariffs from the sale of those crops are used to fuel New England factories, shipping trades, railroads, and business interests. If it wasn't for the south's ability to grow and sell crops, they'd be of no use at all…" He stopped as John Jay joined them. "Mr. Jay, congratulations on your new appointment as the Chief Justice of the Supreme Court."

Jay nodded politely.

"Seems you have been doing a lot of negotiating in Europe, it is good to have you back."

"Thank you, Mr. Hamilton. It was a long six years across the Atlantic establishing our country as an equal power to those in Europe. And once you established the Debt Act, promising our government would pay them back, it was clear to them we are indeed worthy of equal standing. Though I must say, using their model of government, including never ending debt, was a stroke of brilliance. I never thought the agrarian south would go along."

"Oh, they didn't. Just a few who were convinced into changing their votes made it all possible. Patrick Henry and Richard Lee are positively fuming over the State's debt deal, even after I relieved Virginia of a large part of their apportionment."

"It seems they are in solidarity with their southern brethren." Wilson said while chuckling.

"Please excuse me gentlemen." Jay looked uncomfortable with the demeaning remarks. He joined other guests.

Oliver Ellsworth with champagne in hand joined Hamilton

and Wilson. "It appears the bond scheme was a terrific success. Many here have done extremely well."

"Of course they have, now it brings them ever closer to the fold. I must say you two did me one better. Last year's Judiciary Act instituting judicial review now helps us control the entire judicial branch of central government," Hamilton responded.

"It was our only option since that power was not granted in the Constitution. Keeping silent about it when the judicial branch was established was the key. Had we debated these powers in the Convention, I have no doubt judicial review would have been strongly rejected. Now, the states have no choice," Ellsworth added.

"Everything I'm now doing was rejected," Hamilton joked.

"It is amazing how not one delegate at the Convention, including James and myself supported any of your ideas, yet you are implementing them all now with your Treasury position in the Federal Government," Ellsworth said.

"The entire southern contingent is up in arms," Wilson said in a demeaning tone.

Hamilton had a wry smile. "Yes, poor fellows. They have no clue just how much the New England states and New York rule the roost. Having the capital set up in the District of Columbia, that is after ten years in Philadelphia first, seemed to seal the deal. It was really no price at all for the north, though some were not pleased with me until I assured them of the upcoming *National Bank* and corporate welfare deals I will be instituting. How could they complain? This is free money extracted from the south and given to them? It was simply too much to pass up. Jefferson really is the fool."

"Just so long as we have the support of New England and good relations with England as a trading partner, the north really is running the show," Ellsworth responded. "I would however, like you to show a bit more respect for Jefferson even if his ideals are in direct conflict with our own."

"Yes, yes…of course, Mr. Ellsworth. Let us join the others." He gave Wilson a quick nod to gather Ellsworth and intermingle.

Wilson nodded. "Join me, Oliver?" He motioned to join others in the room.

"Thank you, Mr. Wilson."

Wilson and Hamilton gave each other nods of approval and smiled as they all mingled with their fellow conspirators. The room was full of the who's who in political life in the north, those being centralized government and *Nation State* advocates.

October 1790 - London, England

It had been almost 70 days since they sailed from New York having just reached the port in London. Lord North and Church were just disembarking.

"Church. Fetch us a coach at once. We must see the King immediately."

"Yes Lord North."

He did as was asked and in short order their baggage was on a coach. Church spoke to the driver and they were on their way. The two men sat across from each other and were silent for some time.

North broke the silence. "You do understand, Church, that I am not well favored with the King right now."

Church pulled a satchel out of his belongings. He opened it and took out a flask from one of the pockets. "Here. This is a present from the Praetor. It's a favorite brew of his that can comfort in times of stress. A special blend it is." He handed it to Lord North.

North hesitated and then took a long swig and gave it back.

"Yes, Lord North. Your joining the King's hated rival James Fox of the Whig Party in '83 was a big disappointment with him. Especially after you failed him during the American secession from the English Empire. And, having the distinction as the first Prime Minister to be forced from office, well, you'll be living with that the rest of your life."

This whole conversation took North completely by surprise. "I'll thank you to remember that I am your superior officer and you shall not talk to me in this manner. Do you understand?"

"Well, that's just it…Lord North," and with that he handed him the satchel he was holding.

North opened it and took out a letter.

"Recognize the writing?"

"The Praetor's." he said as he was reading. His face grew grey as he looked up at Church.

"Yes, it seems both the King and the Society of Praetorians have had enough of you. You are to resign from Parliament immediately."

North was in shocked by the letter. "But the Praetor never mentioned anything to me."

"And why should he? Isn't it clear enough? Had you succeeded in the poisoning attempt on King George two years ago, your fate would be far different than it is now. The King was quite strong to stay alive with the arsenic you used. The stories of his temporary madness were actually good reading. Too bad you failed to kill him."

Lord North started feeling strange. He was dizzy.

What is happening to me?

"Yes, quite strong isn't it. Absinthe mixed with a few other herbs. Has quite a kick to it. Personally, I have not tried it, but I am told that in very small quantities, the person who drinks it can experience very intense hallucinations. Drink it in a large swig…as you just did, and it goes so much farther, so much faster." Church had a broad smile on his face.

Lord North was in a drug-induced convulsive state with his eyesight now fading rapidly. He started sliding off his seat.

"Now, now, Lord North…you really should watch what you drink."

◊ ◊ ◊

Church caught him and laid him back on the seat. He took some strapping in the coach to hold him there.

They rode on until they reached Wroxton Abby, Lord North's residence in the country.

"Driver…driver…it seems Lord North has taken ill. Please get some help."

Several male servants came out to meet them and took Lord North inside. Others unloaded his baggage as Church waited. A relative came running out of the house.

"What has happened?" she shouted as she approached him.

"It seems Lord North had some sort of seizure while en route. I don't know what to make of it." Church answered as if perplexed with the situation.

"What should we do?"

"Do? Why call his physician, of course. What else would you do with a sick man?"

The woman ran back into the house.

"My, my," said Church to himself. "Just look at this mansion."

It was a huge home with sprawling grounds.

"Pity you won't be enjoying it much longer. And any doctor they get will certainly not help. Enjoy your blindness and eventual death North." He turned to the coachman. "Take me to London," he said climbing in.

February 1791 - Capitol, Philadelphia, Pennsylvania

Washington, realizing the rift between north and south was growing, called a meeting in his office.

Hamilton knock on his door.

"Please come in and sit Alexander."

"Thank you Mr. President." He sat in a comfortable chair next to Washington's desk and only then realized Jefferson was seated on the opposite side.

"I have gone through both your *reports* on the constitutionality of starting a *National Bank* and Jefferson's interpretation of it being unconstitutional. I must agree with Jefferson, Randolph, and Madison. Unless you ignore the Constitution completely, this is something we cannot pass."

"But Sir, we are already using private banks to deposit funds. This just means we will own a share in the banks' with which we decide to do business. I have already selected which banks they will be. Mr. Jefferson believes we only have enumerated powers. You know, we must have *Implied Powers* as well, otherwise we cannot function effectively and…"

Jefferson cut him off. "*Implied Powers* Mr. Hamilton is not in the Constitution which means you must have an amendment for a change in government structure. Enumerated Powers means restricted, that is only the few powers the states give central government. *Implied* means, you can do whatever the hell you want to do with impunity. You're just making it up as you go along! I know what you mean to do, but this goes far beyond your capacity.

"We have enough trouble on our hands now with your new Federalist Party. We were not supposed to have a political party system at all. The Constitution was written for a *non-party system*, not a two-party system. Now it's being forced on us and you are the one driving it."

Hamilton ignored Jefferson completely. "Mr. President, I know it seems like that, but unless you allow me freedom to institute this new government, we will be hog tied just as we were with the Articles."

"The President has already given you far too much power, Mr. Hamilton and I see where you are leading us. Your Imperial English model was rejected at the Convention. Now you mean to institute it anyway, regardless of what the people think."

Washington watched as the two work through their respective sides.

Hamilton continued to ignore Jefferson. "Sir, government is about the ability to protect the people. Unless we can control our monetary supply, we will be vulnerable to outside influences."

Washington knew Hamilton had overreached his authority, but he also knew the government had to control the money.

Jefferson continued lambasting Hamilton. "There's another problem, Mr. Hamilton. This central bank is a windfall for northern business interests just as your bond scheme was. The south knows this. It's a dangerous game you're playing with central government, leaning heavily towards northern interests."

Hamilton finally turned and attacked Jefferson. "Mr. Jefferson, your solution is decentralization. That will never do. It is folly to think the people can govern themselves. Give me one good example of success keeping government close to the people."

"I'll give you thirteen."

"Thirteen what…Colonies? So weak they need central government to protect them? If it wasn't for central government, we would have lost the war. Sovereignty only exists here, in the Capitol…the *united Nation State*."

Jefferson looked at Washington with an expression of complete exasperation. Then he continued his assault.

"That would be thirteen independent countries, Mr. Hamilton. Further, we won our secession, our independence from the English Empire in spite of the central government, not because of it. The militias of the independent states were the victors, not your *Nation State.* Sovereignty is reserved for the states, and if any so choose to leave this alliance, they have the right to do so. It's the only way to keep this colossus you're making under control."

Hamilton responded in kind. "You have no clue about who ran and won the war! The General and I were there…first hand. Where were you? A state Congressman…a Governor who allowed the fall and burning of Richmond! Your home ransacked and properties burned…"

"Okay Hamilton, that's enough." Washington was out of patience. "Attacking Mr. Jefferson is no way for the head of the Treasury to act."

"You're right Sir. You know I get energetic about these things. My apologies Mr. Jefferson."

Jefferson gave him a glare and then looked at Washington. "Mr. President I shall be leaving. Consider what you know to be true. I can only offer what I and several others consider to be unconstitutional acts.

"Central government is not an entity unto itself. It is an alliance of states…of countries. The people will decide the fate of the states through their representatives, not the Treasury Department.

"And Mr. Hamilton is well aware of the central government's limited powers. To give us a single voice in foreign affairs, not to regulate and run the economy, and certainly not to enrich the wealthy he has attached to it.

"The states and their people are in charge. Central government has no business being in business or fooling around with business interests. If it ever does, it will be the end of liberty and freedom in our states.

"Oh and one more thing. I know Hamilton is working on several other *reports.* He should leave governing to the representatives of the several states, not himself. We have now heard of an attempt to use tax money or borrow money for infrastructure like roads and canals. There is no grant of power in the Constitution that allows this. Private business is working with the states in these regards, so hands off the till!" He looked squarely at Hamilton as he was finishing his assault. Once finished, he turned and left.

"Well Hamilton, you handled that well," Washington said sarcastically. "And what was that attack on Jefferson's character? You know Benedict Arnold's defection to the British and the Praetorians was responsible for those actions. There was little Jefferson could do once the traitor turned."

Hamilton remembered back to his youth, when Arnold met him at the pier in Boston, as he was collecting his thoughts. "My passion Sir, is to make this young country into just what you asked. I'm giving it a government for the people."

Washington now had a choice to make. Was he going to centralize government into the hands of a few? Or was he going to keep to the code of the states and allow them to be independent? "You make my position hard to defend Alexander."

"My apologies Sir, but you have to make a choice. You must either allow me to continue to build our central government into a strong enough entity to defend ourselves against the European powers, or allow this chance to pass and forever be haunted by the fact that the states will fall."

"I know what choice to make. I don't need you telling me."

"I know Sir, but what can we do in central government to help the south? I mean they are agrarian, you know this. You yourself are agrarian. A central government is a direct threat to them. You know this, but you agreed to help form our new government. Now you are telling me to back off. If I do, it will mean the end of the *nation*."

"The *nation*, as you call it, is being formed on the backs of southern culture. They will be subservient to the whims of northern mercantilism. You know this. All these regressive tariffs you're proposing affect the south negatively."

"Sir, if this is the wrong road, then tell me what we can do?"

"Well…I don't know how to effectively mend the divide. I'm surprised they have remained in the Union this long. It was only having the Capitol down in Maryland that kept them in it."

"And that is the only reason we are still together. You know they wanted two Capitols, one in the north and one in the south. It almost passed Congress. It would have set up two different countries. Neither side trusts the other. Sir…it will come down to choosing sides. You must choose."

Washington thought for a moment. "I will choose my course though not easily.

"And is it possible for you to keep your hands off the economy? Internal improvements are not our responsibility, nor is creating jobs. You have already spent a ton of money creating Tax Department jobs. You know as well as I do that the only way to pay for those jobs is taxation of the private sector. For every job we create, it takes money out of the economy. That means the private sector is taxed more to pay for the tax collectors to go and take their money. Doesn't that sound like a big waste of money and time?"

"Sir, it is the only choice. We both know it. The people cannot protect themselves unless we have the power to protect them. My resolutions will protect them. Taxation is necessary to run government. The more we grow, the more we need to tax."

Washington was tired of this argument and changed topics. "We must all be willing to compromise if we are to live united."

◊ ◊ ◊

Hamilton said nothing. Compromise was the last thing he wanted. He knew it would weaken his position. He knew a compromising government was a weak government. And, he knew Jefferson felt if the people had to compromise then it would mean giving up freedoms to government so that all would have a lesser voice and tyranny would follow.

"Your thoughts?" asked Washington.

"Sir?"

"I have a compromise for you. You know this whole *National Bank* issue is unconstitutional no matter how loosely you interpret the document."

Hamilton knew he was right, but it was the only way he saw to institute an energetic government.

I have to convince him!

"You increase the size of the District of Columbia and I will sign the legislation to pass the Bank Bill, but it must be a twenty-year charter to see if it even works."

Hamilton was caught totally off guard with this proposal.

What on earth is he talking about?

"Let me show you." Washington pulled out a map of the District and placed it on the table. "Look."

He put his finger on the boundary of the District. Then he moved it down to another point equaling some three miles of territory. "You enlarge the District to this point and I'll sign."

Hamilton now knew. Washington owned property near the boundary line he was pointing to and he meant to have it border the District directly. It would increase the property value even more than the Dinner Table Compromise had done.

Hamilton had him. "Agreed. I will get Congress to enlarge the District."

He knew Washington wanted a strong central government, one strong enough to stand up to the English and French. The President needed him to set it up and no one but Hamilton had the audacity to do it.

Chapter 27

June 1792 - Monticello, Virginia

It was the first major meeting of the Absconditus Verum Society since its inception. They had been corresponding and keeping detailed notes, each his own, since the Convention and had all built up small groups within each state bound to their cause. Jefferson and many others had joined their ranks, and was hosting at the main house of Monticello. Robert Yates, Lansing, Madison, Bedford, Henry, Lee, and others, had hoped that Washington would embrace at least some of their positions.

"Hamilton and his Federalists continue to consolidate power into the Treasury Department," Jefferson said. "Washington won't even listen to any other voice."

"His army of armed Treasury Agents cover all the states and ports and drain the people through his tariffs and taxation schemes," Yates replied. "Why did we even bother to have a Constitution written? As bad as the document is, Hamilton is butchering it."

"That's because of his warped interpretation of it. He simply makes it up as he goes along and then writes these convoluted *reports* to Congress to have them make all his schemes Constitutional with no basis in law or fact, yet they become law through his minions in Congress. Almost everything he has done is unconstitutional and we all know it," Jefferson replied.

"There is nothing warped about that man. He is cold and calculating in everything he does," Lee added.

"And now it's apparent he had this legion of corrupt Americans at his beckon call. He no sooner got into the Treasury Department and all of a sudden there were hundreds of tax agents. He obviously had them ready and waiting for the takeover."

"Can you imagine what the United States will look like in a few hundred years? The states will only be extensions of a colossus Federal Government. All hope of keeping true state sovereignty will be extinguished. The federal and state governments will be saddled with an insurmountable debt brought on by the Federal Government whose only check of power is itself. It will get to the point where the people, the average working class, will be so burdened with debt that the whole system will collapse. Then their children and children's children will be forever paying off debts they never incurred themselves. Their burden thrust upon them by generations of the weak-willed that refused to stop the behemoth they created." Henry said.

"Where are we to date?" Bedford asked.

Madison had brought a list. "Three tariff bills each increasing the amount from the last, and an unconstitutional centralized bank that Hamilton uses to draw in more power. More bond schemes meant to enrich the wealthy in profits while binding them tighter to the Federal Government. The northern industries are receiving free corporate welfare money from Congress to support their companies. I have no way to stop all this. Here is the crux of the situation. If Congress uses *Implied Powers* towards the General Welfare Clause, the Government is no longer a limited one-possessing enumerated power, but an indefinite one, subject to only a few restrictions. Hamilton's *Implied Powers* have already destroyed the Republic we just set up!"

Jefferson realized the chasm between the north and south was growing ever wider. "They are draining the money supply from the south every day through an elaborate system of duties, tariffs, and excises. All of these regressive taxes are meant to hit the working class and the poor the hardest. The tariffs we charge on imports go to the central government and are then handed out to Hamilton's cronies in the north. This makes it very difficult for the entire agrarian population, north or south, to afford goods and supplies as imports cost more because of the tariffs.

"Many of the goods exported from the south are hit with retaliation tariffs in other countries. This reduces the amount of products those countries normally import. I fear this will only get worse as the Federalists continue to control central government.

"The Hamilton Whiskey Tax has been a debacle since its inception in '91. Many poor farmers in western Virginia and Pennsylvania use whiskey as a form of bartering for goods and services. They cannot afford the costs of shipping the raw goods to the east.

"Is this the government we created? Stripping the people of their property, liberty, and freedoms? Hamilton grows central government by the day. He creates more and more government jobs and creates more and more taxes to pay his employees. The people are being less represented than ever. The elite aristocrats have total control over the central government."

All the men realized everything that was happening. They were losing the very states and alliance they had worked so hard to build and protect.

"What are we to do? We kicked out one tyrant in King George and now we have a tyrant in Hamilton who is ten times worse. A greater group of the people are now poorer than ever and the few elitists are consolidating money and power at the top, the top in league with Hamilton. He sells more and more bonds to them and then pays them interest to do it again and again. He is amassing more debt than any country on earth," answered Patrick Henry, angrily. "And, what's worse is he believes the middle class, the very fabric of the workforce and our entrepreneurs should be taxed as high as possible. In his words, *'taxing the middle class encourages them to work harder to retain their standing.'*"

"We all know this enriches only the central government and the rich, to use the people's hard earned property, or wages, to prop up who they wish among corporate partners and thieves. *'The middle class can never be taxed enough.'* is his response," Gunning Bedford had finished off the thought.

Jefferson responded. "He is indeed an enemy of the Republic form of government. Our only choice is to continue to keep records and bring all that is done out to the people, even though our organization must stay hidden to protect both ourselves and the truth. We also must expose what is happening because we all have an interest in this tragedy. For now, the best way is through the power of the press and local community meetings.

"Our position, while the one that was meant to be, is also one of difficulty to have and hold. The very nature of decentralization weakens our position against the strong central leviathan government of the elite. Their position allows them to have and control everything while telling the people that we are the ones trying to destroy their *indivisible Nation State*."

"Then we must build a political party ourselves or we will be ever under the boot of the Federalists," Madison said. "And I have just the man, John Beckley, who has already started to build this base. If we want to have any influence at all, the people must be shown the truth. Right now the Federalists make all the laws, run all business of the Congress, and the economy. That fool truly believes government's job is to run everything, not only foreign affairs, but domestic affairs, the economy, internal improvements, social engineering, and the destruction of the states. Central government was never meant for any of those, save foreign affairs, and even there, they are supposed to represent the several states, not some *nationalized central government*."

Jefferson agreed. "And with that note, I will say that I'm thinking of resigning as Secretary of State. I cannot defeat Hamilton on any issues with President Washington. My efforts are being wasted in the position as I watch his destruction without chance of changing anything. And I'm sick and tired of watching Hamilton run everything. The man is the very definition of a Colossus. He means to marry us with England and forever fight with France and every other country that is against the English Empire."

"We're all sorry to hear this," Bedford said. "You were the one hope of keeping Hamilton and the Federalists at bay."

"That hope must now lie in the Absconditus Verum Society behind the scenes and in the formation of loyalists to the states and Anti-Federalists against Hamilton and his Federalist juggernaut."

"There are many in all the states that do not approve of what this alliance of states is becoming," Yates said. "Many, even in the north, do not approve, though our voice there is in the political minority. The greater majority of the people however look to the Absconditus Verum view of government as the one true form. Our way forward is clear. We must stop Hamilton by all political means possible. We must save our Republic."

"What Republic?" Henry asked. "That died the moment Hamilton took office. We live in Hamilton's imperial monarchy and he is the puppet master pulling Washington's strings."

"Then we must hope to share what we can with all who will listen," Yates said. "Meanwhile we can only press Washington to clip some of those strings for now."

"There is one more very troubling set of events," Jefferson said. "It seems several states have had sensitive documents stolen from their archives. These include many of the Convention affirmation documents. I just got confirmation on this report earlier today and over thirty people have been killed who have been working with us. If this is the case, and it is not simply the politicians behind this, the Praetorians are indeed gaining power. We must stay as loosely affiliated as possible. It is the only way to protect ourselves. Go to your states and find out what you can about those documents. Bring me the news as fast as possible.

1794 - Congress Hall, Philadelphia Pennsylvania

James Wilson and Hamilton were sitting in the Treasury Department's main office, Hamilton's office. He had pulled Wilson into his web of deceit and treachery many years earlier. He needed another close confidant since the demise of Lord North and decided Wilson was up to the task.

"I have the Jay Treaty Mr. Hamilton, just in from England," the currier had only just arrived.

"Splendid, splendid," Hamilton replied. "Thank you, Mr. Parks. I have several letters that need to go out. Will you see to it?"

"Yes Sir," he replied and took the notes going quickly on his way.

"So Mr. Wilson, now that peace is finally settled with England again, we must make sure to break the efforts of Jefferson and Madison. Their attempts to bring French commerce and imports to the states can now be completely cut off. This Treaty gives us total open trade relations with England and will stop the Anti-Federalists from any more attempts to restrict it. And so, as to make sure our industries continue to grow, we must continue to support them financially."

"Sir, the King has never found out about your attempt on his life?"

"That got buried with Lord North," he responded looking hard at Wilson. "Guard that tongue of yours."

Wilson quickly changed the subject. "So what's next?"

"More taxes and tariffs of course. We must continue to have capital available to pay interest on securities, at least enough to keep the bondholders and foreign debtors happy. Meanwhile, another raise in tariffs and excise taxes will be needed."

"Sir, with all due respect, I'm not sure the south can sustain much more in the way of tariffs and taxation."

"Of course they can. Let them produce more and sell more to make up the difference."

"That would mean another increase in the slave trade."

"So…what do I care of slaves? Besides, most of the northern shipping fleets benefit greatly with an increase in importing slaves."

"But some in the northern states are looking for emancipation. You know we already have several policies against it."

Hamilton looked incredulously at Wilson. "Are you just humoring me? Do you really think I care about what the goods are? The slaves will eventually be emancipated peacefully, just as slaves have throughout modern Europe. Meanwhile, I don't care what the cargo is. They can bring them directly to southern ports, it doesn't matter, so long as my force of armed revenue marine ships and Treasury Agents can enforce payment of tariffs and excise taxes for any and all goods imported or made domestically. It just means more slaves or goods and more revenue. You really do need to look at the broader picture Wilson. Having said that, what is your point?" Hamilton stood and went to the window in his office.

Wilson said nothing.

"After all, our focus is building a new American Empire," Hamilton said as he gazed outside. "Mr. Wilson, do you know the meaning of the words Federal Congress?"

"Yes, it means the representatives from the several states."

"Anything else?"

"I don't think so."

Hamilton continued to gaze out the window. "Having it in that worthless piece of paper they call the Constitution gives me great challenges in my plans, because it also means; a formal meeting of representatives who belong to different countries. You do realize the states still hold to the belief they are independent countries and they send representatives to the central government only to make sure each country is protecting all its rights and those of its citizens."

"Yes, I see what you mean. That makes perfect sense since each state agreed to the Treaty of Paris with King George, and he did list them all as independent countries."

"Why do you think he did that?" asked Hamilton.

"I'm not sure. Perhaps they had no real distinction. They were colonies, states, and countries at the same time."

"No, that's not accurate. They were colonies, but cast away that title after victory. They called themselves states because the countries in Europe call themselves both countries and states; the state of England, the state of France, and so on. So the state of Virginia is really on equal terms with any other country just as all the other states are."

"Begging your pardon, Mr. Hamilton. I don't see where you're going with this."

"It was really a brilliant stroke by the King. By keeping them divided, he was keeping them as weak as he could. He knew if they formed an *indivisible Nation State*, it would quickly eclipse the British Empire. It's because of this damned piece of paper. The state rights advocates at the Convention were able to remove the word *nation* and replace it with the United States. That was more shrewd than I thought. You see, like my generous interpretation of a *living* Constitution, it also allows Jefferson to keep the claims of state/countries living as well. It validates nullification and secession along with those damn documents. I guess I can't have everything," he said, chuckling to himself.

"What difference does that make? Everyone knows the states have those sovereign rights. There is no argument on that point at all. So long as we control the money supply with your *National Bank*, we control the states. Besides, we all agreed and signed the Convention documents stating that the states kept all their sovereignty. You can't strip them of those rights unless you can get your hands on the rest of those documents."

"Yes, you're right about that. Perhaps it's time to put them to the test, a test of state strength…yes. Let's see just where the states are in the matter. I really do need to crush the life out of them to really have a chance to fulfill our ambitions. And I believe I have the perfect solution."

"What would that be, Sir?"

Hamilton was not ready to share his plans with Wilson, at least not yet. He changed the subject. "Tell me James, what is happening on our western frontier?"

Wilson gave him a quizzical look. "What do you mean?"

"You know exactly what I mean. It seems you have been doing an awful lot of land speculating, buying up vast tracts of land that have no current value. I also know Aaron Burr is doing the same thing. To what end are you two looking for?"

"Just looking to the future. I have no dealings with Burr. He's in Jefferson's camp."

"Nonetheless I know what both of you are up to and unless you tell me, I will make sure those lands never have value. And my understanding is that you have borrowed a lot of money for this venture?"

Hamilton knew Wilson had been borrowing heavily and purchasing land.

Wilson offered his explanation. "I have it on good authority that King George plans to populate the western lands and form new colonies to our west. Since the English still man and maintain several forts on our western borders in violation of our peace treaty, he means to gain another stronghold in America. This is no direct threat to the states, besides the Spanish and French already own most of the continent. He's looking to keep a balance of power between European Empires and, losing the Colonies hit England a lot harder than originally anticipated, especially now with all these trade restrictions between the states and Europe. Every country in Europe is competing for our trade. Having new colonies to our west ensures the King we will continue to do business with him."

"I see. That makes good sense, but why are you risking so

much?"

"You know perfectly well why. I never got the position Washington should have given me in the court. I'm tired of being an Associate Justice on the bench. I should be the Chief Justice. You know that."

"Yes…I know," Hamilton was being coy with Wilson. "I know everything about the dealings of the King, except this one. He has not shared this vision with me. That is strange don't you think? I mean being the point man here in America. You would think I would be a part of the plans he is making."

◊ ◊ ◊

Wilson fell silent. This was not supposed to even be discussed. That was part of his agreement, but he knew Hamilton's close association with the King and now found himself caught between them.

And what of Aaron Burr? What part did he play in all this?

"Sir, I really don't know what to say. I did not know this concerned you so much,"

"Well Mr. Wilson, you may now consider me a partner, though a silent partner. I will allow this to continue, however you must increase your holdings and I am to be granted 50% of all gains you make. This will pay for my silence."

"Sir?"

"You heard me. Now go. Get out of my sight. I don't want to see you again. You shall deal with my subordinate from now on. I will send him calling. And now if you don't mind, I have other business to attend. You are excused."

Wilson was dumbfounded and stood motionless.

"Didn't you hear me? Get out!" Hamilton yelled. He hardly ever shouted.

Wilson left at a loss with what had just happened to change his life, and not for the better.

◊ ◊ ◊

"Parks!' Hamilton yelled.

Jeffery Parks came running into the room. "Yes Sir?"

"Send out a dispatch to both of the Morris's. I want a meeting scheduled immediately."

"Yes Sir…right away Sir." Parks scurried out of the office.

Hamilton went and looked out the window talking to himself. "So the King has decided to leave me out of this? We will see about that. It's about time I take matters into my own hands concerning the English Empire. And Burr, he will wish I never found out."

July 1795 - Philadelphia, Pennsylvania – U.S. Capital

Hamilton was meeting with President Washington in his office. "Mr. President, may I have a word?"

"Yes of course, Alexander."

"Sir, Jefferson and Madison have been forming quite a coalition these last few years and my concern is they may make a real challenge in the election next year. You are stepping down and I fear Jefferson's camp will pull down everything we have accomplished."

"Alexander, you know I have never favored a two-party political system, and you also know I have never forgiven Jefferson for all his attempts to undermine what you and I have done. I personally will never speak to the man again, yet I also know how different the Federalists and Anti-Federalists are.

"Unfortunately, we must allow what we have created to work this all through. If it is the intent of the people that they decide to move in a different direction, then so be it. You and I cannot force everyone to be repressed just to satisfy our own ends."

"I understand, Sir. It's just that I have put my whole life into raising up this new *nation*," he said, depressingly.

"Now Alexander, you shall be remembered for instituting a totally new government and you shall have praise much more than you know. I should chance they will say it is Hamilton's Republic they live in, not Washington's, even though I have been in the forefront of this exercise."

This was a direct attack on Hamilton and he knew it. Washington spent every hour working to keep, and further improve his social standing.

"Yes Sir. Sir, we do have another pressing matter. I have been unable to extract the Whiskey taxes from many on our western frontier, particularly in western Virginia and western Pennsylvania. My agents have been unable to enforce the taxes, and we need those to help fund the Federal Government."

"What do you propose?" asked Washington knowing full well he would not like the answer.

"We must go out there in force and make them uphold the law and pay the taxes. If not, I fear many other factions will do the same."

"Do you mean to march on them?"

"Yes Sir and I need you to lead the way. You will be the only one not questioned with these actions. If I lead the way, Jefferson will squawk until the cows come home about state sovereignty.

"Once this is done, even this once, it will show the nation that the Federal Government can and will enforce the laws it enacts. If not, we will simply become the new King George who could not enforce even minor taxation."

"I am very hesitant about this."

"I understand Sir, but this uprising is like a large wave and growing every day. Soon a tidal wave shall crest us from the west and that would prove ill in protecting our Eastern shore at the same time."

Washington thought long on this and then responded. "One of the many taboo issues of the Federal Government is never to invade a state, no matter what the reason. It was always left up to the states and Federal Government to work out their differences and if they could not, then allow the state to secede or nullify Federal edicts. You know this. We agreed at the Convention."

"I understand Sir, but how can we have the power to levy taxes and not have the power to enforce them?"

You could see it in his eyes. Washington was dreading this action from the start. "Yes, but I know those people. They are but poor farmers and use whiskey as a form of bartering and paying for goods between themselves. Most are very poor. How will this look? Marching on them and demanding taxes on that same whiskey they trade amongst themselves?"

"I understand your feelings Sir, but like Jefferson has said, '*Do not treat one group of the citizenry different from another.*' This would mean if we tax others and they pay, then we must also tax everyone else."

"Don't play words with me, Hamilton. You know very well the context of his quote and its meaning is the direct opposite.

That was to never take ones property and give it to another, meaning we should not take anyone's property. Your suggestion is we make arbitrary tax demands on the people to take their money and property and then force them all to give it to the Federal Government. That is tyranny in its worst form. Taking the property of one and redistributing it to others. This sounds like a Praetorian view."

Hamilton ignored the inference. "Sir, I understand. But how do you suggest we collect the tax?"

"The people must be willing to pay the tax to support the Federal Government to do its job, and the only job we have is representing the people of the several states on foreign affairs. That means they are willing to pay for protection. The central government should only be as big as the citizenry and states are willing to make it. I fear all your meddling in the economy is coming home to roost."

"But then we are back to our old Articles of Confederation,"

"No, we have already risen above that threshold. But I fear we are taking too much. It seems all central government legislation is doing is making the rich even richer and draining the life blood out of the middle and lower classes."

"General, you know my position on this. It is the working class that keeps our economy going. In times of need however, they must work harder and be taxed more. It is the only way we can keep the Federal Government going. We now have a large debt and the deficit grows each year. We must make sure the Federal Government has the money to function. We cannot let this moment pass because if we do, the people will know they can still control the Federal Government and you know the people are not capable of governing themselves. They must have the aristocracy in control. Otherwise the *nation* I have formed will collapse and the people will be at risk, defensively."

The General, while holding Jefferson's position finally relented.

Chapter 28

May 2018 - Staunton, Virginia

It was nearly 2:00 a.m. Brooks couldn't sleep, especially after the dining room encounter. He sat back in the comfortable chair he had claimed in Ms. Sanders' sitting room to the side of the fireplace. The embers that were left gave a warm comfort.

He was soon joined by Emily and Dean who were also restless after the day's events. They were pressing him to continue their history lesson.

He continued with the story about the Whiskey Rebellion that he started in the car ride back to the farm that evening.

"So in 1795, within a few months, Hamilton conscripted over 12,000 troops. Many were officers from the Society of the Cincinnati, though not all. Both cavalry and infantry would be used. Once they formed enough ranks, they headed from Philadelphia westward. Most were dressed in their finest military clothing, making the exercise look more like a grand parade than an army looking to crush a large rebellion."

"I did hear about the Whiskey Rebellion, but I didn't realize the Federal Government invaded a state." Emily responded.

Johnson joined them. "I can't sleep either," He sat in one of the chairs.

"I'll tell you why in a moment Emily." Brooks said smiling, knowing she hated to have to wait for him to come back from his now famous tangent storylines.

"As they moved on past several Pennsylvanian towns, the people became terrified at what they were seeing and word went out well ahead of the troops.

"When Hamilton's army did finally arrive, there was no one to fight. The few who resisted paying the taxes simply melted away and out of site. Hamilton was most disappointed as this was his first chance to really lead an Imperial American Army into battle.

"Washington meanwhile realized the entire affair was blown way out of proportion, as were most of Hamilton's ambitions, so he left for home ahead of the troops. Hamilton though now needed something to validate this bold move so he arrested who he could find, whether actual resisters or not, it didn't matter. He needed to show a victory somehow.

"Some twenty-two men were rounded up and Hamilton sat as head justice and jury in the field. He tried and convicted them all of treason, set death sentences on a few, and imprisonment on the rest. Then he marched the army back and thanked the Cincinnati for their support to end the resistance. Soon after Washington had to give all the resisters amnesty to keep his own reputation clear of this unfortunate event and they were released."

"So Hamilton's plan was a disaster." Dean said.

"Actually, Hamilton's plan was a success because he was able to show the states the power of the Federal Government to invade any of them at any time for any reason."

"Just another usurpation of power." Emily responded. "Tell me, other than what we all know about John Adams, where was he during all these events. I remember he had pushed for independence many years earlier. Didn't he also have influence as Vice President?"

"Vice President John Adams was furious over this entire exercise and the bad feelings he had against Hamilton as Washington's favorite turned to vicious hatred even though they were both Federalists. Adams had always felt he should have been the one working with Washington to create the Federal Government. He had almost no role at all in anything taking place. The Vice President had almost no power except to preside over Congress and cast deciding votes in case of a tie. He sat and brooded for eight long years as Hamilton built his empire all around him, and he kept interrupting Congress with his own ranting. He really was a pain in the neck to everyone around him…always skulking about and miserable because he was powerless to stop anything. He thought of Hamilton as *'a bastard immigrant.'*

"Hamilton did resign in '95 due to the exposure of an affair he was having. Aaron Burr, who long disliked Hamilton, threatened to go public, but by that time, Hamilton's Republic was firmly entrenched,"

"What was the Jay Treaty?" Dean asked.

"It was made during war between England and France to keep America a neutral observer. Hamilton wanted more trade with England so he could collect more tariffs. Jefferson and Madison wanted a trade embargo against England until they fulfilled their commitments to the Treaty of Paris more than a decade earlier. The British still held forts on the western frontier in direct violation of the Treaty. The chief problems were American vessels in the Caribbean and Atlantic. Whether they were bringing goods to or from Europe, they were boarded by both countries and many Americans were conscripted into European navies without consent from anyone.

"That was the delicate balance and problems that the Jay Treaty was meant for, except Hamilton wrote the instructions for the Treaty for Jay to follow. They were exclusively pro-British and anti-French. So for the next several years, American-French relations deteriorated to the point of war by 1798. It was a *quasi-naval war*, almost exclusively fought in the Caribbean."

"Okay. Enough, please," Johnson said. "Rather boring isn't it?"

"Not at all," Emily answered. "How can we possibly regain the Republic if we remain ignorant of our history?"

"I agree," Dean said.

"Well, perhaps we need a break," Brooks said, standing up to bid them goodnight. "It's getting rather late and tomorrow we'll need all our energy."

Emily and Dean retired for the evening.

Johnson stayed.

◊ ◊ ◊

Brooks sat back down in the same chair.

Johnson sat facing him. "You okay, Joseph?"

"Yes, yes, that was a bit of a scare though."

"Sorry, I didn't know it was Trumbull and that Tim actually saw him. I would've had another agent assigned." Johnson offered.

"Perhaps it's better this way. I need to keep Trumbull on his toes, and Dean's anger will help." He thought for a moment. "Can Dean handle it?"

"Yes, I'm confident he can, and I'll speak to him again. He's a rare find, an excellent agent for one so young. I'd trust my life with that kid."

"Then that's settled."

Brooks stared at the fire and then focused on the odd inscriptions throughout the mantel. "Do you know who's who in this fight? I mean in the government," he asked, breaking the silence.

Johnson paused. "Well, you know it's against protocol to discuss such things."

"Ben, we need to know who we can trust. This is in the open now, just as it was during the Civil War."

"And you know what happened, right? The President wiped out ninety-five percent of the Verum in a matter of a few years. Look how long it's taken us to recover, and only because we were lucky. Had the connection between slave and owner ever been made, it would have meant the end of it all."

Brooks gave him a quizzical look. "Slave and owner?"

"A tale for a different time. One past through my ancestors."

Brooks decided to let it lie for now. "I feel this is the turning point. If we don't recover the documents soon, the Praetorians will hunt us down and kill every member. The sheath of secrecy is off and we've been radicalized."

Johnson was quiet for several moments. "Perhaps it's time you met our senior members."

Brooks was just looking for some names from Johnson, not the source. "Really? Have you met them?"

"Yes…though few have for security reasons. Their families keep to themselves. They don't see too many people these days, and now with what's happened…I don't know."

For Brooks it was now or never. "Ben, give us a fighting chance. Let's see them and work on our strategy going forward. I know our loose affiliation has protected us in the past, but it's time to coalesce. Strength in numbers is our only hope now."

"I don't know, Joseph. We don't have the numbers you think we do. Most of our influence has waned in the government. The two parties have complete control. The people seem more than willing to have government take care of them. I think perhaps the window of opportunity has gone. The partisans keep the people separated and the politicians keep the Praetorians in power."

Brooks leaned forward and with an impassioned breath said, "We must try. We owe it to every American that has sacrificed themselves in something they believed in. Liberty must prevail. This is the last place on Earth people have any chance to live in 'real' liberty and freedom. If we fail, the sins of our generation will be the ruin of our children and their children."

Johnson was now staring stared at the embers in the fireplace. "If we do this, we have to finish it. If we can't, then all hope is lost."

He paused as the fire found a portion of a log and flared up. "Tell me what you know about Mr. and Mrs. Miller, or I should say Yates."

Brooks was hesitant. He had asked for names and now Johnson was pressing him for information.

Did I make a mistake bringing Ben in?

He had to act on faith as time prevented investigation. "I don't know them personally. Sheriff Lucas would be your best source for that information. Maybe we should have him join us."

"No, it's too late for that." Johnson answered.

"I can tell you Emily has a background in architecture and the Romans use of it."

"Really? That can be of considerable value should the time come." Johnson rose and started playing with the fire using the metal fireplace rod.

"I don't know. I'm thinking we should keep her safe. Have her stay here. The exposure might be too great at Monticello. If the Praetorians find out, we're there…perhaps we can communicate our findings to her here." Brooks was battling what his gut was telling him to do, and that was putting her in harm's way if she joined them at Monticello.

"No. She's coming with us. Without her husband, and with the skill set you say she has, we'll need her close. Quick decisions will be critical if things escalate."

Brooks didn't respond. Now that he knew Johnson was his senior in the Verum, his decision was the final one.

"What about Richard Yates? Did you know him well?"

Brooks could tell Johnson was now vetting him, not that he minded. In fact, it gave him some relief to know what side his superior was on. He sat back in his chair and relaxed.

"I did. We explored many sites together. He was extremely intelligent and his knowledge of history unparalleled in the field. I'd say if he wasn't of the Yates lineage, he would have wound up in the education system and perhaps followed the marching orders of institutional education. His loss was too much for us to overcome. The last twenty years have produced nothing of value." He was watching Johnson continue to play with the fire.

Johnson turned and looked at him. "Which is why we must use all our resources." He paused. "Yes, I guess it is time I ask if you can meet. It is up to them of course, being our senior society members."

"What do you know about them?"

"Only that our senior member is a direct descendant of another Founding Father. I know I told you earlier we had few resources. Actually that's not true. We have more resources than you think. But as far as who we can bring in right now…no one, my old friend. We're on our own unless we can find something of value. We can afford to coalesce to a point, but too much too soon would be too great a risk."

Brooks knew he was right. He remembered the few times they thought they had a good lead and brought in extra help only to find out they were on the wrong track. One time it cost them several lives. He couldn't expect any more.

As they both headed upstairs for a few hours of sleep, Brooks thought he heard someone downstairs milling about. He stopped halfway up the stairs and listened. He knew Ms. Sanders had gone to bed earlier that night.

Is someone up? Did they hear what we said?

Failing to hear anymore sounds, he went to bed.

◊ ◊ ◊

Ms. Sanders crept back to her room and slipped into bed.

◊ ◊ ◊

The next morning, Brooks, Johnson, Dean, and Emily, left Staunton and soon reached Monticello. Once again they had them close down for the day. This was a calculated risk that might raise suspicion, but they had no choice. It was posted on the internet again, but this time listed as repairs in the main house.

Trumbull was there to meet them.

It was another brisk morning and they all dressed accordingly. Brooks carried a large satchel with a strap over his shoulder. In it he had the maps, sketches, and drawings from the farm, as well as the diary and the key.

Dean had a bag of tools; hammer, magnifying glass, awl, rags, a brush, screwdrivers, and other small tools.

As they entered Monticello, they laid out all the maps on a large table in the entryway.

Trumbull looked at Dean who seemed uneasy at his presence.

"Mr. Dean, I know I can't change the past, but I am trying to help. Hundreds of families have been touched by the battles between the two Societies. I need to know you won't do anything rash."

Dean looked at Johnson then back at Trumbull after Johnson motioned him to do so. "Yes I know. We have to move forward and this is much bigger than any one of us. I'm not happy about it, but I won't do anything stupid."

"Agreed." Trumbull was scanning the room.

The rest started looking through the maps.

Several minutes ticked by before Brooks asked, "let's hear what information you have, Trumbull."

"It's the riddle of the code."

They all had a look of shock on their faces.

"Mr. Yates and I talked at length about his childhood before I left. His memory was returning quite quickly as he got better. It seems the trauma of the accident shook his memory back to the original accident. While his father had spent so much time researching and making detailed notes, they both only found the secret on the day Richard Yates was killed."

Trumbull looked at Emily. "Your husband had that secret locked deep in his subconscious. Since then, many have overlooked something that was right here all the time. He said his father used to hide objects by the days of the week. Somehow this trick had come to Richard over the years. James was never really sure when it started, but he realized it at about ten years old. Then it became almost a game for the two of them.

"That was when I had first started to follow Richard. James also said that the answer to the code was in the basement. He couldn't remember any more than that. In fact, he wasn't even sure if he knew the clock was involved until recently. The code must have come to him the same time he was piecing his memory back together."

Trumbull looked up at the Great Clock. "That's the piece you've been looking for."

Brooks stood, mouth agape. He stared at the clock that had been handcrafted to Jefferson's exact specifications.

"The clock?" Emily asked.

"Yes. Do you see the weights?"

There were no weights below the clock.

"Look to the corners."

Surrounded by a large assortment of early American artifacts, along with many other features that filled the main entrance, they focused on the front corners and where there were two ropes hanging down with an odd set of weights attached to them."

"I don't understand," Dean said.

◊ ◊ ◊

"Then go and get the ladder there, and I'll show you," Trumbull said with a snarky inflection as he pointed to the ladder leaning on the left wall. He immediately realized his offense and offered, "if you would please," in a softer tone.

Dean glared at him for a moment, then went and got the ladder.

"Those ropes in each corner go up and then are threaded horizontally into the sides of the clock." Emily offered as she pointed them out.

Dean had fetched the ladder that was used to reach the Great Clock.

Trumbull leaned it against the front wall just under the clock. "Yes, Mrs. Yates. Now look on the side wall next to the weights on the right."

Trumbull watched as they all did and they could see them hiding in plain sight.

"Days of the week," Brooks looked astonished by the sight.

Trumbull looked at Emily. "That's right. Your husband pieced it together yesterday."

"Now, since it's nearly ten o'clock and today is Wednesday, we can solve the riddle. As you noticed, the weights have been setup to show the days of the week. They're now down to Wednesday."

He pointed to the weights on the right. "Looking up, we can see the days on the plaques start with Sunday...and the bottom is Friday."

Friday was the lowest plaque visible. There was a hole on each side meant to allow the weights to go below the floor.

"Mrs. Yates, if you would be so kind as to go to the front to your right, and Johnson, the same on your left. Dean, I need you and Brooks to go down into the chamber directly below this one."

They all did as they were instructed. Once they were all in place, Trumbull climbed up to the Great Clock. It started ringing which caught him off guard and his foot slipped. He grabbed the sides of the ladder to keep himself from falling.

The gong had been used to sound to the workers. There was a face to this clock outside as well, though with only an hour hand.

Once the tenth gong sounded, Trumbull looked at Emily. "Please, Mrs. Yates, Johnson, pull the weights down to the floor."

They did so.

"Now, Brooks, pull the weights through the holes and set them on Saturday. Dean, level the left height with the right," he shouted for the two below them.

"All set." Brooks yelled back.

Trumbull opened the glass cover and turned the hour hand backwards until it set at eight o'clock. The gongs started again.

Once the last sounded, Trumbull opened the face to expose the inner workings. It was filled with gears of all types and sizes.

"It's not working," Trumbull said and as he did he noticed a circular bar set horizontally behind the center of the mechanism that reached out to two pins, holding the bar in place. He had to act fast or lose the opportunity. While the ropes were sliding out the sides, he saw he needed to release the center bar. He reached in and turned the bar clockwise until it released the pins. They slid back, allowing the ropes to release totally. They had one more foot of length on them before they were totally extended. Immediately after, they were lowered to full length, another large horizontal bar within the works set inside the wall moved to the right towards the side wall.

A loud sound boomed in the next room and then again farther out. Then several sets of gears and metal bars were heard going down and towards the south end of the house.

"Down here!" Brooks yelled.

They all joined him. "This is where I thought I heard the noise."

"Me too," Dean confirmed.

Brooks pulled the diary from his satchel. He flipped through several pages. "Here it is:

Only time will tell when the key to the cypher is shown;
Look up, then down, walk long, follow sound
Look sharp, no fear, eagle's eye, shows it's here
Iron fist, moves the wall, follow hall, do not fall
Iron Gate, blocks the way, with the key, it will sway
Use the rules; take it slow, mark your way, or you will stray
Even in, to begin, odd it is, to show what 'tis
Up or down, you will go, choices sound, you're center bound
Don't go back, for it's a trap, move ahead, or you'll be dead

Iron Gate, blocks the way, with the key, it will sway
Once you're there, the truth lays bare, read and see, our great folly
Take it up, take it out, use the rules, or you'll be fools
Never safe, never seen, show the truth, to all foreseen
Use the rules, to escape, find the light, or doomed to fate
Don't go back, for it's a trap, move ahead, or you'll be dead
Use the rules; find your way, the Iron fist, will show the day."

He looked up at the group. "We need to go into the South Dependency."

They all followed him through the basement hallway and ended up in the kitchen. They were going slowly as they looked at the ceilings, walls, and floors for any clue. Finding nothing yet, they went out of the kitchen and into the next room, then the next room, then the third room, which was the public ladies room. Still nothing was amiss.

The last room was the men's room. The inside stairway was blocked by a locked door, and they had to go around to reach the upper level. They entered the South Pavilion. It had some small tables, chairs, window dressings, and a large bed - all reproductions of the early 1800s.

They examined everything and found nothing.

"Well, I don't understand," Emily said. "Why wouldn't all that noise coming downstairs have shown up somewhere? Did we miss something?"

"No, not in any of the rooms, anyway," Dean offered.

"Brooks, repeat what you read," Trumbull nodded and pointed to the diary.

"*Only time will tell when the key to the cypher is shown;*
Look up, then down, walk long, follow sound
Look sharp, no fear, eagle's eye, shows it's here."

Trumbull thought for a moment. "Time will tell is a clock."

"And look up means the Great Clock," Emily added.

"Then down, walk long, follow sound," Johnson offered. "So it means the sound came down and we needed to walk through the south cellar hallway into the South Dependency."

"We've done all that." Dean said.

The South Dependency was the lower wing in the basement. It housed the kitchen, the cook's quarters, a smoke house, and originally two small rooms for servants; until they made those rooms into public restrooms. All the rooms faced the south and, because of the contour of the hill, one could walk outside. There was no hallway connecting them, so they needed to exit one room in order to enter the next.

They had done so and were now on the upper level in the South Pavilion above the men's room.

"No more clues to the passage?" Dean asked.

"No." Brooks continued to flip through the diary.

"Then the answer must be downstairs," Trumbull concluded.

"Why do you say that?" Dean asked as he walked around the pavilion bedroom.

"Because no clue has us coming up to the main level." Trumbull headed back down, followed by the rest.

They searched all the rooms again. Still nothing. They ended up in the kitchen.

"It must be here somewhere," Johnson determined.

◊ ◊ ◊

"Okay…let's look at this logically." Emily was trying to piece the puzzle together. "The clues didn't tell us to stop anywhere along the way. It says,

Look sharp, no fear, eagle's eye, shows it's here."

"I don't see an eagle's eye painted anywhere," Dean said as he glanced around at the walls.

She continued. "Perhaps it's not painted. An eagle can spot its prey from high up, so if an eagle looks sharply from the sky, it can see its prey. The eagle has no fear when diving for the catch. It must be outside."

They all went back outside and looked up at the two-story Pavilion.

Emily, however, was looking at the lower level. Something clicked in her head. "Let me see those sketches of the original renovations again."

"I have them here," Brooks started flipping through the papers as he looked in the satchel. As he did he pulled out each one pertaining to the bath.

Emily started taking them one by one. "No, no, no…" She was handing them to Johnson. "No, no…" She stopped.

"This one. This one is the renovations sketched from before and after the bath renovations."

Dean's face lit up. "Let me see!" He stood by Emily looking over the parchment.

"Look…this last room." She pointed to the men's bath part of the drawing. "It was changed. It originally had a doorway to the south. The doorway now is to the east and a window replaced the doorway."

They left the kitchen to examine the South Pavilion lower level.

Dean was looking up at the south wall. "But I don't see anything here."

"No…it's this lower wall. It has to be…" she touched the window and then the bricks below it.

They all looked closely at the lower side of the south facing wall.

"You know, in '87, when I was watching Richard and James at this very spot, it seemed like James had found something. That was what caused them to leave that fateful day…" His voice trailed off.

Johnson, still holding several sketches interjected, "Look, it looks like they raised the ground level up to a point that they had to remove the door and insert a window." He pointed to a sketch and then the window.

"Yes…do you think part of a secret doorway might be buried here?" Dean asked.

"I don't think so," Brooks responded. "If it was, then it would have been found back in the 1940s when they renovated. It must be somewhere else."

Emily had gone around the building to the northwest side. The ground was sloped so one could climb up to the upper level. This was the same hill her husband used when he was a child.

She scanned the brick face. Dean joined her and started looking as well. Brooks, Trumbull, and Johnson all went up to the Pavilion to take another look inside.

They searched for thirty minutes, but no one found anything. Soon they were all standing in the back yard, which had a wandering path and benches, as well as a small pond.

The path was surrounded by a variety of flowers that were in bloom. Reds and yellows, purples and pinks.

The day had warmed up. Their surroundings were calm, almost serene, and they took a break sitting on nearby benches.

"What do you think?" Dean asked.

They were all quiet. Emily was thinking of the puzzle before them.

"What about the riddle, Brooks?" Trumbull asked. "It must have something in it we missed, or perhaps it's here in the back yard. Maybe a secret door is hidden in one of the flower beds?"

Brooks took out the diary and read the lines pertaining to a possible secret location.

"*Look sharp, no fear, eagle's eye, shows it's here*
Iron fist, moves the wall, follow hall, do not fall
Iron Gate, blocks the way, with the key, it will sway."

Emily got up and walked halfway up the slope, sitting down in the cool grass. She looked far to the west and south at the rolling hills of green. Patterson Mountain was high above Monticello and she spied a road winding its way to the top. Wisps of clouds were inching across the sky. She closed her eyes and a slight breeze crossed her face.

The others were in earshot of Emily.

"I don't understand," Dean said. "It must be right there in the Pavilion."

"Mr. Dean, I've been looking through this diary for a very long time. There's a reason no one has found the keyhole," Brooks offered.

"But we've solved the first part," Johnson offered. "That's farther than anyone else has gotten. I mean, just knowing it's here at Monticello."

"Yes, and we know that the Pavilion is clearly holding the next secret," Trumbull added.

She looked back at the men.

Brooks handed the diary to Johnson. "See if you can find anything else."

As Johnson looked through the diary, Emily turned back to the south and thought.

It must be here. I'm missing something. We need to get this done. I want solve this so I can go home.

She closed her eyes and leaned back against the hill. Visions of the girls danced in her head. James was with her. It was a time before this nightmare. They were happy. Life was good.

And now? Are the girls alright? Is James healing? I have to get home.

Chapter 29

Another thirty minutes passed as Emily continued to think about all that had happened to her family. She looked up the slope at Johnson, who was still scanning the diary. Trumbull left to check the front yard side of the hill for possible threats. Brooks was in deep thought on a bench.

Dean came down and joined Emily on the slope.

"I'm sorry about your parents, Mr. Dean. I know what you must have gone through. My girls being kidnapped was horrible for me and with James being shot…"

"Thank you, Mrs. Yates."

"Please call me Emily." she did her best to smile.

"Okay, Emily…and I'm Tim. Not an FBI agent right now, just a man trying to find some answers." He paused. "So, what do you think about all this? I mean that there might be a whole different history of the country that was hidden from the people. Agent Johnson has taught me a few things I never knew."

She sat up and engaged him. "It's more than amazing. It's very troubling to think how much has been kept from us. Even though a lot of this information is already out there, the government has kept so much from being taught." She looked at the side of the Pavilion.

"I know. I think the people will want to know the truth, don't you?" Dean asked.

"Many, yes…but many are so addicted to the system and what it gives them, they will defend it no matter what the truth is. Think of how many are getting financial aid or health coverage or pensions from the government. Most only care about what they're getting, not who the government is taking it from. I don't know if we can change things even if we do find all the additional evidence." She continued looking at the brick wall again as she was talking.

"I tell you what…Emily…I will make it my life's mission to share the truth. I'll show everyone how much the government has hidden from us. They'll listen. They must listen." His toned changed to one of determination.

She looked at him and smiled. "I hope you'll convince them. I'll be happy just getting my family together again, and I want…to…" She looked back at the pavilion. Suddenly her expression was one of total excitement and shock at the same time. "My God!"

"Ma'am? What is it?"

"Look there…just there below the top of the grass." She pointed to the bottom right of the brick wall's southwestern side, two feet from the corner. She stood up as she was talking.

He strained to identify what she was talking about. "I don't see it."

"I do…Brooks, Johnson!" she yelled. Both came running. "Look!" She pointed again and then move closer and pushed the grass down.

Indeed, a small crack had been created in the mortar between two bricks towards the right edge of the wall at ground level.

Emily brought her hands to her face in amazement.

"*Look sharp, no fear, eagle's eye, shows it's here.*"

Brooks was the first to take a closer look. "The mortar is pushed out from behind. I need something to punch through it. Dean, some tools if you please."

Dean ran up the slope, grabbed his bag and returned. He handed Brooks an awl and small hammer, just one of the many provisions he brought.

Trumbull came running back along the side the Southern Dependency, showing up out of breath.

Brooks carefully punched through the mortar and created a hole about two inches in diameter. He hit something that sounded like metal.

"The hole goes totally through this wall. I can't see anything though. I need a flashlight."

Dean dug one out of his bag. "There it is." He handed it to Brooks who looked through the hole he had made.

"What is it?" Emily asked.

Brooks looked at the slope, then the hole again, then the slope. "It's a keyhole." He looked at the position it was in. "When they back filled and raised the slope, half the door was buried below ground. This looks like it's just below the inside stairs. If they had raised the ground any more, this would have never been found."

Brooks pulled the key out of his satchel. Since it had a rather long handle, he was able to fit it all the way into the keyhole behind the brick outlay. He tried several times to turn it, but was not able to. "Seems to be jammed."

"Let me have a go," Trumbull said

Brooks handed him the key. He inserted it again and jiggled it back and forth. "I've found over the years that these things need some careful encouragement." He continued to jiggle it, trying clockwise, and then counter clockwise. The key was slowly rotating farther and farther each way until it finally turned and clicked. There was a loud sound of something dropping within the wall that hit the lower floor line. The wall itself shook and cracked, revealing a brick laid outline of the top half of a door. It slowly pushed inward as they all backed up.

Once clear of the outer wall, the door slid to the left on channels built into the stone of the hill. Dust billowed out of the opening. Someone had fashioned the mechanism to open with the outer brick lines intact, showing no signs of any openings before.

"This was specially made to prevent others from finding it." Brooks concluded. Trumbull handing Brooks the key.

"And it's the next line in the riddle.

"Iron fist, moves the wall, follow hall, do not fall.

"The Iron fist is the key in your hand." Emily pointed at Brooks' hand.

Once the air cleared they could see stone carved out below the under part of the stairway as it wound downwards. It was a shallow depth, some four feet. An opening was on the left. Brooks peered in with a flashlight. The tunnel turned left. It was hewn from solid rock, the stairs crafted above a layer two feet thick.

"It goes to the left, so the tunnel is actually under this slope and behind the men's room back wall. That would explain why they never found it even during the reconstruction. Had the renovation in the 1940s removed more of the stairwell and the rock beneath it, this passage would have been found back then. We have to slide down to the floor level. It's about three feet below the entrance," Brooks said.

Emily's heart raced with anticipation.

This is it! We found it! Oh I can't wait to get back home. My girls, James.

Brooks went first with flashlight in hand. Dean handed each a flashlight from his bag and one by one they entered. Johnson and Dean helped Emily down safely.

"The men's room behind the wall on our right was where the original kitchen was before the remodeling," Emily offered. "It's on the plans we looked at before."

They turned to the left and entered the tunnel, following the northwest wall line of the lower Pavilion. It was filled with cobwebs, dust, and all other sorts of things one would find in an old tunnel buried for hundreds of years.

Brooks lead the way, followed by Dean, then Johnson, Emily, and Trumbull was the rear guard.

As they moved, Emily reached out to the right side of the cave. The rock was uneven, as though it was hewn with picks and hammers.

They were moving to the northwest and down as far as they could tell based on where they entered and the fact that the tunnel was strait. The grade was a slow decent. Fifty feet in, they reached bars that blocked their way. Within the bars was a gate with another keyhole.

"What are the chances that this key works both doors?" Brooks asked.

"*Iron Gate, blocks the way, with the key, it will sway*," Emily said.

He tried the key and indeed it fit. He turned it and opened the gate with a loud, long squeak. There was a sliding sound behind them. Light was fading from the entrance.

"This gate must be connected to the outside door. It just closed," Trumbull was the closest to the front door.

"I wonder if the hidden brick faced door can be seen on the outside now?" Dean asked.

After the gate, the tunnel went both right and left but not forward.

"Which way do we go?" Dean queried as he looked back and forth.

"What's the next line in the diary?" Trumbull kept looking behind them.

Johnson read:

"Use the rules; take it slow, mark your way, or you will stray
Even in, to begin, odd it is, to show what 'tis."

"Even in? What does that mean?" Dean asked.

"And what are the rules?" Emily added as she stood next to Johnson and looked at the diary.

"Ben, let's have a look." Brooks reach for the diary which Johnson handed off. He turned several pages, then stopped.

"It means we need a code to find the right tunnels. And there is a code in the diary. Until now it's been useless to us. Here, look. There are two strings of numbers followed by a second set."

He showed them the diary page:

18 16 14 4 10 20 18 2 26 4 ~
5 15 9 19 17 9 13

----

4 26 2 18 20 10 4 14 16 18
13 9 17 19 9 15 5

"It has numbers in rows. Even numbers in one row and odd numbers in the next…see?" Books pointed them out.

"So, which way do we go?" Trumbull continued to look behind them, scanning the tunnel.

Emily watched him and her anxiety heightened. She finally asked. "What is it Trumbull?"

He turned and faced her. "Just keeping an eye out. We should have left someone to guard the doorway."

"Do you think the Praetorians know that we're doing?" her heart raced again.

Are we safe? Why isn't anyone staying back? What if they know?

Brook's interrupted them. "Let's not jump to any conclusions." He reached for the diary and Johnson gave it to him.

"Let's see." Brooks went back to the riddle. A few moments passed. "I have no idea which way to go. Perhaps the way is on one of the other encrypted pages."

"Doesn't the diary have a map of a labyrinth in it?" Emily wanted the solution now. She was getting antsy.

◊ ◊ ◊

Brooks thumbed through the pages. He'd done this hundreds of times already and knew every page almost verbatim. There were still several blank pages at the end.

"No, there's no map. I've gone through this diary countless times."

"Well, then, what are the rules?" her anxiety was showing in her voice.

"What should we do? Should we continue?" Dean looked overanxious as he took a few steps into the left tunnel.

"Anyone have a compass?" Brooks inquired.

"Yes…" Emily reached into a small bag and took out a compass. She handed it to Brooks. "Ms. Sanders gave it to me before we left. I'm not sure why."

He looked at the needle. He shook it a few times and looked again. "This is pointing to the left." He shook it again.

"What is it?" Johnson looked up from the diary.

"It's pointing to the left."

"So, left is north," Dean answered from the mouth of the left tunnel.

"No, left is southwest. We followed the tunnel straight in after the corner. We were heading northwest towards the back yard. We should be below the walkway or near it." Brooks shook it again.

"Then the compass is broken." Trumbull move up and joined them.

"Perhaps…Dean, do we have another compass?" Johnson looked towards Dean in front of the left tunnel.

"I should have one in my gear…hold on…yes, yes…here it is." He dug it out of his bag and gave it to Brooks.

"It's pointing the same way," Emily said as she was looking over Brooks' shoulder.

"So what does that mean?" Dean continued to ask questions.

Brooks knew. "It means there's a magnetic field in here that's disrupting the compass. Johnson, try your cell."

He took it out and held it up. "No signal."

"That means all communications are blocked as well. It must have something to do with the iron ore in the hill. It's a ferromagnetic material. It seems to be creating a local magnetic field," Brooks said.

"And you would know this how?" Emily inquired.

"It's in the records at the Jefferson Library."

"So once inside the hill, we're on our own," Trumbull concluded.

"Yes," Brooks looked to the left, then right. "Unfortunately there's nothing in the records to help us. Jefferson kept this part of the estate totally private."

"Okay then…let's do this." Johnson looked both ways as well.

"My gut tells me to the right," Brooks stated. "Right heads us back towards the house."

Brooks had gone on many trip of exploration with Richard Yates. As he looked around, he was having flashbacks of certain trips they went on involving caves.

This one feels different. Something about this hidden, elaborate find is different. I haven't felt this uneasiness before. Is it Trumbull causing my trepidation? Is Johnson really who he says he is? And what about Dean? Richard and I always went alone. I think we have too many players here.

◊ ◊ ◊

Emily was unnerved by this whole unknown. She looked back down the tunnel to the door and thought.

Let's just go back until we figure this out. What if we get lost?

Brooks, Johnson, and Dean started down the right side tunnel. Emily didn't move. She looked at her watch.

Something's wrong.

She took it off and shook it, brought it to her ear and listened. She looked at it again.

Something's going on.

Trumbull came up next to her. "What is it?"

He caught her off guard and she jumped back, holding her chest. She looked at him and a chill ran up her spine.

"Shall we join them?" he inquired. "Not to worry. I told your husband I would look after you."

This help calmed her nerves a little. She was still scared of Trumbull.

What if this guy is still a Praetorian*? He could kill us all in here and no one would ever know about it.*

She had a tremendous urge to bold for the door.

No wait. I need to hold it together. I need to be strong. We have to get this done so I can go home.

She shook it off and nodded. They headed to the right, catching up to the others.

This tunnel was more level than the last. It was not straight however, as it slowly turned to the left. Emily noticed the walls were still fairly rough, hewn from the rock with pick axes and chisels. The floor was smooth though, like poured concrete. Some twenty feet in they came to an opening on the left.

"Well?" Emily inquired, anxiously.

Brooks decided. "Let's keep going forward for now."

They continued on and past another opening to the left, then another, passages opened to either side as they made their way down the main tunnel. Each opening was shallow and went to the right, or left, or both ways. They slowly walked down the main path as it continued bending slightly to the left.

"We keep going to the left, and we've now passed over ten openings," Johnson said. "We should stop and think about what we should do next."

They all agreed.

Emily looked at her wrist watch. "How long have we been in here? My watch is either fast or slow. I have no idea how long. It seems like forever."

"I'd say about five or six minutes or so." Brooks answered.

"My watch isn't running right." Emily shook her forearm around.

"Same with mine." Dean was looking at his watch as well.

Brooks offered. "It could be the magnetic field in here."

Johnson cut in. "I suggest we keep track of time the best we can. No telling how long we're going to be down here."

"Emily, where would you say we are in relation to the back yard?" Brooks inquired.

How am I supposed to know? Stop, think. We headed Northeast. The tunnel is curving to the left.

She answered. "I think if we're still under it, then we're going around the perimeter. With the slow turn to the left being constant, yes, the perimeter."

"I agree." Brooks gave her a nod.

"What does the compass show?" Dean asked.

Johnson gave him a firm response. "Dean, they aren't working, ok?"

Emily watched as everyone seemed on edge.

Everyone except Trumbull.

Brooks cut in. "Let's just take a breath. I know we've been bending to the left which would move the compass to the north. However, just in the last few feet, the compass completely changed direction. It's now showing we're going southeast. There's just too much magnetic interference. The iron ore deposits. There's more than one magnetic field in here. It purposefully makes a compass useless."

He looked at the diary.

"*Use the rules; take it slow, mark your way, or you will stray.*"

"We better pay more attention to the riddle. We should map our way, otherwise we could get lost down here forever." Dean offered.

"You're right," Johnson acknowledged. "For all we know, we've already gotten lost."

"No, I don't think so," Trumbull said. "We should go back to where we started to make sure we can indeed get out.

They started heading back. Trumbull was now leading them back and Brooks was on the tail end of the group.

Emily was thinking about the riddle and what the next part meant.

Don't go back. Don't go back!

"No, wait!" She stop abruptly. "What was that next phrase?" Emily asked.

"*Even in, to begin, odd it is, to show what 'tis,*" read Brooks.

"No, no…the one after that."

"*Up or down, you will go, choices sound, you're center bound.*"

"And the next?"

"*Don't go back, for it's a trap, move ahead, or you'll be dead.*"

"Oh, no…" She looked at Brooks.

"Well, we can keep going forward, but our chances are not good, not good at all." Johnson offered.

"Then let's go back," Trumbull said.

He no sooner got the words out of his mouth when they all heard machinery within the walls. They all stopped and listened.

Emily and Dean had their arms out as if to stop a moving object on both sides.

It was metal, like gears, but then the sound of rock scraping against rock. The tunnel behind them was being sealed off by a wall sliding across from the right. They had to act fast.

"Run!" Trumbull shouted.

They all dashed back through the sliding wall before it fully sealed off the tunnel.

"Jesus!" Johnson said as he was catching his breath. "We need to get back out before this happens again."

Emily was totally freaked out. Dean looked extremely anxious. Brooks and Trumbull were both rather calm.

They carefully backtracked, looking for any sign of some evil trap waiting to ensnare them and finally reached the Iron Gate.

Emily let out a huge sigh of relief.

"So now what? Obviously the traps are still working," Dean asked.

"We need to get out and rethink our strategy," Brooks answered..

"I don't know…I think this may be our only shot at this," Johnson offered.

The sound of another set of gears and walls moving within the maze echoed off the walls, though not close. Then there was a different noise. It was rock scraping, but the mechanisms were squealing as if under tremendous strain.

"That's not good," Dean said. "What do you think is causing the traps to go off?" His eyes were wide as if he was still an excited kid.

"Time," Trumbull said.

"*Only time will tell when the key to the cypher is shown.*"

Brooks thought about this.

Time. Time. Jefferson was always working with it. The great clock.

"Based on his proclivity towards inventions and, in particular, the Great Clock and its devices, I'd say he instituted a timing system into the maze. Jefferson must have used timing mechanisms within the labyrinth to change its configuration. This makes sense. It would allow him to use the least amount of space to create a large enough puzzle to thwart those who would enter without his permission."

"And that would mean?" Dean asked excitedly.

"That would mean it will reset once all the timing devices have gone off," Emily said, as she was finally calming down. "That would allow whoever did enter with permission the chance to go through the maze, use the center room, and then get out in a relatively short period of time."

"So then we wait for all the walls to realign to their original positions?" Dean asked.

Emily's architectural proclivity started to surface. "Yes. And I would venture to guess there are several moving walls. Yet with all those openings we passed it would only take one or two walls to completely force a change in direction and into another section. The key is which ones are traps and which ones actually need to move in order for someone to get all the way through."

"Well, until we can find something to help us get through those tunnels, it will be blind luck finding anything," Johnson said. "Meanwhile, let's get back outside for some fresh air. Since the outside door is closed, there's no fresh air coming in. Unless…Jefferson build a ventilation system."

They went through the open gate and down the entrance tunnel only to find the door was closed.

Emily remembered the two doors acting together when the Iron gate was opened. "The door closed when the gate opened, remember? We need to go back and close the gate."

"I'll get it," Trumbull said as he took the key from Brooks. He was only gone a few minutes when the door moved inward and slid open.

Emily was ecstatic. She moved to the front. Brooks and Dean helped her climb out.

The sun was bright and the sky clear. A cool breeze came out of the west.

She went part way up the sloped and plopped down on the grass on her back, extending her arms out to her sides. Her hands filtered through the grass. It was as if it was the first time she had ever felt grass. She was giddy with delight.

Trumbull was back by the time the others were outside. He climbed out and they were all looking at the opening.

"How do we close it?" Dean asked in his now routine anxious voice.

"There must be a lever or switch," Trumbull said, reaching inside the opening. "Here it is."

He pulled a lever on the right side towards the top. The door moved once more towards him as he stepped away. It lined up with the brick outline and slid forward.

"What should we do now?" Dean asked.

"We must break the riddle of the labyrinth," Brooks said.

Trumbull, brought them all back to reality. "What about this outside door? We need to be very careful about getting things back to normal before we leave. Otherwise it won't be long before the Praetorians find out what we're doing."

Dean was examining the sides of the door, running his hand along the shapes of the bricks. "That's amazing, you can't even see where the edges are."

"Yes, it looks good," Brooks said. "The only sign is the keyhole area at the grass level."

Emily watched the men. Johnson was looking around at the landscape. Trumbull was spying out any possible hidden space they might be waylaid.

"Now what?" Dean asked.

"Mr. Dean, so many questions. Let's start thinking about answers," Johnson said rather impatiently.

Emily, Johnson, Dean, and Brooks all hung out on the slope.

"I'll be back." Trumbull said as he headed the front side of the house."

He returned some twenty minutes later.

"There's no sign of any activity. The hill seems secure for now," he reported.

"And there's been no sounds coming from the labyrinth. I think once the main door is closed, or the Iron Gate, the system goes dormant," Brooks said.

"I believe I figured out what the other squealing sound was," Johnson said. "It must be one of the ceiling sections being lowered. That means if you're in the wrong place at the wrong time…"

"You'll be crushed," Dean finished off the thought.

Emily could tell they all now knew the horrible danger that existed down in the labyrinth.

She decided to refocus. "Let's hear that part of the riddle again."

Brooks read from the diary:

"*Use the rules, to escape, find the light, or doomed to fate*
Don't go back, for it's a trap, move ahead, or you'll be dead
Use the rules; find your way, the Iron fist, will show the day."

"Shall we try again?" Emily asked. "I think enough time has passed to reset the system.

"But what do we do when the walls move?" Dean asked.

"We must decide now. Either we go in and work our way through, waiting for the walls to reset, or we head back to the farm and try to figure this out."

"We must try. Jefferson would not have made this to entrap others forever. Can you imagine the stench that would cause? I mean decaying bodies," Emily said.

"Well, that's a pleasant thought," Trumbull said sarcastically.

He immediately realized his tone and looked at Emily. "Pardon me…it's part of my witty charm."

Emily gave a soft laugh.

"The walls would only delay someone, not kill them, unless they didn't get past one," Brooks offered. "The ceilings are the real worry. It depends how far down to the ground they go. Either way, we could be facing long periods of waiting in an area closed off. Air might be a real problem. If it seals off the air flow, we could suffocate. The other thing is we need to stay close so that we don't get separated by a wall or worse. A wall will crush someone if they couldn't get through in time."

◊ ◊ ◊

Trumbull kept I wary eye out for any potential danger. He knew the habits and protocol regarding the Praetorians. This was the second day Monticello was closed and he knew it was a prime target, ever since the accident all those years earlier. They had endless resources to station Agents all over the world.

"I think we need to try. Sooner or later the Praetorians are going to get suspicious about the closings. I know when I was there, they kept Monticello as a high priority target." Trumbull knew the time window involved. "I bought us a distraction back in Horatio, during the kidnapping, but not a lot. This may be our only chance."

"I'm not going back in there," Emily said as she shook her head. "No way. Not until we know it's safe."

"I'll go." Dean chimed in.

"I'm going." Brooks said. He looked at Johnson, who was clearly hesitating.

"Oh what the hell." Johnson finally said.

Trumbull decided it might help if he was not around Dean. "I'll stay with Mrs. Yates. Keep her safe." He said as he looked at her.

He could tell she wasn't too thrilled about it as she looked down to avoid eye contact.

Dean slid down the door drop, then Johnson, and last Brooks. They quickly disappeared.

It was an awkward moment for Trumbull, hanging back with Emily. He knew she was uncomfortable around him.

"I'm gonna take another look around, make sure it's safe."

"Ok," Emily nodded, holding her hand up to block the sun that was in her face.

◊ ◊ ◊

Dean took out a pad and pencil and they moved forward again, mapping out the tunnels.

He was in Heaven. He always enjoyed investigative work, starting in his younger years, and thrown into the fray when he watch Trumbull kill his parents.

His adoptive parents shared many of the tales they had from the Absconditus Verum world. Johnson started mentoring him soon after the event, making sure he attended college. He studied criminal justice, forensics, and cybercrime, grooming himself to join the FBI.

He worked his way through the ranks quickly and on his own merits. This was the first time Johnson brought him on a case. He was trying his best to do his job at the highest possible level.

As the three of them reached each intersection, they took turns vetting them out. He kept notes on every turn.

But this was proving more difficult than they thought, for those tunnels had even more intersections. On top of that, they started finding split tunnels with narrow half width stairways, barely wide enough to go up or down. These were heading downward and they tried a few, but then they had even more choices to go left, right, forward, down, or up.

As they went, the sound of metal gears cranked. Stone was moving. Some faint and others closer.

"Well?" Dean would ask each time he heard rock to the annoyance of both Brooks and Johnson.

This time they heard a wall closing in the distance behind them.

"And that would be sealing us off," Dean concluded.

"Let's keep moving," Johnson said.

Dean was noticing as he mapped, that each tunnel, in addition to bending to the left, was also turning at ninety degree angles. So each tunnel turned left and right as they went. This made him feel as though they were doubling back in some tunnels.

He was having trouble getting it all down on paper as he held his flashlight, the pencil, and the pad. On top of that there were so many turns, he was running out of space to put them, needing to use additional pages. It was becoming harder to keep track.

"Guys, we really need to stop. I'm having trouble keeping all this straight. I don't want to get us lost, and right now I'm starting to get disoriented.

Another wave of walls moving could be heard, including one just around the corner in front of them.

Even though his watch wasn't accurate, it was close enough to guess the time.

"I'm guessing the walls move about every ten minutes. That's the fifth move and we've made like forty turns, counting the dozen or so times we went straight."

"Ok let's get out of here," Johnson said. "Obviously this truly is a complicated labyrinth. There's no way we can hope to find the right path this way. And we risk a section that can crush us."

"I agree," Brooks said. "Let's head back."

"But what about the traps?" Dean questioned. "I thought it was incredibly lucky we got back last time. Now we are at least three times as far from the entrance and we've gone through several different levels. And the walls have already moved behind us more than once."

"Why on Earth would anyone spend the time making this tunnel system?" Johnson asked.

"I think because what awaits us is so important, Jefferson felt the need to have no one but a very few reach the center room," Brooks surmised.

They backtracked using Deans notes until they reached a wall blocking them. Dean figured it was forty five minutes before the wall retracted. This happened two more times before they reached the Iron Gate. They waited twenty minutes for one, and thirty for the other.

"Thank you, Tim, for your mapping skills. We would have definitely gotten lost," Brooks acknowledged.

"Well, until we can find something to help us get through those tunnels, it'll be dumb luck finding the right way," Johnson offered.

Brooks relocked the Iron Gate and the front door reopened at the same time.

They climbed out one at a time, Trumbull pulling them up. Dean hesitated in grabbing Trumbull's arm.

They looked at each other for several moments before Trumbull said, "do you want my help or not?"

Dean gabbed his arm and got pulled up and out.

Trumbull reached in and pulled the lever. The door moved once more towards him as he stepped away. It lined up with the brick outline and slid forward.

"What took you guys so long?" Emily asked.

"Too many choices to make, and we got stuck behind a few coming back." Dean answered.

"Any suggestions about the keyhole? Chances are very small someone would actually find it unless they're specifically looking right at it," Johnson reasoned.

"I think I can fix that," Dean had an idea. He went into the cook's room and came out with some small pieces of broken mortar and brick. "We should be able to put this mixture into the hole to hide it from anyone not specifically looking at this one spot."

"Very good, Tim," Johnson said.

Dean put some of the mortar he found into the hole and indeed it did hide most of it.

As they made their way to the front entry, Dean was explaining all the mapping to Emily.

"I did the best I could. Next time we go in, I could sure use your help keeping track."

Emily smiled and nodded.

"I'll reset the Clock and pull the clock weights back up to where they should be now that the door has been found," Trumbull said. "Gentlemen, if you would."

He climbed up the ladder, as Dean and Johnson pulled the ropes up from the basement level. They continued feeding them up as Trumbull was pulling on them.

"Make sure to reset the weights where they belong." Dean offered, to no one's amusement.

Trumbull just looked at him and shook his head.

"I think it's about three thirty." Dean said softly as he looked at Johnson, who couldn't help but smile.

Once everything was put in place, they exited through the front door.

"I suggest we go back to Staunton and give that diary a good once over." Brooks suggested. "We should also call the Sheriff and see if Mr. Yates can tell us anything more to help us to the next step. Oh, and one more thing. Perhaps it's nothing, but I believe we need to be a little more cautious at the farm. I'm not sure, but I have an uneasy feeling there."

Dean wasn't sure what he meant. He was about to ask when Johnson turned and shook his head from the passenger seat.

I'll ask Johnson later.

Trumbull rode alone and followed them back to the farm.

On the ride back Dean continued going over the notes with Emily, turning them this way and that, like trying to put a puzzle together.

The group is really counting on me to help solve this. I've got to stop thinking about Trumbull. Park it. Bury it. Everything's too important. I just have to be ready in case Trumbull does try to stop the group.

Chapter 30

May 2018 – Monticello, Virginia

They reached the farm, got their gear, and headed inside. Johnson took Dean aside and they chatted for a bit.

Emily couldn't hear what it was about. She guessed it might be about their hostess. She understood Brook's inference in the car.

Do I trust her? How will we really know?

For now there was nothing she could do, so she focused on the tasks at hand.

Once settled, refreshed, and in the sitting room, Emily took out her computer, set it on a coffee table. She sat on the floor and went online to see just what the balance of Federal power was from 1789 to 1801 and beyond.

Dean joined her.

She started reading aloud. "According to this article, John Adams had managed to win the Presidential Election in 1796 mostly due to Washington's popularity and Hamilton secretly trying to rig the elections. It says back then, even if they had a running mate, there was still technically no party system. The top two in votes became President and Vice President, even though they might have had opposing views."

Brooks arrived and sat down.

She continued. "Hamilton tried to rig the elections to have Adams finish second in the votes to his running mate Thomas Pinckney of South Carolina. Everyone found out. Pinckney was one of the few Federalists from the south. The Federalists, however, didn't want another southerner as President or Vice President. Jefferson was running as the Anti-Administration candidate, which was the Anti-Federalist Party."

"That's right," Brooks said. "The educators in central government use the term Democratic-Republicans. This incorrectly leads people to believe Jefferson started the Democratic or Republican parties. In fact, it was the Federalists who labeled the Anti-Federalists as Democratic or Jacobin. It was their attempt to link them to mob rule and the radicals of the French Revolution, ergo Napoleon. Since the

Federalists wrote history, well…now you know why so many historical events are hidden or were written by people wanting to create as false record, a lie.

"Now Jefferson's group did start calling itself the Democratic Republicans, but not until the election of 1800. And it was not to institute democracy. It was to restore the Republic. Understand that they all agreed there was a place for a majority vote, but only at the local community level. From there the rule of law and representative government was the core of the Republic. Any majority vote at a higher level resulted in the minority being forced to live under majority rule. That's the tyranny of democracy and what we have today. It not only forces so many to live under other's ideology, it also creates compromise which takes freedoms away from everyone on all sides."

"I found a quote here from Adams," Emily said. "In a letter to another Founder, Adams explained what he thought of democracy;

'Remember, democracy never lasts long. It soon wastes, exhausts, and murders itself. There never was a democracy yet that did not commit suicide. It is in vain to say that democracy is less vain, less proud, less selfish, less ambitious, or less avaricious than aristocracy or monarchy. It is not true, in fact, and nowhere appears in history. Those passions are the same in all men, under all forms of simple government, and when unchecked, produce the same effects of fraud, violence, and cruelty.'"

"And yet so many are so proud and under the delusion that we're a democracy, even though in reality, we're a Republic," Dean answered. "Emily, can you find out how Hamilton's actions worked against both his desires and Adams?"

Emily was searching for the information. "Here it is. Hamilton's actions backfired. Too many Federalists didn't want Pinckney in so they voted for Adams and Jefferson. They all had two votes back then because each man was essentially running by themselves."

"So Adams still won," Dean said.

Brooks explained. "Yes, but Jefferson was second and missed the Presidency by only three electoral votes. Adams was furious at Hamilton yet again. However, the positive for the Federalists was that Jefferson was now in a no-power position, just as Adams was before him. Jefferson spent most of his time as Vice President at Monticello.

"Meanwhile, the Federalists were in a full-fledged battle with the resurgence of the Anti-Federalists, who had made several gains in both houses of Congress. This was where the real two-party system began to emerge, even though the top two in votes would be installed from two different parties."

"And let me see..." Emily said. "Okay, Jefferson's party had taken control of the House from 1793-97. Lost it through Adams' Presidency and then reclaimed control for the next twenty four years. The Senate was a bit different. The Federalists held control through both Washington's and Adams' terms. All the damage Hamilton did was accomplished by the end of 1794. He left the next month."

"My God," Dean said, "All that damage in five short years!"

"It is pretty amazing isn't it," Brooks answered.

July 1797 - Eastern Long Island, New York

The Praetorians were not able to outflank Adams in the Presidential election and the Praetor was not happy about it. "Church!"

Benjamin Church came into the chamber as he always did now, from behind the Master chair.

"That fool Adams is now starting to damage our plans. It's time we take over. I was hoping to stay behind the scenes, but Adams is forcing my hand."

"Who do you suggest?"

"Someone who can run the government from a Cabinet position. I don't know. It must be someone who is not associated with the Society of the Cincinnati. We need that military arm to join us, but I cannot have them moving in to take control themselves."

Church gathered a list of potentials. "Sir, here is the list of Nationalists. I broke it down to show you who they are and which ones attended the different meetings and Conventions.

"Now, we have Richard Bassett listed here. He was at Newburgh, the Annapolis Convention in '86, Constitutional in '87, Ratifying in Delaware, is not a member of Cincinnati, is a lawyer, and banker,"

The Praetor said nothing.

"…next we have."

"How long is this list?"

"There are quite a few listed here."

"Give it to me. I will look through it and decide. For now, we must play nice until the election agitation calms down. But we need to lay the ground work. Adams is not well liked within the military…and we can use that to our advantage.

"He knows Hamilton controls most of his Cabinet and it will be easy for us to replace one of them. Adams is keeping close to the vest now and I fear he will attempt to undo some of our accomplishments."

"Sir, I don't think he can get much done now that the Anti-Federalists have made gains in Congress."

"Oh he will, somehow. The problem is Jefferson's ilk is also working against us. I'll kill them all before they can take away our goals."

"Sir…" Church hesitated.

The Praetor looked at him. "What is it man?"

"Sir, when will we take total control? It has been many years now and I was wondering about the timetable."

"You are? Or is someone else?"

Church was afraid to speak.

"Tell me Church …you can tell me."

Church looked up to the Praetor. "Sir, you know I serve two masters…and King George is getting very impatient. He wants a timetable for the return of the states to the Empire of England.

"He does, oh that's right, you are his emissary now," the Praetor thought for a moment. "Didn't he just get a great concession from the Jay Treaty?"

"Yes Sir, but he is disappointed you have not taken total control. I'm sorry Sir…he said you have become erratic. You have been using the King's funds for many of your operations and…he wants results, he wants them now."

"We're not ready to take control yet. Having Jefferson installed as Vice President means he might gain control of the Presidency if something should happen to Adams. Our hands have been tied for the moment. You go to England and tell your precious King that I have no timetable for him. He must wait just as I am. Meanwhile, he should keep his thoughts to himself. And if he wants to communicate with me, it must only be through private correspondences. Do you understand what I'm saying?"

"Yes Sir."

"Good, then get on the next ship and give him a message; but only from the letter I will write. You shall never speak openly about my alliance with the King. If you do so and I find out, you will never live to tell the tale."

Church bowed before the Praetor and left.

The Praetor thought long and hard about just who he could trust to step in and take control. He studied the list Church had given him. The name jumped off the paper when he came to it. "Of course…yes, he will do it. He's perfect for the task and he owes me a great favor."

◊ ◊ ◊

Once returned from England, the Praetor had Church track down his choice. It was James Wilson of Pennsylvania, the Constitutional Convention attendee that Hamilton had kicked out of his office some years earlier. He was perhaps the most learned person in politics at the time of Ratification and was instrumental in much of the final writing of the Constitution.

He coauthored the Judiciary Act with Ellsworth and was selected as an associate judge to the Supreme Court in 1789, the year the court was first started. Many personally bad choices with investments in land speculation however, left him impoverished and twice sent to debtor's prison. The Praetor believed this once great man, though they had a falling out some years earlier, could rise again with his help and join them in their quest for power and an American Empire.

It took Church some time to track him down. He finally did, in Burlington, New Jersey. He was shocked to see his deteriorated condition when they met privately. It was at the dockyard.

"My God Wilson, what's happened to you? You look awful."

"It's Washington's fault. I was to rise to Supreme Court Justice. He promised me," he said in an excitedly panicked voice.

Church asked, "The Praetorians are looking for someone with your qualifications to run the government behind the scenes, but now," he shook his head and rose to leave.

"No…no…the King…King George. I told him I could help. He betrayed me. All that land I bought he said would become prime real estate, the plan to bring British colonists to settle our western land. He told me. He said he could not be seen in these actions. I told him I would. I believed him. Now…now look at me. I'm wanted by the creditors. They want to put me in debtor's prison again. I can't. I can't…"

Church now was sure Wilson was the wrong choice. The brilliant mind seemed wasted away. "You know what James? I think it best we skip this business. You have enough troubles, than to get involved in anything else."

"No…no…yes…yes…no, wait. I know I can help. I do know. The Praetor, yes…yes…he will help…"

"James, the Praetor wants you to work with him, like you did before. Do you think you can get cleaned up and return to government?"

"Oh yes…I…I can help. Please…help me…please."

Church looked at him hard. "Okay James. We must have your word. If you betray the Praetorians, or the Praetor, you know what he will do."

"I swear, I swear…no tricks?"

"No James, no tricks. The problem is Adams."

Wilson looked him in the eye. "But how can I do that? All those years working with Hamilton and now I have no rank, no honor left. Adams hates me as much as anyone."

"Then think of this assignment as an opportunity to restore your lost honor and it can make you wealthy once again. Now James, we have a chain of command in place. I am your superior. The Praetor will contact you through me. He told me to tell you this up front. Can you work with me as your superior?"

"Oh…yes…yes, I will, yes."

Church decided. "Okay…first things first. The Praetor's biggest concern is where you ally yourself. He has held you very close to him in the past. He needs to know about Aaron Burr."

"Burr? I have no allegiances to Burr. As far as my allegiance goes, it is to the Praetor, yes, always to him."

"Okay James, come with me and we'll get you cleaned up

and looking proper. Whether you think it or not, most of our friends still honor you, and many know it was the King that betrayed you. Have some faith. Come with me."

Wilson now knew he was involved at the highest level with this most important task. "I guess I have some influence after all."

"It would seem so," Church said. "But be sure, it will not be me, but the Praetor that you will answer to if you fail."

"Yes, of course. I understand, yes."

"Good. Then let's be on our way."

May 2018 - Staunton, Virginia

Ms. Pamela Sanders announced a late lunch was now ready. "Please come into the dining room everyone."

Emily, Dean, and Brooks went in and sat. Johnson and Trumbull soon joined them. They were all sitting in the same chairs as the night before.

Emily carefully lined up her utensils as always. The spacing between them was exactly the same to the naked eye. Her precision was flawless.

Brooks had his mind on other things, *I need to keep this group working together.* He was hoping Dean would not escalate anything.

"Are we good?" he asked as they all looked at him. "Can we all work together? We can't afford personal interests to get in the way." He looked squarely at Dean.

"It's ok. I'm ok. I put the past away. I agree. Let's work together." Dean offered in 'let's move on' tone.

"Good, then let's move forward." Brooks felt in control for now.

Ms. Sanders brought each a plate of greens, and southern barbeque.

"So…what happened to the conspiracy?" Emily asked Brooks.

"It never materialized. Hamilton retreated from political life once the scandal of the elections had come out. He had no choice. He was lucky he wasn't imprisoned for vote tampering," Brooks said. "The Praetorians decided it was too risky for a coup attempt, but it really didn't matter. Adams made a major misstep. By allowing Washington's Presidential

Cabinet to continue on, and not changing any of the economic policies, Hamilton still ruled behind the scenes.

"Wilson, who was well liked by those who had served from Washington's time, regained some political recognition. He frequently met with Cabinet members in secret and continued to make policy through them and Congress, the Praetor's policy of course, though Adams was also keen on a strong central *Nation State.* Unfortunately, Wilson again fell into heavy debt and was on the run. He became a huge liability because of his knowledge of the Praetorians.

"Treasury Secretary Oliver Wolcot had succeeded Hamilton after being his second from 1791 to 1795. Hamilton met with him more than Adams did, and Adams' misplaced trust in the Cabinet ensured his own demise.

"Hamilton pretended to leave the political scene and worked at his law firm in New York City for several years. He now had his own liability in Wilson, fearing he might expose the coup they had planned so he sent Church to take care of him."

"What? Wait a minute; you're getting me totally confused. Why are you talking about Hamilton and the Praetorians together? Hamilton had already told Washington he was not working with them," Emily said.

Brooks looked at her and Dean. "Now you have one more piece of the puzzle."

Dean's face lit up with astonishment. "You mean Hamilton was working with the Praetorians?"

"Mr. Dean, Hamilton *was* the Praetor."

Emily responded. "My God…Hamilton had an army of Praetorians and he was infiltrating every aspect of government."

"Yes, both Federal and state. He needed to find and destroy any documents that exposed this truth. These are another part of what we're looking for. We believe Hamilton kept records of all that was done. He penned everything, was a fanatic about writing every detail down. It's our belief that somehow those documents fell into the Verum Society's hands, possibly from Church, because when he disappeared, so did the documents."

Emily and Dean were both silent.

Brooks gave them a moment and continued.

"By 1798 Adams had so outraged the French, we were close to war. The Jay Treaty bonded us as trading and supply partners with England. Adams stopped paying back the French debt we still owed from our Revolution because of the French Revolution. The French took these actions to mean we were allied with England, and while we held to our neutral position, it was now clear Adams intended to aid the English. So France started attacking American cargo ships and seizing goods headed for England. The French did offer a backroom blackmail deal, the XYZ affair, which Adams refused.

"Then Adams asked Washington to build a strong central government army because America's non-existent navy had no ships. They sold them all off by 1785. Washington's health prevented him from leaving Mount Vernon, but he pressed Adams to have Hamilton at the helm. So Adams had no other choice but to ask him, even though he despised him. Hamilton took command and started building our first permanent National Army to lead an invasion of French and Spanish colonies in North America. He already had several pieces in place through the Societies of Praetorians and the Cincinnati.

"Spain was allied with France at the time and he had visions of invading France as well. Hamilton was finally getting his chance for glory on the battlefield. What he didn't know was Adams was secretly working out peace terms behind the scenes. When Hamilton was finally ready to carry out the invasion, peace was reached. This was just one more reason Hamilton and Adams hated each other so much."

"I never heard about not having ships. I thought we always had ships," Emily said.

"Not at that point until Congress finally acted and was granted twelve ships to be armed. Eventually they had added the Treasury cutters totaling about twenty-five vessels. This naval war was fought mostly in the Caribbean."

"But I don't remember us going to war against France," Emily asked.

"That's because we didn't, well not officially. That was the naval war I mentioned last night. No proclamation of war was ever given by the Congress. Now you know why today's

Congress doesn't make proclamations of war, at least not with the last three. Adams started the trend of ideological Presidents usurping that power way back in 1798, although that is still in dispute to this day by our political elite and historians."

Chapter 31

May 2018 - Staunton, Virginia

They completed lunch and helped clean up. Once finished they sat back down at the dining room table. Emily now had the diary.

"Is it a cypher?" Dean asked.

"There are still several cyphers we haven't been able to decode," Brooks said as Emily flipped the pages. "Without a cypher key or keys, it's hard to imagine we can solve this."

She found the page with the number sequences on it.

18 16 14 4 10 20 18 2 26 4~
5 15 9 19 17 9 13

----

4 26 2 18 20 10 4 14 16 18
13 9 17 19 9 15 5

"We don't have the algorithm to decode it," Brooks said.

"What if the numbers correspond to letters?" Emily asked.

"We've tried that, like one is an A. We tried moving the numbers to other letters in both directions."

"What does that do?" Emily asked.

"The number one moved one letter to the right means that one would be the letter B. We worked it from one letter all the way through the twenty-six letters in both directions. It was still gibberish."

Emily placed the diary on the dining room table, pulled out a notepad, and started working on the cypher.

Brooks changed the subject. "Trumbull, how long will it be before the Praetorians figure out what we are doing?"

"Based on their track record, which is not very good, I would say that we must be done no later than tomorrow night. Having Monticello closed for a third straight day will certainly be a red flag. They've probably already sent out an agent. While it's one of dozens of sites, it is a rather important one because of what happened twenty-five years ago. Now with the panic and killings, it makes it even more attentive to their eyes."

"What if we have them open normally?" Johnson asked.

"I would guess that might ward them off, but they probably

will have an agent search Monticello again."

"So if we get there early and go into the labyrinth, closing the door behind us, it should shield our presence, at least everything but the keyhole." Dean asked.

"That would probably work until we need to get out. Once an agent goes there, he will continue to monitor the site for several days, if not weeks. That door is loud when it opens, loud enough to bring someone to investigate the noise." Trumbull answered.

"Then we must solve the maze tonight or we'll miss this opportunity until they give up surveillance." Emily offered.

"Yes, that'd be the only way to proceed without being detected. Well, I mean there is one other way. I could take care of any agents that do come looking. That would buy us some more time, but not much. They have to check in on a regular basis. They were hot on my trail several times over the years, sometimes almost catching me."

Emily interrupted. "We need to call James. He might be able to help."

"Yes Emily. I'll call," Brooks went into the sitting room to make the call.

Emily wrote down the string of numbers and had Dean make a copy for everyone.

"I've got to go out to the barn and check on the horses. I'll see you in a bit," Ms. Sanders said and headed out the back kitchen door.

"Emily, I have Pete on," Brooks motioned for her to come into the sitting room.

She joined him as he handed her the phone. He went to the dining room to join the others.

"Pete?" Her voice shook.

"Hi Emily. How are you holding up?" Pete said in a calm friendly voice.

"I'm okay. How are the girls and Thomas, err I mean James?"

"They're doing well. James is recovering very well. The girls have been well comforted since I brought him here. I'll put him on."

She was getting more anxious and upset as Pete talked.

"Emily?" James asked.

"Yes James," she trembled as her voice broke. "How are you and the girls are doing?"

James was even keeled as he spoke. "Oh Em, it's ok. We have a great support team. I'm getting better by the day. The bullet missed my main artery which is why I'm recovering quicker that we thought. Amanda wants to talk to you. Here she is."

Emily's heart started pounding. She brought her other hand to her mouth, holding the phone close, closing her eyes.

"Mommy?" Amanda asked in a cautious tone.

"Hi sweetheart…oh…how you are doing?" Emily was trying to check her emotions but was weeping softly as she opened her eyes.

"I'm being very brave mommy. I'm looking after Sara too. She still gets a little scared."

"Oh darling, I miss you so much."

"I miss you too. Pete said we're going to go to a different house today. He said it keeps us safe if we move around. Do you want to talk to Sara?"

"Yes honey." She checked her grief, trying to stay strong for the girls.

"Here Sara. It's mommy." She heard Amanda through the phone.

"Hi mommy!" an excited Sara burst out.

"Hi sweetheart. Mommy misses you. Are you helping your sister?" She stopped weeping and sniffled, rubbing her nose with her hand.

"Yes mommy, but I'm scared. I don't know all these people staying with us."

"I know," she paused trying to hold back her tears. "Daddy is there and Pete and Mike. They will protect you okay?"

"Okay mommy. I love you."

"I love you too sweetheart."

"Here's daddy."

Emily heard James take the phone and say "Ok Sara, it's ok. Go help your sister and Mike."

James started. "Emily. I gave Brooks more information. I hope it helps. He said you guys found a secret set of tunnels under the back yard. It's a labyrinth. I remember my dad talking about one, though we never really worked on it together and he had no sketches of one. He did tell me that there was a code within the cypher that's in the diary. I told Brooks, but I don't know the cypher key."

She sniffled again, wiping tears from her face. "Yes, he's with the others working on it now. We hope we're close to finding something. Brooks has a lot of information about the Absconditus Verum, you know, the Society you're a part of."

"Pete filled me in about the Verum and about the Praetorians now trying to stop us."

"Brooks has been sharing what he knows with us," she said.

"I know. Hopefully we can find it and bring it to the people. It's only through them that we can regain control of our own government. I don't know how that can happen, but we must try. I'm sorry about everything that's happened. I'm sorry it's you and not me."

"Oh James…I love you." She paused, then said, "It's so strange calling you James."

"Yeah, I'm trying to get used to it too. I wish I was there to help. You take care."

"I'll be alright. I miss you and the girls terribly. Hopefully we can see each other soon." She was finally calming down, getting her emotions in check.

"I love you Em. We'll get through this. I'm almost well enough to travel. Pete and I will be joining you soon. Mike and Agent Waxman will be looking after the girls. They'll be safe."

"Okay, just as long as I can talk to the girls wherever they are."

"Yes, we'll be in direct contact with Brooks on a daily basis. They've formed a contact chain, or rather they had one in place and they're using it now. I know about all the killings. I just wish this was some other family that was torn apart and not ours."

Emily could hear the regret in James' voice. She could tell this was hitting him hard.

"No, you don't mean that," she said.

"Well, I do mean it, but I wouldn't wish this on anyone."

"I know James."

"It's time to use those architectural skills of yours. I think they may come in handy at some point."

Emily hadn't even thought about work or architecture.

"We'll talk soon Em."

"I love you, goodbye."

Emily stood and stared at the fireplace. It was difficult, keeping her emotions in check. She hadn't noticed all the handcrafted design work in the mantle before. There were letters carved out of the wood. They were Greek and Roman, Latin, French, Spanish, and others she didn't recognize. Some were large and some very tiny. It was quite beautiful.

After a few moments, she joined the others. They were writing, each trying to break the code, the secret to the labyrinth. She sat down and stared at the numbers on her copy.

"How's your husband and the girls?' Johnson asked.

"They're safe and James's getting better."

"That's good to hear."

"Yes," she was drifting into thought as she looked at the page.

They worked for an hour or so before Dean stood up and walked to the kitchen, flipping his pencil back to his papers on the table. "I can't get anywhere with this. I need a break."

Emily could tell he was getting frustrated, though he hid it well.

◊ ◊ ◊

He went into the kitchen, where Ms. Sanders was standing at the counter, preparing the evenings meal. She stopped chopping a cucumber.

"Mr. Dean, can I get you anything?" she asked.

"Yes…please. A drink."

She opened the refrigerator. "How about some apple cider?"

"Yes…that'd be great."

Pamela poured him a cup. "Come, sit with me."

They sat at a small kitchen table.

"Ms. Sanders. How are you involved with the Verum Society?"

"Well, my husband had genealogy from the original founders. We really didn't know much other than to host members now and then."

"Aren't you afraid for yourself?"

She thought for a moment. "No, not really. We committed to the Verum and I'm proud to be a member, anything that might help to reveal the truth. Our country is such a mess. We know it wasn't set up the way we have it now, but most Americans don't. Such an important piece has been lost."

Dean looked at her curiously.

She smiled. "Yes, I've done some research too. It seems most of the governmental foundation that was in place at the beginning has been swept away. Jefferson wouldn't even recognize what we've become."

"But it seems other Founders would," answered Dean. "Agent Johnson has been tutoring me about what happened in the beginning. Many Founders were not the men we thought they were. Several were nationalists, I think.."

"Some were even worse. A few wanted a monarchy and no representation for the people. The aristocracy was to rule just as it had been in England."

"Well, yes, but I've been thinking. Times do change. We must also change with the times otherwise we can't grow. With the birth of technology, science, math, and social questions, we couldn't keep an old government that was outdated," Dean said. He sipped his cider.

"Is that what you think has happened?" she asked as she got up to attend a pot on the stove.

He turned his chair to face her. "To tell you the truth Ma'am, I only know what I was taught and what Agent Brooks told us. He has my head spinning every time I'm around him. His knowledge of history is astounding."

She answered without looking at him as she continued preparing food on the stove. "Ah yes, and that's because he's a historian. His work in the FBI has allowed him and Mr. Johnson to learn many of the secrets of our past and the Praetorians." She stopped and looked at Dean. "Spend every minute you can with him and learn as much as you can."

He nodded. "My big question is he seems to only be talking about one historical view, perhaps biased towards what we've all learned in school."

She was bouncing back and forth from the counter to the stove. "I don't know Brooks that well, but by what you're saying, I'd guess he's trying to share the other side. The side the Verum believe is the correct one. I don't think he's interested in an ideological debate where partisans simply entrench even more without listening to the other side.

"Just turn on the radio or cable TV. You can hear the babble everywhere else. He's showing you that there is indeed another view, one that the partisans won't talk about. The Absconditus Verum."

As Dean watched her preparing the food, he decided to get up and help. He stopped for a moment passing the kitchen door. There was a ramp over the steps.

He looked at Pamela and was just about to ask.

She cut in. "That helps with my arthritis. I am always going to the barn and back. It helps ease the pain."

Dean looked through the kitchen window that was in the front of the house. He did the math and realized they couldn't see the ramp going up the front walk. He thought for a second and shrugged it off, moving to the sink. "Here, let me help you."

She smiled and handed him a strainer to hold in the sink.

"Ma'am, I understand a bit better now. I guess we all have been so wrapped up in the current form of government we have, most don't even conceive that things were so different back then. Everyone seems to be stuck in the now, and they think all other possibilities are conspiracy theories."

"Yes, just as the government and media want them to believe."

He smiled and she returned one back. He spent the next few minutes with Ms. Sanders before returning to the dining room. He had to help break the code and they were running out of time.

◊ ◊ ◊

Another hour passed. Emily got up every now and then, and circled the table, checking on the others progress or lack thereof. Once in a while she would reach down and straighten papers.

Each in their own time took a break to stand, or stretch.

Emily thought about Brooks' remark regarding Ms. Sanders. She popped out of the kitchen several times with snacks and cider.

She seems the perfect hostess. If she is a Praetorian, then it's an Academy award performance she's putting on.

Still she overheard Trumbull and Brooks whispering remarks about her.

Was she hiding something? Perhaps she was being too nice to cover something up.

Several more hours passed and they kept at it. Emily, however, wasn't writing much down. Something was working in her head. The numbers somehow made sense in some fashion, though she didn't know how.

Architecture…architecture…that's the key, but how? How do these numbers correspond? I know somehow it does.

She'd finished the first row of numbers and had written the corresponding letters below them. It was jumbled but there were several repeating sequences. She wrote the second row and again there were several repeating sequences, though they were completely different than the first row. She continued to try different strategies, but each row was the same; different letters with sequences. making no sense. She stared at it.

What if I use the substitution rule? Something, something is here. Find it, mix it match it…mix it…mix it.

She moaned in frustration as she looked around the table. They all looked at her. She was just getting up when…

"Perhaps it's time I joined you," said a man in the doorway between the dining room and the kitchen.

The men jumping to their feet as they all looked at him. He was in a wheelchair and Ms. Sanders was standing behind him.

"Please let me introduce my husband, Richard Yates."

Emily was shocked and she saw the stunned faces from the rest.

"My God…Richard?" Brooks asked.

"Yes Joseph."

"But, I don't understand. We were never told you survived."

"It was for the protection of all including my son." He scanned the room and locked eyes with Trumbull.

"And here I thought you were dead all these years," Trumbull smiled.

"Yes William. And I have been tracking your movements since that fateful day. Made quite a mess of things haven't you,"

"Of course, would you have expected anything less?" Trumbull said.

Emily recognized Trumbull slipped back into his impetuous tone.

"I suppose not. I was quite pleased actually when you decided to change sides. I was sorry it was so long and so many of our comrades were killed. I do thank you for leaving my son alone. It seems you even helped him recently."

"I did and you're welcome."

"Richard. We found the secret to the Great Clock and the labyrinth." Brooks said.

"Yes, yes I know. But first I would like to meet my daughter-in-law." He said as he hand gestured for his wife to push him closer to the group.

Emily came round the table and went to him. "Very nice to meet you Sir," she said as the moment caught her. "God, if only James was here."

"I know," his eyes showed how much he had missed not being able to share their lives. "My son has done quite well for himself. A beautiful wife and two girls…" he fell silent. They were all quiet for several moments.

"Richard, this is Agent Ben Johnson and this is Agent Timothy Dean," Emily nodded towards each one as she introduced them.

Richard gave them each a welcoming handshake. "Welcome both of you and thank you for joining us, we can never have enough help.

"Tim, I'm sorry for your loss. I know what it is to lose someone so close. Thank you for allowing Trumbull to help us." Richard motion to him and to Trumbull as he spoke.

Dean nodded politely. Emily caught what he had just said though didn't say anything.

"So, it's time to figure out this puzzle," said the now Mrs. Pamela Yates.

"Yes…Yes…if you please dear," Richard motioned for her to pushed him toward the table.

Dean slid his chair over enough for Richard to join them at the table. Johnson grabbed Deans papers and moved them.

Once he was at the table, the rest of them sat, except for

Pamela. She returned to the kitchen.

"Don't fret Emily. I hear you're quite good with puzzles. Perhaps together we can solve this next step," Richard said.

"Well, I think it's here in this numerical sequence, though I haven't been able to place it." She showed him the numbers they were all working on.

"Because you don't have the key," Richard stated.

"Yes, that's right," Emily answered.

"But you do have the key, don't you?" Richard reached out with his hand.

She gave him a quizzical look.

"I mean the actual key to the door."

"No, Mr. Trumbull has it." Emily looked at Trumbull.

"Yes, here it is." He took it out and handed it to Richard.

"Ah yes," he said as he held it in his hand. "This brings back memories. I held this long ago trying to figure out its secrets. Once you've found the central chamber, the path behind you will close, therefore, you must exit through a different series of tunnels. This key unlocks the chamber. It's all in the diary. The numbers are the guide to get you through the labyrinth."

"And you've known this all along?" Brooks asked as he picked up the diary off the table.

"I was never really sure it was Monticello. I never found the entrance. The riddle was passed down to me from my father, but only now that the labyrinth has been entered would I reveal this about the key. The key was no good to anyone unless they had broken the riddle and entered the labyrinth. When you found the entrance yesterday and came back, Pamela heard you talking."

"I don't understand," Brooks said. "I've found nothing in the diary that could break this numbers cypher."

"Because the cypher key it is not in the diary." He looked at Emily. "It's here," he said.

She got up and collected the key.

She gave it a good once over as she slowly walked back to her chair. She remained standing. Nothing was there that she could detect as she turned it over and over by its oval handle. "Am I supposed to see something on this key? I don't see anything."

"Look at the teeth." Richard encouraged her.

The men all watched in anticipation.

"Do you know what it is?" Dean asked Richard.

There were three teeth protruding out. She inspected them carefully. Still nothing. "This is just an old skeleton key." Emily concluded.

"That was the hope. The key would not easily reveal its secret. Try again, and this time use your architectural knowledge." Richard nodded to her.

"Why not tell us?" Dean pressed.

"Because if you have any chance at all of getting through those tunnels, Emily must be able to decipher the key herself."

She kept looking at it as she turned it again and again. Then she stopped, holding it up and horizontal. "Is this a one?"

"It is."

"Where!" Dean said with a burst of excitement.

"Here," Emily said as she pointed to the first tooth. "A Roman numeral one, though masked and rounded. It's no surprise no one noticed it before."

"And the next?" Richard asked.

"Not a number. Not a Roman numeral. No…is this Greek?"

"Well done. You are indeed special. When James was young, he was very good with puzzles."

"Yes, he still is," she answered as she was fixated on the key. "This looks like a Greek number ten. See you can tell by the reverse J with the small tab on the top left."

"Excellent."

"The last tooth appears to also be Greek…a three."

"That is the cypher key." Richard offered.

"One, ten, three?" Dean asked as he came over to examined the key. Emily handed it to him.

"Yes," Richard answered. He had a broad smile as he watched Dean and Emily.

"How does that work with the numbers we have?" Johnson entered the conversation. He motioned for Dean to bring over the key. He was on the other side of the table.

"Well, that's been the one thing I haven't been able to solve. I've tried using these three numbers for every conceivable answer, but haven't been able to get anywhere."

"Can I see it again?" Emily asked as she went and got it, then sat in her chair. They all watched her as she examined the key.

She looked at the group. "I don't have any answers to this," she said knowing they were expecting some instantaneous solution. She looked at Richard. "I saw your mantle in the other room. Quite beautiful with all the foreign and many ancient letters all crafted in their styles of old."

Richard smiled as he knew she made the connection. "The mantle is not part of the puzzle. I carved it all out in the hopes of finding the cypher key. Sometimes if you look at something while working on a project, the visual can help stimulate a solution. I spent countless hours in there working on the cypher, but was never able to…well, anyway…"

"Well then, perhaps some dinner and we can start again," said Pamela as she entered the room, brushing off crumbs from a striped apron she had put on.

As Emily ate, she watched the others conversing amongst themselves. It was another wonderful meal, and even better to her as Richard had now joined them.

"You truly amaze me Richard," Trumbull said.

Emily recognized respect in Trumbull's voice.

He continued. "I was standing there watching you die. And here you are twenty-five years later."

"Well…what's left of me." Richard cracked a small smile.

"Please do tell us what happened," Emily asked.

"As for the accident, I was pulled from the car once they were able to free me. They got me to the hospital and stabilized. My legs never did come back. Fortunately, the engine had missed making any serious damage to my insides. It took a year to recover. I met my lovely wife during that time. She was part of the Verum Society already and helping with my recovery. We've been together ever since. She's sacrificed much for me."

"Oh, don't listen to him. I don't regret one single minute," she said smiling.

"As for my son…well the Verum Society had decided it was too risky after what had happened. Joseph had the diary and the key. We decided to lay low and perhaps ride out another generation, so we got no closer to finding anything. I had the secret to the key cypher, but nothing else. I never did figure out the Great Clock even though it was right there in front of me all those years."

"James did," Emily said.

"Yes, it seems this last accident, or rather this attempt…somehow it came together for him, the pieces from the past. Your hostess has filled me in on everything you've done to date. I think I always knew he could find the answer. He was such a smart boy…" his voice trailed off as Emily could see the pain in his face.

"He is every bit your son," Emily said also getting emotional. "I am very proud of him and of you…" She paused. "These things happening behind the scenes all these years and so important to everything we hold dear."

"Well, what some hold dear," Trumbull said. "I've seen the other side. They believe they have the right to rule over the people. They've stopped at nothing to keep this power and they will do everything they can to make sure it stays that way. Fortunately, you have an ace in the hole," he said pointing his fork at himself.

"You really are infatuated with yourself," Brooks said smiling.

◊ ◊ ◊

Trumbull smiled back and continued eating. "This is just delicious."

These guys have no idea, the danger they're in. We must get this job done tomorrow. I feel we may be too late already.

Chapter 32

May 2018 - Staunton, Virginia

Emily and Dean helped Pamela clean up. Dean rekindled the fire and soon they were all in the sitting room. Everyone sat except Trumbull and Dean. They were each behind a chair taken by the women, opposite each other.

Richard was both excited and anxious about this group and their mission. He'd never had this much help at the discovery end of a quest.

"I do love a nice fire. Helps take the chill out of the air," Pamela said, as she got up and played with the logs using the fireplace poker. A few pokes and she was sitting again.

"So, how is it you're back here in Staunton?" Trumbull asked Richard. "Very smart moving out here to the farm. I didn't know it was you I was watching those last years with the Praetorians. They thought you were just another Verum member. The last place they'd expect to find you is right back where you started."

Richard gave him a small smile. "I can be quite clever you know."

Trumbull couldn't contain a small laugh at the thought of Richard's clever deception "My old boss was furious when I left. Their whole ground operation had to be restructured. The man who replaced me is very good. I've encountered him twice, the second time he *killed me*." He looked at Emily and gave her a slight wink.

"Yes, we thought it best after you *killed me* to move out to the farm." Richard said, playing on Trumbull's fatal muse. "Having a new assassin take your place allowed us to make the change and go undetected," Richard responded.

"That was wise because I believe the Praetor is obsessed with you," Trumbull gave a good chuckle as he said this.

"So now that you know all about me, it's time we find out about you isn't it?"

"I think we need to get back to figuring out the labyrinth," Brooks said.

"You're quite right Joseph," Richard answered, though his curiosity was burning about Trumbull. "Young Dean, if you would be so kind as to retrieve everyone's notes.

Dean brought their paperwork and copies into the sitting room. "Perhaps looking at this from a team effort instead of individually might help."

They spent the next few hours working on the puzzle by sharing all their notes. They still were no closer to solving it. It was 8:00 and time was slipping away from them.

Emily worked on an algorithm to solve the code on her computer tablet. Her app started processing and was running the numbers. "This could take some time. I'm in the dark here with this app and if it will even find a solution. I've used it before, but I had more information."

"Then in the meantime, let's take a break," Johnson said.

Everyone placed their sketches on the coffee table.

"Do we have time to take a break?" Dean asked.

"Yes, and I have something to show you. You'll need a strategy tomorrow," Richard said. "I've been thinking about that for some time now and believe unless we find otherwise, you must use all our resources."

"What does that mean?" Dean asked.

Richard turned to Emily. "You need to keep track of directions in the labyrinth. I think you'll need more than notes to do it. We have an idea to help track where you've been in the tunnels. And we associate this process as the spider method?"

"A spider?" she asked.

"Yes, it mimics the web qualities in two aspects." Richard was speaking with his hands as well as he used his fingers to illustrated a web from the center outward. "So what are the two aspects?"

"Well…he can feel a presence in the web and follow his strands anywhere on it."

"Yes, and if an intruder trips up on our device, you will know it even if you are several tunnels ahead."

"And the other?" she asked, not knowing the answer.

"You'll have the solution to returning to the starting tunnel if you need it. Just like a spider knows how to return home," Richard answered. "And that's what you need to do. If the solution is not found before you enter the labyrinth, you must map out the route as you go, but you must also leave a trail each and every way so that you can keep moving towards the target while being able to retreat. And the target is the center."

As Richard spoke, he watched Dean pacing back and forth behind Emily.

Is this kid going to be able to work with Trumbull? I can't have him going in if his motives aren't true to the mission. Trumbull might make it impossible.

"Sir, with all due respect, we were down in there today and there were endless choices to be made. It would be sheer luck for us to find the secret chamber," Dean continued pacing.

Richard caught Johnson out of the corner of his eye motioning Dean to stop pacing.

"Nevertheless it's your only course," Richard answered.

"Richard, the traps are functioning," Emily said shaking her head. "According to Deans account, the walls change every ten minutes. Not all of them at once. They seem to be on a sixty-minute rotation. They were stuck behind one more than half an hour. I don't think mapping or a bread crumb trail will help once the configuration changes."

This was a new development for Richard. He thought about it. "That's why you'll need to use the method I described."

She shook her head. "It won't matter. We can find our way out because we map the twists and turns, backtracking. Once the configuration changes in front of us, we have no bearings to use; no way to know which way to go. It will still be blind luck,"

Richard motioned his confidence to Emily. "It'll work for retreating, don't worry. The bigger challenge is finding your way to the center and getting out."

"It seems we really need to break this code once and for all," Johnson said.

Richard knew he was right.

All these years, and I still have the problem of finding the center.

"Emily, how certain are you this algorithm will work?" he asked.

"I've set it up cross referencing the coding in the book with the paths we take. Once we have enough data to enter with the twists and turns we make, it will help eliminate possible choices as we move forward. That should narrow our time and hopefully give us and accurate course to take."

Richard looked at his daughter-in-law. He could see she was confident in her algorithm. "I have a feeling you'll get it right." He smiled and then looked at Trumbull.

Richard gave Trumbull an affirming nod. Trumbull nodded back. Richard knew the success of this mission would lay at the feet of the assassin if the Praetorians showed up.

They only have one more shot before they lost the opportunity. I've been out of touch with Praetorian *movements longer than I wanted. I need to talk to Trumbull alone.*

"Then we need to make sure we have enough provisions in case we're down there for a prolonged period of time," Brooks said.

Richard answer quickly. "Yes. I knew if I ever did find the secret to entering the labyrinth and didn't have the cypher decoded, I needed an alternate plan. Dean, can I see what you've got so far?" He motioned for Dean to collect and hand him the sketches.

Just keep this kid's head focused will help de-escalate the Trumbull factor.

He was going through they're sketches as he spoke. "Jefferson was very bright in setting this all up and I know they spent a lot of time forming the maze; however, there are far fewer choices than you suspect, young Dean. The labyrinth cannot be more than two or three levels deep. It was more for making someone abandon the effort as opposed to endless choices. I've studied everything Jefferson wrote about and studied all his sketches in architecture. I may be wrong, but I believe not. Tell me Emily, what do you think of Dean's map?" It was the one that caught his eye the most. He handed it to her.

"Well…I know based on how the tunnels were constantly turning, it's a circular maze. I would guess it's no more than two hundred feet in diameter," she answered.

"So you have a finite area to cover. Now here's the important part. How wide were the tunnels?"

"I'd say about six feet?" Dean interjected, looking at the others.

"Yes, I would agree…about six feet." Brooks said.

"Okay, good. So based on those numbers, how many

tunnels do you think are on each level?" Richard asked, looking at Emily.

"Well, it's a guess, but at about six feet wide for each, I would say you can draw about ten circles inside each other until you get to the middle. Of course, these are not uninterrupted. You would be sent in all directions similar to a circular maze puzzle. Let me draw it out," she said.

Richard handed the notes to her. "Please go have a seat in the dining room and work on it." As she left the room Richard continued. "Young Dean, since you mapped it out, would you help her?"

He nodded and joined Emily.

Once they were in the dining room, Richard turned his attention to Trumbull. "You need to tell us everything you know about the Society of Praetorians."

For the next hour, Trumbull paced and talked non-stop. The history he laid out was beyond anything Richard had even imagined.

When he finished, he sat down. "God, that was exhausting," He took out a handkerchief and wiped sweat from his brow. "I never took the time to realized how much I actually do know. To grasp everything that had been done from the time I joined the Praetorians to the present. Besides that, I don't know too much about their history," Trumbull added.

Richard did, and he knew even more than Brooks, being one of the highest ranking members in the Absconditus Verum. "Alexander Hamilton founded the Praetorians in 1777, the year he became aide de camp for Washington during the war. Most of the Founders didn't know of his involvement. Others joined him for power and glory. He used this position to gain great power. He was in constant contact with all the military leaders, the Congress, and most of the state governments.

"Within the year, he was the one writing most of the correspondences instead of Washington. The General looked over the ones he asked for, but he didn't know the extent of Hamilton's reach into every facet of the American government and society. The amount of information Hamilton accrued in those first years was staggering, and he was only twenty years old at that time.

"Imagine a foreigner moving to America and within five years running the country. That's what Hamilton accomplished. He was basically giving orders to Congress and the military. Washington's trust in him was absolute. That's why he allowed Hamilton to set up the new government after the Convention. Washington suspected something wasn't quite right all along, but couldn't see past his trust in the man. He simply couldn't see or hear the pleas of Jefferson and Madison to stop Hamilton.

"Now, I believe many of the documents from Hamilton's scheming are in the center chamber. Those along with all the others will provide an astounding amount of information that has never come to light. The Praetorians are running scared for a reason. One, or even a dozen old documents, they could marginalize. Hundreds are a totally different story. If we can bring these out into the open, it would effectively reveal the incredible fraud perpetrated on the American people."

"You really do believe they exist don't you?" Trumbull asked. "You know I never really believed all this. I mean once I left the Praetorians I was hoping for something to bring them down."

"It's there Trumbull, it's there," Brooks said.

"Tell me about this Praetor," Richard asked.

"Last I knew he was meeting with his leaders overseas. Since I've been here the last several days, I'm not sure just where he is now," Trumbull answered.

"He's not there. He's in New York," Richard offered.

"So…he changed plans," Trumbull said.

"What of this man? Does anyone know who he is?" Richard asked.

"No one in his Society. He's the Praetor, but I doubt any know just who he really is. I believe like your Verum Society, they keep things close to the vest."

Richard turned his wheelchair and peeked into the dining room. Emily and Dean were still at the table working on the labyrinth plans. Richard motioned for Brooks to keep an eye on them from the doorway. He was still in earshot of the others. Johnson and Trumbull moved closer to Richard, flanking his wheelchair.

"Who do you think he is?" Brooks asked quietly.

Trumbull lowered his voice as well and slightly leaned closer to Richard. "Well…based on all I've discovered over the years and the fact that I was able to track him several times, though at great risk, a gut feeling tells me he may be a direct descendent of an original Praetorians Society member."

Richard was surprised to hear this. None of his research pointed to a Founder descendant. "That doesn't make sense. They weren't based on genealogy. It was power and glory that attracted their members. Why would you think he's a descendant?"

"There were only a few places he went that weren't directly involved in his quest for power, though I wasn't able to ever track him to any place in particular," Trumbull answered.

"Do you remember where they were?" Johnson asked as he peaked over Richard's head, looking to the dining room.

"One was in Illinois, and the other in New York. You say he's in New York. Perhaps we can catch him there," Trumbull offered.

Richard was concerned about this new information. He could tell the others were as well.

Trumbull continued. "Richard, he wants the documents as much as you do. He's mad with his lust for them. To him they are more power than anything they've done, for he can hold them and keep them secret, taunting the Verum. He really is mad."

"That can be useful," Richard whispered. "Brooks, I think we can keep him occupied and off the scent if he's so focused on me."

Brooks nodded from the doorway.

Richard thought for a moment.

Is he really that worried about me? It doesn't make any sense. I've been in hiding forever. Do I offer more information? How much do they know? No, I can't. But if they know of the others involved, it might just help. What time is it?

He looked at his watch. Ten O'clock.

We'll be up all night if we don't get the team ready for tomorrow.

He was fidgeting with his wheelchair, slightly moving it forward and back without changing position. Then he decided.

"Here's our other concern. We have two other teams out there right now; one in Connecticut and the other in South Carolina. Those are the sites we've narrowed down to in the last few days. But we haven't heard from Connecticut. I fear the worst. I've sent another member out to see what's happened. The team in South Carolina is stumped as well."

Brooks cut in. "Richard." He gave him a slight gesture to stop talking.

A moment later Emily and Dean joined them with some notes.

Emily showed Brooks what they had. "Here's a sketch we can use to map the tunnels. I made four copies in case there are four levels. This will give us a much clearer picture, though we're still in the dark as to the real size of the labyrinth. And I don't know if the algorithm will work once we're inside."

Richard decided it was time to show them. "Well then Joseph, if you would. Pamela can use the break by having you push me."

They all went out the back door, down the handicap ramp and to the barn. The team looked in disbelief at what was well hidden.

"My God Richard, a full command center?" Brooks said.

The barn, while ordinary looking on the outside was anything but inside. It looked more like an FBI control central with all the technology on display. A large round table in the center of the room had a dozen technicians working on computers. Around the perimeter were tables and storage units for a large-scale operation. Several other Verum members were busy with the equipment and other important tasks.

"We've been up and running for some time. I knew it would probably take an extended effort to secure what awaits us,"

Dean went over to a large pile of supplies on one of several folding tables. "There's enough twine here to stretch to Texas. What's with the odd color."

The twine was a deep red and brown.

Richard smiled. "Yes and you'll need it to keep to your way and mark the tunnels. You might get to a point where you need to leave a crumb trail or in this case a twine trail so you'll always know where you've been. There are canteens, food containers, extra lights and plenty of batteries," he said as he pointed them all out.

He paused as a fellow Verum member approached. "Gentlemen, Emily, this is Jonathon Jennings. His sister was an *au pair* for me in Staunton. And this is the rest of the team." He motioned towards the others who were busy working.

Some were on computers while others carried equipment here and there.

Jonathon was shaking hands as Richard continued.

"He's the foremost authority on historical document handling. My hope is that he'll have lots of work in the days ahead. We have a clean room below this one."

As they moved from table to table, each member of the team stopped and picked something up. There were flashlights, belts to hold tools for the tunnels, the tools themselves being awls, small hammers, cleaning cloths, wire cutters, and such.

Richard wheeled himself over to another table. "And here are the most important pieces of equipment."

On the table were oddly shaped backpacks. Trumbull grabbed one and tossed it to Johnson.

Richard continued. "If you do get to the chamber, you'll need these to hold all the documents. Each pack will hold six cylinders to store any documents you find. Each cylinder will hold about ten documents without wrapping them too tightly. It's my understanding that it's a trove, so I thought at least four of you should wear them. There's a Velcro cover to keep them in place."

The packs were rather large, some two feet wide, two feet high and one foot deep.

Trumbull picked one up. "These are really light."

"Yes and the lower section of the packs are accessible to store your equipment. You'll need food and supplies"

He moved to the next table. "These cylinders are lightweight plastic with a screw on top; you'll be able to fit six of these in each pack.

"And there are oxygen tanks for all with masks," as he pointed them out. "I know there's an air system designed into the maze, but some areas might have collapsed over time."

"How large do you really think the labyrinth is?" Dean asked.

Richard hesitated. "It could just be a few hours or…"

"A few days?" Emily finished his sentence.

Richard nodded. "You need enough supplies to last 24 hours. If you haven't been able to reach the central chamber by then, you'll need to come back out for more supplies."

"We need to make sure we use the bathroom and go in on a full stomach." Emily stated.

"Practical thinking," responded Richard. "It's good to have a woman in the field. You have toiletries in the packs."

"We'll be monitoring Monticello from here. Cameras are already set up near the top of Patterson Mountain," Jennings offered.

"How…if we're underground?" Brooks asked.

"Well, the hill is made mostly of iron ore and clay with calcium. This will block all communications. It's the prime reason no one ever found the labyrinth. Radar and electronic signals can't penetrate it effectively. At this point, no one has any idea the labyrinth even exists except us. So you'll be on your own, I'm afraid. Our monitoring will be outside and we'll do our best to watch your back, though we can't be too close because it might disclose your position," responded Richard.

One of the Verum members entered the barn and approached Richard. "Sir, we're ready to get everything into the vehicles," the member said.

Richard turned to Emily. "I suggest you bring any architectural tools you may need should the occasion arise. We have a wide selection of equipment over at that table." He pointed as he spoke.

She nodded and went to gather tools.

Richard turned to Trumbull. "Trumbull, a word, if you please."

Richard motioned Trumbull to move to a spot so they would not be overheard.

"Trumbull, you'll need weapons. We have some small semiautomatics that will fit into the side pockets of covert clothing we prepared. We have it on good authority that the Praetorians are mobilizing a team near Monticello."

"Understood. I had a feeling they'd be close. I'll do everything I can to keep them safe. It shouldn't be a problem until they realize you found the tunnels. Once they know, the hammer will come down."

Richard looked at Emily across the barn. "Should she go?"

"She has to. She's our best hope of finding the secret to the maze. I'll protect her."

"If she dies, our hopes may die with her."

"She won't."

Richard paused for several moments. "You see that table to my right?"

Trumbull looked to the table. "Yes."

"Those are booby traps. Made out of plastics and colored like iron ore. If you have to, if the pursuit is too strong, use them. They're easy to set up and will stop them cold."

"Richard, I don't know where Victor Shaw is. Do you?"

"I think he's in Europe, but I can't be positive. He's eliminated many of our members since you left. I would guess he's your equal when it comes to killing."

"My concern is if he shows up at Monticello, things could get really ugly in a hurry."

"Then get the documents out as soon as you can."

Chapter 33

1798 - Trenton, New Jersey

James Wilson was escaping his creditors with the help of the Praetorians. He was bound for Edenton, North Carolina, and Church was seeing him off.

"James. Thank you for all your help. I will contact you soon so that you may come back and enjoy life here in New Jersey."

"Thank you Church. I will be waiting for your correspondence."

Church took out two small flasks from his coat and handed one to Wilson. "A present from the Praetor for your services. A toast to our success."

They both opened their flasks and had a drink.

"Well then…I must be off," Wilson said.

"Yes. Have a safe and healthy trip James."

Wilson climbed the gang plank and boarded. Church boarded his coach. "Driver, New York." A small smile grew into a malicious one. He knew the Praetor had poisoned Wilson's flask. It was just another loose end that needed attention. "Sorry James, old friend," he murmured to himself.

Wilson arrived in Edenton in a state of madness. He died a few months later. No connection was ever made between Wilson and Church. The Praetorians continued to tie up loose ends and keep Hamilton insulated from any accusations. His plans were moving forward and he had total control of the Federal government.

1799 - Monticello, Virginia

Thomas Jefferson was meeting with the Absconditus Verum Society at Monticello.

"Gentlemen, John Adams has now committed to build a large centralized American Army and Navy sufficient enough to invade the rest of the continent. However, the Federal Government has no authority to conduct this war without the consent of Congress, meaning our state representatives. He also has no funds to support it. He resisted Hamilton's input, but Hamilton forced his hand because of his tremendous influence in Congress and Adams' Cabinet. Hamilton's suggestion to create a National Property Tax and bind every single person who owns land, housing, slaves, and all other property to central government has passed Congress and his army of tax collectors is on the prowl."

Madison added. "Since the Federalists still hold power in Congress, they passed this War Tax scheme. So now tax collectors are routing citizens in every state, forcing them to pay this new tax that was passed through Congress with virtually no input at all from the people. Some people are paying, others are resisting. It seems the structure in which the amount owed was so ill conceived, is has produced many to stand up and cry foul. The tax structure is based on how many windows are in a house and what their sizes are. The more windows in the house, the higher the tax. The larger the windows, the higher the tax."

Yates broke in. "That's unconstitutional! Congress only has the power to tax based on consent of the governed and in proportion to population. This is just another example of usurpation by the elite. Again, the people have no say. I know for a fact that acceptance of this legislation is in the extreme minority in New York."

"It has been blasted by Virginia too," Patrick Henry answered. "This Congress with Hamilton working behind the scenes is slowly but surely sucking the life and right to govern out of the states and the people."

"And since the Alien & Seditions Act prohibits the people from speaking out against the Federal Government, if you do so now you'll be jailed. This is a direct attack from the Federal Government against the 1st Amendment of free speech and the right to assemble," John Lansing added.

"Well, right now we have an armed insurrection in Pennsylvania," Thomas Mifflin offered. "Hamilton's leverage with my creditors has forced me to move from Philadelphia to Lancaster."

"But you're the Governor of the city Thomas," Gunning Bedford declared, incredulously.

"I am, but against Hamilton's tax collecting army and his coalition of bankers, merchants, creditors, land speculators, loyalists to the crown of England, and his influence in Congress, I stood no chance defending myself."

"If he can force a sitting Governor out of the city, then surely he can do it in every other state," Robert Yates said.

"Well Virginia is one state the Federal Government will never influence, or invade!" Richard Henry Lee answered. "Hamilton's brashness will only go so far. Many in Virginia are also not paying this new Federal War Tax."

"Then we must stand together and have all the states resist," Jefferson said.

"I can tell you this. The New England states are happy to pay the new tax. It protects their interests. Trade with England is all they care about and this tax to support a war against France only strengthens their position. You will be hard pressed to have any New England states go against the Federal Government. They mean to rule Hamilton's *Nation State* and keep plundering the south to increase their wealth, businesses and power," John Langdon of New Hampshire added. He was one of the few northerners who went against the north's power in the Federal Government.

"So what's to be done?" Bedford asked.

Jefferson looked at them all. "We must continue to resist all these tax schemes forced on us by the Federal Government. Henry, Lee, Madison, and I will hold Virginia true. Pennsylvania is the key right now just as it was during the Whiskey Rebellion. If they can force the central government to abandon the tax and back down, then we shall ride that wave along with the Seditions Act, and our Anti-Federalists should be able to sweep into power. Then we can start to undo all the damage Hamilton and the Federalists have done. Our government is not even a shadow of what it was supposed to be and we must restore the intent most of us shared in the 1770s.

"Central government must only be a representation of the states, not the reverse that Hamilton has set up. Right now, we have Adams who sees himself as King George and his aristocratic cronies ruling over us. And behind the scenes, Hamilton is still pulling all the strings. Only through the education of the people can we hope to straighten the course of the American states. We must fracture this *Nation State* Hamilton has built and return the power to govern back to the states and the people. It is the only way America can survive. So let us fight to restore the Republic for which we stand."

◊ ◊ ◊

Hamilton was now ready at the helm, waiting to go off to war, when John Fries started a Rebellion against the War Tax in Pennsylvania. While support grew and more resisted, Federal authorities arrested Fries, and some thirty others to stand trial for treason. They were all found guilty and with a Federalist frenzy, sentenced to be hanged.

Before the hanging however, Adams stepped in and pardoned them all. He knew Hamilton had overplayed his Federalist hand yet again and now Adams was concerned about the next election and having the Federalists maintaining their power.

Around the same time a peace treaty with France was completed. Hamilton was beside himself. So enraged was he that he dismissed all the southern soldiers at the camp to return home and took part of the army, which was stationed in the District of Columbia, and positioned them to march on northern Virginia. It was some five-thousand strong. He was determined to show once again that the Federal Government was the supreme government of the land and the states were mere satellites of his *Nation State.*

But Virginia was not sitting idly by. They had watched Hamilton's actions and their militias were ready to resist should Hamilton's army invade. Militias were also sent from Kentucky, Tennessee, and both the Carolinas. Word was sent to Georgia, but they had not yet confirmed support and troops. In all, they had some two-thousand men.

Both armies were positioned towards the most western part of the District of Columbia. Hamilton was at the lead on horseback ordering his commanders to make ready as he told them "Virginia wants to secede from the Union and it is our job to stop any such attempt."

An army core of engineers built crossing structures to reach Virginia over the Potomac.

Hamilton spied across and could see several of the front lines of the militia hiding in the woods. He smiled and said to himself. "Jefferson, your time has come. Your precious Virginia will fall and the south will be ever a subservient minion to New England and the north."

Hamilton slowly crossed one of the bridges just erected. His troops started crossing the bridges. His commanders however were stationed in the rear on high ground as was proper military decorum at the time. They watched anxiously.

Hamilton's glory in battle was here and he would not sit back and watch.

I will forever be the man who saved the American Nation State he thought to himself as he slowly crossed the river.

Suddenly a rider came up to the commanders in the rear. "Sir!, Orders from President Adams."

A commander took the orders and read them out loud. "The army is to stand down. Peace with France has been reached. News of the army's invasion of Virginia has reached my attention and it must be stopped. Hamilton must come to the Capitol at once."

"God help us," a commander said. "How can we stop him?"

"Corporal, sound the general retreat," another said.

The horn sounding the retreat was heard towards the back end of the units. The men stopped moving forward. They called out to soldiers ahead of them to do the same. Several more horns were sounded. Within a few minutes, the news and the sound of the retreat had reached the front. The men on the bridges stopped. The militias also heard the horns and slowly came to the edge of the woods. They were no more than 200 yards from the river. Everyone stood still and silence was all around.

Hamilton stopped. He looked at the militia and then swung round and realized what was happening. Fury rose in his heart. "No!" he shouted. "No retreat! Forward men, that is a direct order!"

The men looked at each other, confused.

A lone rider had now made his way up to the front of the lines. "General! President Adams has ordered you to stand down."

"No! I shall not. We must show these southern rebels that we are in charge. We must put them down and show them their place in our *Nation State.*" He turned and continued moving across the bridge. He had almost reached the bank on the Virginia side. He turned back again and saw that no one was advancing.

It was over, finished. His hopes for glory since his childhood were gone in an instant. His face was one of a man angered to madness.

"General. It's over." One of his commanders was now on the north side of the bridge. "It's over."

He glanced back at him, and then at the militias, then he turned his horse and went back over the bridge.

A roar came from the woods as many were now walking out into the open.

Within the army ranks there was a great sigh of relief.

One could hear the shouts from across the river. "Go home Yankees! Yankees go home!"

While the young southern soldiers were celebrating the events of the day, a small group of veterans from the Revolution were more reserved. They were together near the right flank of the militias. "This *will* happen one day," said a veteran. "The divide between the north and south has grown great and I fear the south will one day have no choice but to defend itself from the aggression of the northern states.

◊ ◊ ◊

It was several days since the incident in north Virginia as a dark hooded figure approached Mount Vernon on a rainy night.

Washington had been out checking on his farms. The weather was cold as he returned to the main house. He ate and retired to bed with Martha.

The dark hooded figure stealthily entered the house and the bedroom undetected. The Washington's were sleeping soundly as were all their servants. The figure approached the General and stood by the bed. Fury was in his face. He took a small bottle out of his pocket. From it he extracted some of its liquid and dripped it into Washington's mouth.

He spoke to himself in a hushed tone. "I could not leave this to my subordinate. You require special treatment," he said as he stooped over him. The assassin stood once Washington had swallowed the poison in his sleep. "I have been in your shadow long enough. Now you will miss the rise of a new order." He slipped out and disappeared into the night.

Washington woke early the next morning with a severe sore throat. Throughout the day it worsened and by early Saturday morning had turned into a full-blown illness. The doctors tried every cure they could think of for a cold and possible pneumonia as none were aware of the ingested poison.

General George Washington, the man who saved the American colonies from English rule, died that same evening.

May 2018 - Monticello, Virginia

Emily, Dean, Brooks, and Johnson had finished all preparations for their quest and were back in the sitting room.

Emily was looking at the key and she wanted Brooks to continue. "I need to know more."

Trumbull and Johnson were resigned to hearing another history lesson.

"In '98 when Adams had made the decision to build a National American Army and keep ties with France severed, his positions were being constantly attacked by the press, mostly the Jefferson controlled press. Adams' own Federalists controlled 75% of the news in those days with the Anti-Federalists authoring the remaining 25%. There was virtually no neutral press back then. Very similar to today, though even back then they claimed to be independent and neutral."

"I know our media today is very partisan. I also know that all those partisans claim to be neutral. I could not name one neutral news outlet today," Emily said.

"Yes and it was the same back then. Just like the recent attempts to snuff out the dissenting voice with legislation like *Internet Neutrality* or the resurrection of the *Fairness Doctrine.*

"Most Americans think our earlier history of news was much more neutral. Nothing could be further from the truth. All through American history, the press was used as a tool of partisanship and it was brutal during the Adams and Jefferson Presidential run. But what happened in 1798 eclipsed everything our Founders could ever imagine.

"Adams decided to attack the 1st Amendment directly. The legislation was called The Alien and Sedition Acts. His Federalists Congress passed the Acts, four separate laws, the last being the Sedition Act. It was directed towards any writings disparaging or at odds with the central government policy. This gave him the power to shut down any dissenting voice in the press and he enforced it by jailing publishers."

"So he was squashing free speech?" Dean asked.

"Yes, though he claimed it was to protect the views of government especially during times of war. If dissent was allowed to be published, it might act to stop the demand of partisan loyalty to blindly following the *Nation State*. At least that's what they hoped would happen."

"Wouldn't you want that during war time?" Emily asked.

"On the surface, you do want to show solidarity. However, if you stop one side from free speech, even though unconstitutional, the other side must also stop the slander. That was the doom from this law and it destroyed the Federalists for fifty years. For their media continued the relentless attacks on Jefferson and the Anti-Federalists.

"Jefferson and Madison each wrote resolutions meant to challenge this usurpation of power by the Federalists. They were the Virginia and Kentucky Resolutions. In them they spelled out the restricted powers of Federal Government and the rights of the state republics, which hold that the United States is made up of a *voluntary Union* of states that agree to cede some of their authority in order to join the Union, but that the states do not, ultimately, surrender their sovereign rights. These rights once again were the state's rights of sovereignty which included nullification and secession.

"This became the central issue in the elections of 1798 and 1800. A tidal wave swept through the voting and the Federalists were swept from power. Jefferson became President and the original intent of many of the Founding Fathers would finally get its turn. Later on, it was clearly established that Adams and the Federalists had indeed implemented unconstitutional laws.

"The irony is that the Supreme Court never got the chance to use judicial review. Had they, they would have found some way to make Adams' law Constitutional. Most of the judges were Federalist appointments and most held very political views right out in the open."

"But I don't understand. I thought judicial review was part of the judiciary power of the central government." Dean asked.

"And based on what happens now, you would certainly think so. But it was not a power granted in the Constitution. It wasn't until the Judiciary Act, the year after the Convention, that judicial review was born out of a Congressional law. In 1803, in a case before the Supreme Court, judicial review was used by Chief Justice John Marshall. He gave his court omnipotent power to decide what was Constitutional and what wasn't. The ideology you see in today's Supreme Court Justices was just as prevalent as Marshall's court, perhaps even more so then.

"The point is, even though the Federalists were driven from power, the courts that they had set up and judges they had installed had lifetime appointments. This meant that in the people's own government; they had no power to elect judges because a major defect in the Constitutional guidelines gave that power to the central government. The judges took power and never gave it back. Marshall's court ruled over everyone for thirty years. The only counter balance was that the Anti-Federalists kept getting elected by the people to offset this omnipotent body of judges who believed they had the power to decide all things in government including now most of our social issues."

Emily thought about this. "But didn't Lincoln and Roosevelt do the same thing as Adams by enacting laws to squash dissent in the press?"

Brooks nodded. "Now you know a bit more about the desire for power and control over the people by the few powerful elitists. It goes on today and you see it all the time in our political machinery."

"That's enough for tonight Joseph," Johnson said. We really need to get some sleep. We need to be on the road and get there before dawn breaks.

Emily was lying on her bed and knew she needed rest to start fresh in the morning. There were so many things she'd seen and heard, yet she was calm. Knowing James and the girls were safe was very comforting, and as much as they were in danger, she felt more confident than she ever had in her life.

This is such an extraordinary event. People have been killed and my family in danger, but I really feel I can help. People all over the country can live better, freer lives, if we can find what the others say are hidden. Americans can regain control of their government and restore the balance of power, perhaps even improve much that is now wrong, and I'm a part of it.

I just hope to God the Praetorians don't show up.

Chapter 34

May 2018 - Monticello, Virginia

This was perhaps the most important day in Emily Yates-Miller's life. She got up early, got ready, and met Pamela in the kitchen preparing breakfast. It was four in the morning.

Her anxiety was high as she worked on her algorithm at the small kitchen table. She was scared. Scared of the thought she would get trapped in the tunnels, or worse, die a horrible death.

Trumbull opened the kitchen door and walked in.

She jumped up in surprise. "Christ Trumbull! You're going to give me a heart attack!"

He smiled and said, "If you're surprised by this, just wait until we get into the labyrinth."

"Very funny," she answered sarcastically.

Pamela brought two coffees to the table. "Now you just make sure you protect her from any danger."

Trumbull sat and politely answered. "I shall do everything in my power to protect her."

"If you don't, you'll have to answer to me." Pamela said as she winked at Emily and gave her a small smile.

"Pamela, where's Richard?" Emily asked.

"Oh he's already out in the barn, getting everything ready for when you return."

"Tell him not to get his hopes up just yet. We may not have anything." Trumbull offered.

It wasn't long before Dean, Brooks, and Johnson, made it down to the dining room.

They had eggs, bacon, toast, and coffee.

Soon they were on the road to Monticello in two Jeeps. Johnson, Dean, and Emily rode together while Brooks went with Trumbull.

"How's that algorithm coming along?" Johnson asked Emily as they started out.

"I'm still tinkering with the program itself. It's the traps that are the problem. The labyrinth layout changes and I don't know how to get the software to calculate it beforehand. We're going to need to be in the tunnels so I can enter the changing information as we go. I think it's the only way it will work."

"I'm confident you'll get it right. We have faith in you Emily." Johnson assured her.

It was five-thirty and still dark as they reached Monticello. Once unloaded, Brooks and Dean took the cars part way down the hill and hid them off the road, close enough for a quick escape if need be.

They brought their backpacks and supplies around to the Southern Pavilion's lower side. Each was now loaded up with tools, lights, food, and small oxygen tanks, as well as other items for the expedition.

The sun was just starting to brighten the sky.

"Brooks. A word if you would," Trumbull said.

Brooks nodded to Johnson and gave a small wave for him to bring the others around to the tunnel door.

Emily's was peeking around the corner as she watched the two men speaking just out of earshot.

What on earth are they talking about? And why in secret?

She turned away, looking at Dean and Johnson.

A moment later Brooks and Trumbull came around to the hidden door.

"Are you ready?" Brooks asked as he took out the key. He sounded a bit rushed to Emily.

Her heart raced.

They all nodded. A turn clockwise and the door pushed inward and to the left.

Once inside, Trumbull used his flashlight to show Brooks where the door closing lever was. "There it is, just there, in the corner."

Brooks went over and pulled the vertical bar, some two-feet long and two inches in diameter. The mechanism responded and the door was starting to close. Trumbull kept looking outside until it was completely closed.

"Do you think this will keep the door shut once we open the gate?" Brooks asked, again in a rushed, almost panicky voice.

"That's what I'm counting on," Trumbull answered.

He motioned them all forward. "Let's get through the gate."

"What is it?" Emily asked the question but did not want the answer.

"Move!" Trumbull said in a quiet yet panicked tone. He took out his revolver.

As they made their way down the tunnel Dean, Brooks, and Johnson all pulled out their weapons.

"We've got trouble," Trumbull said as he grabbed Emily's arm and started running with the others.

"Trouble? Ow!" Emily reacted to being pulled forward.

Brooks opened the gate just ahead of the rest.

They heard the gears, but not behind them. The outside door stayed closed when the Iron Gate opened. Brooks smiled at Trumbull and they lowered their weapons.

"BOOM." The outer door blasted into the tunnel.

Debris broke loose from the ceiling and walls and rained down on them, leaving a plume of smoke in its wake.

"They're here!" Trumbull yelled.

They all scrambled through the gate and around the sides of the tunnel.

Brooks and Johnson on the left.

Emily, Dean, and Trumbull on the right. Emily was peeking around the corner.

They heard footsteps running towards them.

Flashlights were bobbing and swaying.

Emily couldn't pinpoint anything, though there was a glow from the outside door behind the agents, even though it was around the corner.

"That's far enough!" Brooks yelled.

The Praetorian agents abruptly stop in their tracks and moved to the side walls.

"Agent Brooks," a voice called out.

Emily's heart was pounding, her breath short, hands shaking.

"I'm a Praetorian Captain," the loud voice identified himself. "We want to spare the lives of you and your comrades. Please come out now."

"I would have considered doing so a few days ago, but with all the killings, I must decline!" Brooks shouted back.

"That is unfortunate. Losing key members of your organization will greatly damage the Absconditus Verum. We would hate to see that. Especially the young lady."

Emily watched as the men positioned themselves to ward off an attack.

"I'll bet you would," Brooks answered in an antagonistic voice.

"You have no choice. I'll give you one minute to discuss it with your associates." The commander said.

Emily could hear soft footsteps coming ever closer. She wanted to run, run down the tunnel.

Brooks and Johnson looked at her, Dean and Trumbull. They shook their heads. No one was giving up now.

Emily moved back and sat against the wall.

"Trumbull, how many do you see?" Brooks asked quietly.

"Shh." Emily said forcefully, yet quiet, "They'll hear you!"

"They're not close enough to hear us." Trumbull responded, his eyes fixated down the tunnel. "There are seven in all in the tunnel, four on the left. Who knows how many more outside? I'm surprised they sent this many agents. Things have definitely escalated. Our best chance is to crossfire, but make sure you don't hit the open gate."

Brooks and Johnson nodded.

"Are you ready, Dean?" Trumbull asked.

"Yes…yes, I'm ready." Dean said.

Emily could tell his adrenalin level was maxed out by his response.

She looked at Trumbull as she started crying.

We're all going to die!

Trumbull touched her should and Dean's as well as he said. "Take a breath. Slow down your heart." He focused on Dean. "You must be calm enough to shoot."

Dean took a few deep breaths. "Yes…okay. I'm ready. So much for leaving a bread trail."

"Your minute is up, Brooks!" The commander shouted.

"We're still deciding." Brooks nodded to the others.

"No more…" was all the commander got out.

Dean and Trumbull swung round and opened fire. Emily saw Brooks and Johnson do the same.

Bullets were flying everywhere, some ricocheting off the Iron Gate as Dean was firing first and aiming second.

They were fortunate the ones coming back hadn't hit any of them.

There was some return fire, but not much.

They all swung back behind the walls.

"How...how...many did we get?" Dean asked, visibly shaken with the encounter.

Agents were still sending a few shots at them.

"Five down," Trumbull said. "Including their Captain."

The shooting stopped.

"I suggest you two head back out!" Brooks yelled.

The agents looked at each other and started retreating.

"Sounds like they're leaving," Dean said. He glanced around the corner and confirmed it. "They are leaving!"

"We need to close that gate," Johnson said. "Another explosion like the outside door will bring the entire ceiling down. They know that so I doubt they'll risk a collapse over their own heads. Closing the gate could give us the protection we need."

Dean nodded to Johnson as if it was an order to do so. "Close the gate, close the gate." He said to himself.

"Wait, what?" Trumbull asked as Dean started moving.

He swung around the corner and forward to grab the gate.

"No...no, Dean!" Trumbull yelled as he reached out to stop him.

Several shots were fired.

Dean stumbled backward.

The two retreating agents had been joined by four others. They were advancing again.

Trumbull grabbed Dean by the collar and swung him around and into Emily.

She was still sitting against the wall with her hands on her ears trying to block out the noise.

Dean dropped to his knees just in front of her.

He looked into her eyes.

It was dark, but she could she blood from several body shots stained his shirt.

He coughed as blood gurgled up in his throat and out his mouth. "I'm sorry, Mrs. Yates."

He coughed again, spewing blood onto Emily. "Please make sure you get the truth out to the people."

Emily was weeping as she reached out and touched his cheek. "I will, Tim. I promise I will."

He fell forward into her lap.

She screamed. "No! No!"

She heard the other three were returning fire at the Praetorians.

They swung back again.

"Shit! Shit!" Johnson said. "Is Dean hit?" He looked at Trumbull.

"He's down…He's dead."

Emily softly cried behind him.

"We got five of them," Brooks said, "One left."

"Sons of bitches!" Johnson swung back into the tunnel and opened fire, walking forward.

The last Praetorian was fleeing down the tunnel as Johnson took him out.

Trumbull bent down on one knee and lifted Timothy Dean off of Emily.

She shut down, hers hands covering her face. She couldn't stop crying.

Johnson closed the gate and returned.

Trumbull stood up. "We must move. They know this is the main target. More agents will follow."

He helped Emily to her feet and the other two moved Dean's body next to a wall. Johnson took everything Dean had on him: gun, backpack, wallet, and money.

Gears started, and a wall came out of the right side of the tunnel a few feet in front of them.

◊ ◊ ◊

Trumbull could see Emily was in shock. "Move, move, move!" He pulled her through just before the moving wall sealed them off.

They moved down the tunnel, but soon had to stop as the first of many choices presented itself.

"What now?" Johnson asked. "We have all this equipment and can't leave a trail for their agents."

"I don't know," Brooks said. He attempted to give Emily the Key.

She was still visibly shaken, though she had stopped crying.

He finally placed the key in her hand and closed it. "Emily, all our hope now lies with you."

She didn't answer or even acknowledge him.

"We must move!" Trumbull said.

"Up there! A side tunnel! On the left!" Johnson yelled.

Trumbull took Emily by the shoulders and helped her walk forward.

They entered an opening on the left, and then went to the right. Another left and right. Next was a right, then left.

"This is far enough," Trumbull said. "Brooks, you need to map our way, or we'll get lost in very short order. If Emily's calculations are correct, we've got just under an hour before that first wall moves again so for now the agents are blocked."

"Unless they use more explosives," Trumbull said.

Brooks took out the pad Dean was using and mapped their first several choices.

They moved more cautiously.

Emily was moving on her own now but Trumbull could tell she wasn't over the event.

She walked, looking at the key the whole time. She seemed in a trance, not paying attention to where they were headed.

She started murmuring "Tim, that young boy. What can we do? It's hopeless. We'll all get killed. My girls…Thomas…lost. It's all lost."

The men stopped. Trumbull watched as she walked right passed them.

"Emily?" Brooks asked.

She didn't answer. Brooks gently grasped her arm and she stopped, staring straight ahead.

"Trumbull, what's their next move?" Johnson asked.

"They'll hold control of the exit. They won't venture very far even after that wall moves. Instead, they'll wait us out. I would guess they'll have dozens of agents surrounding the entire hill before long. I would check our communications if we can, though I'm pretty sure they won't work with the iron ore in here."

"Emily…" Brooks moved in front of her.

◊ ◊ ◊

She started sobbing. She reached out and hugged Brooks as though it was the last thing she would ever do.

I'm going to die.

Dean's last words were haunting her.

He's Dead. We all are.

Brooks held her until she eased up, and then held her arms as he stood in front of her.

"Emily, we need you."

Her blank stare began to fade and she finally made eye contact. A moment passed.

No, I'm not going to let them kill me. I have to be strong. Strong enough to help with the mission. Strong enough to save them all if I can.

She came out of her fog with a nod.

"Alright?" Brooks asked.

She shook her head. "My girls." She started crying again. "What if I die? I want to see my girls."

"And you will, Emily. You will. I'll make sure of it," Brooks said.

"Try your phones" Brooks instructed.

Trumbull and Johnson both tried, neither had a signal. Emily looked at her handheld tablet. No signal.

"You won't get any signal on those." she said quietly. "The hill is mostly iron ore. Signals won't penetrate it. Remember, that's why no one ever found these tunnels."

Gears cranked, and walls moved within the system. Nothing changed in the immediate area.

"Looks like we have some time," Johnson said.

"Yes. Probably all the time in the world," Trumbull said "The key now is for us to use that time and find our way."

"Then we must make several more choices ahead and hope luck is with us," Brooks said.

They started down the next tunnel.

◊ ◊ ◊

Stu Beverley and his team of six Verum members had left the barn and were now watching Monticello from Patterson Mountain. They had installed several long range cameras the day before. These were wirelessly connected to monitors in the barn.

He had a clear view of the Southern Dependency.

Stu called Richard just after the Praetorian agents entered the labyrinth.

"Sir, did you see?" Stu asked.

"What's happened Stu? We saw that explosion at the entrance." Richard answered.

"Praetorians entered the labyrinth just after our team. They blew the door clean off. I believe there was a skirmish. Several agents went in, and then several more. I'd say about a dozen or so. None of them came out. I must assume our team's been captured or they're being tracked. There are at least twenty agents on the property."

"Then we must be prepared to help them in an escape, or stop those agents if our team finds the center chamber. We have views from all four cameras on our monitors."

"My Alpha team will stay here for now. My Delta sniper team is at the ready," Stu answered confidently.

◊ ◊ ◊

The Yates' barn command center was teaming with activity. Absconditus Verum members were getting ready for the possible arrival of the hidden documents. Some were on computers. Richard went to the one Hal Davis was using.

"Hal, can we zoom in with those cameras? It would help to get a closer picture."

Hal worked his keyboard, hitting the keys fast and furiously. Soon the four camera shots were zooming in on the monitors, one in each quadrant.

"Look, sir, there." He pointed to one.

"Yes…Stu, we have a close-up now. What's your assessment?" Richard asked.

"The Praetorians have already mobilized. Several more agents have moved to the doorway. They're securing it." Stu answered.

"I've contacted our Verum operatives in the area as well. We may need to engage them directly." Richard answered.

◊ ◊ ◊

Emily and the team stopped as they hit a dead end.

"I'm going back to set up some traps," Trumbull announced.

"No, you can't," Johnson replied. "What if a wall blocks you off from us?"

"That's a chance we have to take, otherwise they can catch and kill us." Trumbull left with a small box from his pack.

Emily had come around since Dean's death. She was a bit more focused. Had her emotion in check. "Brooks, I just realized the wall movements are different than yesterday. We haven't heard any of the ceilings move. I believe when the Praetorians blasted the door in, somehow it changed the timing system within the labyrinth. "I'll have to re-start the algorithm and hope the system reacts in some reasonable fashion."

She watched as Brooks and Johnson checked every wall around them.

Trumbull returned twenty minutes later. The box he was carrying was empty. "There's no way they can get through that mess. We won't be followed unless they're willing to lose a lot of agents, and those agents are all hired hands. I wouldn't blindly go in knowing death was imminent. The Praetor will have a lot of resistance from the agents."

"But they'll bring in a bomb squad at some point to disarm everything you've set up," Johnson said.

"They will, but with the walls in a constant state of flux, it'll be awfully hard for them to find us."

"And for us to find the right way," Emily said.

Brooks was flipping pages in the diary. "I know that somewhere in here is a key to these walls. Jefferson must have known there was a chance to be followed and from what we've been able to decipher, it's in the diary."

Gears cranked. The wall in front of them slid to the left.

"Well, for now we must move forward," Johnson said.

Brooks was mapping their way as they went, making careful notes when walls moved. Johnson was walking with him.

Trumbull was next to Emily, protecting her from any sudden event and to keep any Praetorian agents at bay if needed.

They continued moving forward. The strategy was to go forward if that was a choice at each intersection. Then, if that direction was not available, to move right, left, down, or up, in that order. If they hit a dead end, they would backtrack and enter each side tunnel to sort them out. Brooks kept recording every choice, every turn.

Emily continued to enter the data Brooks was recording. Each time a wall moved that they saw, she entered it in. The algorithm was struggling with each new entry.

Two hours passed, and they hit another dead end. This was proving impossible. The movement of the walls simply made all the dynamics change with each event. They had yet to go down to another level, trying to eliminate as many choices on the main level as possible. They decided to backtrack.

Eventually they got back to where they'd started and rested a bit while waiting for yet another wall to move.

Emily, now resigned to the endless maze, took the key out and examined it again as the algorithm ran on her tablet.

The walls and the booby traps had effectively stopped the agents cold and near the entrance. Trumbull had set up all kinds of devices. Nothing large enough to cause a collapse, but clever enough to stop any advance. They included bursts like small land mines, poisoned darts, shrapnel, and small laser cannon. The plastic parts made them impossible to detect until too late. They also had motion detectors built in and their colors blended perfectly into the iron ore and red clay.

As they waited Emily continued to tweak the program, sitting next to Trumbull. She finally asked, "Can you tell me about my father in-law?"

Trumbull thought for a moment. "Well, it was when I'd first joined the Society of Praetorians. Richard had already been searching for the lost documents over many years. His quest was more like a hobby, though, than anything else. He would work his regular job all week, which was in historical data, and then would spend time in the evenings or weekends exploring and documenting everything he did. He settled in Staunton to give James a permanent home and allow him to have school years that weren't interrupted by frequent moves."

"And why did you join that Society?" she asked.

"Because I had become one of the best assassins in the world. I originally was contracted by western governments that targeted extremists, either religious or political. I was well paid and believed I was helping to defeat our enemies. Once I started to really dig deeply, however, I found I was indeed working for the very faction I was supposedly killing off. That was many years later. I quit five years ago. They believe one of their agents killed me in a car crash two years ago. I set it up to look that way. He was my replacement, Victor Shaw, and is every bit as good as I am. From then on, I have been wreaking havoc globally on their Society. They never found out it was me, though I think the Praetor and Shaw both suspect I'm alive."

"The Praetor?" Emily asked.

"Yes. The one who runs the Praetorians Society."

"Who is he?"

"I believe he's a direct descendant of a Founding Father, though I've never been able to track it down."

"So it was your job to follow Richard Yates?"

Trumbull took out a pocket knife and started flipping it over and over in his hand as he talked. "Yes. I started in '88. It was two years after that when the accident occurred. We actually got to know each other a little bit. He knew I was following him. Something had been irking me even from the beginning. I watched his trips with your husband, then a small child. They had such a good time together, and I guess that was the closest I'd ever come to having a family. Perhaps that's why I let him know every time I was around. Aggression in those days was rare…it was more of the societies just monitoring each other."

"So you were there the day of the accident?"

"Yes. Brooks and I were both there. I was only supposed to be the backup at that time, though I was already much more skilled than the lead agent. They were at Monticello in the morning. The day before, I saw James acting as if he had found a clue. Anyway, they did indeed have a lead that morning, but because the agent was there, I made sure Richard saw me. That interrupted his quest and sent them on their way, and the car crash. I was torn between my job and their quest. I chose my job, though, and spent many years eliminating Absconditus Verum Society members." His voice trailed off as he looked at Brooks and Johnson.

"You mean killing them," she said.

Emily continued to work on the algorithm as they talked.

Trumbull continued. "Yes…Anyway, I followed behind the agent to the school. Once the car chase started, I got behind

Brooks. I would've stopped the agent if I had the chance right then, but the traffic didn't allow it and Brooks was ahead of me. Richard's car was hit in that intersection head on, pinning him in the car. Brooks had already gathered James, the key, and the diary. I killed the agent and tried to find Brooks, but I was unsuccessful. They had moved everything out of the Yates' home by the time I got there.

"After that, I had the Praetorians switch me to Europe. I felt something was going on between the two societies much deeper than what I was told, so I decided to let it play out without my intervention. The next eighteen years, I continued with my work in Europe. I did come back to the States a few times for an assignment. I was the best they had."

"Was one assignment Dean's parents?"

He didn't answer.

She knew this was eating him up inside even with all the killings he had caused. "Did you ever find out what happened to James?"

He gave her a surprised look.

"What is it?"

"You called him James."

She thought for a moment. "Perhaps hearing it so much in the last few days has…it kind of fits him, now that I think about it."

Trumbull continued. "I knew he went to a safe house, but nothing more until I intercepted a message just last week. Two agents working in Europe were given instructions to go to Texas to kidnap your girls. I couldn't stop the kidnapping, but I did track them to the house where they took the girls. I was able to rescue them and kill the agents."

"So what do you think of all we're doing now?" she asked as she continued working on her tablet.

"I think there is indeed something hidden. I never thought so, and even fought my boss about the validity of the quest. That's when I quit. The Praetor had me chased for years, mostly by inept goons, but eventually he pulled his best off another assignment to go after me. That was Victor Shaw. During our first encounter I wounded him pretty good. He wears a patch on that eye now. My fake death kept him off my trail for a while. I think he now believes I am alive. I've killed many of the Praetorians' agents since then. He knows I'm the only other one who could do this with the skills we both possess.

"I thought it never mattered if the information came to light. Now, I believe it may affect their global empire and they're doing everything they can to stop it. Their resources are endless, and your Verum Society has been greatly damaged by recent events. I do have one hole card however, and if I'm right it will prove deadly for them."

"What hole card?" she asked.

"That, Mrs. Yates, shall stay secret until the time is right."

A wall finally slid open, and they entered a new tunnel. As they walked, they talked about her girls, her work, and James' involvement in the Verum Society. The moving walls kept them alert but not panicked. They had time to react if they needed to. It took a full minute for a wall to slide all the way across. None of the ceilings had changed. While they walked, she looked at the key while running the algorithm on her tablet, entering in each new event, hoping somehow it would give her the results they desperately needed.

Brooks and Johnson stayed close by, probing a few tunnels. There were several more wall changes while they did this, but nothing to separate them.

Upon their return of investigating a tunnel, Johnson said, "Most are dead ends, but who knows? We could've already gone by the right choice."

"We did discover something. Not all the tunnels are hand crafted. We saw a lot of natural rock that was not touched by any cutting tool," Brooks said. "But if we never make it out, the truth will die in here with us."

They stopped for a moment to decide on the next choice.

Emily noticed Johnson seemed preoccupied.

"Are you ok," she asked.

"Oh, just thinking about Timothy. He was a good kid, a good friend. I trained him from the start. He was a good FBI agent and an even better Absconditus Verum member."

Brooks tossed him the diary. "Something to keep your mind occupied."

Gears cranked.

Emily pondered possible outcomes if they were successful.

I wonder if the people even want to know the truth. What if we find it and they just won't listen. All this will be for nothing.

As she though, they heard an explosion in the vicinity.

No one spoke.

I wish these Praetorians would just give up and leave us alone. And I wonder what's going on outside? Are the Verum in charge, or are the Praetorians waiting to capture us?

Chapter 35

Gears cranked, and walls moved. It was nearly eleven o'clock in the morning and they had no idea just where they were in the labyrinth. They broke out a snack and ate in silence. They were already weary from the day's journey and it showed.

Each took turns looking through the diary as they moved and stopped, moved again, and stopped again. They were convinced the page listing the numbers was the cypher holding the answer.

Emily kept at it, working on her notes and the notes Brooks had kept as they went. "I just…this took years to carve out."

"Jefferson had work going on here for almost fifty years," Johnson said.

"But he wouldn't have started this until at least 1792, when he returned from Europe after the Convention and the Praetor's initial scheming," Brooks answered. "Even so, he still had thirty years. And the natural uncut walls and passages certainly helped speed the process."

"This is truly a work of genius. Think about the complexity of the machinery necessary to make this work and yet be able to keep the overall project relatively small and manageable. These walls are what amaze me. The ability to have them move, slide into new positions. I don't know if you guys noticed, but most of the walls are not moving. He set the sliding ones into the grounded walls at ninety degree angles so they simply change the configuration each time they move," Emily said.

"So it would be like using the same maze on paper, but changing some of the barriers or walls and trying again," Johnson said

"Yes…yes. That's a good observation, Mr. Johnson." She took out her original sketches of the circular maze and started working on them through the choices they had already made.

There was concern on Johnson's face. "Trumbull, what do you think they'll do? Are we safe here?"

"For now, but eventually they'll start finding ways to get past the traps I set. I think the moving walls will keep them at bay;. I have no doubt about that. No one wants to get lost in here."

"No one but us," Emily said, half listening as she stared at her screen.

Trumbull couldn't help but smile. "Those agents won't just sacrifice their lives as guinea pigs. Things are different than they used to be. Soldiers no longer sacrifice blindly unless they believe they'll save or protect others. This is not a bunch of suicide bombers we're dealing with and perhaps that's a good thing. The encounter in the first tunnel showed they would attack if they believed they had the advantage. Now all the rules have changed."

◊ ◊ ◊

The lead Praetorian agent was getting ready to send in another team. There was great resistance. Four small teams from his unit had gone in and no one came back. A bomb squad team went in last, but to no avail.

"Jones, I gave you an order to get in the tunnel and find them," Hays, the Commander said.

"I'm not going in…Go in yourself."

Hays pointed his gun at Jones. "You will go in."

"Shoot me, but I won't go in there." He flinched with a look of shock on his face. Blood was running down the side of his head. He fell towards the tunnel opening.

Confused at what just happened, Hays looked around. A lieutenant pulled him to the ground.

"Sir, we got fire from the hill!" He pointed to Patterson Mountain.

It was Beverley and both of his teams. The Alpha team, positioned on the slope of Patterson, kept shooting until they forced the Praetorians to seek shelter behind the Southern Dependency on the upper level. A dozen lie dead near the entrance. None of them sought shelter in the tunnel. Several other agents could be seen moving in that direction. The Delta team was already maneuvering close to Monticello's southwest slope.

The Praetorian Commander phoned the Council. "Sir, we have real trouble here. We're pinned down! They're on Patterson!"

"You're to stay there and control the situation," he said sternly.

"We're retreating and regrouping."

"No! You are to stay and fight until you have control."

The Commander hung up. "This is way beyond our control. The public will be on this soon. We can't contain it. He won't listen. I'm bugging out of here. I'd advise you all to do the same."

The remaining Praetorians fled to the front of the property.

◊ ◊ ◊

The Delta Team successfully reached the South Dependency.

Beverley called in. "Richard. It's a mess here. We're clearing the labyrinth entrance. You need to call in some favors if we hope to contain this. For now, no one can see this battle, but it's only a matter of time before someone does see it, or hear it."

Richard wanted to assure him. "Okay, Stu. Keep a watch for now. We'll do what we can from here."

"Yes, sir." Stu looked at his second. "This will get a lot worse before it gets better."

◊ ◊ ◊

Back at the barn, Richard asked, "Jonathon, make the call. Tell him we have engaged the Praetorians at Monticello. We need him to make ready to intervene,"

Jonathon nodded and went to make the call.

Richard spoke softly to himself. "We must give them time to complete their task or we'll lose this window, perhaps forever."

It was all they could do for now. Richard knew the Praetor would think twice before exposing their operations. At least he hoped so.

◊ ◊ ◊

Emily and the others had gone down a level and were quite far from the entrance. They had stopped again and Emily caught a short nap.

She woke with a start and looked at Trumbull. "What's happening?"

"Nothing down here."

She looked at him curiously. "What does that mean?"

"It means events are unfolding above that we have no control over, so we must press on. I've been listening and there is quite a firefight going on."

"I'm sorry, .I dozed off."

"No need to be sorry. It's been a difficult day."

She remembered Dean's face, looking at her. Grief washed across her face. Trumbull reached out and helped her up.

"Let's get moving." he said softly.

She nodded, and they started again in a yet another new direction.

It wasn't long before Emily stopped. "I don't know how you guys do it, but I really need to go."

"There's a toiletry kit in your pack," Johnson said.

"Someone could have told me a lot sooner than this," she snipped.

"Richard did, in the barn…We'll be just up ahead," Brooks said, smiling.

◊ ◊ ◊

The Praetor was stewing in his seat.

The Praetorian Council was assembled in their headquarters. Because of what happened when Trumbull defected five years earlier, they were forced to move from their New York City penthouse suite. They were now in the old subterranean hidden stronghold in eastern Long Island that the King's Pawn set up all those years ago. The Praetor was in the main chair, and the Council was seated as they once were. The Senator's and Shaw's chairs were not occupied.

The Praetor received a call from Shaw.

"Apparently there were Verum members who infiltrated our leader's meeting. One of them shot and killed the Senator," Shaw said.

This was troubling to the Praetor, but he had even more pressing matters. "Shaw, we need you at Monticello now."

"So it's there?"

"We don't know…" the Praetor responded. "Hold on Shaw." He put the phone on speaker.

The Praetorian's field commander, Russ Thornton, had just entered the main chamber. "Sir, there was small-arms fire at Monticello. The Verum team must be pretty far into the system by now. We were securing the entrance but took fire from Patterson Mountain. Our second unit is down except for the Commander. Evidently, he fled. We're tracking him now. The third unit should get there soon. The Verum have a team securing the entrance to the tunnels. For now, we have no way to stop them or even contact our agents. Communications are down in the area. Nothing will get in or out."

"Shaw, how soon can you be there?" the Praetor asked.

"By eight o'clock tonight." Shaw hung up.

"So, they think they have found the site. This must be true…" The Praetor thought for a moment. "If they have found the way in and out, we can wait for them and then take whatever they do find. Commander, have our third unit allow them to work, but they must take back the entrance to the tunnels. Once they have, secure the property. And send in an air unit to flush that team off Patterson. If we control the high ground, then we'll see where they do come out."

"Sir, what about the press?" his new second in command, the General, asked.

"I'm not concerned about the press. We'll just send out what the news is, and the media will cover this just as they've always done, from our perspective. After all, these are the same terrorists that caused the worldwide panic the other day. They will be marginalized."

"Sir, the Verum are just a bunch of laypeople. They have no tactical training." The World Bank Executive added.

Thornton cut in. "That's how they appear, but they're clearly more than what they show. Many of their members have just been killed, yet they press on. This is a highly organized group. Far more than in the past and they have units holding superior positions in the field. We must make no mistakes. Our air unit needs to take Patterson Mountain."

"Make it so." The Praetor ordered.

Thornton nodded to a guard near the door to relay the command. The guard was soon on his way.

"Sir, why don't we just blast it? The collapse will destroy whatever documents are there," the Admiral asked.

The Praetor gave him a hard look. "I want those documents! And I want them undamaged! Those documents are all that keep the people from knowing the truth. Whoever holds those documents holds all the power. We cannot overcome that kind of damage. The documents are raw power in their hands. I will not risk having them find a way to safety with the Verum and, if we blast, they might still get their hands on them. I won't risk it unless it's our only choice and that'll bring worldwide attention that we won't be able to hide. We risk a tremendous amount of exposure by blasting Monticello, and then we'll really have a major media problem."

Thornton was treading on dangerous ground as he held his resolve. "What will? Do you mean terrorists have taken over Monticello and mean to blow it up as a symbol of the American nation?"

"Monticello? What, in comparison to the World Trade Centers? That's stretching a bit, isn't it?" the Praetor snapped back.

Thornton didn't reply.

"Yes, I thought as much…For now we'll keep them pinned on the property and let them bring the documents out. Then the Society of Praetorians will finally bring down the Absconditus Verum once and for all."

"Yes, Praetor." Thornton answered.

"Make the arrangements. I can't trust anyone else until Shaw arrives. You and you alone shall command and carry out this mission until then. Go now. Take command at Monticello. Shaw is on his way and will meet you there. Our Praetorians are to do nothing more but secure the property and detain any Verum members they catch. No killings, understand?"

"Yes, sir. I shall leave immediately."

◊ ◊ ◊

Emily enter more data into her tablet.

Come on. This stupid program isn't solving anything!

The choices continued to change as the walls moved. They were now in a completely new area.

"What do you think?" Emily asked.

No man made signs of anything were in sight, yet the floor was still fairly smooth and level.

"I'm guessing no one needed to go through this area to find the center room," Johnson replied.

"Agreed," Brooks said.

The tunnel they were in end in an open area.

Brooks was first in line. He stepped out of the tunnel.

"Whoa!" He held out both arms to stop anyone from passing him. "Trumbull, get those high intensity lights out."

Trumbull pulled two small but powerful lights out of Dean's pack and brought them to the end of the landing.

At first they couldn't see anything, the lights were so bright. Then their eyes adjusted.

Awestruck, Emily said. "My God."

They were at the top of a precipice where the tunnel had come out, overlooking a vast underground cavern. The bottom dropped out of sight. The lights danced off the walls of all sizes and shapes.

Emily heard water flowing below them.

"Now, there's something you don't see every day," Trumbull remarked.

It was extraordinary. No underground caverns in Virginia could compare.

"This isn't the way," Brooks said as he motioned both right and left. There was no way to continue forward.

They headed back, but were forced into another section by the moving walls.

All the while they were exploring, Emily was thinking about and looking at the key and adjusting her algorithm. While no solution was there, something was nagging her.

It's here...It's right in front of me, and I can't think of what it is. The answer is in this key, but how? Where? Richard, James, I need help. Everyone is counting on me, but I can't figure this out.

"Wait!" Emily stopped short.

"What is it?" asked Trumbull, grabbing his holstered revolver.

"Look." She point into a tunnel on their right.

They all looked.

"I was sitting there at some point."

"That's because we're backtracking," Johnson said

"No, we haven't backtracked. We looped. We just came from this tunnel." she pointed to their left. "The problem is this opening to the right wasn't here the last time. A wall must have been blocking it. That means we went another way to reach those caverns."

She looked at her notes. "I can't find it, but I know we were in that tunnel earlier today."

She looked at her watch and shook it. It showed 2 o'clock. She knew it wasn't accurate, but close enough.

"We need to stop and wait for the wall in front of us to move. Otherwise, I think we'll end up near the Iron Gate, not the direction we want."

They decided to stop.

"Can we have a watch since we'll be here for a while?" she asked.

"I'll take the first watch," Trumbull offered. "Brooks, how long have we been in here?"

"It's been around eight hours I think," Brooks answered.

"Trumbull, can you give us an assessment? What do you think the Praetorians are doing?" Johnson asked.

"Well," he brought his hand to his face and rubbed it. Then he was moving and pointing as he talked. "I was sure we would have encountered them by now, even with the devices I set and the wall movements. Superior numbers would give them the ability to cover a lot of ground in short order. Perhaps the traps I set…I'm not sure. I know the Praetor's methods quite well from all those years in their Society. He won't blast the hill unless he has to and only as a last resort."

"Well, that's reassuring." Emily said sarcastically.

"All his power is bent on having the documents. That would mean…" Trumbull pondered.

"He'll wait for us to bring them out." Brooks finished the thought.

"So we find the most important discovery since the beginning of our country's formation and just hand them over?" Emily asked. "And what about Richard's teams? Can't they protect us?"

"They can if they control the property." Johnson answered. "And that's more possible than you think."

Brooks gave him a quizzical look. "What do you mean?"

"Richard has more backup and protection than you would think."

"How do you know that?" Brooks queried.

"I know…I know because we're not the only society working towards this goal."

"What?" Emily said, flabbergasted.

Trumbull looked at Johnson. "You know about them?"

Brooks eyed both of them. "All right you two. Let's have it. I think Emily and I have a right to know just what the hell is going on."

"Damn right!" she added sternly.

"You first." Trumbull said as he looked at Johnson with a small smile.

"What society?" Brooks asked impatiently.

Johnson looked at him and shook his head. "There's a Special Forces unit. They're a unit in the military. Fully trained and operating. Only a very few in government even know they exist, and those few are in the Absconditus Verum. We do have some people in the government. We have to. It's the only way we've been able to keep track of the Praetorians. The Verum made this decision a long time ago, during reconstruction in the south after the Civil War.

"You already know Joseph and I are in the FBI." he said, looking at Emily. "We have members in all the departments, though we don't make policy. Our numbers are few. There are two million people working for the government. Some of our members in government have been killed by Praetorian agents just this week. When we were ready to go on this quest, I contacted the head of our order. He made arrangements to have our Special Forces team in position. Richard was obviously in the loop as well, though I didn't know it. They're out there…somewhere right now trying to give us a chance to escape. So, all hope is not lost. We're stronger than the Praetor thinks."

"And stronger than we were led to believe." An angry Emily concluded. "I'm finished with all this secrecy crap. If you really want to make a difference, then you need to come together as a group and show everyone that there are

Americans willing to restore the government we were meant to have."

"I wish it were that easy." Johnson answered. "Secrecy is the only thing that has kept the Verum Society together. If we do go public, it can only be with sufficient proof. That's what we've been lacking. That's why we're here, Emily. So we can finally come out of the shadows and share what we have with the people."

She was silent, trying to figure this all out. Most of her life had been so open and honest. This was new to her.

"Okay, Trumbull, your turn," Brooks said

"You just heard it, and I'm Johnson's contact."

"What else?" Emily asked.

She looked at him, probing his conscience. "Sooner or later you need to come out of that singularity you've been living in. Perhaps now's the time."

He looked at her and broke a small smile. "Perhaps you're right, but until we can find these documents and get to safety, my explanation will have to wait. Johnson knows that."

She looked at Johnson.

"He can't, Brooks, tell her why he can't."

Brooks explained. "It's because of the structure of the Verum. Our strength has always been in our loose affiliation. If we try to show a unified front without the proof we need, we'll be marginalized and it would put too many other members at risk. Then, it wouldn't matter if we had the documents or not. The Praetorians would wipe us out to protect their power."

"But don't you think the Praetorians will marginalize you, anyway?" she answered. She started pacing in front of the men. "If they own the government and the press, what can you do to overcome that?"

"Emily," Brooks continued, "You're a brave warrior now, but still have much to learn. This goes deeper than what you know, what I've told you these last few days. It pushes much harder against the establishment than you think. The forces of the Praetorians control so much that we are but one small problem in their large world. Help us solve this labyrinth so we can get to safety, if we have the chance. Time is working against us now. The longer it takes, the less chance we can be helped from the outside."

She wasn't satisfied but she knew in her heart that these men were doing everything in their power to bring the truth to the people. She had to trust them.

"Okay," she said softly. "I'll do what I can."

"A ten-minute break and then we need to move. I'm still not convinced they won't enter the maze and if we're back to an earlier spot they might be nearby," Johnson said.

◊ ◊ ◊

"Sir…Sir!" yelled Jonathon as he looked at the monitors. "Beverley's Delta Unit is retreating from Patterson. Looks like helicopters are attacking. From what we can see here, they shot one down but lost the position. One of our cameras was lost in the crash."

◊ ◊ ◊

Beverley's alpha team was ambushed by reinforcements of the Praetorians. They retreated back down onto the southern slope of the property, below the gardens.

He was looking through his field glasses at Patterson and called in. "Richard, we had to move. They just took control of Patterson, though the cameras are still undetected. Praetorians have returned here and have secured the entrance. We need to act."

"Okay, Stu, we'll turn up the heat as best we can. I'll call you back."

◊ ◊ ◊

Richard knew more help was needed. He'd been resistant in the past to call the current leader of the Absconditus Verum Society. But this was a critical juncture in their mission. He'd contacted him the night before just in case they needed more resources.

He made the call. "Sir, it's time. Our team is in the labyrinth at Monticello. Praetorians have taken control of the entrance as well as the high ground on Patterson. One of their helicopters is down. We need to bring in more assets. Hopefully, the attention this causes will force them to retreat, unless they really *are* ready for a war."

The Verum leader responded. "The FBI has Monticello locked down. Are you guys going to be able to get them out?"

"We can, sir, if you send help." Richard answered.

There was a brief silence.

"Help is on the way." The leader hung up.

"Mr. Yates, our Units are on the move." Jonathon said.

Richard nodded as they watched the monitors.

He called back. "Stu, reposition below the south side of Monticello's gardens near the western end."

"Got it. I hope you're right about the location."

"I hope so too." Richard's grave look showed the entire team what the risks were.

"Hal, what's going on with Praetorians communications?" Richard asked.

While monitoring Monticello, the Verum team at the barn was also blocking the Praetorian ability to communicate with jamming devises set up in the Monticello area.

"We're still blocking them, though I don't know how much longer we can. It's tricky keeping our teams up while we block them. If they find our blocking equipment on Patterson, they'll regain communications." Hal was working furiously to continue disrupting Praetorian communications.

It was only a few minutes before broadcasts were being heard in the barn from a variety of news stations.

"This is breaking news. We have just learned that a helicopter has crashed near Monticello, the former estate of President Thomas Jefferson. Our initial reports link this episode to the killings two days ago. We advise everyone to clear the area. I repeat, we have a helicopter crash at Monticello. The FBI has locked the area down."

Several other stations, both radio and TV, broadcasted a similar report.

"Let's see him get out of this predicament." Richard was not smiling. "Two can play at this game, Praetor."

◊ ◊ ◊

"Okay, here we go." Stu and his men were moving to the location on the southwestern slope for cover and to help in any rescue effort. "Stay alert…and follow me."

"Yes, sir" said his Alfa Team lieutenant answered.

They moved stealthily from the bottom of Patterson Mountain and up the Monticello southern slope.

◊ ◊ ◊

Richard was hoping to force the Praetorians actions into the open. He was right. Within minutes, word reached not only all of America, but Europe as well.

◊ ◊ ◊

Assassin Victor Shaw was still in southern France and had just reached a private airport where a Praetorian plane was waiting. "Ready the plane. We leave at once."

"Sir? Where is the Senator?" a Praetorian agent guarding the plane asked.

"I'm afraid he won't be joining us. I need to get to the States as fast as possible."

The Absconditus Verum were much more organized than he had thought.

Trumbull. It must be him, but how? Who is he working with? The Verum are just a pathetic band of vagabonds. He must be helping them organize.

"Trumbull," he said under his breath. "I know it's you. You fooled me with your apparent death in our last encounter. I should have killed you five years ago! I'm afraid once I reach the states your little quest will come to a quick end."

Chapter 36

May 2018 - Monticello, Virginia

They were on the move again when the wall in front of them slid open. Emily asked to continue about the events that unfolded during the late 1790s as they walked. It was an effective way to pass the time without constantly thinking about the dreary day they had gone through and what lay ahead. Emily kept at the key trying to find its secret.

Brooks was only too happy to continue. "The Election of 1800 was between Adams/Pinckney and Jefferson/Burr. This proved to be the most important vote in the first 90 years of America as a Federal Republic. Hamilton was still very influential even if no longer in office. Because of the Alien and Sedition Acts though, Adams' Federalist Party was severely weakened and waves of Anti-Federalists were elected. For the Presidency, it was a battle between Jefferson and Adams again. The elections took some six months and South Carolina was the last state to vote.

"Praetor Hamilton's new scheme to have Adams' running mate Charles Cotesworth Pinckney get more votes and become President, was exposed during the elections. Because of yet another attempt to rig the election, Jefferson and his running mate, Aaron Burr, ended up getting more Electoral votes than both Adams and Pinckney. In fact, the vote was a tie. Hamilton had also written a pamphlet deriding Adams' character that became public and fractured his Federalist Party.

"South Carolina had the final say in who would become President. Their Anti-Federalist Party decided to have one member abstain a vote for Burr, but they botched the vote and it was still a tie. That meant it went to the House of Representatives.

"Once the Federalist candidates both lost, they threw their support to Burr. Each state was allowed one vote. There were sixteen states total. A minimum of nine was need to get elected. Jefferson received eight votes and Burr got six. A split occurred in two states so their votes weren't valid. They took the vote over and over thirty-six times.

"Hamilton finally got a few members of his own party in the South Carolina delegation to abstain. They had been voting for Burr. He believed Jefferson was the lesser of two evils, knowing Burr had schemed with King George behind his back as well as exposed his affair.

"Jefferson was elected thanks to his biggest adversary, though he didn't know it at the time, and Burr became Vice President. Hamilton's scheme, found out later by Burr, furthered his hatred of Hamilton.

"Burr originally told Jefferson he would run but wasn't interested in the Presidency, yet when the tie took place, he didn't back down and that created animosity between the two men. Had Burr won, his alliance with the King could have turned the states back over to England in some fashion, or at the very least, there would have been a permanent trade agreement and alliance against France.

"Perhaps the biggest miscalculation of all was that the people themselves finally understood the tyranny of Praetorian Hamilton's *Nation State* and used the elections as a referendum to kick the Federalists out. At that time, the power of the people still held great sway in local and state politics. Their Federal Senators were elected by the state legislatures and that helped the people keep what power they could, to control central government.

"That's what we are hoping to restore, government of the people, by the people, and for the people, except I'm not talking about Lincoln's version. The 17th Amendment changed how we elect senators. It's now just a democratic majority vote."

◊ ◊ ◊

"Mr. Yates, sir…look." Jonathon pointed to a monitor of the entrance to the labyrinth. Praetorian reserves now flooded Monticello.

"My God. I was hoping the press release would make them retreat, not advance. Get me Stu." Richard's mind was racing. *How in the world are we going to deal with these numbers? I have to save the team.*

Jonathon got Stu on the radio. "Uh, Stu?" he asked in a frantic, panicked, question.

"Do you see them?" Richard asked Stu. "Are you in position yet?"

"I see a lot of movement at the entrance. We're in position on the southern slope. We can't try to retake the entrance from here." Stu and his second were peering over the top of the southwestern part of Monticello's back yard. They could see the house to the east as well as the Southern Pavilion.

Richard had to think fast. "Stu, there must be twenty Praetorians at the entrance. Stay put for now. Make sure you're well hidden from Patterson. They can't know we've staked out that area."

"Will do." Stu answered.

◊ ◊ ◊

The new units of Praetorians had secured the entrance of the labyrinth, but still had no instructions on how to proceed. Word from New York had not reached them.

"Who's in command here?" yelled the current Praetorian Commander at the entrance, Agent Stillwell.

"Sir, no one, sir." replied an agent.

"What happened to the other team?" Stillwell was trying to look into the entrance tunnel through the debris from the original blast at the door. Agents were everywhere, moving this way and that, trying to spy out any possible threats. Two agents appeared coming out of the tunnel.

"They took off." The same agent replied.

"Bastards. We need to go in with force, and we need to do it now!" Stillwell commended.

"Sir, communications are down." One of the agents from the tunnel answered. "There's no way to communicate in the labyrinth and we can't reach headquarters. He motioned towards the entrance. "We have no idea which way to go down there. It's an intricate maze with moving walls.

"So no orders are coming in?" Stillwell asked, as he paced back and forth. He looked up at Patterson Mountain and pointed. "What about up there? We hold the high ground right?

"Sir, no orders are coming from anywhere. Yes we have the high ground for now, but they shot down one of our helicopters." The agent was standing next to Stillwell looking up at Patterson.

"Then this is a field decision. I'm in command now. Get your unit ready." Stillwell tasked.

"Yes, sir."

Stillwell talked to several other agents as they approached him. He directed some to the front of the house, others to scan the lower part of Patterson. He wanted to make sure there was no counter offensive from the mountain.

Two more agents approached with papers that had notes scribbled on them. He looked up, and started pacing again. *This is my chance to rise up and become a top-level Praetorian. All I need to do is bring them out.*"

June 1801 - London, England

Hamilton entered the King's chamber. The king had demanded a face-to-face meeting after the American elections.

He was not happy at all. "Praetor Hamilton, I need to know what our next move is. We've lost the elections, the worst possible person is the President, and we lost both houses of Congress."

"This was a setback I know, but Burr was the last one I wanted as President. Why don't you see that?"

"Why? Do I have to tell you why? Not only have you bungled yet another election, you made sure our mortal enemy is in office. What's going on in that head of yours? I can no longer even guess what you're thinking. The problem, Praetor, is we have no strength in any office and you made sure our trade relations are going to deteriorate because of Jefferson!"

Hamilton paused for a moment. "I have been thinking about this for some time now. Since we are temporarily the minority in the Federal Government, we will use the judiciary to continue our plans," He looked at King George who was not buying this for one minute. "Oh come now, you can't expect to rule on high without a few setbacks."

"A few setbacks are expected, but this is sheer blundering! I already had Aaron Burr ready to get elected. He was the choice you idiot."

Praetor Hamilton would not have taken this aggressive behavior from anyone else. "Burr is an idiot. I know about your plans with him and Church, buying western lands to start a new colonization project. That is a worthless quest. The states will simply keep pushing your colonies farther and farther west, just as they are doing with the native Indians."

The King leaned forward on his Throne. "That, Hamilton, was none of your affair. Now you've messed everything up. It will take me years to regain the American states."

"Perhaps if you had included me in your…"

"Oh shut up. I have no more to say to you on this subject. You are to return to New York and sit there. Sit there and watch Burr rise above you. Your power is now taken. You are no longer Praetor or my pawn. Burr is now Praetor and he will carry out my plans. Being Vice President gives him great positioning in the government, and I will use the judiciary to advance control, but you will not be a part of it. You are broken, your *will* no longer matter. Go back to your wife and live out your years in the purgatory you yourself have made. It will give me great pleasure to see you suffer."

Hamilton seemed quite calm for the circumstances. He was already working on a new plan to destroy Burr and Church.

"Well man, don't just stand there, get out." demanded the King. "Guards, make sure he's on the next boat for America."

Two guards came over to escort him out.

His mind was already racing. *That weakling North should have killed the King when he had the chance!*

Eastern Long Island

"Do you understand the mission and the message?" Benjamin Church kept murmuring to himself. "Do you understand the mission and the message? Idiot. He's ruined everything. Praetor Hamilton, Praetor Hamilton. I'm done with him."

Church entered the secret Praetorian chamber from the front. No one was in the hideaway. He went directly through the main chamber and into the archives. His special rank as Hamilton's second gained him access. There he found all of Hamilton's correspondence from the time he became aide-de-camp for Washington until his recent departure for England. He gathered up everything he found and escaped with them.

He knew the King would now kill him because of all he had done with Hamilton. The King had found out about his part in the attempt North made to poison him. There was nothing left for him in the Society of Praetorians. Now he meant to expose them and bring them crashing down to try to regain what little he could.

<u>May 2018 - Monticello, Virginia</u>

Brooks, Johnson, Trumbull, and Emily started using their oxygen tanks as several of the tunnels were proving thin air.

It was now six o'clock, twelve hours since they had first entered. Not even luck, it seemed, was helping them find the central chamber. What was even worse, they continued entering tunnels they had already been in, a vicious circle with endless designs. They stopped again. Most of their time was spent in silence.

Brooks walked over to each member, checking equipment and oxygen levels in their tanks.

Johnson, pacing, continued pouring over the diary.

Emily sat, made herself as comfortable as she could, and decided it was time to talk. While the information she was learning was important, she still didn't have a grasp on what they would find, and how it could somehow change the future. "What do you think is happening outside?"

"The Praetorians are firmly entrenched, I would think." Trumbull answered. "They're waiting us out. We have nowhere to go. If they had come in, we might have crossed paths by now. I think that we're so far into the labyrinth, the chances of meeting are pretty small."

"I hate to tell you, Mr. Trumbull, but we were in this tunnel before." she replied.

"I know, just trying to stay positive." He gave her a small smile.

Emily knew was for her sake. "I still don't understand this whole labyrinth. It seems beyond scope that the Absconditus Verum Society would have built this thing. If they ever wanted to have a meeting, it would take days just to make it to the chamber."

Brooks answered as he continued checking equipment. "Actually, it wouldn't be long at all if you have the direct route. I've been thinking about that for some time. I don't think they met down here. I now believe they met in the house and had documents sent to the chamber by a slave or house worker. There was less chance someone else would find it, especially if it were a large meeting. Too much risk of exposure. Jefferson trusted very few with this entire project, let alone outsiders. His whole focus would have been to keep the documents secret, keep them safe, away from prying eyes."

Trumbull looked at several of the tunnels entrances into the one they were currently in. "Well, what about this timing system? Sooner or later, the mechanisms will no longer have power to move the walls, right? I mean, just what is powering this system?"

Brooks paused what he was doing to answer. "I'd guess the power is coming from an underground waterway with a turbine system. This was all setup before electricity."

Several walls moved in the distance.

Emily eyed Trumbull as he got up and started pacing.

"Then this won't matter," he said as he walked past Emily.

"What?" Brooks asked. He had now stopped checking equipment as he looked at Trumbull.

Johnson stopped pacing and looked up from the diary. Emily turned towards Trumbull as well.

"I found something out just before all these events happened. There was no use telling anyone since the focus has been on the documents." Trumbull started.

He paused. "It seems there is indeed a treasure trove hidden, but it's not only the documents. The Verum Society accumulated and kept a vast fortune in case they needed to try to recapture their own government. They would have needed enough money to reestablish stability in short order or chaos would have ensued and England, France, or Spain might have used the opportunity to conquer the fragile country."

Emily watched as Brooks looked stunned.

"How did you come by this information?" Brooks asked. "Very few know this."

"The Praetor knows. He confided in me several years ago. I believe it was an attempt to keep my interests, that is before I left them."

Brooks looked at Emily before he answered. "I understand the strategy. It only makes sense. Such wealth would be instrumental in stability as well as funding for defense from foreign influences. However, Trumbull, I don't think the treasure is here. There are three separate sites, two still hidden. Hiding the treasure here as well as the documents would prove a risky move. I believe the treasure is at one of the other two sites."

Trumbull nodded. "In any event, the Praetorians believe a vast treasure might be here. So that should protect us from a radical move on their part." He looked straight at Emily. "They wouldn't collapse the labyrinth and risk losing the chance to recover a hoard of treasure."

She was caught off guard by the comment, giving him an astonished look. *Oh great! The hits just keep on coming.*

Trumbull turned and headed down an open tunnel.

She looked to Brooks, trying to brush off the unnerving news. "Do you know where the other sites are?"

"Connecticut and South Carolina," Brooks answered, "but we don't know for sure if these are the real sites."

"Then this is all for naught? And what do we need old treasure for," she asked?

Johnson got up, walked over and entered the discussion. "Emily. This will make a difference. The world has changed from colonial days. Back then, you needed time and money. Now, you only need enough exposure of the events to start a cascade towards the truth. We don't *need* the treasure, but finding it helps put all the pieces to the puzzle together. It confirms the Verum did indeed hide everything precious to them back then.

"But there does need to be a linchpin in order for the events to actually unfold in today's world. Look at what's happening now. All the scandals in Federal Government. All the intrusion on people's lives. I believe this is the moment in time when the people really can make changes to their own government."

Trumbull return in a full jog. "Brooks, we need to get going."

"What is it?" Emily asked, distraught.

"Trouble," was all Trumbull said.

She heard distance sounds from the tunnel Trumbull had just come out of. She jumped up, picked up her gear, and followed Johnson down another tunnel. Brooks and Trumbull were behind her.

They jogged for a bit, then slowed to a walk. A wall close behind them rumbled closed. She took a breath and stopped, knowing that wall would stop any immediate threat from that direction. The men stopped as well, listening.

Brooks gave a sign of relief, nodded and they continued forward.

Emily pulled out the key and started looking at it again. She stared at the teeth.

Why would Richard say the teeth were the answer? They've been no help at all. What am I missing?

As she fingered the teeth, a thought came to her. Her OCD kicked in as she examined the key closely. The others, realizing she had stopped walked up to her.

"Brooks, take a look at these three teeth and tell me if you see something different." she handed him the key.

"You remember I had that key for many years and never even figured out the numbers."

"Yes, but look at the teeth."

He did so, turning the key several times. "Nothing."

"I think I might have found something. Look at the spacing between the teeth."

He did so, but shook his head.

"This key was specifically made to appear as though the three teeth were evenly spaced showing three different numbers. I think, while miniscule, the second and third ones are slightly closer together." She pulled out an architectural ruler and magnifying glass from her backpack. "I had a feeling these might be useful." She took the key and measured the spaces. "See here."

Brooks looked through the glass as Emily held the ruler in place. "I see perhaps a tiny difference, hardly measurable."

"Close, but it is measurable. One tenth of a millimeter."

"Okay, I'll take your word for it, but what does it mean? In those days, the spacing was probably not well done in the making of the key."

"But for this one, I believe the spacing is there for a reason. It means the first number is a one, and the second number is not a ten followed by a three. It is the number thirteen. Now, if my guess is correct, I will plug the two numbers into the cypher code."

She took out her tablet, which still hadn't decoded the cypher, and brought up her copy of the code numbers in the diary, then inserted the two numbers into the algorithm replacing the three already in the program. The software started processing. A page came up that was in numeric rows and alphabetized both to the right and down.

"Oh, my God! It's working!" Her adrenaline was pumping, hands shaking, as she almost dropped her tablet.

The others gathered around her.

"The first row starts with A in the first position going through the alphabet. The succeeding rows moved the letters one space to the right."

They all looked at the chart.

"You showed us this program already," Brooks said

"Yes, but now we may get some different results. The first number is 18. The letter on the first row in that position is R."

"So that would be a right?" Trumbull asked.

"I'm guessing, but yes I think it is."

"Well, at least we had the first choice correct." he said, not hiding his sarcastic tone.

"Yes…now, how many choices do we have?" Emily queried.

"You mean all the numbers?" Brooks responded.

"No, directions. Look at the first row. If we allow for every choice and check the row, we find out the first is an R for right." She held her tablet as they all looked from behind her.

"Ben, the diary numbers if you please." Brooks requested.

Johnson opened the diary to the specific page.

18 16 14 4 10 20 18 2 26 4 ~
5 15 9 19 17 9 13

----

4 26 2 18 20 10 4 14 16 18
13 9 17 19 9 15 5

"So, our choices should be right, left, straight, up, and down the stairways?" Brooks asked.

"Yes," Emily answered.

She sat down to focus. The men squatted next to her.

"Now, the second number is 16 and in the 16th position on the first row, is the letter P. We don't have a choice of direction there so we must look to row two. The 16th position is O. That's also not a choice. But something we either talked about or was in the diary indicates using alternate rows."

Brooks took the diary from Johnson and read the rhyme,

"Only time will tell when the key to the cypher is shown;
Look up, then down, walk long, follow sound
Look sharp, no fear, eagle's eye, shows it's here
Iron fist, moves the wall, follow hall, do not fall
Iron Gate, blocks the way, with the key, it will sway
Use the rules; take it slow, mark your way, or you will stray
Even in, to begin, odd it is, to show what 'tis
Up or down, you will go, choices sound, you're center bound
Don't go back, for it's a trap, move ahead, or you'll be dead
Iron Gate, blocks the way, with the key, it will sway
Once you're there, the truth lays bare, read and see, our great folly
Take it up, take it out, use the rules, or you'll be fools
Never safe, never seen, show the truth, to all foreseen
Use the rules, to escape, find the light, or doomed to fate
Don't go back, for it's a trap, move ahead, or you'll be dead
Use the rules; find your way, the Iron fist, will show the day."

"Okay. Even in, to begin." She said as she was turning over the thought in her mind. "See all the numbers on the first row of the cypher are even. And the odd numbers are in the second line."

"But what does that mean?" Johnson asked.

"I've been thinking it meant just what it looks like, even numbers in and odd numbers out. But that's not the case. It means we find the answer to the even numbers in the odd rows. Those are the 'rules' from the passage. So, if we use the odd number rows, we should be able to break the cypher."

Emily worked row three. "Now, number 16 in the third row reveals the letter N."

"N? What way would that be?" Trumbull asked.

Emily thought for a moment.

This has to be the cypher. I'm sure of it.

"I don't know. I'm missing something."

"It was a good try, Emily," Brooks offered.

The men stood up and stretched. Emily was silent. She looked at the screen.

It has to be here. It has to be.

She followed column 16 downwards in the chart. Row **5** revealed an L-left. Row 13 a D-down. Row 22 was a U-up. The last clue in the column was row 25, an R-right.

She knew row 22 was eliminated as an even number. This left three choices: left, down, and right.

"Guys, I know I'm right. We need to go back to the Iron Gate and try this code."

The men looked at each other and then to Emily.

Johnson's eyes widened. "Go back! Are you kidding? Praetorians are in the maze. No way we can go back."

"It's the only way." Emily stated.

"Can we even find our way back to the Gate?" Brooks asked.

Emily was confident. "Yes. I have all our notes right here. Because we've been constantly looping, we're close. Guys, trust me. This is our best hope and I know I'm right."

"If you can break the cypher, we'll go back to the gate. But expect a lot of resistance, and we must make sure to turn off all the devices Trumbull set," Brooks instructed.

Emily was now entering in all the information about the moving walls. She was getting close, she knew it. She worked all the numbers down through the rows. There were still many choices, but only a fraction compared to what they had gone through. She also added one more possibility, F-forward in addition to S-straight, just in case it was one and not the other. This left her with only a few pages of code. It also would be whittled down once choices were not available at certain intersections.

She put her tools back, adjusted her back pack, and turned to the first tunnel they had to go through. "I'm ready. We can head back. I'm confident we can find our way once we get into the correct tunnels."

"Lead the way, Mrs. Yates." Trumbull quipped with a smile.

She went first, and he motioned the others to get their weapons ready.

They were indeed headed back to the gate. A dozen different tunnels, a few stairwells, and a wait for two walls to move got them within earshot of the entrance. All thanks to Emily's mapping of their journey in Dean's notepad. She kept working on the cypher as they went.

They were incredibly lucky there were no encounters with Praetorians.

They were about to turn a corner when Trumbull held up his hand.

"Stop." He said in a hushed tone. "This is where I set the booby traps. Wait here."

He silently crept around the corner with his flashlight on a low setting. He didn't return for several minutes.

"What's happening?" Emily whispered.

"Just wait." Brooks looked at her. "You remember that several of Trumbull's devices went off right?"

"Yes…so?"

"So, when he comes back and we go, you need to hold onto my pack and walk directly behind me, focusing on the pack."

"But what's the…" She just realized there would be body parts up ahead. "Oh…ugh."

"That's right."

Trumbull returned. "Okay, I cleared the way. Emily, there are several dead agents in the tunnel. It's an ugly scene."

"She'll be okay. She's walking behind me." Brooks answered.

"I suggest you keep your eyes closed," Trumbull instructed. "Let's go."

Trumbull led the way. He stayed to the right wall, avoiding as many body parts as possible. He had done a good job making a narrow path. There was blood everywhere, on the walls, floor, even the ceiling rock.

Emily kept her eyes tightly closed until they reached the end of the tunnel.

"Okay, Emily, which way?" Johnson queried.

"We just came around that corner behind us," Brooks pointed back to their last location.

She looked at her tablet. "A left and down that tunnel brings us one turn from the gate."

As they approached, they started hearing voices. The Praetorians had moved into the tunnel system, though not very far.

Emily feared the worst. They would get captured and the documents as well as the treasure trove the Praetor wanted would be in his evil hands.

They stopped once they were close to the Praetorian agents, and Emily opened Dean's notepad. Brooks took a good look at the numbers page.

"It looks like we need to go through one more tunnel and then turn left. From there, we can start at the second number of the cypher," she said.

"That puts agents between us and our goal," Trumbull interjected.

They started slowly as Trumbull and Johnson went ahead of Emily and Brooks. They approached the last opening, and Trumbull slipped around the corner.

He returned dragging a dead agent. "We need to go now."

Emily's jaw dropped.

◊ ◊ ◊

Stu Beverley and his team were scanning the situation from below the garden. "Richard! There's a lot of activity up there. Something's happening. Agents are entering the tunnel."

Richard looked at the monitors and indeed there were dozens of agents entering the labyrinth. "Stu, are you in danger of being seen?"

Stu was still on the top edge of the western side of the back yard. "No, we're secure here and their focus is totally on the entrance." He motioned two Delta agents toward a flanking position on the lower south side of the hill.

"Stay put. I know the exit is there somewhere near your position, buried, though I can't be sure."

"Okay, we'll stay as long as we can. If they find us, though, things could get real messy."

"Understood," Richard confirmed.

◊ ◊ ◊

Richard steered his wheelchair over to Hal's station in the barn. "Make ready all our available members. We'll need to create a diversion on the east side to allow Stu's team to work undetected."

Hal nodded as his fingers frantically worked his computer keyboard.

Richard gazed around the inside of the barn control center. Several dozen members were performing all kinds of tasks. He thought, *I can't believe this is really happening, on my watch. I can't let the Verum down. We must succeed now. If we don't, I fear we might not survive. Everything is at stake. Everything the forefathers envisioned our country was to be. We have a chance to be a Republic once more. I have to make it happen.*

He made the most important call of his lifetime. "Sir, it's now or never. We must bring all assets to bear. Are they in position?"

"Yes, Richard. All the teams near your location are standing by. What are the chances for success?" answered the head of the Absconditus Verum Society.

He paused before answering. "I believe in them sir."

Chapter 37

May 2018 - Monticello, Virginia

Trumbull, Johnson, Brooks and Emily silently entered the main tunnel, which was a right turn from the Iron Gate. It was the first choice in the cypher. It was time to trust the algorithm Emily had so carefully put together and they simply didn't have time to map it all out. There was no pursuit yet, but they couldn't dally.

They came to the next choice which was the second on the cypher, number 16. Emily looked at her tablet and scanned down the row. There were no stairs, so those were quickly eliminated. There were only two choices, left or straight/forward. She looked at the possibilities. L-left was on row 6. S-straight was on row 24. There was one choice to go…F-forward on row 11. She pointed for them to continue forward.

The next choice was only left or right. Again, she scanned the chart with the next number, 14. L-left was on row 3, R-right was on row 21.

She turned to the group. "This could be either way. So far, we have row 1 and row 11. The choice is row 3 or row 21. So it could be either one by either alternating between lower odd numbers and higher ones, or it could be the addition of ten to each choice and rotating back into the top of the chart."

"Then this choice should help us decipher the rest of the code?" Johnson asked, scanning the choices in front of them.

Trumbull was now the rearguard.

Brooks held the diary open to the cypher page as he stood next to Emily watching her work the tablet.

"Yes, at least this first section." Emily pointed to the tablet while answering Johnson's question.

"Then let's try right. It worked the first time," Brooks instructed.

They all agreed. It wasn't very far in that they realized it was a dead end.

As they turned to go back, a wall started to appear directly in front of them.

"Move!" Trumbull directed in a soft firm voice.

They outran the wall before it closed completely and ended up back at the third choice tunnel.

Once past the encounter, the team formed a small circle.

Johnson shook his head, looked at Emily, and nodded. "It's ok, you got this. Where to?"

A Praetorian agents walked around an opening behind them. He stopped. Emily was facing him and could tell he wasn't expecting an encounter. His gun was holstered.

"Down!" Trumbull shouted as he turned and fired. A head shot put him down.

Emily put her hand to her face to muffle a scream.

They heard commotion down the tunnel they had just come through.

"They know we're here!" Trumbull said as he motioned them forward, taking the rearguard once again.

The sound of footsteps were much closer and they saw lights coming down the tunnel.

Emily now knew the cypher was alternating lower and upper odd rows for the coded numbers. They ran down the tunnel to the next choice.

"It's left!" Emily burst out as she quickly found the number 4 on row 13. They ran down that tunnel to the next intersection. Emily looked at her tablet. Number 10, row 5. "To the right."

They all moved. It was not long before the pursuers were farther and farther away. The Praetorian agents had to make choices at intersections too and most had probably now entered unknown paths. The amount of agents, however, was now tenfold so they could cover many intersections and choices.

The next intersection was number 20, row 15. She pointed forward, then number 18 row 7 and F-forward again.

"Wait, wait," Brooks, leading the way, put out his arms to stop them. "We've made six choices from the first seven numbers. How come we haven't gone up or down?"

"Because the intersections we've come to don't have those choices." Trumbull answered.

"So what do you think that means?" Johnson asked.

"I believe it means the chamber is on this same level. All the other choices up and down were for entrapment. We'll soon find out." Emily concluded.

Gears cranked, walls moved.

"Go, go!" Brooks directed.

Up ahead was a turn to the left according to the code. They just made it through before it sealed off.

"Now what?" Johnson asked, scanning ahead.

"That should buy us some time. The agents will need to find another way or wait for that wall to open."

They moved down the tunnel to a dead end.

"Not good," Trumbull whispered "What now?"

"We have to stay here until something opens. I don't know what else to do." Emily's emotions surfaced as she put her hand on her chest, trying to calm down.

Hold it together. They're lives on in my hands. Stay focused. You've figured out the cypher. Just get them to the finish.

The team stayed silent while Emily worked on the changed maze for what seemed like forever, though it had only been ten minutes. Gears cranked, and the wall to their right opened.

"Well, do we go?" Johnson asked as he peered into the tunnel.

"Wait, it's processing." Her eyes were glued to the screen.

The algorithm was processing. She shook her hands as if it would somehow help the program.

"We're out of time, Emily," Brooks said.

She looked at the screen. Nothing. She shook her hands again. Still nothing.

"Well?" Johnson asked as he was already part way into the right side tunnel.

She could wait any longer. She had to use her instincts, what her gut was telling her. "Go right."

They did and wound their way around several corners and tunnels they had not been in before. The Praetorians behind them started hammering, trying to break through the wall that separated them earlier.

"Wait…we need to stop." she said as they came to another choice, right or left.

"We must be very close," Brooks guessed. "There are only two choices left."

"Yes, but that wall blocking our way changed the maze again."

She had one more part of the code to decipher.

Do we turn right or left? Which passage brings us to our destination?

The agents had stopped hammering on the wall behind them.

"Which way?" Brooks asked anxiously.

"Wait a second." She held up her hand.

There was a small explosion down the tunnel from which they had just come.

"Those idiots will bring down the whole place!" Trumbull headed back down the tunnel. "I'll hold them off us as long as I can."

Her algorithm was still calculating. "Come on…come on." She tapped the touch pad again, no results.

Several shots came from behind them, including return fire.

"We need to go now!" Johnson yelled.

"It's still processing. The moving walls keep changing this damn code." Her height of frustration was only matched by her adrenalin level. Her hands were shaking. She hit the touch pad again.

The sound of several shots echoed off the walls. Trumbull came back around the corner in a full run towards them. He continued to shoot at the agents on his tail. "We need to move!"

A sound of gears cranked within the walls of the tunnel. Walls that were hidden started to move out from the side walls to block their way from going right or left. Their escape was getting cut off.

Emily shouted at her touch pad. "You piece of…" The numbers started reorganizing. Four moved up into the placement area at the top of the screen. "Left! Left!" she yelled as they all lurched towards the left opening.

Johnson was closest and went through first. Brooks grabbed Emily and shoved her past the opening, diving after her. Trumbull was still in a full run as bullets zipped past him. He jumped and turned sideways in the air as he barely slipped past the wall before it closed completely. Bullets ricocheted off the other side.

Everyone but Johnson was on the ground. He was already moving down the tunnel. The ground shook. They heard more walls moving. Dirt and dust filled the air as the labyrinth continued to change. Then the horror was unleashed. Screams…human screams from the area they just escaped. It was one of the old traps. The agents were getting crushed as the ceiling was descending. Their screams became muffled, and then there was silence.

Loosened rock fell from above, covering them as Emily dropped the tablet and raised her hands above her head. Several small chunks of stone pelted the ground all around her.

Brooks, who had managed to get up, pulled Emily to her feet. They were gagging and coughing as they ran down the passageway toward the central chamber.

More gears moved and the rock roof just above them and ahead started to cave in. They scrambled to a side wall, trying to avoid the debris.

It was no use. The entire system was now compromised. Trumbull pulled Emily down and used his body to cover her. Johnson and Brooks were several yards in front as more debris fell. The entire tunnel was filled with a thick bank of dust and loose rock.

They're chocking and coughs became muffled.

The gears went quiet. The sounds of moving rocks stopped.

The scene was one of heavy destruction. No one was visible. They were buried under shards of debris.

July 1801 - Monticello, Virginia

A carriage pulled up to the house and was met by Jack Jouett, the very man who saved Jefferson and several legislators from the British on June 3, 1781. Jefferson, who was governor at the time, fled Richmond as Benedict Arnold, the traitor, captured and burned it. British General Cornwallis' spies had intercepted a message saying the governor and legislator fled to Charlottesville, the town near Monticello. His ride was as famous as Paul Revere's. He saved them all and had become a state hero.

Now, he was on special assignment to protect Monticello as

Jefferson was President. He often traveled with him as personal bodyguard and clever spy.

"You there," Church called out.

Jouett came down the front portico to meet the carriage.

"What's your name?" Church asked.

"I'll have yours first."

"Benjamin Church," he answered.

Jouett was surprised and alarmed. He pulled a pistol. "Not the one working with the Praetorians?"

"The very same. And now, I shall have yours."

"Jack Jouett. Why have you come?"

"I know you as well. The famous ride that saved Virginia's legislators, and if I'm not mistaken, Jefferson as well. You are indeed someone trustworthy. I have documents from the Praetor's personal archives. They contain all their dealings with the King, political figures, government employees, military personnel, and especially spies."

"And, why would you give Jefferson all this?"

"Because I'm done with Praetor Hamilton and the King. My life no longer holds value and the King has a death warrant out on me. I have very few acts left and I decided to act with some honor in my last days, though I shall be known only for the horrible deeds I have committed."

Jouett gave him a long look before calling several house servants to come and take up the crates in the carriage. He personally checked the contents of each making sure this was not some ruse. They both looked on as they were taken into the lower south wing.

When the last was moved, Jouett engaged Church. "Can you tell me anything the documents might not reveal?"

"Yes. The Vice President is a Praetorian, and might perhaps become Praetor. The king even now is breaking Hamilton."

Jouett was completely surprised by this, but acted in a calm manner. "That's very interesting, anything else?"

"Isn't that enough? The rest of the Praetorian names are within the documents."

"I see. Well this was a most unexpected visit. Do you know what you'll do?"

"I plan to travel to England. I have unfinished business there. I shall not return to America."

"Well then, I hope you can reconcile what you've done."

"I hope so too. Thank you for receiving me. I know I have placed these in good hands. Just be aware that Hamilton will be missing them when he returns from England. These must be kept somewhere absolutely safe."

"Thank you. I'll take care of them."

Church climbed into the carriage and was never seen again.

May 2018 - Monticello, Virginia

It was several minutes before anyone moved. Trumbull was the first to dig his way out. Bruised and beaten, he seemed intact with no broken bones. They had dodged a major bullet as the debris, while voluminous, didn't have many large chunks of rock. He dug down and pulled Emily out. She'd been mostly shielded by him and appeared in good shape, considering the circumstances. She reached down, picking up the tablet.

They both walked forward and saw a hand sticking out of debris. Quickly, Trumbull dug down and helped Brooks and Johnson escape. Emily stood, resting on a side wall.

"Are you alright?" was the first thing Brooks said, looking at Emily.

"Yes. Mr. Trumbull took most of the hit."

"How about you, Johnson?" Trumbull asked.

"I'm okay." He winced. "But I think my shoulder may be broken."

Trumbull pulled out some bandaging, from a medical kit in his backpack, and created a sling for Johnson.

They checked all their equipment and found that only two lights were broken. Somehow, Emily had protected her computer tablet from damage. She checked it, and it responded. It once again showed the left turn they had taken just before the cave-in.

Once they had time to catch their breath, they started moving forward. While there was a lot of debris, the walls and most of the ceilings were intact. The debris was limited to the outer surface of the rocks so there were no holes of any kind. They did have to climb over and go around some mounds that were more than a foot thick.

"We must be near it or on top of our destination," Brooks said.

Another thirty feet and around the corner, they hit a dead end. No opening of any kind on any side.

"Okay, Emily, this is it." Johnson offered.

"We're sealed in, aren't we?" she asked.

"Only until you give us the next clue." Trumbull answered, with a feeling of confidence.

Brooks started scanning the walls. "Here!" He brushed away cobwebs and dust and there was a small latch built into one of the walls.

They all looked at each other.

"Let's do it," Emily nodded.

"Well…here goes." Brooks turned it counter clockwise.

It moved ninety degrees. Latches and gears could be heard within the walls. The sounds darted around them within the side walls and back through the tunnel they had just come from. Next, it was the sound of stone moving... lots of stones moving, both near and far along with the faint screams of human voices.

"My God!" Brooks shouted as they moved into the center of the small room. "The entire system is moving this time."

What was once a system that moved a few walls every ten minutes was now moving everything that could move at the same time. They listened to the system struggling as sliding walls were trying to push debris as they closed. They heard more agents scream behind other walls, some close, others in the distance, until an eerie silence hung in the thick and dusty air.

The team moved back around the corner they had come from. The tunnel was gone, just a wall blocking the way back, sealed perfectly on both sides. The debris on the floor had been crushed into small stones.

"That's it. The latch triggered the traps. I would say everyone in the tunnels is dead or trapped, including us." Johnson surmised.

Brooks looked at Johnson. "A kill switch."

Johnson paused. "Yes! I'd say maybe the first of its kind. Meant to protect the user from pursuit."

"Fascinating." Trumbull was examining the lever closely.

Emily watched as he looked intrigue by the ingenuity involved. He turned and caught her eye.

"What a perfect killing machine," he said proudly. His tone changed. "That won't sit well with the Praetorians. I'd say we have very little time before they start a full-scale invasion of the hill. They'll dynamite once they know it's been sealed, even if it means damaging the treasure."

"Oh, great!" Emily exclaimed, in a hopeless tone.

"Johnson, Trumbull, look around for some other mechanism." Brooks was already looking, "If we can't find anything to open, we need to see if any air is getting in here."

They scanned the entire area. No latch, no air flow, nothing. Brooks broke out the air tanks again, and they each strapped one on. Trumbull helped Emily with hers. Brooks did the same for Johnson. They sat on the floor.

Emily gazed at her tablet again. After she keyed in the final sequence, the tablet reconfigured the way through the labyrinth. They were now where the last number on the first row would have brought them.

"We finished the top half of the code. We need to figure out how to find the way to the next set. The small tilde after the number four must have been meant to use that latch. That's what you've been looking for, Brooks. It wasn't in another section of the diary, it was with the numbers."

"What the hell is a tilde?" Trumbull queried.

"It's that swung dash after the four in the first line of numbers," Emily explained.

"Well, I can rest easily now that I know about that symbol." Trumbull said in his trademark sarcasm.

Emily rolled her eyes and looked at the algorithm. Brooks was studying the diary, and Johnson was scanning every inch of wall for something that would open the next sequence. Trumbull had an odd expression on his face. Emily could tell he was still not quite over the tilde answer. She couldn't help but smile.

It was another ten minutes and nothing moved. She checked the time. "It seems that latch has stop the ten minute reconfigurations. Perhaps we can get out of here without any more walls changing."

They still had their oxygen tanks on. Brooks checked his indicator. It was down to fifty percent.

Emily was immersed in thought as she watched the tablet screen. "The first number on the second set indicates down."

"Yes, but we must find a way through one of these walls that will lead to a stairway." Trumbull answered.

Brooks started reading the riddle again:

"Only time will tell when the key to the cypher is shown;
Look up, then down, walk long, follow sound
Look sharp, no fear, eagle's eye, shows it's here
Iron fist, moves the wall, follow hall, do not fall
Iron Gate, blocks the way, with the key, it will sway
Use the rules; take it slow, mark your way, or you will stray
Even in, to begin, odd it is, to show what 'tis
Up or down, you will go, choices sound, you're center bound
Don't go back, for it's a trap, move ahead, or you'll be dead
Iron Gate, blocks the way, with the key, it will sway
Once you're there, the truth lays bare, read and see, our great folly
Take it up, take it out, use the rules, or you'll be fools
Never safe, never seen, show the truth, to all foreseen
Use the rules, to escape, find the light, or doomed to fate
Don't go back, for it's a trap, move ahead, or you'll be dead
Use the rules; find your way, the Iron fist, will show the day."

"What was the last part of the riddle we used?" Johnson asked.

"Let me see it." Emily reached for the diary and Brooks handed it to her. "Here. Even in, to begin, odd it is, to show what 'tis."

"And the next line?" Johnson inquired.

"Up or down, you will go, choices sound, you're center bound," she read as she started to ponder a possible answer.

"Okay, so it's telling us to go to the center room." Brooks concluded.

"Is this the center room?" Trumbull asked.

They looked around to not even a hint that anything had once been kept there. The area itself was only twelve by twelve.

"No, this can't be it," Brooks offered as he walked the perimeter. "It must be a lot bigger than this."

Emily looked and read aloud.

*"Up or down, you will go, choices sound, you're center bound
Up or down, you're center bound!"*

"So that means...?" Johnson asked, looking at the walls. He winced and grabbed the sling.

"Up or down, you will go, choices sound, you're center bound. It means we have to continue by going up or down." Emily was convinced she was right.

"Yes...yes." Brooks answered. "And, since we're on the main level, we can't go up, but only down."

"Yes, and the answer is in the middle of the room-center bound. It wasn't a clue for the center room, but for us to start the next level!"

"There's so much debris and dirt here, it must be underneath," Emily surmised.

Brooks and Trumbull started brushing aside the rubble. As they did, a small circle in the floor appeared, no larger than a silver dollar.

Trumbull looked up. "Okay, before we push this down, we need to have all our equipment together."

They quickly gathered their things. Brooks pushed the button. Nothing happened. He pushed it again, harder. They noticed a slight rumble, the sound of moving rock.

Emily lost her balance as the floor below her dropped. Trumbull caught her hand and pulled her safely to his side. They watched as step after step appeared going down into the darkness.

"Okay, we need to move quickly. I don't know if we have enough oxygen to linger and get out," Brooks directed.

They went down to the next level, and Emily quickly got them through all the choices now that the algorithm was working properly. They turned around the last corner, and there it was...

◊ ◊ ◊

Stu called in from the top of the back slope at Monticello. "Richard, we just had what we initially thought was an earthquake. I think the old traps in the labyrinth went off and trapped or killed a bunch of Praetorian agents inside. Our team must have found the point to set them off."

"Any chance they survived?" Richard asked as his voice cut out.

"We don't know. Until we get some kind of signal from them, it's a guessing game."

"We'll go on the assumption they're going to get out. Make sure your team is ready." Richard instructed.

"They must be getting fairly close by now, if they survived the traps. We can't stay here much longer as they're starting to expand the perimeter. I'd say another few hours before we need to bug out to avoid detection." Stu continued to direct his team, coming and going, to and from, secret locations around the back yard.

He kept a lookout from the south side of the hill. "Some fifty agents have gone in and only the last two came back out. One of my Delta team monitored the sounds made from the traps going off and they realized the Praetorian agents will not be coming back out. Any communication they had set up is also cut off, so they're no closer now than when this all started."

Richard answered. "Stu, we've heard rumors that the Praetor's main assassin might be close, so keep an eye out for him. If we can take him out, we should. It might be our only chance. Keep me posted. Meanwhile, have two of your best sharpshooters setup wherever it looks safe in order to protect your position, should it be compromised. I also want them keeping an eye out for the assassin."

Two of his best circled to the northwest and into a tree line where they climbed and had a clear view of the back yard of Monticello.

◊ ◊ ◊

The plane landed and taxied down the runway towards his personal hanger. Soon Victor Shaw was on the road heading to what was sure to be his destiny.

Chapter 38

The Old Praetorian Chamber, Eastern Long Island

The Praetorians managed to break through the communications blackout the Verum had setup.

"I want that entire hill covered!" yelled the Praetor on the phone. "No one gets in or out without us knowing."

The Praetor sensed he was too close to miss now.

An agent in charge after their crushing defeat was on the line. "Sir, we had fifty men in there and only two made it out." Even the esteemed Agent Stillwell hadn't survived.

"My orders were to wait them out!" The Praetor was not open to discussion.

"I know, sir, but communications were down until now."

"What's your name, Praetorian?"

"It's Agent Kroger , sir."

"Well, Agent Kroger, don't do anything stupid until Field Commander Thornton arrives, understand?"

"Yes, sir."

"You are to call me once you catch them."

"Yes, sir."

Several council members had just arrived at the old stronghold. Each took a seat around the original table Praetor Hamilton had forged hundreds of years earlier. Several conversations were taking place between them. It seemed they lacked the cohesion critical to running an 'on the ground' strategy. The military officers on the council were helpless to run a group of agents they knew very little about.

◊ ◊ ◊

Commander Thornton had arrived and was at the labyrinth entrance. Agent Kroger met him there.

"God, what a mess. Kroger, you better not let them escape or we're both done for, got it?" Thornton said sternly.

Kroger nodded and followed Thornton through the debris surrounding the entrance.

"Yes, sir. The Praetor said we must wait until they come out. After what just happened, I have no idea if they're even alive. We've now lost almost seventy agents." Kroger filled in the new commander.

Once through the debris around the entrance, they walked up to the lawn. The yard itself had sunk several feet in many places. Some as large as six feet in diameter. There was a large pile of explosives positioned in the center of the yard on a pallet, where the ground was still intact.

"This is a nightmare." Thornton declared. He called the Praetor. "Praetor, the entire labyrinth structure has been compromised. We need to work our way in to see if we can even get them or the documents."

"Then blast your way in and get what you can. We'll worry about the cleanup later," the Praetor ordered.

◊ ◊ ◊

The Praetorians had taken Patterson Hill earlier that day and were using it to spy out any attempt of rescue or escape. They hadn't discovered Beverley's units or any other Absconditus Verum members anywhere, but they continued to monitor. They had managed to break through the communications black out as one of the Verum devices on Patterson, which had been damaged in the helicopter crash, gave out.

No information was let out about what was going on at Monticello since the crash. The media was chomping at the bit from the bottom of Monticello hill. The Verum didn't want the press, good or bad, and Richard assumed the Praetorians felt the same. This allowed both sides to firm up their positions and make ready for any upcoming action or event.

◊ ◊ ◊

Johnson, Brooks, Trumbull, and Emily, made their way down the circular stairwell into an anti-chamber. They paused and stared at their newest deterrent-an Iron Gate between them and what they hoped was the central chamber.

Emily's anxiety was at a peek. "This must be it."

She handed Brooks the key, and he unlocked it. With a loud squeak and a strong pull by all three men, the gate gave way.

"Won't they hear the noise?" she asked.

"It doesn't matter now." Johnson stated. "But I think we're far enough underground to avoid detection."

"Then let's get to work," Brooks directed.

They all went through the gate and entered the center chamber. The room was filled with old tables and a few chairs-cobwebs everywhere. It was hard to see with only their flashlights.

Johnson went along the stone surface to the right. "I found a torch holder!"

Emily used her flashlight to scan all the walls. "Yes, there are several of them."

"And I found some torches," Johnson had bumped into a table filled with them, almost knocking it over. He handed them out.

Brooks took out a lighter and lit each torch, the team put them on the walls. As each was set, more and more of the room could be seen. It seemed circular, fifty feet in diameter. The walls did not form a perfect circle, however. They meandered around in the shape of an oval. Many of the walls had shelves carved into the stone. The room itself was hewn from solid rock that was buried in the hill of Monticello. There were several tables, shelves, and bookcases. Old papers were everywhere: maps, charts, and letters. Many were in poor condition as time was consuming them. Dozens were on the floor.

Emily was awestruck. "My God!"

The shelves were filled with parchments, artifacts, and trinkets of wealth. They had reached the center chamber.

There was one large desk in the middle of the room. It was surrounded by tables that were all covered in documents.

"This is not the meeting room some thought," Johnson deduced. "You were right, Joseph. It looks like a document hold, only for the storage of papers and other valuables. They must have met in the main house and had the documents sent down here to be cataloged and stored. They have chairs about. The time it took to catalog all these must have been immense."

A large octagonal chest made of glass with a bronze alloy frame was on the center desk. It was filled with scrolls and parchments.

Brooks took a closer look. "Because of this chest's location, these parchments would have been either from the last meeting to be cataloged or the most important ones in the room."

Emily's palms started to sweat. *Could this be the resting place of the documents we've been looking for?*

They all started going through the parchments nearest them. Brooks was trying to figure out how to open the chest.

"Here are notes from the first and second Continental Congresses!" Johnson exclaimed.

"I have treaties with most of the European countries over here." Emily was beside herself with enthusiasm.

They continued to find artifacts from every event that took place since the 1640s, the first of the English Colonies. Most of the Colonies had governmental structures that had been set up and implemented, the majority of which were faith based and centralized within each community.

"Most of these are copies made from the original documents," Johnson surmised, "But I don't see anything I haven't seen before."

Brooks had gotten the octagonal chest open and was looking through the contents. "I think I found something," he stammered."

The others joined him.

"These documents look like correspondence between the New England States and Jefferson from 1803 to 1815…see the dates?"

A distant bang was heard above them. They were out of time.

◊ ◊ ◊

"We better gets this cleaned up and get out of here," Trumbull said "There's very little time to waste." He looked at the room. All this time he never really believed it existed, yet here they were.

They spent the few minutes removing everything from its storage spaces and rolling parchments and placing them in the protective tubes in their packs. They took everything of value they could find and carry. When they had finished, the room was barren of most items of value, both documents and trinkets. They were each loaded down to the point of struggling just to walk.

Another bang went off, This time it sounded a bit closer to their position.

Brooks yelled. "Everyone out now!" just as debris started falling from the ceiling.

◊ ◊ ◊

Perched on the back yard southwest slope, Beverley watched as the Praetorians started setting off explosives. "Richard! They've started setting off charges on the back lawn above the labyrinth."

"Can you move into position?" he asked as he watched the monitor in the barn command center.

Stu did a quick survey. "Yes. They're focused on what they're doing for the moment."

"Then we must hope luck is on our side. We'll create a diversion. The undiscovered secret back door of the labyrinth should be up by the old Joinery chimney. From the chimney, look directly across Mulberry Row and it should be in the side of the hill."

Stu looked down the slope from his position and saw the old chimney. "I see it. How do you know it's there?"

"I have the sketches of the maze Emily made. She has the exit in that area."

Stu hung up. "Men, get ready to move."

The Delta members, who had not gone to other points on the hill, grabbed their gear and readied to go. There were eight in all.

"I'm leading the way. Stay low and out of sight." Stu instructed.

They had with them a large camouflage tarp which four team members held taut from the corners. The rest of the team was underneath. Once they reach Mulberry Lane near the old chimney, they got down on their knees and waited for whatever Richard had up his sleeve.

◊ ◊ ◊

Richard called Jonathon and Hal over to his station. "This is it, guys, . Either they're going to be there or we miss this window. Put everything into motion."

"Yes, sir," they both nodded and went back to their stations.

Each contacted their outside sources and, within minutes, there was more action at Monticello than it had seen since the Civil War. Verum team helicopters flew towards Patterson Mountain and opened fire with tear gas and small explosives. They weren't looking to kill everyone, but they were looking to drive them from their positions. It was happening just as Stu Beverley's team started to move. The perfect distraction.

◊ ◊ ◊

Field Commander Thornton was monitoring the explosive charges going off on the lawn. The sounds from the mountain pulled his attention and the rest of the Praetorians on the backyard.

He called the Praetor. "Sir, they're driving our unit off Patterson!"

"Is there any action anywhere else?"

"No, sir. We've been getting farther into the labyrinth from the yard with explosives, but haven't found anything. This is going to take some time unless we scrap the mission and blow everything up."

◊ ◊ ◊

The Praetor was burning with anger. As much as he wanted those documents, he wanted to keep the Verum from escaping with them. He looked to the other Council members, who were seated at the old stronghold council chamber. "Well? You're all here for a reason. Do we destroy everything?"

"Forget about the labyrinth for now." His new second, the General, responded. The Praetor promoted him after the assassination in France. "They're up to something. This is a distraction, or a way to keep us from seeing what they're doing. Look for activity somewhere else."

The members were all engaged in different expressions, some nodding while others shook their heads and grumbled.

"Anyone else?" the Praetor asked.

The rest of the men fell silent. What had once been a chamber of great intellect and military skills was now filled with corporate executives, politicians, and former military commanders past their prime, none of whom had any field experience.

"We really do need Shaw to clean this up." The General finally said.

The Praetor was seeing, perhaps for the first time because of the Verum resistance, their inability to manage an uprising. They were skilled in banking, the stock market, lobbying, and crony capitalism. They were able to run governments from back rooms in secret, addict the people to entitlements and government handouts. The weakness of the people was their strength. Now, even though they were involved in several military actions throughout the world, they just didn't know how to run an actual military operation. Their only other strength was to hire hit men and have them do all their dirty work. He needed to call for assistance, something he dreaded doing.

Finally, the Praetor called the commander on the ground. "Proceed, but cautiously. If they're alive, then bring them in. If not, find whatever you can. You need to make sure everything, and I mean everything, is cleaned up. That includes every agent. Try to keep the damage to a minimal amount."

◊ ◊ ◊

Field Commander Thornton had his orders. Try to work into the labyrinth, clean up the mess they make in doing that, and remove all traces of dead agents. "We need to bring in several medical emergency units. There's a Praetorian unit in Richmond. Get them here," he ordered Kroger, who was standing beside him.

"Yes, sir." Kroger made the call.

◊ ◊ ◊

Thornton no sooner got the words out of his mouth when a skirmish broke out on the front lawn. Another Absconditus Verum unit had taken position near the front walk. Six Praetorian agents ducked for cover in the Northeast Portico, the front porch. The Verum team was using communication jamming devices again to keep the Praetorians from coordinating any plans. The Verum meant to keep them occupied for as long as they could.

◊ ◊ ◊

"Kroger!" Thornton yelled. "Get a team up there and see what's going on. Bring a small unit with you."

He nodded and selected four men. They hurried towards the house.

◊ ◊ ◊

The Praetor called Shaw. "I need you to get there as soon as possible. The situation is out of hand, and we need to wrap it up as soon as possible."

"I know. I'm in contact with them. You really screwed this up big time, didn't you?" Victor Shaw's disrespect came through loud and clear.

"Never mind that, just do your job." The Praetor was fuming.

"I can't. Your actions prevent me from saving the situation. Perhaps next time you'll consult with me before you make any decisions." Shaw had a demining edge in his voice.

"How dare you take that tone with me! Just get down there and fix it. That's a direct order, Shaw." The Praetor stood up and acted as if he wanted to reach into the phone and throttle Shaw.

"I'm killing everyone I find." Shaw responded.

"No! We need as many captured as we can!"

There was silence on the other end.

"Shaw!"

The line went dead. The Praetor slammed the phone on the stone table and it shattered.

Shit! Another phone! As he remembered back to the encounter with Trumbull.

The room was quiet until the General dared to ask. "Well, what did he say?"

The Praetor glared at the council. He was overly concerned with the deteriorating situation. "Have we become so feeble that we've lost focus on actually engaging the enemy?" he paused, "He's going to kill every Verum member he can."

"What do we do now?" the World Bank Executive asked.

"We hunker down until we know what the situation is." the Congressman responded.

"No. You must stop that team inside! I don't care how you do it, just do it!" the Interpol Agent blurted out.

"No! We cannot contain the situation if we continue to escalate the encounter." The General surmised.

The Praetor looked at the FBI Director. "Is this going to destroy Monticello?"

"No, but it will open the labyrinth so we can finally get inside."

"Do it." The FBI Director responded.

"No!" the Congressman yelled. "If you do, it will bring so much attention to our hidden Society that we shall surely be exposed."

A full-scale argument erupted. It lasted for several minutes as the Council threw verbal insults at their fellow Praetorians.

They finally made the decision. The Praetor called Field Commander Thornton, but communications were being jammed.

"Can I get someone to find those jamming devices so I can get through?" He scowled angrily.

"Praetor, we're not the ones jamming. It's the Verum." The Admiral chimed in.

◊ ◊ ◊

Trumbull knew they had to find the exit and fast. The events outside were going to end them all if they didn't hurry.

"Now what?" Johnson was doing his best to carry a full pack with a broken shoulder and one good arm.

"Well, we need to find the solution to the exit tunnels," Brooks said, "We need to go over the end of the riddle again." He took out the diary. "Okay, so we're here…

Once you're there, the truth lays bare, read and see, our great folly
Take it up, take it out, use the rules, or you'll be fools
Never safe, never seen, show the truth, to all foreseen."

"So, that part is completed," Johnson said

"Yes. Now here's the rest:

Use the rules, to escape, find the light, or doomed to fate
Don't go back, for it's a trap, move ahead, or you'll be dead
Use the rules; find your way, the Iron fist, will show the day."

Emily punched in the number for the exit route on her tablet. The algorithm responded quickly. "We take that other passage on our left."

They all started to make their way, though slower now that they had overflowing packs. It wasn't long before they reached a tunnel that was totally collapsed.

"Now what?" Johnson struggled, almost falling to his knees. Brooks caught him in time.

"You're kidding, right?" Emily responded with anger in her voice. "I know it's near the old chimney, but now I don't know how we get there. This was the way!"

"We have to go around and find another way out. Hopefully the fact that some of the walls move can actually benefit us." Brooks answered in a calm tone, holding out his hand, face down. "Let's just keep calm and figure this out."

Trumbull wasn't pleased with this proposition. "They're working their way in with explosives right now. They'll get to us a lot sooner than we can find the way out." His voice firm and determined.

There was a slight sound, almost undetectable. It was a low frequency musical note.

"Shh…listen," Emily directed.

It sounded again, then again, in five-second intervals.

Trumbull watched as Johnson was concentrating on the sound. "You know what? That's a signal from someone outside." He took out a compass. It was pointing in the direction the sounds were coming from.

Brooks looked at Johnson's compass. "Really? Your compass working?"

"Yes. Or, well, I don't know, but it's showing southwest and southwest gets us to the southern slope. We should follow the sounds. Brooks, you said you knew where the exit is." Johnson winced and adjusted his pack.

"I said I believed it to be towards the southwest. That's what Emily's drawings indicated."

Trumbull couldn't wait. "People, we need to move! Just follow the sounds. He disappeared into a southwest tunnel."

◊ ◊ ◊

Emily watched Trumbull leave. "What if it's the Praetorians?" Emily asked as her enthusiasm quickly dissipated. "And as we've seen, many of these tunnels double back. Even the correct path did that several times." She tried adjusting her pack, struggling to get it balanced. It was overbearing. "There's no way I can carry all this for an extended amount of time. I wish Tim were here…"

Brooks decided. "It's our best chance right now, and we don't have time to waste. Emily, we'll take turns with your pack. Let's go."

As they entered the southwest tunnel Brooks yelled out. "Trumbull!"

"I'm up here!" he yelled back.

They quickly caught up.

He pointed to a tunnel. "That's a dead end." He pointed to another. "That one too."

There was only one choice left. He nodded to Emily and started ahead.

They continued on, though slower, and started mapping the route again as Emily's algorithm worked through the choices.

She came to a halt. "Wait! Of course. Why didn't I think of this earlier? I can figure out which way we're going based on the turns in the algorithm."

"How can you with no reference point?" Trumbull asked.

She punched in data. "I have a reference point. We came in going northwest. Now…if I add that to the program and have it…yes, yes. Okay. This tunnel is going southwest.

They hurried down the tunnel in the direction of the steady rhythm from outside.

◊ ◊ ◊

Field Commander Thornton stood next to the pallet of explosives in the back yard. The sun was fading in the west. There were a half dozen gaping holes in the yard. Several gave no results as the collapses block any way to get into the maze. Only one was accessible. Several agents have gone in.

It was another hour before the Praetorians were able to get past the communications jam. He finally got the latest orders. Agent Kroger returned from the front yard and approached him with a detonator box in his hand.

"It's a stalemate up front. Both sides are dug in. We have three agents left up there," Kroger reported. "And, besides us, there are four in the tunnels."

Thornton had to make the most important decision of his life.

Do I just blow it up? That's what the Praetor wants. Everything will be lost. And there's no way I can clean this mess up. What an absolute waste. Hundreds of years comes down to this?

He finally decided. "Pull them out of the tunnels. We're going to collapse the system with these explosives."

Kroger climbed down the gaping hole made by one of the blasts and soon returned with the four Praetorians that had been using small explosives to make their way into the labyrinth, though they had made little progress.

They all walked along the explosives leads back to the labyrinth entrance below the South Pavilion. It lay in ruins.

Kroger set the primer and flipped on the detonator switched. His thumb just above the blast button. He looked at Thornton, standing in front of him. Thornton nodded.

It was the last thing Kroger did. Bullets rained down on them from Delta sharpshooters in the trees and from the long distance of Patterson. He was shot through the head at least twice in an instant. The surprise jolted Thornton backwards and behind rubble, luckily to cover.

◊ ◊ ◊

Part of Beverley's Alfa Squad had just retaken Patterson. Stu was still on the crest of the southern slope to the west of the labyrinth entrance.

Two shots from the trees put down two Praetorians next to Thornton, while the last two dove back into what was left of the entrance. They were the four from the hole in the yard.

Thornton was the only one left outside. He was lying flat on the ground, trying desperately to use what little cover there was. The Delta Sniper team spread out around the perimeter of the backyard as they had started advancing with the explosives activity. A Delta leader took aim at the wires going to the explosives.

Stu watched through his rifle scope. Thornton dove over to the detonator and was just about to push the button. Stu fired from the top of the south slope and caught Thornton in the side. He fell forward and hit the button. It was too late. The connection was gone. Two shots from the Delta member had severed the wires to the explosives. A sniper shot Thornton twice in the neck, and he was dead only moments later.

Another Delta sniper who was surveying the grounds with binoculars shouted., "Sir! There's an agent in the cuddy of the house!"

One could see the attic window facing the backyard was broken and a weapons barrel was aimed at the explosives. It was a grenade launcher.

"Take him out!" yelled the team leader.

The Praetorian got off the shot before they could react. It found the mark. Delta sniper bullets littered the window and all around it. The grenade hit the explosives and the entire hill shook.

Stu Beverley stood, frozen in place, mouth agape, watching helplessly as the explosion went off. He called Richard. "We've secured the backyard and have them pinned down in the front. Richard, there was a large explosion. It came from the backyard. Can you see it?"

◊ ◊ ◊

Richard was leaning over Jonathon, eyes fixated on the monitors in the barn. "Yes, Stu, I see it. They set off explosives."

The backyard had a fifteen foot wide crater in it. The explosives, collapsed the entire center of the labyrinth. The Praetorians finally had a way in. The problem for them was, there were no Praetorians left to go in. At least none willing to.

"I see part of your Delta team heading to the impact point." Richard continued. "Get me a status report as soon as you can. And send in a team to catch any remaining Praetorian agents that might be in the entrance to the tunnels. They still look intact from our camera view."

◊ ◊ ◊

Emily's algorithm and the tones weren't leading them out yet as they had to double back several times. Two more walls blocked their way before they made real progress. They ran around several corners and another choice had to be made. They couldn't hear the tones any more.

An explosion from above and to the east had them scrambling to the sides of the tunnel. Everything in the system was teetering on collapse, but it somehow held mostly intact.

They clung to the walls as the dust settled.

"That came from the center room area," Brooks observed.

"Yes, they're trying to open the system from directly above now, hoping we haven't cleared it yet. This is another panic move. They're risking everything, including major exposure," Trumbull offered.

Suddenly a massive blast hit the top of the Monticello property.

"Run!" Brooks yelled.

They rushed through more tunnels, which were descending sharply towards the southwest, as more and more of the system collapsed behind them. They had to guess on directions as the algorithm couldn't keep up with their pace. Soon they reached a dead end. Luckily the tunnels stopped collapsing just behind them.

"You've got to be kidding me!" Emily yelled. "What the hell was that?"

Johnson looked at Brooks. "It has to be."

"I can't believe it," Brooks shook his head.

"Believe it." Trumbull answered as he frantically looked for an escape.

"Well?" she asked.

No one answered. They backtracked as far as they could, but the tunnels were almost completely collapsed. It was a few minutes before everything went quiet.

"What happened?" Emily asked.

"That was a drone strike. No amount of explosives would do that. It collapsed most of the system and the ceilings. That descent we just made puts us about fifty feet below the upper tunnels," Trumbull answered, still looking for an exit. "If we were any higher in the system…"

◊ ◊ ◊

Richard watched in disbelief as a drone flew over Patterson and launched a missile, hitting the center of the backyard. A massive explosion followed at the same spot the dynamite was set off. The backyard lay in ruins, most of it a gaping hole.

He quickly called. "What's your status, Stu?"

Stuart Beverley was down, as were most of his team. Richard looked at the monitors as they showed the destruction.

"Stu!"

"Yes…yes, I'm here." he answered in obvious pain.

"Are you alright?" Richard yelled.

Richard found Beverley on one of the monitors. Jonathon zoomed in. Stu rolled over and got to his feet. He was only part way up the yard from the southwest. The contour of the hill saved him from oblivion. Most of his team wasn't as lucky. The blast vaporized several members as others lay in grotesque pieces throughout the yard. The remaining Praetorians still embedded at the entrance to the labyrinth were also killed. It was all visible on the monitors.

"Sir, what was that?" Stu was shaking off the concussive effects of the explosion.

"A drone strike." Richard looked at the monitors as the smoke slowly cleared.

What had been a small hole was now an entire collapsed upper portion of the grounds. The house itself was spared any significant damage. The top level of the labyrinth in the center was gone. Rubble filled whatever was left of the center room.

"And our team inside?" Beverley asked, wobbling, reaching out to balance himself.

Richard's emotions rose to the surface as he fretfully said. "Alive, I hope, and heading for the exit. Start probing the area around the Joinery. Find that back door."

Stu staggered back down the southern slope. "Yes, sir. We've started sending the pulse signal. Hopefully, it will help them directionally."

"Only if they figure out the exit path." Richard answered. "Hopefully they found something that will guide them. Stu, pull everyone out except a small detail. This just went public."

Several other monitors in the barn lit up with newscasts.

"We just been witness to a massive explosion on the grounds of Monticello," said a live newscaster stationed well below the grounds that were blocked by government officials. "It looked like a craft of some kind, possibly a drone , launched a missile. We can't tell where it hit, but I can tell you there is pandemonium here."

◊ ◊ ◊

"I have to stop." Emily wrested her pack off and put it down. She sat in silence for several minutes, surrounded by rubble, as the men scoped out possible exits. She was in deep thought.

I'm missing something. We have to have the escape route. What is it? Can this even work, now that so many choices have been destroyed?

She looked at her tablet, which had gone into sleep mode, and brought up the algorithm.

"Do you have something, Emily?" Brooks approached her through debris.

"I don't know. I'm taking a look at the algorithm again. Perhaps something I missed. The direct route was blocked. I'm trying to find an alternate."

"Meanwhile, we need to decide what to do," Trumbull said, "They blew up the yard. It probably exposed some of the tunnels. If so, Praetorian agents will now be in the labyrinth and perhaps very close."

"Then I need you to backtrack and see," Brooks directed.

Trumbull was soon gone, looking for trouble.

Emily stared at the algorithm, lost in thought. Brooks and Johnson checked all the gear.

Brooks started talking to Johnson in a hushed voice, but Emily was able to overhear them. "You realize our air supply is cut off."

"Yes. That collapse affected the entire system. I would say no more than thirty minutes of air left. We have perhaps an hour left in the tanks." Johnson whispered.

"My assessment, as well. What do you think is happening up there?" Brooks asked.

"Well…since the blast, everything's gone quiet except that low tone that we're hearing. That's from a Verum team. It was set up years ago as a signaling system for contacts and directional feeds," Johnson offered.

"So we must assume our Society has control of the area."

"Yes, at least the southern and western hillsides." They were back checking for exits. Rubble was everywhere, but the tunnel they were in was still passable.

Johnson took out the compass. "I think Jefferson set up a magnetic field near the exit. It's been pointing southwest much of the time."

"That makes sense, although without the algorithm, it keeps sending us to dead ends. We must be south or west, but we've double-backed with some choices into tunnels that simply stop," Brooks said.

"I think we need to go back to the central room. Hopefully, if we do have control up there, they can get us out that way." Johnson deduced.

They both looked at Emily.

"She's a remarkable woman," Johnson said "Her courage alone is remarkable. Can you imagine being thrown into all this and still be able to function…and help no less."

Emily look up, smiled and shook her head at the compliment, as she continued working the algorithm.

Brooks gave Johnson a small smile. "Let's go."

"What's going on?" she asked as she stood up.

"We're going to try to make it back to the chamber. Perhaps the explosion opened an exit for us," Brooks said "Any luck with the algorithm?"

"No. It doesn't make any sense. There's something I'm missing. Too many blocked passages."

"Then we need to get going."

"Don't bother." Trumbull returned as they were about to go. "It's sealed off. Unless the Verum members can cut through solid rock, we won't be going that way."

"They won't do that, chancing another collapse from either cutting or blasting," Brooks concluded.

"Then we're stuck here," Johnson said dejectedly.

Emily looked at her tablet, thought for a moment, and said "No, we're not. Brooks, can I see the diary?"

He handed it to her as she passed him the tablet. "It was so easy I completely overlooked it, the riddle. The exit is not expressed in one of the lines, but the entrance is.

"Even in, to begin, odd it is, to show what 'tis.

"This was the key to mapping our way into the chamber. The algorithm is set up to alternate lines and odd or even numbers. If it holds true, then the exit must also be in the same way. I just flip the lines from last to first and reverse the numbers from first to last. I know this changes it completely, but based on how it's structured, I believe the author did the exact opposite to go to the exit."

"Okay, then where to?" Brooks asked.

"We must go back to the center chamber and start from there," she answered.

"We can't. The way is blocked," Trumbull said.

"Well, how far in is it blocked off?" she asked.

Trumbull thought for a moment. "You know, I think it's blocked from the chamber to before we made our first choice. Which as I recall was quite a ways away from the center on the maze. It may not be totally caved in."

Brooks handed the tablet back to Emily and put the diary in his pack.

"Well, then, let's get going." Johnson was already trying to put on his pack again. Trumbull helped.

They found their way back to the starting point, thanks to Johnson and Emily's directions. They could no longer hear the lower tones pulsing, which they expected going in the opposite direction. Emily ran the algorithm, and they made their way more or less southwest. The blocked tunnel was not the right way, after all.

They soon picked up the low musical tone again. It was becoming more prominent as they made their way. The compass was pointing towards the exit, if there still was one. This route had no stairways, only a constant steep grade going downward as they twisted and turned around the tunnels and intersections. They moved through each row of numbers rather quickly and within thirty minutes they were at the last intersection.

Emily struggled with her pack as they went, then noticed it was getting harder to breath. "Wait guys." She attempted several deep breaths and looked at the men. They started struggling as well.

Brooks and Trumbull helped each other pullout their face masks tucked in their packs, and each put his on. Trumbull then helped Emily as Brooks did the same for Johnson.

Soon they were breathing normally and continued.

"I suspect we will encounter a heavy resistance if the Praetorian agents control the hill. We better be ready. And we are risking a tank explosion if we do hit trouble." Trumbull handed Brooks and Johnson their weapons.

They turned the corner and encountered another Iron Gate. Brooks used the key, and they entered the escape tunnel. It also sloped downward and was a lot longer than the first tunnel. Trumbull led the way followed by Emily, Johnson, and Brooks.

Johnson explained as they walked. "We must be outside the perimeter of the system by now. This route was made to avoid detection from the main house."

It was a long tunnel, more than one hundred feet. The steep pitch actually helped them with their packs, and momentum moved them forward.

Emily stopped as she heard the musical tone directly above them. The men did as well.

They looked up at the ceiling.

"What do you think?" Brooks asked.

"Continue ahead," Trumbull answered.

Several hundred yards and they reached the end of the tunnel, which was blocked by the same kind of door as the original entrance to the labyrinth. Trumbull stopped, followed by the others.

They all dropped their packs, except for the oxygen tanks. Brooks helped each strap them around their waists with Velcro attached to each tank.

Brooks had the inserted the old key. The door mechanism strained to push outward. "This door swings out instead of in. There's a lot of resistance outside. It's jammed."

Trumbull took the key and tried as well. "Something is so wedged against the door, the machinery can't force it open. It must be buried into the hillside."

"What can we do now?" Emily asked.

"Johnson, try your cell phone. We might be close enough to the surface to get a signal," Brooks said as he backed away from the door.

Johnson made a call. There was a lot of static. A voice answered on the other end, but they couldn't communicate. It was too broken up. "I can't get clear enough reception."

"Keep the line open," Trumbull said.

Johnson nodded.

Trumbull pulled out Dean's rifle from his pack, removing the clip. "I'm going to let them know we're here. Verum or Praetorians. It doesn't matter now. We have to get out. "Ready?"

They all nodded. Emily's heart rate rose with each moment.

Trumbull used the butt end and whacked the metal door. They listened. The noise outside continued uninterrupted. He whacked the door several times in succession.

A moment later Emily heard a faint sound coming from the other side of the door. "That sounds like digging."

Then the music stopped.

Trumbull hit it the door again. They all listened intently. They could hear digging, but nothing else.

"Trumbull. Hit the door once, hard." Johnson instructed.

He turned and did so. They listened. Nothing.

"Again." Johnson said as he moved next to Trumbull.

Another blow to the door. They listened.

One note played.

"Now hit it twice."

He hit it twice and two notes returned.

"My God, they are up there!" Emily shouted.

Emily looked at Trumbull and Johnson. There seemed to be a signal between them as they nodded at each other.

What's going on? Is this all a trap? Are they working for the other side? No. It can't be. They killed all those agents. But maybe it was a ruse and casualties meant to fool us. Oh, God, does Brooks know?

She moved next to Brooks in a panic.

"What is it?" he whispered.

"What if?" she whispered back and nodded towards the other two.

He shook his head, as if signaling her thoughts were misplaced. She took a breath of relief but cling to his arm.

They tried the door several more times with no luck.

"This door won't open until the outside is cleared," Brooks said.

Several tones sounded above them in alternating code.

"What's that?" Emily asked.

"Morse code," Brooks said "My Morse is rusty. I can't make it out….you guys?"

Both men shook their heads.

She looked at the three of them. "So, no one knows Morse code? You're kidding, right?"

They shrugged their shoulders, looked at each other, and then at Emily. She shook her head in disbelief.

"Every movie I have ever seen about people trapped uses Morse code to save them as the last resort. Everybody in government knows Morse code right? So you're telling me two government men in high ranking positions don't know the code? Brilliant." She slid down and sat against the wall.

"I guess we wait." Johnson said rather sheepishly.

"Should we look at the documents?" Emily asked. "What if they're not with the Absconditus Verum? In case we're caught, we'll at least have the hidden information."

"The documents are the only way to bring out the truth. Without them, we won't be able to prove anything," Brooks said.

"Shh." Johnson said quietly. "I hear something outside."

There was a sound, a rustling noise. Then there were two, or three, all at the same time.

"It sounds like they're getting close to the door." Johnson surmised.

"It is," Trumbull confirmed.

"So we're caught!" Emily said in an angry tone.

"Emily, chances are heavily in our favor those digging are on our side," Brooks assured her.

He looked at the others. They each raised their weapons, just in case, waiting for the encounter. They still had their breathing tanks going as the air was continuing to fail. It was another few minutes of rapid shoveling until one of them struck the door, then another. A pause followed. Then three soft taps…a pause, three more taps. Johnson tapped three times back.

"Brooks, try the key now."

"Are we safe?" Emily asked.

Brooks looked at Johnson and Trumbull. They both nodded.

Trumbull turned to Emily. "Stand behind us."

Brooks turned the key. The door struggled but pushed outwards. A rush of air came in the tunnel along with dust, dirt, and the setting sun. It was hard for them to see as they shielded their eyes even with their oxygen masks on. The door only moved a few inches to the side, then stopped.

"Johnson?" said a voice from outside, though not too loud.

"Yes, it's us," he responded.

"We need to clear more dirt to let the door slide fully open."

"Okay." He turned to the others. "It's our team."

"I hope you're right." Emily was peeking around Trumbull.

It took another ten minutes before they opened the door halfway. Two operatives slid through sideways, dressed in covert gear. Brooks still had his gun pointed at them. Emily was holding her breath.

"Joe, trust me," Johnson said to Brooks.

"You'll need to take off those packs. There's not enough room. We'll collect them and the rest of the gear." said an operative.

"Thank God." Emily said as she let out a sigh of relief.

She removed her breathing gear as did the others. Emily's eyes adjusted from flashlights to the evening light. The moon was now shining brightly in the east. They were pulled out of the tunnel one by one as just enough of the opening had been cleared. Emily stood still and felt a gentle breeze blowing. Once her eyes adjusted she could see they were facing southwestward. The hill sloped slowly down.

"Ma'am, Stu Beverley. We thought the tunnel ended at the Joinery." He pointed back behind them and up the hill to the old chimney. "Up there on Mulberry Row. Did you hear the musical tones?"

"Yes." answered Johnson.

"We're just below the southern point of the gardens."

Emily watched two more men also in full covert combat gear move past them down the hill.

"It's okay, Mrs. Miller.," said one of the men as he passed.

"We're clear, sir," an operative said to Beverley. "The blast on the lawn somehow only exposed the center of the system below."

The door was now fully dug out. The rest of their gear was brought out by two operatives.

They all looked up the hill. It was some five hundred feet to the top. The spot where the Joinery once stood next to Mulberry Row was above them. They were in an area that gave them natural cover from any Praetorians that might still be lurking around. Emily looked back towards the tunnel. The entrance was buried into the hillside. Several men in suits were dead and lined up on the ground. She assumed they were Praetorians.

"Where are the rest of their agents?" Trumbull asked.

"The ones still alive left. Our team in the front pulled back ten minutes ago and they fled." Beverley answered.

"You created a diversion?" Brooks asked.

Beverley nodded. "Let's get you guys to safety."

◊ ◊ ◊

Johnson called a Verum member in the Virginia government to make arrangements on cleaning up the disaster at Monticello. A portion of Beverley's team would stay to oversee the work on what had become a major battleground.

Beverley brought them down the west side of the hill to two vehicles below the garden hidden from prying eyes. They loaded the gear and the packs. Soon they were driving across the fields to safety. Emily leaned on Brooks. The adventure from hell was finally over.

I hope James and the girls are safe, she thought as exhaustion caused her to drift off.

◊ ◊ ◊

Beverley called. "Richard, we have them and we're moving out."

"Yes, Stuart, we saw them on the monitor. Is everything else getting cleaned up?"

"As much as we can for now. Johnson called for more help. This will take a large effort to hide what was done here. All the agents on the outside are being cleared. Richard, they lost over seventy Praetorians, possibly more." Stu answered.

"Understood, we'll be here when you arrive."

Chapter 39

July 1801 - Monticello, Virginia

Jack Jouett was charged with hiding the Praetorian documents in the main house until word had been received back from Jefferson. A private letter was delivered the next day.

'Sally knows the Absconditus Verum chamber on the grounds. Have her lead you into the secret tunnel system currently under construction below the backyard, and store them with all the other documents. Make certain to catalog each and every document within the journal of documents located in the central chamber.'

Jouett and Sally Hemings brought the Praetorian documents into the central chamber and stored them with the other documents.

◊ ◊ ◊

Jefferson had accumulated years of documents regarding the Praetorians, and the Constitutional Convention, but this proved to be the evidence that could be needed if he decided to pursue a due course in justice and have *'a very large number of government officials charged with treason in dealing with King George and undermining the new Constitutional government.'*

◊ ◊ ◊

Jefferson, Madison, and Monroe met at the Capital to decide what to do. In the end, they spoke with each and every tainted member of government as well as the private sector and agreed to keep all things hidden until such time as one of them or the Praetorian Society should ever look to the ruin of the United States Republic government ever again. They pledged an oath both to secrecy and not to pursue the corruption that Praetor Hamilton had created.

They met privately with Aaron Burr as he had become the new Praetor while holding the Vice Presidency. He agreed not to pursue any Federal office ever again. He would be allowed to return to New York and if he so chose to be in local government where Jefferson said,

'He can do little harm at the local level as the people are ever watchful but if he did turn to corruption, then his community had the right to dispose of him in whatever manner they seemed fit to pursue.'

Over the years, many Absconditus Verum Society members brought other items of wealth to Monticello and they were stored in the chamber. They also selected two other sites in the hopes that if anything was found, they still had evidential support from them. Many of the documents were copied and sent to the others sites, but not all. Each site had originals of critical documents.

2018 - Eastern Long Island, New York

Several hours passed as the Council continued to argue. It was clear each Council member had a different view on how to proceed.

A messenger showed up with a written message.

Finally, the Praetor stood. "Quiet! I have heard quite enough!"

The Praetor read the message. "It seems our defeat at Monticello is complete. Only four Praetorians out of eighty-three survived and those are low level agents. The main Verum forces have left the grounds. We still don't know if they found anything, but I must assume they would have stayed until they retrieved their team that went in, if they survived."

It was signed by the local Praetorian outpost near Monticello.

"Then, we need to contact the media right away. If the Verum have the documents, they must be marginalized to make the documents irrelevant." The Congressman responded.

The FBI Director spoke. "If they had such an organized unit at Monticello, then the evidence must still be close. I say we mobilize all our units in the Virginia area and try to track them."

"We're going to do both." The Praetor looked at the Congressman. "Write the news. Make sure to include the killings from this past week. Marginalize them."

He had just finished his sentence when another figure came into the chamber. He was granted access by guards posted at the door. He came forward.

The Praetor stopped talking and looked at him. "Well, Shaw, what the hell happened? You were supposed to go to

Monticello and keep our operations from failing. Now we have this huge loss, thanks to you."

Victor Shaw gave him a menacing look. "There was no way for me to stop the carnage in Virginia. It is you, Praetor, that has failed, not me."

"How dare you take that tone! Report all you know and do it now."

Shaw looked around the chamber. "This really is a pit. How humiliating it must be for you pathetic wimps to have to endure such conditions. Is there any reason one of you on the Council has not taken command?"

"We all know our place, Shaw." The Admiral. "And you would do well to remember yours."

Shaw relaxed his look and smiled. "You know, that's what the Praetor's lieutenant said in France…that is before I killed him."

The Praetor watched as terror seized the Council. He too was scared to death.

Shaw crossed his arms into his overcoat and pulled out two automatic weapons.

"Guards!" the Praetor yelled as he ducked for cover.

There were two guards behind the Praetor's chair and two at the entrance. Shaw quickly turned ninety degrees and all four were on the ground, filled with bullets. He turned back and looked at the Council. Four members hadn't moved. they were frozen in their seats. He sprayed them with bullets as they screamed. Three others had shrunk down under the table and were all dead with another spray from Shaw as he crouched to see them.

When he stood up, he took a bullet in the chest. Another whizzed by. The Praetor was the only Council member armed, though he was a business man, not a soldier. He had slipped behind the royal chair.

Shaw staggered backwards as the Praetor got two more shots off, both missing badly.

The Praetor rose and advanced.

Shaw returned fire with a short burst hitting the Praetor in the legs. He screamed and dropped.

Shaw walked over to him and kicked his gun away.

The Praetor screamed in immense pain. He looked up to see Shaw standing over him with a smile on his face.

"How does it feel? I imagined the original Praetor was in similar pain when he was shot. He at least died in a duel. But you know, since I'm such a nice and empathetic person, I will relieve you of yours." He shot a short burst into the Praetor's chest.

◊ ◊ ◊

Shaw turned, and fifty agents who had been in the front corridor entered the room. He had not been idle these past several months. He had been coordinating the takeover.

"We're with you, Praetor.," said one, and they all raised their weapons. "Hail Praetor Shaw! Hail the new Praetor."

Four of the lead Praetorian agents stepped forward.

"We've been looking for new leadership for a long time. These idiots all held onto power too long. It's time to start anew. We pledge ourselves to you as Praetor.," a lead agent pronounced.

Victor Shaw went around the large round stone table and sat down in the Praetor's chair. "The first thing you can do is clean up this mess. Then we will have a meeting and a new order shall rise. We shall now rule through power and fear, and all those who oppose us shall meet their fate."

Chapter 40

It took the Verum members over an hour to get back to the Yates homestead as they went stealthily, mostly on back roads. As they approached the farm, Brooks nudged Emily awake and pointed at two men standing in front of the house. She knew them immediately and tears of joy rolled down her face. As they were going up the drive she recognized everyone else she had met outside. Once they parked, she ran from the car and threw herself into Thomas-James' arms.

"Oh, Thomas."

"Em…"

Emily was careful not to hurt disturb his neck bandage as she brought her hands to the sides of his face. They embraced. She broke down with joyful tears. They kissed and hugged, then kissed and hugged some more, finally reunited.

It was several moments before she could release him. "How are the girls?"

"They're here." Thomas-James pointed to the front door where Amanda and Sara came out, followed by Agent Waxman and Deputy Wilson.

Emily fell to her knees and opened her arms.

"Mommy, mommy!" they both yelled as they ran.

When they reached her, she hugged them both, one in each arm. They hugged her back as she stroked their hair softly.

"Amanda, Sara." She hugged them tightly. "My girls. Oh my girls are here and they're safe." She said, sniffling, as her eyes filled and her nose began to run.

It was almost surreal. A perfect reunion with her family, one that, at times, she'd thought might never happen.

Thomas-James stood over them with his hands on their shoulders.

"Let me look at you," Emily tenderly moved the girls out of their hug so she could see them. The most beautiful sight in the world. She sniffled some more and hugged again.

In a few moments, Emily looked up. "Hi Pete. Thank you, thank you."

She reached out, and he held her hand. He didn't say anything, but she could see him holding back tears.

"If you would, please join us in the barn," Richard said as Pamela wheeled him by.

The cars the team had taken to Monticello were parked in a hideaway next to the barn command center. Johnson was getting medical help for his shoulder inside.

They all entered and Richard brought them down to a room below ground. It was a 'clean room' below the main level and had sophisticated equipment everywhere. A team of specialists were already receiving and logging the documents and delicate parchments. They were carefully scanning them one by one. It was a time-consuming process and would take days to sort out.

Emily looked on as she held Thomas-James' hand, girls standing in front of them.

◊ ◊ ◊

Brooks and Richard were watching the events unfold. There were six individuals sitting around a large circular work station. Scanning stations lined the perimeter along with storage compartments. The information being scanned was then sent to the center table monitors.

The Monticello team and Yates family stayed for a short while and then headed into the house. They gathered in a large living room. They celebrated for over an hour.

Richard was in heaven. His lifelong search for the truth was realized. He was getting constant updates on the documents. His reunion with his son. His granddaughters fussing over him once they found out who he was.

"Emily my dear, you have proved a wonderful daughter-in-law and a very special Absconditus Verum Society Member. By Brooks' account, you saved everyone more than once."

Emily smiled, but then her happiness faded.

What is it? Richard asked.

"Everyone but Tim." She looked over to Johnson, who was sitting quietly to one side.

There was a sadness in his voice, as a parent who'd lost a child. "I will miss him. His bravery and dedication to the FBI and the Verum will be remembered." His voice shook.

"There was nothing you could have done." Brooks consoled him.

They all paused for a moment to remember their fallen comrade.

Emily broke the silence, in a soft tone asked. "Richard, can you tell us just where we are with everything? Do we have all the documents you need to reveal the truth?"

"It looks very promising," he replied.

"Good. I hope the American people are willing to look at more than what they are offered now. I think many are so fed up with Federal Government that we might just start breaking the current paradigm and the Praetorians' hold," Brooks offered.

They continued on with the celebration well into the night, including a wonderful dinner and plenty of storytelling. Emily heard all about the kidnapping from the girls. James told them how Trumbull had saved the day with both the girls and himself. They all relaxed, having their fill to eat and toasting the success of the mission.

It was two in the morning when Jonathon came into the house. "Sir, we have some of the more sensitive documents ready for viewing."

"Well, then, let's take a look, shall we?" Richard motioned for everyone to join him.

Emily and Thomas-James brought the girls and the rest joined them. They were now on the main level of the barn command center looking at the monitors. Documents were displayed on all the screens.

The girls headed for tables that had dozens of old artifacts. Thomas-James stayed with them.

"Well, here's what we have so far." Hal said, who was monitoring the scanned documents and cataloging them on his computer. "Sir, I think this is one you were specifically looking for."

Brooks wheeled Richard over to the monitor Hal pointed to, and they took a look. Trumbull and Johnson joined them.

"My God." Richard exclaimed. "Look at these. This is a set of letters exchanged between King George and several of our Founding Fathers. Private letters." He started reading one to himself mouthing the words. "Jason," he called out to one of his technicians across the room. "We need all these in chronological order. It will give us the timeline we need to see how the events unfolded."

"I'm already on that, sir."

He turned to Emily and said. "Jason' one of our young whiz kid and son of a top Verum Society member." He leaned in close as she bent down. "He's a direct descendent of a founding father."

"Richard, look at this." Brooks called, with surprise in his voice.

Emily pushed Richard over to the monitor Brooks was viewing.

Richards studied the screen. "Can this be right? I thought we'd find these in Hartford, not here."

"I know," Brooks answered.

"It seems either these are copies of the originals or they are the originals. We won't know until the lab results are in." Richard concluded.

"What are they?" Trumbull queried as he and Johnson joined them at the monitor.

"These are a series of letters written by all the New England states to President Jefferson. It appears they were asking for a second Constitutional Convention and they were threatening succession."

"A second one?" Emily asked. "There was no second Convention."

Richard pondered. "Apparently, Emily, there might have been, or at least these letters express that course. I have a lot of research about this."

"So, we'll find those in Hartford too?" Trumbull asked.

Richard paused. "We were hoping to. These may be originals or copies. We'll get it sorted out. In fact, we have a team there now. They informed us they did find a secret hideaway, but no word has come in since." He had a look of concern on his face.

"Sir, I don't understand this," Hal interrupted. "According to this, the New England States are looking to secede? My understanding of history was the Southern States made this claim and the Northern States said they had no authority to leave the Union."

"That was some fifty years later when the Congress was totally controlled by the North." Brooks answered. The Civil War.

"That means that the North forgot they were threatening the exact same thing?" Hal asked.

Richard broke a small smile. "Now you know why we are on this quest. These documents, once hidden, hold the truth to events that took place. While you can find information about the New England threat in open documents and the internet, this is the missing piece that validates the States believed in the right to secede. A belief that every politician will tell you is a lie and was not possible."

"Well, then, this is indeed the most important day in American history," Johnson said.

Richard nodded but didn't answer. He continued to view everything on the monitor. Brooks, Trumbull, and Johnson slowly walked around the table. They saw all sorts of documents on the monitors, some short in length, others long and detailed. Many were copies of documents already a part of American history. Many were not.

Brooks stopped at a station looking at the monitor. He read several lines to himself before alerting the others. "Here's one of particular interest." He read it out loud, interpreting it to contemporary text:

"Dear Mr. Thomas Jefferson,

There has been a conspiracy toward our government. King George is in league with a Society called the Praetorians. I have enclosed copies of all the correspondence between them. As you read, you will plainly see they were, in fact, collaborating to destroy our fledgling Republic. I was complicit in these acts and participated in many dishonorable deeds of which I expect no quarter.

Also, I have enclosed information about the Praetor. Let these documents show that he is indeed in league with the King in everything done. He was conspiring against our Republic from the time he left the Constitutional Convention, possibly much sooner. It is my intent to put a stop to this as soon as possible. I realize this will cost me everything in your view and that of the people, but I cannot allow this to continue. Please keep all of these documents safe and hidden.

If I am successful tomorrow, they need never see the light of day. My sincere apologies for bringing my actions so close to your standing; my life is now forfeit for the good of the states and their citizens.

Faithfully submitted, Benjamin Church, 10th of July, 1801."

"And there are two marks at the bottom right." said a technician at the station. "One we know is Jack Jouett's, there, signed the same date. It looks like Sally Hemings is the other. She had no writings we can associate it with, but it certainly looks like her mark with the date 1832."

"That is her mark." Johnson verified as he and the others joined them. "She did sign several documents, though many are still hidden in another location. Her family has been working with the Absconditus Verum since the beginning." He turned and called. "Stu, can you come over?"

Stu Beverley joined them.

"Have a look," Johnson said.

He scanned the monitor, examining every detail in the letter. "It's hers all right."

Brooks was taken by surprise. "Seems I'm the only one without some information. What does that mean?"

"It means that the Hemings family was responsible for keeping many of the records safe and hidden. They did this while at Monticello. It was Jefferson's decision to incorporate them with the Verum. They had no formal name, but all the same, they participated protecting the country." Stu offered.

"How do you know this?" Brooks asked.

"Because I'm a descendant of the Hemings family line."

"What?" Brooks asked incredulously.

"It's true," Richard confirmed.

Stu explained. "We were responsible for receiving, storing, and cataloging all the documents. Somewhere in this trove you have recovered should be a catalog booklet. That was from Sally and her siblings. Then it was passed down. It stayed at Monticello. When other events took place, they set up the other locations working with Presidents Jefferson, Madison, and Monroe. The Verum didn't want all the information in one place. It was too great a risk."

"Okay, I understand their mission, but what about now?" Brooks inquired.

Stu continued. "When it became obvious that our ancestors had to seal everything in at all the locations, we focused on becoming trained as a militia unit. This was kept totally secret. We formed units in every southern state as others joined, and a few in New England. We were taught covertly, and we became a covert unit with great skills. These same units are in place today. We have them all over the country and in many foreign countries. Just like many other families during the Civil War, we have members on both sides.

"The Hemings line has played a critical role in doing what could be done to keep everything safe as well as to protect the Absconditus Verum members. From there, we trained into Special Forces units."

"And now you know about the slave and owner part of our Society." Johnson said as he looked at Brooks.

"Sir! Here's another one you need to look at." Jonathon called from his station.

They all went to see as Emily pushed Richard's wheelchair.

"It's the affirmation papers from the Convention." Richard gasped.

"The ones you noted in the diary?" Brooks asked.

Richard moved close and read, also interpreting the text to contemporary understanding:

"Agreed to this 19th day of June 1787,

We, the delegates of this Constitutional Convention, do hereby affirm our loyalty to the sovereignty of our own states. That it is our intentions to strengthen central government as needs be without compromising any states right of sovereignty. These rights include the right to nullify central government laws any state believes acts detrimentally to their own state.

Further, we affirm that any states may, at any time, secede from any central government of the United States, being from our Articles of Confederation and Perpetual Union where that right currently exists, or any new Constitution drawn up at any time in the future. We further agree that any disputes between states, while having input from a central authority, can decide on their own a due course in remedy.

The states can, do, and shall always have the power to run their own governments without central government interference, laws, or edicts. To that end, any state in the minority of any said settlement retains the rights to nullify such settlement or laws pertaining to their own state so long as they do not impede others states with the ability to move goods through said state freely.

That the central government will not be allowed to raise and hold standing armies at any time other than during war as declared by Congress or to defend the country from invasion of persons not of American born descent.

That the states may, in addition to the covenant of any Constitution, form alliances separate and apart to their own benefit. This shall not, however, override the central government's representative duties to manage foreign affairs.

"This is a critical find. And look, all the delegates still at the Convention signed it. A major piece of the puzzle is now found. This will show that indeed a great conspiracy took place by most of the Federalist Party."

Brooks looked through the diary. "Yes, here it is. Robert Yates referenced this as one of the events that took place. We couldn't confirm it without the document."

"Which means the argument about the States and their original intent and authority is now confirmed. The Praetorians have long held the States had no right to nullify Federal edicts or secede from the Union. This changes everything."

"You realize what this means, right?" Emily surmised, "The entire paradigm of our current Federal Government is based on lies. They stripped the states and the people of their rights to govern as they saw fit. To allow the states to control their own destinies. This changes everything!"

Richard smiled, realizing all this effort, all the risks they just encountered, was reaching into the heart of a person, who until a week ago never understood the importance of true history and liberty. "Now, Emily, you understand why our mission is so important. Why we will show the people, that their very liberty, their choices, must be given back to them. The foundation of our republic is based on the liberty of each and every American. That a political representative, whether congressman, senator, executive, or judge, must protect your liberty above everything they have taken from you."

"I'm still at a loss as to what this truly means." She answered.

"It means, the great American experiment has totally failed the people. and the states. because it has wholly corrupted itself." Johnson concluded.

Richard added. "This Republic was established to insure liberty and freedom were protected by government. The very words we say in the pledge. The very choices that we have been stripped of. Our own choices to live as we choose to live, not as the government decides how we can live. Our representatives no longer defend and protect our liberty. They consolidate power into the few, who make all the laws and edicts, so many choices we may not agree with. Everything our founders warned us about: democracy, the debt, giving up liberties for protection and government programs. It has all come to pass. The concepts of federalism and a republic have been destroyed by the politicians, the political parties, and even the judiciary. They all exceed their limited powers to govern at the expense of your freedoms and mine. We have all become slaves to almighty government through taxation, unfair laws, and the loss of our representation."

"Where do we start?" Emily was trying to change her paradigm, one that was ingrained throughout her live. One that was taught by the very government that had abandoned the true republic for a democracy run by politicians."

"American Federal Government must be brought back to the beginning. You have to start building government based on your liberty and mine. That is the true paradigm. That is the Absconditus Verum Society. The real government we should have.

"These documents, along with many other, can now be put forth for the people," Richard pointed to all the monitors showing dozens of parchments, "But not yet. We still need to see what we can find in the other two locations."

◊ ◊ ◊

Trumbull, while overwhelmed, had some trepidation. "I'm not sure I understand. Who would look at all this and how would it change everything? Don't we still have the same problem with the government and the media? The government won't let this get out and the media is run by the Praetorians."

"That, Mr. Trumbull, is our trump card." Johnson answered. "It must remain secret, but when the time is right, we do have the ability to get this information into the people's hands and then it's a matter of reeducating them to understand that the government we have now is not the government we're supposed to have."

Trumbull didn't mention the card he held. The timing wasn't right and he knew this battle was far from over.

Richard interjected. "Then we can bring down the original Federalist Party's implied powers used to create this colossus nation state of elitists and become the alliance the United States was meant to be. It's the people, and only the people, that have the innate rights to govern themselves. Liberty is a natural right, not one given to us by government."

They spent the next few hours looking over the information.

◊ ◊ ◊

At sunrise, they gathered in the house. No one had any sleep, and Richard didn't want to spoil the celebration. He decided not to share the disturbing information about the Hartford or South Carolina teams. The Praetorians were already starting a counter offensive. They're other teams were in danger. And, he still needed the Second Constitutional Convention documents to seal the Verum's victory and restore the Republic, the rights of the states, liberty, and the American Dream.

◊ ◊ ◊

The Monticello quest was over, but it was only a matter of time before they had to face an even more difficult job. While the Verum had a great victory, the Praetorians still controlled much of the world. They also didn't know Victor Shaw had taken control of the Praetorian Council.

Trumbull had already left the farm, headed for Connecticut.

Epilogue

"This is breaking news. According to sources, Monticello, Thomas Jefferson's former home, where a helicopter crashed earlier in the week, and rumors of a drone strike were spread, is now being treated as both a conspiracy against the Federal Government and a terrorist threat. It appears there was small arms fire on the grounds and up to eighty or more people have been killed.

"Our own news sources have identified two different groups involved. The first is called the Society of Praetorians. The second group involved is the Absconditus Verum Society. Apparently, these groups have some kind of blood feud that's been going on for over two hundred years.

"We have wildly conflicting information coming into our newsrooms and will bring you more as we verify our sources.

"Meanwhile, two United States Congressmen have gone missing. They are New York Congressman Steven Henry and Massachusetts Senator Benjamin Michaels. They were both last seen at Long Island's MacArthur Airport. Authorities are looking for any information that might help in locating them.

"Reports are also coming in that an executive of the Federal Reserve, as well as an executive of the World Bank, have disappeared near the same area. Those names have not been disclosed."

Praetor Victor Shaw had an evil smile on his face as he watched the news from the old stronghold. He was seated in the original Praetor's chair. "Just wait, Trumbull. Soon, the entire Federal Government will come down on you and that pitiful band of Verum members. You're missing the one set of documents that might have really caused us trouble."

The Praetor looked down next to his chair at a large opened box filled with old documents. He read the first line of the top document:

"Met and Agreed,

Congress of the United States, the Second Constitutional Convention, Hartford Connecticut, June 15th 1815...

"I'm sorry Trumbull, but that Verum team you sent to Hartford will not be coming back." He let out a cruel and evil laugh.

Author G.W. Barnes grew up in Connecticut where he began his own artisan contracting business. He's both a businessman and entrepreneur, researching American history for the better part of twenty years. Writing fictional thrillers based on historical facts has culminated in the new series, "Liberty's Dagger".

Made in the USA
Middletown, DE
08 August 2021

45614214R00262